BEST NEW AMERICAN VOICES 2006

BEST NEW
AMERICAN
VOICES
2006

GUEST EDITOR
Jane Smiley

SERIES EDITORS
John Kulka and Natalie Danford

A Harvest Original • Harcourt, Inc.
Orlando   Austin   New York   San Diego   Toronto   London

CONTENTS

PREFACE

Despite constant reports that film, television, the Internet, and other media are dampening interest in reading, especially the reading of fiction, more books are sold today in the United States than at any other time in history. In particular, there seems to be a renewed interest in the short story. Indeed, to judge by the number of anthologies and collections on the bookstore shelves, the short story is back with a vengeance.

Renewed interest in the short story may be attributed, in part, to the flowering of writing workshops in North America that began after World War II, thanks to the GI Bill. Today the AWP (Associated Writing Programs) supports more than 370 member colleges and universities and 125 writers' conferences and centers. As Jane Smiley writes in the introduction to this volume of *Best New American Voices*, "... for various practical reasons, writing programs do concentrate on the short story, and the result, for readers, has been a bonanza—the continued cultivation of a bona fide American literary form that might have died altogether after the great twentieth-century popular magazines, like the *Saturday Evening Post,* ceased publishing. A system has evolved that works very well—writing programs produce short stories and small presses and university presses produce the literary magazines that publish most of the stories. This alternative to commercial and popular culture is intensely fertile— rather like a salt marsh at the edge of the sea."

Many of these writing programs are justly famous training grounds for our best new talents. Consider, for example, that the following writers all came out of the Iowa program: Flannery O'Connor, Wallace Stegner, John Gardner, Gail Godwin, Andre Dubus, and T. C. Boyle, to name just a few. And the Stanford program has produced its own credible national literature with such famous alumni as Robert Stone, Raymond Carver, Evan S. Connell, Tillie Olsen, Larry McMurtry, Ernest J. Gaines, Ron Hansen, Ken Kesey, Scott Turow, Thomas McGuane, Alice Hoffman, Allan Gurganus, Wendell Berry, Harriet Doerr, Al Young, Blanche Boyd, N. Scott Momaday, Vikram Seth, Dennis McFarland, and Stephanie Vaughn.

What distinguishes the Best New American Voices series from other annual anthologies is that we do not collect previously published stories from magazines and literary quarterlies. Each year we solicit story nominations directly from writing workshops. Writers must be enrolled in these programs to be eligible for the competition. Nominations come to us from MA and MFA writing programs like Iowa and Columbia, from fellowship programs like the Wisconsin Institute for Creative Writing, from arts organizations like the Banff Centre for the Arts and the PEN Prison Writing Committee, from summer writing conferences like Bread Loaf and Sewanee, and from community workshops like those held at the 92nd Street Y in New York City. Hundreds of programs across the United States and Canada participate in this process. A directory at the back of this volume lists all of the participating institutions in this year's competition.

Best New American Voices, now in its sixth year, introduces emerging writers. By emerging writers we do not mean apprentice writers but writers embarking on their professional careers. Still, few of the names in the table of contents will be familiar. As in past years, some of our contributors make their debuts in these pages. If our current contributors are not well-known, that is certain to change soon. Many of the contributors to past volumes have since gone on to great success: David Benioff (*The 25th Hour*); William Gay (*Provinces of Night* and *I Hate to See That Evening Sun Go Down*); Ana Menendez (*In Cuba I Was a German Shepherd*); Timothy Westmoreland (*Good as Any*); Adam Johnson (*Emporium*); John Murray (*A Few Short Notes on Tropical Butterflies*); the late Amanda Davis (*Circling the Drain* and *Wonder When You'll Miss Me*); Maile Meloy (*Half in Love* and *Liars and Saints*); Jennifer Vanderbes (*Easter Island*); and Rattawut Lapcharoensap (*Sightseeing*). This is far from a complete list.

For *Best New American Voices 2006* we received more than four hundred nominations. We read all of the nominations at least once, as we do every year, and winnowed these down to a much smaller group of finalists that we then passed on to our guest editor, Jane Smiley. Jane has selected fifteen stories for inclusion in the volume. Her selections make for a diverse, surprising collection of stories whose authors probably have little in common—except that they attended workshops, whether in summer conferences or in degree programs or in arts organizations. The stories speak for themselves.

We would like to extend thanks to Jane Smiley for her thorough reading of the manuscripts, for her professionalism, and for her enthusiasm for this project. We would like to thank our past guest editors for their ongoing efforts and support: Tobias Wolff, Charles Baxter, Joyce Carol Oates, John Casey, and Francine Prose. To the many writers, directors, teachers, and panel judges who help to make this series a continuing success we extend heartfelt thanks and congratulations. To name just a few others: We thank our editor Andrea Schulz for her patience and help; Jenna Johnson, for her constant attention to detail; André Bernard at Harcourt, Inc., for his enthusiasm; Lisa Lucas in the Harcourt contracts department for the obvious and maybe not-so obvious; and our families and friends for their love and support.

—*John Kulka and Natalie Danford*

INTRODUCTION

Jane Smiley

I never write short stories, and as a reader I find them a little scary. A good short story has to take the reader over for a half hour or so, imposing its own mood, sensibility, and events with enough intensity to make a lasting and even unshakable impression. There are, of course, stories I love, such as Stuart Dybek's "The Death of the Outfielder," but there are also stories I love but hate to think about, like Katherine Mansfield's "Miss Brill," in which a genteelly impoverished lady of a certain age goes to a concert dressed in a way she thinks is flattering, and overhears remarks that, the reader knows, must permanently disabuse her of her self-respect, or Shirley Jackson's "The Lottery," which I read in high school and which may have been my first real exposure to plausible evil.

Short stories are hard to write. Good ones have to avoid trick endings, pat endings, clichéd situations, familiar voices. They can neither ramble on nor look too neat. The author must be inventive, but overt novelty, too, is suspect. If I had been the one who set about devising writing programs after the Second World War, I might not have had the fiction programs concentrate on such a difficult form.

But for various practical reasons, writing programs do concentrate on the short story, and the result, for readers, has been a bonanza—the continued cultivation of a bona fide American literary form that might have died altogether after the great twentieth-century popular magazines, like the *Saturday Evening Post,* ceased publishing. A system has evolved that works very well—writing programs produce short stories and small presses and university presses produce the literary magazines that publish most of the stories. This alternative to commercial and popular culture is intensely fertile—rather like a salt marsh at the edge of the sea. Out of this protected but richly populated world has come the flowering of American literature.

A generation ago, naysayers predicted that the products of writing programs would all sound alike, but such a result has not come to pass—the literary culture we have in the first decade of the twenty-first century is multithemed and multivocal. A. M. Homes, for example, isn't at all like Michael Cunningham, though they both went to Iowa. Louise Erdrich could never be mistaken for Michael Martone, though they both went to Johns Hopkins. Richard Price attended Columbia, but his work is not at all like that of Julie Otsuka. How about two from Stanford? Scott Turow and Raymond Carver. The fact is, the history of writing workshops shows that they are not much different from any other sort of literary salon. Enrolled students don't learn to conform but rather to find their own voices and stories, as well as to find colleagues who share their literary passion. In fact, students in writing workshops are more like siblings than clones of one another—they end up developing their differences more than their similarities. In addition, the proliferation of writing programs has led to a radical democratization and regional dispersal of American literature. Aspiring writers no longer need to move to New York to find a literary culture—most of the time, literary culture is as close as the nearest state university or summer writing program. As a result, the variety of U.S. experience and culture is more broadly and skillfully portrayed than ever before.

And so we have a sixth volume of *Best New American Voices,* an anthology of stories hot from the workshop fire and, in some sense, an ongoing justification for the writers' workshop method. Of these writers, we may ask, are they good—are they promising—are they various and compelling? And, as a bonus, do they give some clue about the direction of American writing in the next ten or twenty years?

They are, indeed, various. While there are two stories from Stanford, the others construct a minimap of the United States—one from New Mexico State, one from University of Alabama, one from University of Michigan, one from the Wisconsin Institute for Creative Writing, one from University of Houston, one from George Mason University in Virginia. Their settings are even more various—Vietnam, Bulgaria, Wisconsin, San Francisco, Hawaii, the South Pacific at the end of the Second World War, an aquarium in California.

The question I would really like to ask, though, since they are short stories, is, are they scary? Do they impose themselves and take over?

Let's consider Michelle Regalado Deatrick's "Backfire," which is ominous from the first line: "Think about it: two kids in a car, alone, in late summer." A carefully plotted story, "Backfire" builds from there—pretty soon, after waiting longer than they ever have before, the children, a brother and sister, aged nine and six, are shocked when their mother takes them home from the bank and tells them their father has withdrawn all of the family's savings without her knowledge. She can't even obtain twenty dollars for the week's groceries. But the children remain children—when they get home and their mother goes into her room to figure out what to do, they return to their own rivalries and desires, which turn out to be even more suspenseful, and dire, than financial ruin. Told in a restrained, thoughtful voice, "Backfire" is sad and shocking and inevitable—scary, indeed.

Or how about "Leave of Absence," by Jennifer Shaff? Shaff takes one of the biggest risks of all when she introduces Spock, from *Star Trek*, as a character. Spock, of course, is a walking cliché, so conventional and bland as to be nearly transparent. And yet Shaff's first-person narrator, Lisa, persists in relating to him—as the story opens, she is taking him to the School Bus Demolition Derby at the county fair. He has entered her life in some mysterious way, and it soon becomes apparent that he is not the only novelty she must adjust to—her parents have recently died in an automobile accident and Lisa's mental condition is very shaky. Shaff's introduction of Spock is much more canny than it first seems—she makes him funny and alive and also uses Lisa's interactions with him to delineate her barely controlled grief. The resulting story, carefully and imaginatively worked out, is affecting and poignant.

One of my favorites is the simple story of Alice, Robin, and the first-person narrator of "Alice's House" by Jamie Keene. The story begins reasonably—the narrator awakens suddenly because he hears someone outside his bedroom door in the middle of the night. The intruder turns out to be Alice, his former wife, who has a key and wishes to look around the house before it is sold. But the story comes to turn on the narrator's inability, or refusal, to choose between his failed relationship with Alice and his new and apparently more successful relationship with Robin. The wry and subtle manner in which Keene's narrator explores and exposes his charming fecklessness is quietly alluring.

More exotic is Matt Freidson's "Liberty," which opens in a youth rehabilitation camp in Vietnam and explores the lives of a group of adolescent boys who have been arrested for various crimes—mostly heroin use and drug peddling. Freidson skillfully focuses on the particulars of the boys' lives—their rivalries, their judgments on their teachers, their attempts, once they leave the facility, to find something to do in a Vietnam that is unlike anything most Americans imagine—but his special skill is depicting the world they must make their lives in and implying how history, economics, and culture have combined to nearly, but not quite, destroy any hopes they might realistically have.

All too familiar and, sadly, not exotic at all, is the scene of Andrew Foster Altschul's story, "A New Kind of Gravity." Set in a shelter for abused women, told from the point of view of one of the guards, Altschul's powerful story depicts the everyday tensions and terrors of trying to protect women and children who have little resistance against their abusers. Altschul's crisp, informative, and ultimately tragic tale is a model of narrative tact.

And then there is Jessica Anthony's mysterious and laconic "The Rust Preventer," which ostensibly takes place somewhere in the South Pacific, sometime after the Second World War. "The Rust Preventer," about an isolated soldier who is gradually losing contact even with himself, is the sort of story that should not work but does, owing entirely to Anthony's careful choice of details, cool tone, and masterful development of her protagonist's state of mind.

For suspense, we have Melanie Westerberg's "Watermark," in which the protagonist secretly swims with sharks in the aquarium where she works, although she knows it is dangerous and prohibited. For comic relief, we have "Useless Beauty OR Notes on *Esquire*'s 'Things a Man Should Never Do After the Age of 30,'" by Albert Martinez. For unexpected happy endings, we have Vanya Rainova's "Trampoline," in which Liubo, a Bulgarian man who has apparently given up his dreams and settled upon being a small-time entrepreneur at a dingy Eastern European beach, happens to meet just the woman who knows the very thing he wants to know. For sheer weirdness, we have Amber Dermont's "Lyndon," which manages to combine chilling family dysfunction with a visit to the birthplace and presidential library of former president Lyndon Baines Johnson.

Many of these stories focus on cracked and broken families, and part of their interest is how each asks the reader to look at family dysfunction through the lens of regional idiosyncrasies—the members of the southern family in Sarah Blackman's "The Jupiter's In" don't quite know what to make of their situation, and finally choose to stick together and make the best of small gestures of connection. In Gregory Plemmons's "Twinless," the twin who flees the family home in Charleston, South Carolina, leaves behind a sensuously and lovingly evoked landscape of haze, flower bulbs, ice tea, humidity, fireworks, familiarity. Palpable at the end is the ambivalence of the twin who stays behind, who longs to go but can't stop cherishing home. By contrast, the protagonist of Kaui Hart Hemmings's "Begin with an Outline" must try to understand the motives of her father, a native Hawaiian, who has shown no desire to have a relationship with his daughter, and must also admit that her Hawaiian relatives make her uncomfortable, even though she is beset with a sense that to lose them entirely is to lose a significant part of herself. In Sean Ennis's "Going After Lovely," it quickly becomes clear that in some families, neither going nor staying is the answer. The more the protagonist's father attempts to accommodate his wife's agoraphobia, the more eccentric and frightening family life becomes. Lovely, the sister, runs away and is never found. The protagonist stays home, but in a chilling revelation at the end, he appears to have made the wrong choice, too. In Sian Jones's "Pilot," written with compassion and precision, Calla oversees her mother's prolonged decline as a result of a massive stroke. Neither she nor the reader can quite understand what is going on, but Calla's ultimate act of tenderness toward her mother is to accept what happens rather than to impose her own theory upon it.

When I received the stories I was to read from John Kulka and Natalie Danford, who had done the preliminary screening of the stories sent by writing programs around the country, I noticed that all were ambitious in some way. My own experience as both a writing workshop student and a writing workshop teacher is that the pool of talent is a large one. Some students are exceptionally efficient in realizing their talents at a young age—in every workshop there are students who seem to have a knack for conceiving, or finding, dramatic material that works almost from the rough draft. There are students whose style is fluent and original from the beginning, others who have tremendous psychological insight. There are students who seem to have more application than inspiration, but eventually, through hard work, find inspiration. Workshops are full of protonovelists, who might not understand the form of the short story very well at all, and who don't blossom until their workshop years are long behind them. Workshops are also full of students who don't write again after graduate school, who go on to become editors or English professors or computer programmers, but whose months and years of intense consideration of stories of all kinds and in all stages of completion give them incomparable tools for understanding how fiction works—writing programs have produced many wonderful writers, but, no doubt, even more astute readers. While I was reading those stories I was reminded of the serendipitous and, let's say, accidental quality of every workshop—fifteen students brought together more by chance than by design, with different interests, experiences, and talents, who find something to care about in each other's work. Not all of the ambitions in all of the stories I read came to fruition, as did those of these fifteen, but all were worth reading. That is the best news of all, and a good omen for years to come.

JENNIFER SHAFF

Emerson College

LEAVE OF ABSENCE

When I first discovered Spock in my basement, I made him promise to take me off this crazy planet. I really didn't need to be here anymore, and he agreed to my deal. If I helped him hide his alienness from the general population, he promised to bring me into space, circle the sun with a slingshot effect, and land in the future, with his spaceship. He was scrounging for material to build a communication device and needed rides to the dump, tools from our shed, and my brother's old transistor radio for the wires and circuits. I cleaned off the laundry table in the basement so he could work, gave him my last set of AA batteries, and let him take apart my Mac Classic for the hard drive. The last thing he needed, he told me, was a big, flat piece of metal, and I was happy to oblige him.

But by the time I was driving Spock to the School Bus Demolition Derby at the county fair, so he could cut a large chunk of metal out of a busted bus, I was starting to feel nervous about where I was going and confused about what everything meant. I even slammed on the brakes in front of one of those DO NOT PASS signs along Highway H. "I can't pass this point, Spock!" I yelled at him. "What if there's a hole up ahead and we fall into it?" The sky was turning the pale, smoggy blue of late afternoon, but the warm summer breezes blowing through the car windows were not relaxing me.

"Lisa, there is a high probability that the DO NOT PASS sign means no one can pass you as you drive your vehicle. Your behavior is illogical," he replied.

"I just don't know." I pulled my hands away from the steering wheel, but they were shaking so much, I put them back and gripped the faux leather covering even tighter. "I don't know anything." An emotional man would have recognized my hysteria and tried to calm me with soothing words, but Spock, of course, had no emotions and could barely recognize the dangerous situation he was in—sitting in the passenger seat as I put my idling Ford Fiesta into park in the middle of a road that cut a cornfield in half. Lately, I had been forgetting things I used to know—what highway signs meant, how far to stop behind a flashing school bus, what to do with the dirty kitty litter—things that were somewhat insignificant, but necessary for everyday life. For a moment, I wondered if Spock's mind meld had messed up my memory, confused my knowledge of signs, made me forget important things, but then I remembered my parents' crumpled car in the ditch and I realized the mind meld wasn't that powerful. I wish it had been.

When Spock first landed in Wisconsin, he snuck in a basement window of the duplex I had lived in with my parents and now lived in alone. He must have been digging through old boxes, looking for wires, because the scratchy noises coming from the basement made me think squirrels were getting in again, so I tiptoed down the stairs with the junior-size baseball bat and almost had time to scream when

I felt someone grab my shoulder from behind. Next thing I knew, I was lying on the floor and this old Jewish-looking man was kneeling over me, chanting, and touching my face. "My mind to your mind... my thoughts to your thoughts... my mind..." I didn't automatically recognize him and, for some reason, thought I was eleven years old again and getting in trouble for skipping Hebrew school. Then, all of a sudden, I understood that this strange man was Spock. He had done the Vulcan Nerve Pinch on me to keep me quiet, was doing the mind meld so that we would know everything about each other, and wasn't Jewish, even if he sort of looked that way. "Appearances can be deceiving," my father always said, though he was talking about cars. Maybe it's a good thing Spock did the mind meld, which allowed us to share memories. I probably wouldn't have believed him if he'd just told me he was from the future, but I still wondered if his Vulcan desert memories were blocking some of mine. I wanted to think that Spock had the memories I couldn't access, so I could trust him with confusing highway signs, but I couldn't be sure. He didn't know what to do with the kitty litter either and sent Oscar outside to "drop his excrement in the shrubbery." Oscar didn't come back for a week.

Now Spock peered through my windshield at the sharp curve ahead of us. "In the past when you have slowed your vehicle on this highway to show me grazing, domesticated animals, other cars have driven around you. They 'pass' you. Since passing would be dangerous behavior at this juncture, given the speed capabilities of your automobiles and the curve in the road, it is highly probable that sign refers to automobiles passing other, slower automobiles."

"Yeah, but what if it means I can't pass this point? Don't pass right here—this sign!" I almost started crying. "What if there's a hole up ahead in the road from some old construction?"

For some reason, Spock always considered what I said and gave me one of his thoughtful pauses before continuing. "Lisa, a hole in the road should not cause you to panic."

"What?!" I shrieked as a truck beeped behind us, grew rapidly in my rearview mirror, then beeped again as Spock and I watched it drive around my stopped car and disappear beyond the curve.

"That automobile would not have to engage in an illegal and dangerous maneuver, if you would accelerate."

"You're not worried about a hole?" I asked.

"A hole will not impede the progress of your vehicle."

"Yes it would, Spock! We'd be stuck in a hole."

"Does your vehicle have vertical thrusters?" he asked.

"Up and down?! Jeez! No, Spock! This is a Ford Fiesta. It doesn't go up and down. If we're in a hole, we're stuck. This vehicle has forward and backward. Forward and backward—that's it!" I didn't know why I was so upset. Maybe I was worried that Spock wouldn't find the metal he needed from the side of a dented-up old school bus. Maybe I was worried that he wouldn't like the School Bus Demolition Derby, wouldn't find it as entertaining as my dad and I used to when we went every year and cheered at the first scent of a burning engine.

"Please continue driving forward cautiously for our safety. I can assist you in any difficulties ahead." For some reason, when he spoke like that, I believed him, so I tightened my ponytail by grabbing at two long chunks of hair and separating them until the rubber band was tight on the back of my head, took the car out of park, shifted into first gear and then second. As we gained speed on the empty road, I wiped my eyes on my sleeve, took a few deep, diaphragm breaths, and gradually began to lose my fear of leftover holes. "This is a very quiet road," Spock observed from the passenger seat—using my own words to describe highways with only a few cars. Recently, he'd begun picking up some of my phrases.

"I'm taking you on the back roads to the fairgrounds, Spock—

more scenic and less crowded. Hey," I said. One of his ears was poking out of the knit green acrylic of the Packers hat I made him wear. "Pull your hat down." I suddenly sounded like my own father, shouting out the door for me to wear a hat, scarf, or a jacket over the Wiota Middle School sweatsuit I wear to teach physical education to sixth-, seventh-, and eighth-grade students. I had figured I could live with my parents for the first year of teaching to save for a condo in Evanston, but then the rental unit opened up and I got along fine with my parents, except for my father's fear of breezes and my mother's almost mythic quest to find me an attractive, available, intelligent Jewish male in southern Wisconsin. "Maybe it's not dairy and meat that don't mix, but the dairy state and Jews," I would always tease her. "Oh hush," she'd say and offer potential sons of acquaintances as if simply saying their names got them into jewelry stores picking out diamonds. "Millie Hempel over in Jackson has three gorgeous sons. One is named Ron, I think."

"The Minnie we visited in the geriatric home? How old are her sons? I'm only twenty-four, Mom." When she said not Minnie, but Millie, I leaned back on the kitchen counter and said, "You mean the Millie with the cross-dressing son." My mother, truly confused, set down the ladle she had been using to pour liquid strawberry jelly from the pot into the tight row of sanitized Mason jars and said, "Millie doesn't have . . . what are you . . . ?"

"Stop teasing your mother." My father stood in the doorway, smelling of fresh cut grass and diesel fuel. When I tried to look innocent, he pointed a finger at me and said, "Stop."

"Dad," I said, "I can find my own husband, when I'm ready. I'm living on my side of the duplex and paying you rent, so I shouldn't have to take this. She should hound Martin."

"Your brother's another story. Let your mother love you how she knows," he said with finality as he walked past me into the family room and settled into his recliner. "Preseason Packers tonight," he shouted back into the kitchen to change the subject, so I walked into the family room and sat on the couch. "You know they're letting me coach the football team for sixth graders and it's going to be boys *and* girls. Isn't that great?"

"That's great, Lisa. Very modern. See, Elena," he spoke loudly so his voice would carry into the kitchen. "Our daughter is very modern—that's all."

"Millie's sons are modern!" Mom shouted back in her high voice, which carried into the family room, over to Mrs. Sorensen's house next door, and easily across half the county. "Not modern enough to be cross-dressers, but they're modern!"

Sitting in my car, I wondered if in the future, where Spock lived, men and women played on the same professional sports teams. Would Spock understand human athletic games? He adjusted his hat and asked, "What type of metal is used in school bus construction?"

"You know, I'm not really sure." We had driven into the more populated section of Highway H, so we passed ranch homes set at the end of half-mile driveways and acres of mowed, green lawn. "But like I said, this stuff is heavy because they build the buses strong to protect the kids."

"Do the children have any other protective devices at their disposal during the demolition derby?" he asked in his quiet, not-trying-to-judge-humans way.

I stared at Spock in confusion, forgetting safety and good driving habits. "Oh no, Spock. The kids aren't still in the buses. These are old buses they don't use for school anymore." His eyebrow arched in relief. "These are the crappy, almost broken ones. But the metal—the body is good metal, like I told you. We can get some after the derby. You have your laser thing, right?"

"I have the equipment to obtain the piece I need," he said.

"Good." I laughed at his question. "No kids in there, Spock, jeez...we're not that bad on this planet."

Although I tried to be accommodating, Spock was so exact about everything that he annoyed me, but then I realized a person with his concern for specifics would be good at flying spaceships. Once I asked him what it felt like to die and then come back to life on the Genesis planet, but he reminded me that he didn't have feelings. Before I could rephrase the question to "What was it like to be reborn on the Genesis planet?" he switched topics and asked if I had thought of a way to disguise him. That's when I gave him Dad's Packers hat to cover his ears and some of Dad's old clothes to wear instead of his Starfleet uniform. But he still sounded odd when he spoke, because he called me "daughter" in public sometimes, which wasn't the plan. I wanted him to pretend I was his daughter, not call me "daughter." By the time I started taking him to restaurants, I was used to hearing, "Daughter, please order the appropriate dishes for me." He liked hummus from Café Lebanon, and the tofu from the Chinese take-out place, but not McDonald's salads.

Showing Spock the Earth, or what I knew of it, was sometimes bizarre because the easy places became problematic and the difficult places, the ones I avoided, became even more problematic. For instance, when Spock expressed interest in my religious background, I didn't want to take him to temple, because he wouldn't know what to do. "You could instruct me in the proper behaviors," he suggested as he sat at my kitchen table eating Chinese leftovers. I told him it was too complex. I didn't tell him that I hadn't gone to temple in years. "But my disguise is predicated on my being interpreted as an 'old Jewish man,' as you so often say. Perhaps I should learn more about your heritage." I told him not to worry, but he insisted.

"Fine," I said and rented *Fiddler on the Roof* from the video store, set him up with the remote, a bowl of air popped popcorn, and my brother's old copy of *E. T.* I wanted him to see that we suspected there might be alien life. He could learn about my ancestors and then how humans in the present would deal with aliens.

"Fascinating," he said after the movie marathon. "Should I learn a musical instrument?" He kicked the recliner footrest down.

"No, Spock," I said as I leaned back on the couch. "That's not the point."

"Perhaps if E.T. had learned to vocalize better, he would be pressured to relocate on Earth instead of having to leave the planet."

"Spock! Those are two separate movies!"

"The similarities are remarkable."

Sometimes for a logical Vulcan he was completely dense. "Spock, one is about Jewish people in Russia—like my ancestors—and the other is an alien—like you, from another planet."

"When the winter comes," he asked, "will we be forced to leave the duplex?"

As we drove through another cornfield, I rolled up my window and turned on the air-conditioning. To get to the fairgrounds, I needed to turn onto Route 117, which was right past the pull-off people used when they climbed Thompson's Hill, so I told Spock we could stop there on the way and get a great view of a whole cabbage farm. "I have been curious about Earth's agricultural production methods at this time," he said. I turned onto the dusty patch along the road that everyone parked on, matting down the grass till it gave up and turned to dirt and stones for car tires to crunch over. When we opened the car doors, the sun and dust and weedy smell from knee-high brush hit our senses like a brick wall, like a car hitting a brick wall, like a car hitting another car at eighty-five miles per hour. And I remembered how different walking in a field of weeds smelled depending on if it were day or night, or even noon or 8:00 A.M. The smell was always different in warm weather and I wondered—picturing my parents' car flipped over into the weeds alongside the highway, in the dark, with the tires spinning and the headlights still on—what their last smell was. My parents always drove with the windows open, if it was warm enough. What did the weeds smell like that night?

After our short hike up Thompson's Hill to check out the cabbage farm, and then back to the car, I pulled onto Highway H and then turned onto Route 117. Spock said, "That view was intriguing," and I nodded. "Cabbage has a distinct aroma," he said.

"We'll get that last piece of metal you need, radio your ship, and get the hell out of here. We're almost near the state line." I rolled my window down to get fresh air.

"When we took this route to dine at the Lebanese restaurant, you informed me of the state boundary," he reminded me.

"Oh, yes." I smiled at the memory. "I brought you to Chicago for Lebanese food—good for vegans." He agreed.

The first time I made dinner for Spock, he didn't even know what kind of vegetarian he was. When I asked him if he was lacto-ovo or vegan, he replied that he was Vulcan and I said everybody knew that. What type of vegetarian? He looked puzzled. When I asked about milk, he announced that he consumed dairy products as an infant through breast-feeding, as if we didn't have breasts on this planet and he was some cosmic La Leche representative. Okay, I told him, then you eat cheese. No, he did not. Milk? He refused. Eggs? He asked if eggs were considered "dairy," which frustrated me because I never thought eggs should be on that level of the food pyramid either, I was just asking. My sixth graders always assumed eggs were there because they were white, like milk, and Spock was not turning out to be any easier as a student. I put the box of mac and cheese back on the shelf and found an old can of kidney beans and some rice.

Spock was difficult to live with, and not only because he was vegetarian. I had to hide him from Mrs. Sorensen next door, and it didn't help that she was trying to feed me through my grief with plates of caramel brownies and huge tins of cowboy casserole. Every time I saw her, she would hand me another dish of food and say, "Your parents are with God now, dear." She'd offer to help me clean the house, too, but I didn't let her in. I didn't want her to see Spock. "You're always driving off somewhere," she said. "Where do you go?" I told her I was attending to my parents' affairs and had to go to a bank in Milwaukee. "Oh dear," she said. "Couldn't your brother do that?"

"My brother's busy gardening in Oconomowoc," I told her.

"Oh, is that his business now?" Mrs. Sorensen was trying to be friendly, but looked so nervous around me that I made Spock sleep in the basement for a few days, till she went off to Florida to visit her grandchildren. Then I let him stay in the guest room.

It also didn't help that my friend Joanie always called to check on me when I was boiling dinner. I told her I was fine as I peeled the paper off a can of beans and wiped the top off before opening it. "I've been worried about you since you started the leave of absence," she said. "The kids really missed you at the end of the year. And we don't see you jogging down at the track."

"I'm taking a break from exercising," I told her.

"And Frank was wondering if you wanted to help with his Little League team. It'd be good for you to get out."

"No, I'm taking a break from coaching, too." I dumped the beans in the colander and rinsed off the slimy fluid.

"Frank went over and mowed your lawn, you know. He knocked,

but you weren't there." When I didn't respond, I heard her take a deep breath through the phone. "I'm not the only one worried about you. We just want to help."

"You can't." I started to get angry. "My parents died and I want to be alone for a while. Is that so bad?"

"No, hon." She was backpedaling. "No. You just never wanted to be alone before and your brother didn't stay long and I know that made you sad. I'm here for you, okay? Are you still seeing that psychiatrist?"

"No. He was crazy. Listen, I'm cooking and I gotta go. I'll call if I need anything."

"Promise?" I heard her ask as I hung up.

Spock asked who had communicated with me and I actually told him to shut up, which was rude, but I was confused. My parents had just died and I wasn't angry that they left me in the middle of a huge state with my brother five hours away and a community of people who thought that if I would just coach something, I would feel better. I wasn't angry that I was left alone on the flattest, most boring part of the planet to instruct young children how to throw a ball and eat vegetables. I wasn't angry, just really sad because that's how a person is supposed to be when loved ones die, not jealous, not angry, but sad. Only when I talked to Spock, I didn't feel sad anymore, but sometimes I got angry with him.

When we pulled into the gravel parking lot of the fairgrounds, along with everyone else in the county it seemed, I rolled up my window to keep the dust out and told Spock to do the same. The gravel section of the parking lot gave way to bumpy portions of grass and then dried mud, which spit out sheets of dust. A sad-looking teenaged boy used a white flag to point us to our parking spot, scratched his face with his other hand, and continued walking backward and pointing at the cars that pulled in behind us. Most people came for the School Bus Demolition Derby at night, but some had been there all day getting their animals judged, their homemade sauerkraut tasted, or their nerves thrilled on the carnival rides. Spock stared out at the rows of cars we needed to walk through to get to the ticket booth and into the fair and I thought he might not want to walk that far, so I said, "It's not that far," as I pulled up my emergency brake and turned off the engine.

"I am not concerned about the distance, but am fascinated by the number of fossil-fuel-burning vehicles," he said.

"This is America, Spock." I reached in back for my sweatshirt and my father's old spring jacket for Spock. "This is what we do." I handed the jacket to him and he set it on the dashboard.

"I am not as affected by temperature fluctuations as you are," he said.

"Spock, just bring the damn coat!" My anger scared me, so I turned to look out my window for a moment to see a peaceful horizon. Instead, I saw a woman in the car next to mine, dancing in her seat as she put her car into park. Her lips moved with the words of a song and her eyelids fluttered shut. I thought for a moment of my brother singing along to his Bob Dylan's greatest hits tape as he drove us from the funeral, his voice cracking at the high notes and tears running down his face. I was in the passenger seat of my own car, letting him drive because the funeral director held the passenger door open for me, eyes down, with a hand out for assistance and I obeyed. We had just watched our parents in side-by-side coffins being lowered, by an air jack, into the ground. "Why didn't we get a limo?" I had asked my brother.

He stared ahead, but paused in his lyrical protest against capitalism,

"They're gas guzzlers," he said. "Bad for the planet. Mom wouldn't want that."

As Spock and I walked up to the gate, I tied my sweatshirt around my waist. Since he didn't have any money, I purchased two orange tickets that said TICKET on them from a thin old man in a wooden kiosk. He flattened out two dirty dollar bills before handing them to me as change along with my halves of the tickets. "There's gonna be a raffle." His voice floated from the shadows behind the chicken wire. "So keep your stubs. It's good you got two tickets. Next."

When we walked through the gate, I was momentarily stunned by the flashing lights and mechanical music of the carnival rides. Children screamed as they slid along the seats of the Tilt-A-Whirl, screamed at their parents for more rides, or screamed in frustration in front of the snow cone vendor. I hadn't been around so much motion and noise since I worked the annual sixth-grade field trip to the chocolate factory. I felt light-headed. "Perhaps you need some refreshment," Spock said and I realized my hand was pressed to my forehead.

"No," I tried to say, but his dark eyes stared back at me. "No, you couldn't buy me a soda anyway." I tried to laugh. "You don't have any money."

I staggered forward, down past the row of games where every challenge seemed to require hand-eye coordination and offered something fuzzy and supposedly soft as a reward, past the carousel and the kiddie rides. I tried to start a conversation with Spock to distract me from all the insane pings and whizzings, but my mouth dried up and my words got lost, until we reached the end of the carnival section and I paused to take a breath at the amphitheater entranceway. To cover my confusion, I asked Spock how things worked in the future with no money. He told me there were plenty of resources in the galaxy for all sentient life to share. When I questioned if all parts of the universe were so enlightened, Spock remarked that, unfortunately, many portions of the galaxy still engaged in monetary trade and other barbarisms.

"Oh jeez, Spock. Come on. I smell burning engines. The derby must have started." Although I knew he didn't like to be touched, I pulled on his arm a little, but he didn't move and I could tell he was forming a question. We stood outside of the open-air amphitheater with people strolling past, while the smell of fried doughnuts blended with exhaust. Engines roared and tires screeched in the distance.

"Do you also engage in employment for monetary funding?" he asked.

"Spock," I said. "All the good seats in the bleachers will be taken."

"You have not answered my question."

"Yes, yes. I work." I kicked at the gravel. "I have some time off is all."

"I have not observed your employment and have been here approximately two of your weeks. Perhaps you could explain."

"Spock, I told you." I started walking so he would follow. "My parents died. School gave me time off. That was May, now it's June and I have summers off anyway."

His stride matched mine and he leaned in to talk. "You have not explained your situation in such detail."

I told him that I taught physical education to middle school students who didn't go to school in the summer. But I got the end of May off too because my parents died in a car crash and my principal thought I needed some space. I smiled and added, "Not like outer space, but time alone." I explained how my principal told me to take a leave of absence because she didn't think I was dealing with things very well—thought I was shell shocked or something, and I explained how I was surprised she used those very words: *shell shocked.*

Spock didn't seem to understand, but I didn't want to bother explaining, so I told him how she gave me this card for a psychiatrist, who asked what I thought other people thought of me. Can you imagine? I asked Spock, and he replied that no, he could not imagine. The psychiatrist wanted to know if I was worried about what was happening to my relationship with my best friend, Joanie. I told the psychiatrist that a person who lost both parents shouldn't have to be worrying about other people. I never went back.

"Humans in my time engage in elaborate ceremonies to commiserate the death of a fellow being," Spock said. "Perhaps other people wanted to worry about you."

"Well, my brother came down from Oconomowoc, but he didn't stay. He's busy living in his yurt, being all organic and shit." And for a moment, I no longer saw Spock standing sedately in front of me. Instead, I imagined my brother as he would be at that moment, making red sauce from his early tomatoes, pushing his long hair out of his eyes with the back of his hand and not noticing when some dark, loose strands accidentally fell into the pot. His food always had something extra in it—a strand of hair clinging to the inside of a pasta bowl or yarn fuzz from one of his hand-knit sweaters floating in the soup. He couldn't see beyond the organic goodness of his food to observe rules of general hygiene, and when some of the sauce bubbled over onto the white enamel stove, he'd keep stirring. The sauce would bake onto the warm stove, harden, and he wouldn't even reach for a sponge. Then he'd look through his Plexiglas window, start humming a little ending tune, turn off the burner, and head out for some weeding before dark. He could sing while driving a car or hiking uphill, but he always hummed at the end of a project, not during it—make organic red sauce, hum, clean the bathroom with useless biodegradable soaps, hum, knit a sweater, hum. I could even hear him laying out a tune, as he grabbed his tools from his trunk and headed out into the garden that surrounded his round home—wading through his organic plants, shuffling past the remaining tomato clusters that leaned onto cornstalks, stepping between the soybean and zucchini plants, sticking his fingers deep into the earth to touch the hairy roots of forgotten potatoes, falling to his knees to let the tears come. He would be thinking of Mom in her garden and Dad mowing the lawn. Grieve, then hum. Weed, then hum. His garden didn't have clear demarcations, but his movement through time always did. I wondered if he was thinking of me.

Standing just inside the amphitheater, I turned to tell Spock, "My brother's weird. He can't live at our house because the lawn has pesticides, so he's up north in his year-round tent. You'd think he'd want to be with his sister after our parents died. You'd think he wouldn't want to be alone right now." I started walking as the summer sky began to fade into the white of early evening.

"The memories concerning your family had intrigued me," Spock said, and I stopped at the base of the wooden bleachers.

"You saw my family in the mind meld?" I was shocked. "So why ask?"

"I needed you to interpret your memories." His head tilted slightly and he grasped my father's old jacket in his left hand.

Before I could reply, I heard the announcer's voice blasting out of the metal speaker fifteen feet above our heads. "Ladies and gentlemen! You are about to witness the strength that has carried your children for years! Now, in early retirement, these school buses still yearn for the chance to prove their metal..."

"Let's go, Spock," I said, not wanting to interpret more memories for him or even demand he return them. "Let's go watch the derby, get some metal, then get off this stupid planet."

Spock followed me up the wooden steps and into the middle level of the bleachers, where we sat down. When I was young, my father took me to this derby every year. We quickly learned that if you sat near the top, you might have a better view, but clouds of exhaust congregated at that height, so the middle was best. My mother and brother came with us the first year, then stayed home after that— probably sitting in the garden contemplating the stars and possibilities of cosmic life. Without saying anything, I knew they enjoyed the quiet of the backyard more than the noise of Dad and me screaming and cheering for trucks, old vans, school buses, and anything that would crash over and over again. Me and Dad. We wanted action, burning oil, the sound of metal crushing metal.

Down in the oval arena, school buses circled, beeping and revving their engines, till there was equal space between them on the dirt-packed floor that had earlier been filled with jumping horses, prize pigs, and men tying themselves into harnesses to pull as many tractors as they could. Now it was school bus time. The fleet of school buses circled menacingly, then began slamming into each other. Sometimes five buses were in the ring at the same time and it became a tag team thing with two buses joining forces to topple another by both ramming its side. Other times, there seemed to be so many buses in the ring they couldn't drive forward without smashing into each other. At one point, after we'd been there for about half an hour, there were only two buses in the ring and they turned toward each other, increased their speed, and crashed engine to engine in the center. The metal folded and crunched with such a familiar thigh-buckling, bone-twisting sound that I was surprised to hear a sustained ringing afterward, like a bell made out of school bus metal sounding deep and clear, till it wiped out my vision of Spock and the people cheering for their favorite buses. Suddenly, all I saw was my parents' car in the drainage ditch and the highway barrier bent where the other car crumpled into it. Then I heard the voice of the policeman who'd been standing next to me when I went to the morgue to identify the bodies. I heard him say the driver would be punished to the full extent of the law, so I didn't need to worry. Full extent of the law, and he added something about how we got to take care of these drunk drivers. I saw my parents under those white sheets—just strange lumpy bodies until the coroner on the other side of the glass pulled at the edges to show my father's face, purple and bent somehow, and then my mother's.

The smell of auto exhaust enveloped me, and for a moment I didn't know where I was. I heard someone say "daughter" in a calm voice. "Spock?" I said tentatively. "Dad?"

"Daughter." I recognized Spock's monotone voice. "I am concerned that these school buses will be completely destroyed." I focused again as two school buses drove away from each other. More people were crowding into the bleachers and they were cheering too loudly for me.

"Ladies and gentlemen," the announcer's voice started up again. "These two warrior school buses separate from the battle for a brief moment, returning to their corners of the ring, beaten and bruised, but not conquered!"

"Spock, there's a couple of rounds." I tried to remember what he had asked. "Plenty of school bus metal."

"Will they be completely damaged?" he asked me.

"No." I waved my hand at him and tried to take deep, diaphragm breaths. "The engines won't last that long. See," I pointed as two buses started toward each other from their corners of the ring and crashed head-on again. "They only go like fifteen miles per hour and mostly aim for the engines, which give out before the rest of the body."

"Fascinating," he said as the buses squealed into reverse before hammering each other again. One bus slammed into the other's side so hard, it rocked back and forth and then fell over. The remaining bus started a victory lap around the ring that was cut short when its engine caught on fire. Both drivers scrambled out—one through his window—and ran for the protective shed at the far end, while three men dragged fire hoses into the ring and doused the fire. "See, they have some safety precautions here, and that one still standing has a good body."

By the time the minibuses were circling the arena, my hands were shaking again. I thought to hand Spock a five and ask him to go get us some sodas, but my mouth was too dry to ask, and I couldn't always see him there next to me, as if my peripheral vision were fading and I couldn't stop myself from staring straight ahead at crash after crash of yellow school buses. Finally I couldn't take it anymore, so I turned directly to Spock, and told him we needed to go, but the bleachers had become so crowded by then with cheering fans that I wasn't even sure how to get to the aisle where the steps were. I didn't know if I could move forward, so I stood awkwardly on the wooden plank with my arms out for balance for some reason, till a guy behind me said loudly, "Are you going anywhere, miss? Maybe you could sit down."

"I can't..." I started to say and then remembered how Martin and I used to shimmy under the bleachers when we were young. I squatted down on the wooden plank, then slid under the seat and onto the complex set of bars before swinging to the dirt floor in the shadows beneath. I landed, knees bent to take the stress.

Spock landed next to me, pulled my arm, and said, "This way."

"No, Spock," I said. "No, I think the exit is that way. I need to get out of here."

"We need metal," he said and I had to agree with him. He started a cautious jog away from the exit, down the long row under the bleachers, bending his head down every ten feet at the crossbeams. I stayed close behind him, feeling my heart pound. When we reached the far end of the bleachers, he surveyed the sheds and cement barns ahead of us, searching for the school buses.

"Spock, I think they bring them over there—behind the monster trucks." I pointed to where a tow truck was dragging a dented school bus past large 4x4s gearing up for their sprint into the ring. He scanned the area in front of us for anyone protecting the school buses, suddenly looking more dangerous than he did fiddling with wires in my basement, or peering over paper menus in confusion. Crouched there under the bleachers, looking for the battered school buses, he seemed almost animal-like, powerful, adept at espionage, hungry for school bus metal. I leaned in next to him to study the dusty spaces between cement barns being lit by orange fluorescent lights high above the ground that sputtered on automatically as the sky slid into darkness. His eyes searched for shadows, mentally mapping a dark path to the buses—cross to the overhang on the sheep barn, then twenty feet to the side of a truck parked to unload hay, then a sprint to hide behind the gas pumps near the crumpled buses, waiting for their last ride to the dump. Spock bent his knees, searched the ground at his feet, and grabbed a large stone. "What are you—" was all I got out before he hurled the stone an impossible distance to strike a lamppost. It exploded in a brief spurt of light and smoke before leaving the space in front of us in darkness.

"Now," was all he said before we ran, crouched and low, as one being across the dusty gravel surface. We stopped with our backs pressed to the cement barn and I realized his hand was on my arm, melting through my sweatshirt, leading me into the safety of the next shadow. He no longer had my father's jacket. We ran again.

The next morning I woke with a dusty taste in my mouth and tried to hang on to a dream about school buses flying above the cornfield at the end of my street. My digital clock radio blinked at 7:02 A.M., so I pulled the damp sheets away from my legs, stood up to search my bedroom floor for some clothes, and forced my legs into a pair of dirty jeans. Then I remembered I had left Spock working in the basement, the night before. He had already cut the school bus metal piece to fit into his communication machine and was fiddling with some circuits to make the thing work. He told me when it was operational, he would contact his ship, which had gotten stuck in some other time as it always seemed to do, and then his shipmates would come to this time, pick us up, and head into the future again. Spock just needed to amplify his transmitter to adapt for multiple time waves. It was interesting at night, but in the morning I felt dried out. My palms smelled like the metal bars below the bleachers and my eyes itched. I tucked my Packers nightshirt into my jeans, pulled my hair into a messy ponytail, then made a quick mental list of what I would bring with me into the future: the necklace my parents gave me for my Bat Mitzvah, the sweater Martin knitted even though it was too small, a ceramic bowl from Joanie, my basketball jersey. I wondered how much Spock would let me bring, so I walked down the hall to his room to see if he was up.

I knocked lightly on the hollow door. When there was no response I opened it slowly, saying, "Spock?" but he wasn't there. His daybed was pushed together and his clothes from the night before were folded in perfect squares and sitting on a corner at the end of the bed. The green Packers hat lay on top with its emblem glaring up at me.

"Spock?" I said again to the empty room, thinking that he too had left without letting me say good-bye.

I felt a few hot tears streak down my face. I repeated his name one more time, then ran down the hall, slammed open the basement door, and padded down the cold, cement steps. On the last step, I realized the light was already on and Spock was hunched over his communication machine on the folding table next to the dryer. I stopped at the last step and he turned. "I have already contacted my ship and am waiting for them to adjust the transporters."

"Oh, Spock." Looking at him there in his uniform, without my father's hat, made me feel more lonely, like I was prepared to miss him.

"My captain has been informed that you will be joining us."

Suddenly, the machine crackled and buzzed. The yellow metal piece Spock had cut from the side of the bus rattled against a metal clip attached to my old hard drive and a spark flashed, bright and hot, then was gone. "Spock," a strange voice came through clearly. "We've got the transporters set and are locking down your coordinates. Are you and the young lady ready?"

"Are you prepared to leave?" Spock asked me, but I couldn't respond, so he pressed a button and spoke at his machine. "Mr. Scott, we require a few minutes."

"Right. Scott out" came back. My knees felt weak. I leaned on the wall and slid down to sit on the last cold step.

"Are you unwell?" Spock asked but all I could do was shake my head. "You are crying."

"Spock, I thought you'd left without me."

"I agreed to take you with me."

"I know, but I was afraid." A sob came up through my chest and made a sucking noise as I tried to stop it.

"I am preparing for us to transport together as we agreed. I would not leave you alone."

"I know," I said, feeling guilty that I had doubted him. "I know, but..."

Although he waited attentively for me to finish my sentence, all I could do was stare at the floor and then at him. "Do you remember what I have explained concerning the transporter device?" he asked.

"Yes," I said obediently.

"You will not be harmed, although the sensation may feel odd to you." I nodded. "Are you prepared to leave?" he asked.

"No," I said feeling my hands begin to shake. "I can't go." The machine buzzed again.

"Do you require more time to prepare?"

"No, Spock. That's not it. I don't know...I can't go into space."

"Then I must leave without you," Spock said.

The voice from the machine interrupted us. "Mr. Spock, are ye ready for transport?" Spock looked at me for permission.

"You can go now, Spock." He raised a hand with his middle fingers separated, which I recognized, from his memories, as his planet's special greeting. I raised my hand, too. "Live long," I said.

"Next year in Jerusalem," he said. Then he pressed a button on his communication machine and turned slowly into floating diamonds that sparkled and hummed in my basement before fading completely into silence.

By the end of July, I started jogging again on the high school track. Joanie must have seen me from her window, because she came over with vegetables from her father's stand and made me eat salad. When I said I really wanted to see Martin, she told me to drive up there. I should have driven up there weeks ago, but I started crying and told her I didn't want to drive. I was afraid. So she dumped her tape collection straight from her passenger seat to the driveway, shoved me in her car, and drove me up to Martin's place herself. He was so happy to see me, he started plucking vegetables the minute we pulled in the driveway and almost had a meal planned by the time we stopped the car. We sat in his garden a while before we went inside to cook vegetarian style, and then Joanie drove me home. The next weekend she drove me up again and after that, I could drive myself.

I also started reviewing the new health curriculum for school and called my principal to let her know I was ready to come back in the fall. I told her I was doing well, but I didn't tell her that sometimes memories rush out of nowhere and take over my mind. It's not a bad experience, but it's not something I'd tell my principal. If I sit on the front steps shucking corn, I sometimes see my father out on the gravel next to the road, trying to get the mower to start, or I hear my mother pulling the car into the garage, shouting for help with the groceries as soon as she opens the door. I can't explain how much I miss them. Other times, I shut my eyes and visions flood back from places I have never been—satellites, strange spaceships, rooms filled with odd equipment, but then the memories swirl around and I see the Vulcan desert, stretching out into the horizon. In the distance, Spock walks toward me in robes that flap in the dusty wind, and it's always a relief to see him.

AMBER DERMONT

University of Houston

LYNDON

My father died because our house was infested with ladybugs. Our French neighbors, the Heroux family, had imported a hearty species of the insect to combat aphids in their garden. The ladybugs bred and migrated. Hundreds upon hundreds were living in our curtains, our cabinets, the ventilation system. At first, we thought it was hilarious and fitting for us to be plagued by something so cute and benign. But these weren't nursery rhyme ladybugs. Not the adorable, shiny, red-and-black beetles. These ladybugs were orange. They had uneven brown splotches. When I squished their shells between my thumb and forefinger, they left a rust-colored stain on my skin and an acrid smell that wouldn't wash off. Dad used a vacuum hose to suck up the little arched creatures, but they quickly replaced themselves. The numbers never dwindled. Dad must have smoked a lot of pot before he climbed the ladder to our roof. My guess is that he wanted to cover the opening in the chimney. He'd suspected that the flue wasn't closed all the way. Our house was three stories high. When he fell, he landed on the Herouxs' cement patio, his skull fractured, his neck broken.

For months after his death, I kept finding the ladybugs everywhere. When I stripped my bed, I'd find them in the sheets. When I did laundry, I'd find their dead carapaces in the dryer. When I woke up in the morning, I'd find a pair scuffling along my freshly laundered pillowcases. Then just like that, they were gone.

Long after the last ladybug's departure, I pulled a pair of sunglasses from Mom's purse on the car seat, fogged the lenses with my breath, rubbed the plastic eyes against my chest, and said to her, "You missed the scenic overlook."

Mom swiped her sunglasses away from me. "There will be other stops, Elise," she said.

We were driving through the Texas Hill Country in an upgraded rental car, cruising a roadway called the Devil's Backbone. Our destination: LBJ. His ranch. His reconstructed birth site. The rental car guy had flashed a brilliant smile when he bumped us up from a white Taurus to a monster green SUV. Mom couldn't resist bullying the skinny clerk. "No one screws me on gas mileage. I'm not paying extra to fuel that obscenity. Knock ten dollars off the daily fee." As the car clerk hammered his keyboard and readjusted the price, Mom winked at me.

My mother the investment banker. Every morning, well before dawn, she would maneuver her own Ford Explorer across the George Washington Bridge into Manhattan, cell-phoning her underlings while cutting off other commuters. Mom called her first-year analysts "Meat" and bragged that she, in turn, was known as "The Lion." Mom always wore her long, straightened red hair loose and down her back. She'd sport short skirts and sleeveless dresses, showing off her sculpted calves and biceps. Mom specialized in M&As, corporate re-structuring, and bankruptcy. She traveled a lot. Dad had brain-stormed our presidential sightseeing tours as a way for him to keep me entertained while Mom flew off to Chicago and Denver, dis-mantling pharmaceutical corporations along the way.

"I really think we were supposed to stop at that overlook." We coasted past juniper trees, live oaks, limestone cliffs. As far as I could tell, the whole point of driving the Devil's Backbone was to stop at that particular overlook and view the span of gently sloping hills from the highest vantage point. "Dad would have turned back," I said.

Mom just kept driving. I passed the time by reading snippets from the *Lonely Planet Guide to Texas* and rattling off the names of local towns: Wimberley, Comfort, and Boerne. I flipped down the sun visor, replaited my French braids in the vanity mirror. I'd worn my favorite outfit: red high-top sneakers, baggy khaki shorts, and a T-shirt I'd special-ordered at a mall in Teaneck. For twenty-eight dol-lars, a man from Weehawken had ironed black velvet letters onto the front of a tiny green jersey. The letters spelled out VICTIM. When my mother asked how I got off being so self-pitying, I told her it was the name of my favorite underground band.

The Devil's Backbone reminded me of the shingles sore torment-ing my lower torso. The giant scab resembled a hard red shell. The family doctor had explained how sometimes the chicken pox virus would remain dormant in a nerve ending, waiting for the immune system to weaken before reemerging. He was concerned because he'd never seen shingles in anyone my age. Usually he treated it in older patients or in cases occurring with cancer or AIDS. People closing in or death. I told Mom the shingles were proof I was special. The agony wasn't limited to the blisters on my back. My whole body felt inflamed, as if a rabid wolf were hunting rabid squirrels inside my chest. The doctor recommended ibuprofen for the pain. He gave me pamphlets describing stress-reducing breathing exercises. The first few nights Mom slipped me half a Vicodin and a nip of Benedictine brandy. As I tried to sleep, I heard her roaming from living room to bedroom to family room. I listened. My mother the widow did not weep, did not cry out for her dead husband.

A year after my father died, my mother's breasts began to grow. She developed a deep, embarrassing plunge of cleavage, a pendulous swinging bosom that attacked my own flat body each time she hugged me good night. Mom's belly had pouted. Ballooned. I could detect the domed button of her navel pressing out against the soft silk of her blouses. Her ankles swelled and I became suspicious. Mom was maybe six months into her pregnancy. I did the math. Dad had been pushing dead too long to be the father. I was about to enter my sophomore year at the Academy of Holy Angels. Before school started, I wanted the shingles on my back to disappear, I wanted to tour the reconstructed birthplace of Lyndon Baines Johnson, and I wanted my mother to admit to me that she was pregnant.

With Dad gone, I'd insisted on upholding our family's tradition of visiting presidential landmarks. Dad and I had been doing them in chronological order. We'd sightseen the big ones: Mount Vernon, Monticello, The Hermitage, Sagamore Hill. Weeks before Dad broke his neck, we'd spent a lively afternoon in the gift shop of the John Fitzgerald Kennedy Library, rubbing our faces in the soft velour of JFK commemorative golf towels. The less popular the sites, the more obscure the leader of our country, the more Dad got excited: "Elise, can you imagine? John Tyler actually sat in this breakfast nook and ate soft-boiled eggs from those egg cups." In Columbia, Tennessee, I tore white azalea petals from James K. Polk's ancestral garden while

Dad rambled on about the Mexican War, the "dark horse," and "Fifty-four Forty or Fight." At the Albany Rural Cemetery, Dad and I knelt solemnly before the grave of Chester Alan Arthur. A giant marble angel with voluminous wings towered over us. We prayed to our favorite forgotten leader, the father of civil service reform. One year, we spent Christmas on Cape Cod at a beachside inn that had been a secret getaway for Grover Cleveland and his mistress. Mom couldn't make that trip, so Dad and I tramped by ourselves on the snow-covered sand dunes, plotting my own future run for the presidency. "You need a catchphrase. And a trademark hairdo so the cartoonists can immortalize you."

All day we'd been driving in various stages of silence and radio static. Mom asked whether I'd like to stop for sundaes. I considered patting her belly and making a joke about cravings for ice cream and pickles. I had expected Mom to nix my travel plans for us, but really, I just wanted her to be honest and say to me, "Elise, I can't fly. Not in my condition." Instead, when I said, "Johnson," Mom folded her arms against her burgeoning chest. She swung her hair over her shoulders, and said, "Texas in August? Why can't it be Hawaii? I'm certain Lyndon Johnson loved the hula."

The day before, we'd visited the Sixth Floor Museum in Dallas. Mom and I took the elevator up to the top of the Texas Book Depository. We slowly worked our way through the permanent exhibit dedicated to the Kennedy assassination. Though a glass wall surrounded the actual Oswald window, Mom and I got close enough to size up the short distance between the building and the *X* on the street below. The *X* marked the spot where Kennedy was first hit. I'd always imagined Dealey Plaza as an enormous expanse of traffic and park, but here it was in front of me, tiny and green, more like a miniature replica made by a film crew. One SUV after another covered the

X as the cars drove over the site in perpetual reenactment of Kennedy's last ride. This was the bona fide scene of the infamous crime. Mom whispered, "Even I could make that shot." She hugged me from behind and I felt the baby's heartbeat vibrate through her belly. In anticipation of our trip, I'd begun calling my secret sibling "Lyndon." I asked, "Is Lyndon kicking?" Mom ignored me. Weeks ago, when I'd asked her point-blank if she was pregnant and quizzed her on what she intended to do with the baby, instead of answering the question she told me that her new goal in life was to get me away from "the fucking Holy Angels."

Dad was the Catholic. Mom's family had come over on the *Mayflower.* "Elise, a lot of Yankees brag about tracing their roots back. Always be conscious of your place in history. Most of the people on that ship were poor. Your relatives were the lucky ones with money." Before her parents divorced and squandered everything, my mother grew up rich in Manhattan. Her childhood bedroom had a view of the Sheep Meadow and the Central Park Reservoir. Both of Mom's doormen were named Fritz. When she turned six, her folks hired Richard Avedon to take the snapshots at her birthday party. At sixteen, she'd curtsied before Princess Grace at a charity fund-raiser for retired racehorses. I often felt as though Dad and I were descended from one class of people, while Mom hailed from another class entirely.

My father sold pies for a living. Nominally, he was the vice president of the Pie Piper, his parents' international bakery corporation, but mostly what Dad chose to do was drive his pie truck around the Tri-State Area. Checking and restocking Safeways and Star Markets. Shelving lemon cream, Coconut Dream, and chocolate meringue pies. Dad had a jacket with TEAMSTER embroidered on the back. He liked to brag that he knew the fastest routes in and out of Manhattan, at any point during the day. He knew when best to take the Lincoln Tunnel.

Dad felt that my aristocratic heritage and working-class lineage would make me an ideal political candidate. He cast me as a liberal Democrat and cast himself as my campaign manager. Dad first ran me in third grade for homeroom line leader. I lost to Andorra Rose, whose mother, on election day, made two dozen chocolate cupcakes with pink rosebuds in the center. Dad viewed this loss as a tactical oversight. Our future campaigns always involved the Pie Piper donating dozens of pies and pastries to Holy Angels. In fifth grade, I was class treasurer. In seventh grade, I was student representative to the advisory council on redesigning our school uniforms. Dad imagined I would win the governorship of New Jersey, and from there, if I could find the right Southern running mate, become the first woman president of the United States.

I was twelve the afternoon I caught Dad sprawled out on the Philadelphia Chippendale, one hand holding a silver lighter, the other hand cradling a short ceramic pipe. There'd been a bomb scare at Holy Angels and the nuns had begrudgingly sent us home early. Dad was wearing his boxer shorts and watching a rerun of *The Joker's Wild*. He flung a cashmere blanket over his lap, swung his legs off my mother's two-hundred-year-old sofa, and said, "Honey, come meet James Buchanan." I sat beside my bare-chested father, his blond hair flattened on one side, and watched him twirl his pipe around. "Made this in college. Art class. The clay morphed in the kiln." He showed me the blunt end of the pipe. "Looks just like our bachelor president. His first lady was his niece. Handsome fellow." On the TV, Wink Martindale exclaimed, "Joker! Joker! Joker!" Dad smiled, "Don't worry. Your mom has seen me smoke."

My father confided to me that he'd had panic attacks as a kid. "I'd be paralyzed with fear. Knocked out with it. The only thing that helped was reading almanacs." Dad memorized historical facts, like the years each president served in office, and he'd repeat these dates in an effort to calm himself down. "Zachary Taylor, 1849 to 1850, Rutherford Birchard Hayes, 1877 to 1881, Franklin Pierce, 1853 to 1857." At fifteen, Dad discovered pot.

I loved sitting in the living room while Dad toked up. Marijuana haze drifted around me, settling on the folds of my pleated wool skirt. I'd lean my neck down against my Peter Pan collar and catch the wonderful stink of weed lingering against my blouse. I was a nervous kid. I often threw up before big tests. No one at Holy Angels invited me to their sleepovers anymore, on account of my loud, thrashing night terrors. Even my closest friend, Alana Clinton, often insisted I take a chill pill. I'd attempted hypnosis therapy to treat the warts on my hands, the muscle spasm in my left eye, the mysterious rashes that appeared across my stomach, my inner-ear imbalance, and my tooth-grinding problem. Only breathing in my father's pot smoke truly relaxed me. He never let me inhale directly from Buchanan, but he'd grant me a contact high. Afterward, the two of us would split one of my father's ancestral peach pies. This happened once or twice a week. Mom didn't know.

Mom and I pulled off the Devil's Backbone and stopped for soft serve at a place called the Frozen Armadillo. She got a chocolate and vanilla twist with cherry-flavored dip, and I ordered a vanilla cone covered in something advertised as Twinkle-Kote. Outside in the August heat, the ice cream dripped down our arms. We decided to eat the cones in the air-conditioned rental car. I told Mom my theory about LBJ and the Kennedy assassination. I was convinced that Lyndon was the real culprit. Nothing that big could happen in Texas without Lyndon's approval.

"Motive is obvious," I said. "Who gains the most from Kennedy dying? LBJ gets to be president. Who's responsible for the investigation and subsequent cover-up? LBJ gets to appoint the Warren Commission. There's proof that LBJ actually knew Jack Ruby. All LBJ ever wanted was to be president. Not vice president. He was an old man. Time was running out." I told my mother that there had been talk of Kennedy dropping LBJ from the ticket in '64.

"How do you know so much?" she asked.

"It's Dad's fault," I said.

"You know, your father always wanted to be a high school history teacher."

"What stopped him?" I asked.

"Well, sweetie," Mom said, wiping ice cream off my nose, "convicted felons aren't allowed to teach children."

Mom balanced her own ice cream cone against the steering wheel and turned on the ignition. She headed out toward Johnson City. We drove past brown, sandy hills crowned by patches of cacti with round, thorned leaves.

"Take it back," I told her. "What you said. Take it back."

"You shouldn't idealize your father. You didn't know him as well as you'd like to think."

"From the looks of it," I pointed to Mom's belly, "Dad didn't know you at all." I was deciding between calling my mother a "bitch" and calling her a "fucking bitch" when she chucked the rest of her ice cream cone at the side of my face. The ice cream splattered against my hair and cheek. The wafer cone landed on the side of my leg. I picked it up and threw it back at her. I pulled the top of my own ice cream off its cone and aimed for Mom's chest. She shrieked, swerving the car and throwing back at me whatever clumps of ice cream she could pull from her cleavage. We each lost sense of our target, hurling any ice cream slop we could get hold of. The rental car's green cloth upholstery and side windows clouded over in a sticky, cherry-flavored film. Chocolate ice cream melted in streams down Mom's chest. The black velvet letters on my VICTIM T-shirt soaked up my dessert. Mom drove and swore. She called me ungrateful and threatened to leave me right there on the spine of the Devil's Backbone. Mom didn't notice the bend in the road. She screamed in confusion as our rental car lurched through a very real white picket fence, careening down a hill and into an orchard. She pumped and locked the brakes just in time for us to hit a patch of peach trees.

The air bags did not work. No explosion of white pillow. In that brief instant, as I watched the seat belt jerk Mom back and hold her safely in place, I thought of how the pressure and force of the air bag would have crushed Mom's belly, crippling Lyndon, killing the start of him. Mom saved me from the windshield by holding her right arm out straight against my chest. "Holy fuck," she said.

Mom surveyed me. "Are you all right?" she asked. We got out of the car together, the two of us still dripping with ice cream. We marveled at the damage. A peach tree appeared to be growing out of the hood of our rental car. Mom picked up a pink and yellow fruit, brushing the fuzz against her lips before taking a bite. "You and your presidents," she said. "That's it. I'm through. And you can be damned sure I'm not taking you to Yorba Linda. There's no fucking way I'm visiting Nixon."

I insisted on hiking the remaining mile and a half to the LBJ Ranch. The car was not my problem. I was a kid and this was my summer vacation. I stayed a hundred yards in front of my mother. She played with her cell phone the entire time, dialing and redialing numbers. From her loud cursing, I could tell that there was no service, no way to call a tow truck or taxi. No way to complain to her mystery lover about me. I imagined my mother had many young lovers. For all I knew, she didn't know who Lyndon's father was. I didn't want to think about The Lion having sex. I wanted to remember the Saturday mornings when I'd wake up early, sneak into my parents' room, and burrow a narrow tunnel between their sleeping bodies. I'd trace the beauty marks on Mom's back, naming the largest ones. With the tips of my fingers, I'd smooth out the worry lines on my father's forehead. Their bed was an enormous life raft. I would imagine that the three of us were the last family left in the world. I loved my parents best when they were asleep and I was standing guard.

On the LBJ tour bus, the man sitting closest to the door stood up to give my mother his seat. She smiled and said, "Not necessary." We'd taken turns washing up by ourselves in the ladies' room of the park's Visitors Center. While Mom pulled knots of peanut Twinkle-Kote from her hair, I watched a short film about the ranch, the birthplace, and the family cemetery. The birthplace wasn't really the birthplace. The original birthplace had been torn down. LBJ actually had a facsimile of the house rebuilt during his presidency. He decorated the house in period pieces, but none of the furnishings were original except for a rawhide cushioned chair. The film showed Lyndon in a cowboy hat and sports coat posing on the front porch of his make-believe home. Dad would have loved the film. He would have leaned over and repeated the story about LBJ and the goat fucker.

"Do you know about LBJ and the goat fucker?" I said to Mom. "When Johnson first ran for office, he told his campaign manager to spread a rumor that his opponent had sex with farm animals. When the manager pointed out that this wasn't true, Johnson said, 'So what. Force the bastard to admit, "I never fucked a goat." He'll be ruined.'"

"You curse like your father." Mom sighed.

The reconstructed birthplace was the first stop on the tour. The park ranger/bus driver was a chatty, older woman named Cynthia. She bounced around the bus taking our tickets, sporty and spry in her light green ranger's uniform. A row of bench seats ran along each side of the bus facing a wide center aisle. Another row of seats ran along the back. There were nine other people on the bus: the polite man closest to the door, a pair of elderly, identical twin sisters who wore matching red Windbreakers, a middle-aged German couple toting two large canvas backpacks, and a family of four. The mother and father of the family laughed as their young daughter hugged her baby brother and scooped him up onto her lap. The little blond boy had a crazy cowlick I wanted to flatten and fix. Mom and I sat in the very back row, several seats apart from each other.

As we drove past the banks of the Pedernales River, Cynthia described the Lawn Chair Staff Meetings Lyndon held at his ranch during Vietnam. She told us that Lady Bird had kindly donated all of the land and the ranch to the National Park Service, but chose to live part-time in the main ranch house. I could feel my shingles sore rubbing against my T-shirt, the pain ratcheting up inside of me. I was still angry at Mom. I held my breath to calm myself and ran through dates: "Andrew Johnson, 1865 to 1869, Benjamin Harrison, 1889 to 1893, Warren Gamaliel Harding, 1921 to 1923." Mom leaned over and said, "Lady Bird is shrewd. Putting the ranch into a trust is an excellent way of avoiding taxes."

We drove past lazy orange and white Hereford cattle grazing by the river. An ibex shot out from behind a sycamore tree, and then another ibex followed, and another. The cows ignored the elegant brown and white horned antelopes. Cynthia said, "Lady Bird also runs an exotic animal safari on the ranch. As exotic animals are legal in Texas, hunters can pay the Johnson family to come and stalk rare creatures from the Dark Continent." My mother whispered, "Lady Bird's a genius."

I'd always thought that Dad liked Mom because her mother's maiden name was Van Buren. One afternoon, my father told me how he and

Mom began dating. "You have to be careful with this information," he said. "Your mother doesn't know the whole story." My parents met their freshman year in college. The same day Dad met Mom, he also met another woman, a sculpture major named Lisel. She had wavy black hair, a German accent, and an apartment off campus. Dad liked both women and was stuck deciding whether to pursue Mom or Lisel. He decided to go after Lisel. He was dressed up and on his way to meet the German sculptress for their first serious date when he bumped into Mom. "She'd been playing rugby and she was totally covered in mud and sweat. She asked me if I wanted to take a shower with her. I went back to her dorm." Dad smiled. "And that's the moment when my life began." He said something else about Mom being a sexy lady, but I clutched my hands to my ears and blocked him out.

The reconstructed birthplace was white with green shutters. It was small. Just two bedrooms, a kitchen, and a breezeway. Cynthia showed us the bedroom where Johnson was birthed. A queen-size bed dominated the room. I noticed long, shiny black beetles crawling over the chenille bedspread. One of the beetles flew up and circled past me. Cynthia said, "His mother claimed that he had it wrong. She kept insisting that Lyndon was actually born in the smaller bedroom, but LBJ was adamant."

In the kitchen I saw the rawhide chair, the one authentic piece. I wanted to run my hand over the cow fur. Right by the kitchen table stood a baby's wooden high chair with LADY BIRD etched across the backrest. Cynthia said that the First Lady had been kind enough to donate her own Roycrofter high chair for the replica. Mom mouthed "Lady Bird" to herself and rested her hands on her belly. I pictured a plump, kicking baby fidgeting in the chair. "Mom, if you want," I said, "I could steal the high chair for you."

"What's a lady bird?" Mom asked Cynthia.

"A lady bird is what we in the South call ladybugs."

Mom looked at me. She shook her head. "Those little killers."

Sometimes when I hung out with my dad while he smoked Buchanan, I'd get paranoid. Even though I understood how girls got pregnant, I'd imagine one of my father's sperm magically escaping from his boxer shorts, swimming through his pants, landing on my leg, and inching up my Holy Angels uniform. I imagined being pregnant with Dad's baby, but I couldn't imagine anything after that. In her grief Mom had fucked someone. Maybe The Lion had some Meat after all. She probably couldn't explain her own pain over losing Dad. At least not to me. I knew harboring a baby while I looked on could only make her feel alone. While Dad was alive, Mom was certain I loved him more than her. "The two of you have your own secret society," she'd say. Now that he was dead, Mom was convinced I'd love the memory of him more than I'd ever love her. I wanted to tell her she was dead wrong, but I wasn't sure that she was.

The Johnson family graveyard, nothing more than a small plot of land squared off by a stone wall, stood straight across from the birthplace. Mom and I walked hand in hand in the August heat to the cemetery. Cynthia and our bus mates were still loitering beside the house. Mom told me that Dad had been arrested before I was born. He'd been pulled over for speeding in his pie truck. The cop noticed a Baggie of pot in the ashtray. A very big Baggie of pot. Dad was arrested, tried, and found guilty of possession with intent to distribute. "Your grandfather could have made the whole thing go away, but instead, he let your father do six months in prison. Minimum security, a life lesson. I was pregnant with you the whole time he was locked up."

Mom tucked a wisp of loose hair behind my left ear. "I figured you should know about your father's past, you know, for your political career."

I wanted to tell her that I was sorry. As much as I loved my father, I was mystified as to why Mom, who worked ninety hours a week, would stay married to a man who was happiest when lying down on a couch, a man who couldn't keep his balance on the roof of his own house. A man who could never find his wallet or remember to tie his shoes. A man who panicked every time the phone rang. I would never understand how she had come to love him.

"I'm sorry about the rental car," I said.

"Insurance will cover it."

Mom and I looked out at the family gravestones. The tallest one was Lyndon's.

"Honey, your dad was a wonderful, frustrating, lovely, ridiculous man."

When we reboarded the bus, our tour guide Cynthia smiled and informed us, "You're all very lucky. Lady Bird is in Bermuda this week. The Secret Service has okayed us for a drive-by of the ranch house."

Mom shouted down the length of the bus to Cynthia, "Can't we leave the bus and visit the inside of the house?"

"I'm afraid not, ma'am."

"But that's why we came here," the elderly twins said in unison.

"Sorry, ladies. Those are the rules." Cynthia turned the bus onto a red dirt road.

Without even the slightest look in my direction, Mom shouted, "My daughter has visited every other presidential home in the country. We came all the way from New Jersey."

"Security risk," Cynthia said. "Plus, the ranch house is Lady Bird's primary residence. None of us would want a bunch of strangers trudging through our homes while we were out of town."

"It's fine, Mom," I said.

"Besides, you've seen the birthplace," Cynthia said.

"The reconstructed birthplace," Mom retorted. "Elise, you came here to see the house, and I'm going to make sure you see it." My pregnant mother pushed herself up from her seat on the moving bus, clutched her leather purse, and waddled to the front. Cynthia continued to drive. Mom held on to a railing and leaned into the back of Cynthia's chair. Cynthia shook her head. And then she shook her head so violently that her mirrored sunglasses flung off her face and skittered to the floor of the bus. Mom kept right on talking. She reached into her purse and pulled out her wallet. Everyone on the bus heard Cynthia say, "Ma'am, I am a ranger for the National Park Service. I cannot be intimidated."

While my mother continued to buzz in her ear, Cynthia picked up the microphone on her CB and radioed headquarters. She spoke in a quick, clipped lingo that I did not understand. Then Mom swiped at the CB, grabbing at the spiral speaker cord. The entire bus and I witnessed their slap fight for control over the CB. Neither Mom nor Cynthia could hold on to the gadget, and the black cord snapped and struck against the dashboard console. Mom leaned in and appeared to snare Cynthia in a headlock. None of my fellow passengers moved. The polite man who had offered Mom his seat looked at me and said, "Can't you calm her down?" Mom let go of Cynthia and said in a hoarse voice, "You win." Cynthia announced that the bus would return to the Visitors Center, immediately. We would not be driving by the Johnson ranch house today. The German couple spoke German in quick, violent snatches. The little boy with the cowlick put his hands over his ears and screamed in three sharp blasts before his sister covered his mouth with the back of her hand. I felt my shingles pain run down my neck and arms. Felt the ladybug shell on my back harden.

Mom strode down the length of the bus, past identical fierce glares from the twin sisters. She sat beside me. I shook my head and said, "This is not Manhattan. We're in the Republic of Texas. Pushy doesn't work here."

Mom said, "Don't worry, kid. I got it covered."

Cynthia sped back to the Visitors Center. She tried to calm the agitated passengers by turning on the bus's stereo system and blasting Lyndon Johnson's favorite song, "Raindrops Keep Fallin' on My Head." I stared out the window at the terraced farmland and tried to remember why I ever cared about the presidents. I loved them because my father loved them. Since he'd died I'd been trying every day to reclaim his sense of history. All I'd managed to do was re-create his level of stress and discomfort. The red sores on my back proved to me that I was nothing more than the nervous daughter of a panicked man. That was my place in the passage of time, my inheritance. I could never be president. I was the would-be pothead child of a convicted felon and a whore. I tried to picture my father relaxed, stoned, resigned to his shortcomings. His eyes bloodshot, his smile goofy, a halo of ladybugs flying over his blond head: That was the father I loved.

When Cynthia parked the bus, she pointed to Mom and me and said, "You two stay seated. For the rest of you, I'm sorry but this is the last stop." Mom clutched my arm. As Cynthia ushered our fellow travelers off the bus, I imagined the Secret Service descending upon us. We were a family of felons. I figured the penalty for assaulting a park ranger included a prison sentence. Maybe now, with the threat of incarceration pending, Mom would admit her pregnancy. I was furious with her. She'd ruined our vacation, stained my VICTIM T-shirt, tarnished my father's reputation.

Through the bus window, Mom watched Cynthia confer with a

fellow ranger in the Visitors Center. Mom said, "I told Ranger Cindy to wait ten minutes in case those Germans got curious."

The Johnson ranch house was smaller than I had imagined. The white paint on the outside of the house needed a touch-up. The large bow windows sagged in their rotting casings. Before Cynthia dropped us off she pointed out the security cameras and told us which ones were working. "I'll give you twenty minutes like we agreed. The house is locked, but you can view the grounds and Lyndon Baines Johnson's antique car collection."

A massive live oak stood on the front lawn. Lyndon, or some other hunter, had attached two plaques with enormous stuffed deer's heads directly to the tree's trunk. Mom petted the buck's antlers. I'm not sure what Mom promised or paid Cynthia for our private tour of the Johnson Ranch. Mom believed in cash, and always had at least a thousand dollars stashed on or near her person. She also believed in threats and bribes. With a phone call, Mom could place a lien on your ancestral home or buy you the ostrich farm you'd always dreamed of owning. Mom knew how to bargain. How to make a deal. She was fearless. She knew that she couldn't appreciate the presidents the way Dad and I had, but she could give me something Dad never could. Mom could provide access. She could make things happen. She had what it took to be president.

We walked into the open-air front of the airplane hangar that held Lyndon's cars: a red Ford Phaeton, a Fiat 500 Jolly Ghia, a vintage fire truck, and a little green wagon. The sun had tanned Mom's face. She looked beautiful, victorious. I put my arms around her, rubbed her tummy. "What is it?" I asked. She looked down at me and placed my hand flat on the crown of her belly. "It's a boy."

Inside the hangar, I recognized one of the automobiles, a small blue and white convertible. "This is one of those land-and-sea cars.

An amphibious car. Johnson used to drive his friends around the ranch, take them down to the river, and scare everyone by plunging them into the water. The car turns into a boat."

Mom opened the driver's-side door. "Get in," she said.

We sat in the white leather seats, proud of our hard-earned view of the Texas hills. Mom took out a linen handkerchief from her purse and handed it to me. "Your father told me this thing helped you guys relax."

I knew by the weight and size of the gift that it was Buchanan. I unwrapped the pipe. The bowl was still packed with a small amount of pot. I'd never smoked Buchanan before.

"Your father died too young to have a will," Mom said. "Just think of this as your inheritance."

"I don't suppose you have a lighter." Mom handed me a silver Zippo with Dad's initials. She watched me light the pipe. I coughed. The smoke burned my throat. I offered Mom Buchanan, but she shook her head no and pointed to her belly.

"When the baby's older," she said, "I want you to tell him about his dad. I want him to know where he came from."

His dad.

We sat together in this magic convertible, me smoking, Mom breathing in the air at my side. We needed a new getaway car. One that could take us back home and beyond. Up the Hudson and along the Garden State Parkway. I gazed down the hill to the Pedernales. Mom pointed out a zebra. I laughed. It was just a gray spotted pony. Everything was clear. I would skip Nixon. Dad would understand. Instead, I'd take my little brother to Omaha, Nebraska, then to Michigan. Gerald Ford 1974–77, born Leslie Lynch King. He was renamed after his adoptive father. Ford didn't know who his real father was until he was practically an adult. I'd tell my brother about Ford and all the men fate brought to power, the chief executives, all the fearless men in charge. He'd know that Andrew Jackson was thirteen when he fought the British in the Battle of Hanging Rock. I'd explain the difference between John Adams and John Quincy Adams. I'd give him reasons to like Ike, to be grateful for the Monroe Doctrine, to appreciate the irony of William Henry Harrison dying of pneumonia one month into his term after staying out in the cold to deliver his endless inauguration address.

Mom said, "Now smoke in moderation. Don't get caught. Don't let your grades slip. Promise me."

I could hear the walkie-talkie static and chatter coming from the Secret Service agents. We'd been caught. Mom would certainly be arrested. Cynthia would lose her job. I'd be left to raise Lyndon alone. Dad's pot was strong, but mellow. For the first time in our relationship Mom and I had a deal, an understanding. I began to hum "Hail to the Chief." As the agents approached in their dark, shiny suits, I promised Mom I would tell Lyndon, my running mate and my half brother, all the things I knew about my father, his father.

ANDREW FOSTER ALTSCHUL

Stanford University

A NEW KIND OF GRAVITY

Around one in the morning I go out to the alley with Horace to bum a cigarette and trade the evening's tragedies. I'll pick him up at his cage in the basement, rap on the reinforced glass, point to the clock over his head. We check the monitors to make sure all's clear, no belligerent drunks or clever husbands waiting in ambush. Mattie would fire us both in about a minute and a half if she knew we did this. If she looked back at the night's security tapes, saw the steel door propped open with a brick, the two of us leaning against the outside wall like we were on school recess—she'd have no choice, everyone knows that.

"Play with your own life if you want to," she said when she hired me. She looked me in the eye, shook my hand, but didn't raise her voice. "Don't fuck with someone else's. That's our rule here." Mattie always says things that way—real plain, like she's just talking. But Mattie's never just talking.

I tried to laugh about it with Horace once, my first week on the job, trying to get chummy with the other guard. I did a pretty good impression of Mattie's monotone, her cold half smile, the way she presses her palms together when she's lecturing you. Horace didn't think it was so funny. He unbuttoned his uniform and showed me the thick brown scar where a husband had knifed him on the sidewalk at eight in the morning and taken his keys. Mattie shot the guy in the vestibule, then gave them both first aid until the ambulance came.

It's not that we can't smoke in the building—nicotine practically holds this place together. There are meeting rooms on the second and fourth floors with industrial-sized ash cans that are always overflowing. There's the dingy third-floor kitchen, and there's the roof. But to get there you have to walk down those sad hallways past posters of Paris and the Grand Canyon, ONE DAY AT A TIME in flowing letters across a sunrise. You can hear the women in their rooms, praying or sobbing or talking in their sleep, yelling at their children or reading bedtime stories. Some of the rooms are dead silent. The meeting room walls are cluttered with photocollages and news clippings and needlepoint, third-grade spelling tests and divorce papers and Spanish prayers. Me and Horace like it better out in the alley, where it's just the Dumpsters and the weather, a few minutes of bare freedom.

The women don't come out here. They don't stand on the roof or stroll in the city park or take their kids to Little League practice. Some of them can't even hold jobs anymore, haven't left the building in two, three, ten weeks. When they do leave, we usually don't see them again for a while, until they come back with their noses broken or their elbows dislocated or worse.

"Look at them," Horace says out in the alley. He doesn't have to look up to know they're there—sleepless faces in the windows above, staring out at the shabby buildings, jealously watching us smoke out-side. "Pathetic," he says. "Pathetic specimens."

Horace is on a roll. Sometimes you'd think he hated the women, the way he talks. But he's been here six years. I've helped him and Mattie wrestle a bodybuilder into a four-point restraint, the guy so amped you could smell the crystal. I saw Horace's face while we held down the husband, who howled into the concrete. I don't have to ask whose side he's on.

Tonight he's worked up because he saw on the log that Lucille Johnson checked back in. "You explain it to me, Charlie," he says, blowing out the smoke like it insulted him. "You tell me why a woman like that ought to be coming and going from here, wasting her life in this place. Don't she have brothers? Don't she have a father? And nobody doing shit."

Horace gets especially enraged by black women at Skyer House. He says it's a private thing, the community ought to take care of it. "Woman in my neighborhood gets beat up like that she's not gonna need no safe house. She's not gonna need no restraining order," he says. He flicks his cigarette across the alley, where it bursts into a small orange shower against the Dumpster. "That kinda shit only gonna happen once. You know why?"

I've heard this speech a hundred times. "Because black men know how to treat their women?" I say.

Horace gives a sour laugh. "Black men know how to treat ani-mals," he says. He crosses his arms and nods. I grind out my cigarette with the toe of my shoe.

"Get back?" I suggest, checking my watch. There's a 1:30 rerun of *The Honeymooners* that I don't want to miss.

"Talk about *humane*," he's growling as we head for the door. "I'll show you some fucking humanity."

I kick the doorstop away and try not to look up—even though I know I will, even though I know who I'll see when I do: a seven-year-old girl in Wonder Woman pajamas, waving at me from the fourth-floor window. I wave back, point to my watch, and pantomime sleep, but Camila only stares from behind the bulletproof glass. It's the same every night: I trudge upstairs to my cage in the lobby, and in the monitors I can see her still standing there, a tiny figure looking at the place I've left, while I triple-check the doors and clean my gun and wonder if the day will come when I'll have to kill her father to keep her safe.

The doorbell chimes at seven in the morning and I don't even need to check the monitors to know what's out there: a husband on the front stoop, fidgeting with his clothes, trying not to eyeball the camera. He'll be freshly shaved, maybe wearing a tie. He'll definitely have flowers, red roses from the Korean shop on the corner—they do a hell of a business. Some of these husbands are big, real big; some of them aren't. Some of them look like the bottom of the barrel, some look like accountants. But when they walk past you, you get the same feeling, like a smell they give off, like something hot and rotten has been packed inside them, crammed down into a space too small to hold it in.

Soon there are footsteps clicking down the stairs and April Pittelli floats past the cage in her best dress and an hour's worth of makeup. She's wearing a big smile, despite her swollen jaw, glowing like a teenager getting picked up for the prom—she's leaving, she says, we can give her bed to someone who really needs it. It's what she always says. She stops to give me a hug before I buzz her out. In the monitors, I watch them embrace, her husband crying, smothering her in kisses. They hold hands as they walk away.

The first time I had to let one of the women go, I started arguing with her, incredulous. Mattie shook her head at me from across the lobby. "It's not your decision," she said later. "No one can take care of them but themselves."

It's true. You can't stop them. Even the fourth or fifth time, when they've come back to lay low a while, let their bones heal, their hair grow back—but when that door chimes they practically fly down the stairs. The caseworkers talk about how scared the women are, how they go back because they don't know what else to do, or because they can't support themselves, or because of the kids. But it's the smile that gets me, the way each one throws open that door and falls into her husband's arms. You'd think she really believed this time would be different. You might as well tear up the restraining orders in her file, shower them like ticker tape out the second-story window, make a big celebration out of it.

But then you'd just have to call the courthouse for new copies in a week or ten days, when she comes back in a squad car with cigarette burns on her arms or a high wheeze from broken ribs or, worse, injuries you can't see, whatever spirit she'd had left replaced by shaking hands and a self-loathing so deep she won't find the bottom for months.

When Mariana came back the first time, wearing a neck brace and gripping Camila's hand so tight the little girl was trying to pry it off, I opened the door and put an arm around her to bring her inside. She closed her eyes for a second, and I thought she might cry on my shoulder, but then she pulled away and yanked her daughter up the stairs and disappeared. Mattie called me into her office a minute later and gave me another warning. There's no such thing as positive male attention here, she said, slicing the air with clasped hands. You open the door, you close the door. You see a raised hand, you grab it. You see a knife, you shoot it. These women are not your friends, she said. They're not your girlfriends. They're sick. And let me tell you, you don't want to catch what they've got.

For a while it seemed every woman I dated had an ex who hit. For some it was unpredictable, a kind of reflex—the hard shove in the middle of a fight, the drink thrown against the wall; for others it was premeditated, methodical. It started with Teresa, my old fiancée. Soon after she moved in with me, she told me about her ex, how he used to cry while he wrapped a towel around his fist so he wouldn't bruise her. She sat on the edge of the bed, her back to me, and I held a pillow over my face while she told me how sorry he'd feel afterward, how she believed it was a different person, like something taking over his body.

He put her in the emergency room once, she said, and when she came home the next morning she found him in the bathtub—he had shaved his head and was trying to slash his wrists. When I asked why she didn't let him do it, she closed her eyes and twisted her mouth into a smile, as if there were some things about love I just couldn't understand.

I heard so many of these stories they stopped surprising me. I didn't know what it was about me that attracted women who'd been with such men. I'd have dreams about running into the guy on the street, smashing his face into the pavement. This was when I still worked at the mall. I'd find myself taking it out on some stupid shoplifter, pinning him to the wall by his neck.

What got me was that they all went back. Maybe they'd go into counseling or quit drinking together, but it didn't make a difference, after the first hit it wouldn't stop. None of these assholes went to jail. No one pressed charges. Teresa's ex was the only one who even got ar-rested, and that was because he pulled the phone out of the wall when she tried to call 911. Apparently, pulling the phone out of the wall is a federal offense.

The last thing Horace and I do each morning is put the kids on the bus. The counselors bring them down the back stairs and they file past Horace's cage with their book bags and lunch boxes. When we see the bus pull up in the monitors, we stand outside the steel doors and the kids pass between us. It's almost like any other bus stop, just a bunch of kids going to school—except that these kids barely make a sound, they don't tease each other or complain, and they need two men with guns to make sure they get on the bus all right.

Sometimes a father will be out in the alley, but usually he'll just call to his kid and wave. "Tell your mother I love her," is what they usually say. We have lines painted on the pavement at one hundred feet and two hundred feet, so they can see exactly where they'll be violating their order. Sometimes, watching a father out of the corner of my eye, I catch myself hoping he'll cross the line, give me a reason.

Horace says he's never seen a problem at the bus. The fathers know there's not much to gain here, what with the mothers locked inside and armed guards and all. He says they just come to feel like fathers for a few minutes. Maybe they hope their kid will wave. Maybe they think their kid will run over to them, crying, "Daddy, Daddy!" We have to stop them if they do that.

I've worked out a deal with Camila's caseworker where I'm allowed to pat her on the head before she gets on the bus. She used to run over to me and hug my legs—her caseworker watching, alarmed, I stood there and tried to gently pry her away. Now I'm allowed to say, "Have a good day at school," and she's allowed to blow me a kiss.

Last week her father showed up in the alley. I knew he was there because Camila walked out the door and froze and immediately started to cry. "*Camila*," he shouted. "*Te quiero, Camilita. Tu mamá, dile que le amo."* The caseworker had to carry her onto the bus. I turned to see a middle-aged guy in cords and a fisherman's sweater. I figured I'd get some kind of dirty look or Spanish curses, but he wasn't even looking at me. He just stared at the bus pulling away and gnawed miserably at his thumbnail.

In the evenings things are more informal. From eight o'clock, when I come on, until ten, all the women are in meetings. The night counselors are supposed to plan activities for the kids, but mostly they have them do their homework or watch TV. I sit in my cage with the day's logs and drink coffee, read up on any new residents or watch *Wheel of Fortune* on the little black and white. Eventually, out of the corner of my eye, I'll see half of a face and a few strands of hair peek around the corner of the stairwell. I'll pretend not to notice, looking over the notes on the console, and she'll sneak down the last stairs to spring up at the door of the cage.

"Boo!" she yells, and I pretend to fall out of my chair.

"You shouldn't sneak up on a man with a gun," I said to her once, thinking that was kind of funny, but I could see from her face that it wasn't. Another time I put my hands in the air and said, "Please, don't hurt me!" like it was a stickup. That wasn't funny either. You really have to watch yourself.

Camila brings her homework downstairs and I let her sit in my chair and swivel around and I help her with math. She has her times tables down cold, but she's completely blocked on long division. Last night I had to tell her again that it doesn't always come out even, that sometimes there's a remainder.

"This is stupid," she said, shoving the book onto the floor. She started pressing buttons on my console and I could hear the electric lock on the front door clicking in and out. I quickly checked the monitors, which thankfully were clear, but I still didn't want her fooling with the doors. I picked up the book and the pencil and put them back in front of her, but she didn't stop.

"Camila, you can't touch those," I said, and when she kept doing it I reached out and put my hands over hers—so gently I didn't even breathe—and moved her arms away. "We have to keep the doors locked," I said, rolling the chair back.

"Why?" she said.

"That's the rule. That way everyone's safe."

"But what if someone wants to come in?" she said.

I pointed to the monitors and said anyone who wants to come in can talk to me through the intercom. She knows all this. We've been through it before. She said she wanted to go outside and use the intercom. She wanted me to buzz her inside. When I said no, she said I should go outside and she would buzz me in. She wanted to make sure it wasn't broken.

"I'm not allowed to go outside," I told her.

"You'd get in trouble?"

"I'd get in trouble."

"You'd get a *castigo*?" she asked. I didn't know what that meant, so I just nodded.

We finished the last problem and I told Camila it was time to brush her teeth. The groups were letting out upstairs, the women spilling out of the meeting rooms, high on caffeine and affirmations.

"My daddy wants to visit me," she said, erasing and carefully rewriting her name in the exercise book, brushing eraser shavings all over my console. "He said he wants to take us home."

"You saw your father today?" I asked, trying to sound casual.

"He said he wants to see my room."

I took a deep breath. I'd have to tell her caseworker. Her father's order says he can't come to her school, but they don't have the staff to keep a lid on these things. Last month one of our first graders was taken right out of PE. He was missing for almost a week until they found him, in a motel with his father, two towns away. They were just watching TV and ordering pizzas, like they couldn't think of what else to do.

"He says you won't let him visit me," Camila said.

I pictured her father behind me in the alley while Camila got on the bus. I wondered how many mornings he'd been out there, watching, what it would feel like to see your daughter grab a stranger's leg when you called her. I made myself stop thinking about it—Mattie says the worst thing you can do is let yourself identify with these people.

"I can only let in the people they tell me to," I said, taking back my chair. I tried to say it the way Mattie says it, slow and reassuring. "It's so everyone can be safe."

She crossed her arms in the door and glared. "My daddy loves me."

I pretended to straighten some papers, checked the monitors again. I could see the women in the upstairs hallways, leaning against the walls, on line at the pay phones—waiting to call their husbands, to cup the receiver for their allotted fifteen minutes, whisper how much they miss them.

"I know," I said.

"He does."

I saw Mariana in the third-floor stairwell, on her way down. She couldn't have been more than twenty-five, but she looked much older. Her hair was pulled back tightly and she walked with a stoop, her head tilted to one side like she was listening for something. She never talks to any of the other women. Camila stood in the door of the cage and scowled.

"You're stupid," she finally said.

———

"You need to be careful with Camila Lopez," Mattie said over the phone. She usually checks in around eleven. Now that I'm on nights, I see her only at our monthly supervisions, or when something is really wrong. "Young girls like her behave in very sexualized ways around men. It's how they get attention."

"Sexualized?" I said, too loud. I tried to laugh. "I'm helping her with long division, for Christ's sake."

"Don't be defensive. I'm not accusing you of anything. You're not trained to see these things. You don't know the things I know."

I knew where she was headed. Horace and I are allowed to see the court orders, so we know who can do what—but only caseworkers can read the files. We hear a lot of stuff, but there's always more. I stared at the monitors, at the washed-out olive world surrounding Skyer House, while Mattie talked about positive reinforcement, appropriate buffer zones, and nonverbal cues. I could feel that tightness creeping back, that heat on the back of my neck. At my first weekly supervision, almost a year ago, I told Mattie how angry it made me to think of what these women had been through, what the kids had been through. I twisted a paper clip until it left dark indentations in my fingertips and said if a husband tried anything while I was around he'd end up in worse shape than his wife. Mattie put down my folder and told me to take the next week off to decide whether this was the right job for me. There was nothing angry or disappointed in the way she said it, but nothing encouraging either.

"It's better if you don't care so much," she said. "We don't need another Rambo. That's why most of them are here in the first place."

Out in the alley, I asked Horace if he thought there was anything weird about how Camila hugs me or asks me to pick her up. He propped a foot against the wall and blew smoke up toward the windows.

"Someone gotta treat these kids like kids," he said. "Else they grow up thinking everyone's just as fucked up as their mother and father. Thinking one minute you hug someone, next minute they punch you in the gut."

"Kids are naturally affectionate. You don't want to discourage that," I said, but it came out sounding a lot like a question.

A light drizzle pattered against the Dumpsters and our breath came out in orange clouds. The alley smelled of burned rubber, like someone had just peeled out around the corner. "You ask me, they should lock both of them up, the mother *and* the father," Horace said. "You let your kid see that kind of shit, see you putting up with it, now what kind of damn message is that?

"It's weakness," he said on the way inside, gearing up for another one of his rants. "Nothing makes someone want to victimize you more than you being a victim already. They can smell it. Like a shark smells blood a mile away. There's no blood, you can swim right next to a shark and he just leave you alone. But you show him you weak…" he said and shut the door to his cage. I watched him sit on his chair and cross his arms, his mouth still moving, the hollow sound of his voice rasping through the two-way speaker.

Upstairs, I checked all the doors and windows and put on *The Honeymooners*—Ralph steamed again, Alice shaking her fist in his face. I watched Camila in the monitor, her back to the camera as she stared out the meeting room window. Some nights she stands there for hours, wrapped in her Wonder Woman cape. Maybe she's worried that her father will come to get her. Or maybe she's hoping he will. In the months before Teresa moved out I used to stand at our kitchen window, watching the street. Sometimes I'd see her ex, driving slowly past the building, squinting up at the windows; by the time I got down there he was always gone. Other times, waiting for her to come home, I'd sit with the light off and pray for her car to appear.

After the kids got on the bus I went home and pulled down the shade and slept through the morning. I had the dream again, the one I've been having for months: I'm up on the fourth floor and I've found a room I've never been in. The windows are open, long curtains fluttering, and I don't know if someone's gotten in or gotten out. I rush downstairs but can't make it fast enough, moving in excruciatingly slow motion. That's when I usually wake up, but this time there was more. This time it was Mariana's husband down on the street, and then Mattie was shouting at me from the bottom of the stairs and I couldn't find my gun. "It's the end of the week!" she kept yelling, as though this kind of thing shouldn't be happening and I fumbled at my holster, trying to make it to the bottom but there were so many stairs, and my feet were so heavy I knew I'd never make a difference.

Mariana's been talking to her husband again, hanging off the fourth-floor pay phone every night this week. Her caseworker got it from the night counselor, though Mariana still denies it in their sessions.

"It's the old pattern," says the caseworker, shrugging as the school bus pulls away. "She doesn't really have anyone else, no skills, no experience being on her own. It's either go back to her husband or go back to El Salvador." She looks up at the brick wall and bulletproof windows, the crumpled gray sky. "Or stay here."

He's coming to Camila's school every morning, says the caseworker, giving her notes to bring to her mother. This is how it happened last time, she says. She's called the school, the police; no one acts very concerned.

"There's gotta be something you can do," I say. She looks at me like I have three heads. "She can't just go back. I mean, there's a little girl involved."

"I'm aware of that, Charlie," she says.

"Maybe I should ride the bus with them," I say. "Make sure they get in the school all right."

She looks at her hands. "The school has security guards," she says.

"Hell of a job they're doing."

"I'm just saying."

She leans against the wall, looks at me over her glasses. She's my age, or maybe a little younger, with a face that would be pretty if she let it, if she didn't pull her hair back so tight, if she smiled once in a while. Her nose looks like it was broken once. When she talks, her eyes don't blink.

"There must be something we can do," I say.

"We're doing it," she sighs, and goes right into the spiel. "We're giving her choices. We're giving her a place she can be safe, for as long as she needs it."

"What about Camila's choices?" I say, as quietly as I can manage.

The caseworker doesn't answer. It's not really a fair question. She pats me on the arm and walks inside. I can tell by the set of her shoulders how tired she is. I try to imagine her outside of Skyer House— walking in the park or driving, or maybe out on a date, sipping a drink, hair down around her shoulders. But all I can see is that exhausted expression, the lines at the corners of her eyes deepening each day. I picture my own face in the bathroom mirror. Behind me, my silent apartment, the empty refrigerator and broken stereo, one side of the closet bare where Teresa used to hang her clothes.

I got my job at the shelter when Mattie fired the previous guard, a kid named Trevor. She never told me what he actually did to get fired, but she said she'd always known he wouldn't last. In supervision he'd snicker and talk about irony. It was ironic that so many of the women hung crucifixes in their rooms, he told Mattie. It was ironic that their husbands were out there, living normal lives, while these women were locked up like criminals. It wasn't that he didn't have sympathy for them, she said. Just that he saw them as unwitting, the helpless butts of a cruel joke.

But cheap ironies abound at Skyer House and Mattie won't permit you to underestimate the women. "It's mutually assured destruction—like the bombs," she once told me. We'd just watched an ambulance pull away; one of the women had swallowed a bottle of pills and collapsed at a meeting. You can't stop people from fucking up their own lives, Mattie said. You can't even really stop them from fucking up someone else's, if that's what they want to do. All you can do is give them choices, offer them some scaled-down version of freedom, then stand back and cover your ears when they still decide to push the button.

"Now I'm going to stand there and wave and then you press this button to let me back in," I tell her. I make her point to the button three times, until I'm convinced she knows the right one. "No playing around," I say. "I wave, you push."

But Camila wants me to talk to her on the intercom. She says I have to ask permission.

"No. You just press the button. That's it."

She crosses her arms and spins around and around in the chair. "But you have to pretend I don't know you. You have to ask if you can come in," she says. She stops spinning and puts her arms around my waist. "Please?"

I glance up at the monitors. The meeting room doors are still closed, the sidewalks and the alley empty. Horace is in the third-floor kitchen, taking his first break. "You can't ever tell anyone," I say, showing her how to key the intercom. "I'll get in big trouble."

"Okay."

"Promise?" She nods solemnly.

As I'm opening the front door, I turn back to look at her—sitting in my chair, staring at the console, her lips pursed in concentration. Outside on the stoop, I wait for a few seconds and wave to the camera, press the doorbell, grasp the handle. After a moment, the speaker crackles, but there's no voice. It crackles again, just the tail end of whatever Camila tried to say.

"It's Charlie," I tell the speaker, smiling for the camera. That's when I realize I left my keys in the cage. "Can I come in please?"

There's another crackle of the speaker, a quick clicking in and out of the lock, too fast for me to pull it open. I look up into the camera and wait, and she does it again—in and out—not holding the button long enough to open the door.

"Camila, no messing around," I whisper into the speaker. "Open the door now." But when it crackles again I can hear her laughing, saying my name. The lock keeps clicking, too fast, she's playing with that button like a damned video game, like this whole thing is just a game. Then it stops clicking altogether.

For a moment it's quiet outside Skyer House. The front of the building is patterned with lit windows—if someone looks out and sees me standing here, if they tell Mattie about it tomorrow, I can kiss my job good-bye. "Camila, open this door," I say, trying to keep my voice down, yanking on the reinforced steel. "Open the damn door, or you'll get a *castigo*." I'm starting to sweat. There's still no response, another minute I'm standing out there like a fool, then the lock buzzes steadily and I'm back inside.

"Camila," I'm saying, throwing open the vestibule door, ready to pick her up out of my chair and send her upstairs. But Mariana is standing in front of my cage, holding her daughter tightly by the arm. Camila is bawling, hiding her face against her mother's hip, holding the hem of Mariana's sweatshirt in one hand and hitting her other fist against her mother's leg. She turns to look at me, her face red and miserable, and cries harder.

"She just wanted to see how the door worked," I say, a little out of breath, feeling like I should apologize for something. Mariana looks at the floor, still gripping Camila's shoulder. Her sweatshirt hangs nearly to her knees, over old jeans. She looks so young—she could be anyone, a college girl in a dorm, or someone's little sister. Above her head, the monitors are gray and empty.

"She is a very bad girl," Mariana says quietly. Camila hiccups and sniffles. "She doesn't listen to me, she doesn't listen to her father."

"It was my fault," I say, scanning the console, the inside of the cage. "I shouldn't have let her do it."

"Disculpe," Mariana says. "I keep her in the room. She will not bother you."

"It's okay," I say. "It's no big deal." I reach out to put my hand on Camila's head, but she hides behind her mother. Mariana raises her eyes, and for just a second I can imagine her as a young girl, back in El Salvador, before all this. Then I imagine her upstairs on the fourth floor, in the small room she shares with her daughter, staring out at the alley and wondering what the hell happened.

"She's a good girl," I tell Mariana, who blinks at me from the door of my cage. "She's very nice. Just like her mother."

For a second she looks like she's going to smile. But then, just as quickly, she lowers her eyes and slides past me. She mutters another apology and guides Camila, to the stairs; I sit back in my chair, watch them move through the monitors, climbing back up to the fourth floor, where they'll be safe for the rest of the night.

The next night the front-door chime sounds as Horace and I are heading out for our smoke. I freeze up for a second, sure that it's

Camila's father. I have to grind my teeth and tell my feet to follow Horace back to his cage. I have to remind myself that I'm a professional, I'm not paid to understand.

But the guy outside is white, in his thirties, wearing jeans and a dress shirt. He stands there with his hands in his pockets, whistling at the sky. Through the monitors he seems almost friendly, like an insurance agent; if you saw this guy in the supermarket you wouldn't think twice. He's no one we've seen before, probably the husband of a new client, just testing the waters, seeing how much we'll let him get away with.

Horace keys the intercom. "Sorry, we didn't order no pizza," he says.

"I want to see my wife," the guy says. He looks right into the camera, leans forward so his face grows large in the monitor, breaks up into green pixels. His pupils are shrunken to pinheads.

"Visiting hours are over," Horace tells him. "You got two minutes to find somewhere else to be." He keeps his voice even but firm, exactly the way we were taught. He's really good at it—I've seen him put a guy in an armlock while the wife clawed at Horace's face, drawing blood, all without raising his voice. I don't know how you do that, how you lock those feelings away. I wonder if it comes out when he gets home, if the walls of his house have big divots in the plaster where he punches them, like mine do.

"You've got two minutes to go fuck yourself," the guy snarls into the camera. "She's my fucking wife, you piece of shit."

The clock on Horace's console reads 1:08 and I take out the incident log to start a report. Horace leans back and crosses his arms, trying to wait him out. You never want to get into it with a husband—especially when he's flying on something, like this guy. You keep it friendly as long as you can, let him know the limits, and hope he'll show some good sense and let it go. That almost never happens.

The husband hits the chime again, mashing the button and shout-ing into the intercom. Any minute now, the women will start coming out of their rooms. We'll see them in the monitors—nightgowned ghosts drifting through the hallways. The chime only sounds in our cages, but somehow they just know. It's like a sixth sense.

"Don't make me call the police," Horace says, rolling his eyes. "Make a better decision than that."

"I'm gonna decide to bust down this door and kick your ass," says the husband. He starts pounding against the door, slamming into it with his shoulder. "You hear me, fuckhead?" he screams, pointing his finger into the camera. "When I get in there I'm gonna rip off your head and shit down your neck. I want to see my fucking *wife!*"

"Two points for the shit-down-the-neck comment," I say. "This one's creative."

"Yeah, he a real poet," Horace says, reaching for the phone. There are women in the halls now, whispering among themselves, shooing their children back into the rooms. This will be over in five minutes when the police arrive. The only thing to worry about is whether the husband will catch a glimpse of his wife or not. If his wife goes to the window, and her husband looks up and sees her, all bets are off. I've seen a 140-pound husband throw off three cops after seeing his wife in the window. I've seen a guy make it halfway up to the third floor by scaling the front of the building—his wife beating against the glass, trying to put her arms around him. I couldn't stop thinking it wasn't human, that normal people don't behave like this. I watched him in the monitors, clinging to the bricks until the fire depart-ment came, his wife being restrained by the counselors—they weren't human, they were more like moths hurling themselves against a light-bulb, some frantic, uncontrollable instinct driving them.

This is what Teresa wouldn't say to me, why she couldn't stop going back to her ex, time after time. It's not something that can be explained. It's a force of nature. We were together for two years, and she said she loved me, but I never felt it. They were just words when she said them to me. They had no force.

The cops finally pull up and, after the obligatory struggle—the husband spits in one of their faces, they slam him onto the hood of the cruiser, his legs wild and rubbery as they cuff him—things are under control. Horace and I flip a coin to see who'll go calm the women. I lose and climb the stairs to the second floor, where they're still whispering in the hall and peering out the windows. Lucille Johnson is on the phone already, slapping her hand against the wall, her face smeared with cold cream. I tell them everything's all right, to go back to bed. I keep my hands open at my sides, like Mattie showed me. I maintain acceptable distance. These women know me, know I'd never hurt them, but it's not a question of what they know. I speak quietly and do my best not to look at their open bathrobes, the thin nightgowns and worn sweatpants, the shy smile of a woman who leans against the wall and tries to hide the cast on her wrist.

"Who was it, Charlie?" they ask, their eyes nervous, excited. They grab my arms and ask, "Is he going to come back? Where's Mattie?" I don't know whose husband it was, but it seems like she might have slept through it. If not, if she saw her husband downstairs, it could be an even longer night than it's already been.

When I've finally gotten everyone out of the hallways I remember the cigarette in my shirt pocket. Mattie will review tonight's security tapes, so I open the door to the fourth-floor meeting room, look for a pack of matches. As soon as I walk in I can feel the cold breeze—someone left a window open again—and I'm halfway across the room before I notice Mariana standing in the dark, her nightgown camouflaging her against the curtains. She's standing in the same spot Camila always stands, holding her arms around herself, her cheek damp and reddish silver from the streetlights.

"Are you okay?" I ask quietly. I start to reach out to touch her shoulder but think better of it. Mariana just nods. "It's over," I tell her. "There's nothing to be scared of."

I shut the window and look for a blanket or a robe to put around her, but there's nothing. There's the faintest of reflections in the glass, doubling her face, and the large darkness looming behind her is just me.

"Do you need anything?" I ask. "Is there any way I can help?" As I'm saying it I can hear Mattie's voice in my head, but I just don't believe what she says. I don't believe you can help another human being by not helping them. It makes no goddamn sense.

"You are very nice," Mariana says, her voice barely audible. Her eyes are swollen from crying, the light on her face makes her look girlish and innocent. "Camila, she likes you. She says you are very intelligent."

"She's the smart one," I tell her. "She really is a bright little girl."

Mariana still won't look at me. "It is from her father. He is very intelligent."

I know I shouldn't say anything but I can't help it. "I don't think he's very smart," I tell her.

She starts to say something but stops, and that's when I see that she's holding something, a picture frame that she's pressing to her belly, the fabric of her nightgown taut against her body. I don't have to look to know what that photo is. There's no sound in the room, only the rise and fall of her chest, a siren somewhere in the city, as she holds it out to me.

"I was only seventeen years old," she says, handing me her wedding photo. Her eyes are dark and liquid, her hair tucked behind one small, ringless ear. And as we stare at each other I realize that she hadn't been scared by the commotion outside. She wasn't frightened—she was crying because it wasn't her husband, because he wasn't the one who tried to force his way inside and take her home. She pushes the frame to me, her gaze finally meeting mine, and her need for me to look at that photo, to see in it what she sees, is a tangible force between us, a new kind of gravity, bodies that somehow repel and attract each other at the same time. I look at the security camera in the corner, its little red light blinking slowly. I take her wrists and gently push them away, her skin warm on my hands, my knuckles brushing the fabric of her nightgown.

I open my mouth and all that comes out, whispered, is "Camila." We're standing much closer than we should be, something pushing us even closer; I should move my hands away but I don't. We both take a breath, and I don't know whether in the next instant I'm going to lean down and press my lips to hers or take her small, pale neck between my hands. I don't know what comes over me, but the image is so clear, the moment so imminent, that I snatch my hands away and take a step back; the frame falls at Mariana's feet and the glass shatters.

"Don't move," I tell her, awake now, bending to grab the frame, collecting the shards in the palm of my hand. "Stay here. I can't see it all, dammit," I tell Mariana, whose bare toes are inches from my fingers. "Hang on, I'll carry you out or something."

There are already faces in the doorway, drawn to the sound of violence. I'm on my hands and knees, running my fingertips over the carpet, invisible splinters burrowing into my skin. Mariana snatches the frame out of my hand and then, despite my warnings, walks right past me in her bare feet. I want to reach up and grab her arm, pull her back, ask why she would do such a thing. But I keep my eyes on the carpet, scrounging around stupidly, all I see is a flutter of cotton, the flash of her calves as she pulls the door shut behind her.

A few days later, Camila doesn't come down to the school bus with the others. Horace and I stand in the sunshine of a fragile, early spring morning, and I watch the kids' faces file past. When the bus door closes, I raise an eyebrow to the caseworker, who shrugs and turns away, heads upstairs before I can catch her.

"Smoke?" Horace says, reaching into his pocket. He casually moves between me and the door. The bus turns out of the alley, sunlight warbling off the back windows.

"I think I'll go see what's wrong with Camila," I tell him, but he grabs my elbow as I try to move past.

"Have a cigarette first," he says. "You go in a few minutes." His hand on my arm is friendly but firm, his expression studiously neutral. I know that expression, have seen it on my own face, practiced it in mirrors.

"What's going on?" I say.

Horace looks past me. "What do you mean?"

By the time I'm halfway up the stairs I can hear Mattie's voice in the front hallway and I know something terrible has happened. I take the stairs two at a time, hands clenched, wondering how I could have missed it. At the top of the stairs I nearly barrel into the four people standing outside my cage.

"Good morning, Charlie," says Mattie, taking a half step forward to look me in the eyes. "Can you wait in my office a moment, please?"

Before I can say anything, Camila runs to me and wraps her arms around my leg, pressing her face into my thigh. Her mother calls to her, but she holds on to me, sniffling into my leg. Her father says nothing, frowning and watching her over his mustache, holding Mariana's hand. Mariana says something in Spanish and he nods. He's shorter than his wife, wearing freshly ironed black pants and a collared shirt. Mariana clutches the roses to her chest. Her suitcase sits by the door, Camila's small backpack slumped on top of it.

"Camila, ven," says Mariana, her voice steadier than I've heard it.

Mattie says my name again, but I don't look at her. My hand rests on Camila's head, stroking her hair.

"Hija, ven," says the husband. Camila looks up at me, wanting me to tell her what to do, but I won't take my eyes off her father. Finally, she lets go and straggles back to her parents. Her father crouches to whisper in her ear. She shakes her head, but he turns her around, urges her back to me.

"He said thank you for being my friend," she translates. Mattie has her hands on her hips, watching me intently, but no one can control what's about to happen, least of all me.

"Tell him I'm not his friend," I say.

Camila starts to giggle. "No, stupid," she says. *"My* friend. *Me."*

Mariana starts to say something, but I've already taken a step forward, drawn myself up—it's like I can see it happening, like I'm watching the whole thing, that fucking animal shrinking away from me, trying to get his arms up, but not in time, and the sting of his face against my open hand sends a shiver through me, the sharp smack ringing in the air as he half twirls, slides against the wall, stumbles over his wife's suitcase, and sprawls to the floor. Then I'm standing over him, just waiting for him to get up, just waiting. Camila is crying, everyone shouting, but it all seems to come from somewhere else. For that instant it's just me and him, staring at each other, one of us stronger than the other, locked in a moment of perfect communication.

"Now you done it," says a voice behind me, then arms wrap me in a bear hug. Horace nearly lifts me off the ground, pushes me against the far wall. He stands inches from me, containing me without anger, Mattie shaking her head and Mariana sheltering her sobbing daughter, the roses strewn across the floor.

"Stand right there," Horace says quietly, barring an arm against my chest. "Don't you move." He reaches around and undoes my belt, removes the holster, faces peering from the top of the stairs, tense voices whispering. I stand with my palms flat against the wall, my throat so tight I can't swallow, while Camila's father picks himself up and smoothes out his clothes, reaches for his wife's arm. It's hard to tell who's leaning on whom.

Mattie opens the door and the lobby floods with sunshine. Mariana picks up her howling daughter, her husband's arm around both of them as they walk out of Skyer House. Over her mother's shoulder, Camila looks at me one last time, her face smeared with tears, her eyes wide open and afraid.

The door swings shut and Horace backs off, still wary, ready to tackle me if I try to go after them. "Shit, Charlie, what in hell are you thinking," he says, trying to make eye contact. His voice sounds like it's coming through a tunnel. "You know that motherfucker just gonna take it out on her."

There's noise in the stairwell, women applauding, hooting, and calling down congratulations. "You're my hero, Charlie!" comes Lucille Johnson's voice. I walk back to my cage—slowly, hands in the air so Horace will know I'm not a danger anymore. I sit at the console and find them in the monitors, watch them move from camera to camera, Camila's face buried in her mother's shoulder, her father's arm across Mariana's back. The image skips from one monitor to the next, the angle changing as a new camera picks them up, so for a second it almost looks like they're coming back.

Soon they've passed beyond the cameras. I can see Mattie on the stoop, catching her breath, waiting to come inside and fire me. I can hear her doing it, that businesslike voice telling me it's for the good of the shelter. I can't blame her. I've given her no choice.

She'll say it's for my own good, too. She'll smile weakly and suggest I think about counseling. She'll say it's up to me to decide what to do now. Then she'll ask for my keys and tell me never to come back.

But first she'll bring me into her office and close the door, and from a desk drawer she'll take out the tape from the other night. She'll ask me if I know what's on that tape and I'll nod, unable to speak. She'll put the tape in the player and let herself out, leaving me alone in her tidy, windowless office. And while she's upstairs, setting everything back to normal, I'll watch that tape again and again, sit right up close to the monitor and stare at the grainy image of a man—standing outside the shelter, coming through the door. I'll keep hitting the rewind button, watching him forward and backward, and wonder if that's what I really look like in the flat gray world outside the door.

JESSICA ANTHONY
George Mason University

THE RUST PREVENTER

In all cases, whether or not the corrosion products are pleasing in appearance, whether they are voluminous or slight, the eventual destruction of a product is inevitable unless protective measures are taken.

—*Rust: Causes and Prevention*
E. F. Houghton & Co., 1945

I, your average human male, am sitting with my fingers spread out on a wooden table in a shack in the jungle, wearing trousers that once were khaki, but now have faded to a truculent gray.

I'm not wearing a shirt.

I'm pretending that my hands are the wings of a butterfly, pinned on a cushion. The line of sweat that's been running from my forehead, down my arm, and to my fingertips is about to drip onto the table. The bead holds for a moment, then rolls over the fingernail and begins a small puddle. Today is hot. Yesterday was hot. Tomorrow will very likely be hot.

As a working metallurgist for Hutton & Hutton Research, I can manage many different kinds of products, like Straight Cutting Oils and Bases, Soluble Cutting Oils, Quenching Oils, Heat Treating Salts, Drawing Compounds, Metal Cleaners, and Industrial Lubricants. But here in the shack, I'm strictly Rust Preventives. My job is to receive the metal and iron specimens that the Concessionaires send me every day in large brown cardboard boxes. I open the boxes, remove the specimens, and put them on my front lawn to see how long they can last without rusting. These statistics I enter into the Log.

For the first few months, it felt good to be out in the jungle, working in the shack, helping the war effort. Every week the Concessionaires would send me large brown cardboard boxes with a small note that said, THE CONCESSIONAIRES THANK YOU FOR A JOB WELL DONE with a stamp of an American flag at the top.

Now? Now all the notes have faded. The Concessionaires stopped delivering the large brown boxes a very long time ago, and I've since lost track of the days. *Really* lost track. It could be 1948 or 1949 for all I know, although I'm pretty certain that it isn't 1950. It can't be 1950. That would mean that I've been in the shack for five years. That would mean that I'm forty years old.

But my fingers don't look like forty-year-old fingers.

There are only a few specimens left that have been well prevented and still have all their shine. They are my booty: these ball bearings, M-1 rifles, propeller blades, iron plates, rifle barrels, wrenches, and radio tubes. All the stuff that I've been testing for the time I've been here in the shack in the jungle. I keep the smaller ones with me inside. The rest is left outside, naked, to rust and deteriorate completely from the Natural Forces that surround me: the humidity and the rain. The general moisture.

In the jungle, shiny metals quickly become red and brittle, but unless snapped or cracked by me, they always keep their original shapes. There are a thousand iron ghosts on my front lawn.

Statues poised for disintegration.

I'm worried, because with the absence of deliveries the number of things I don't know has started to outweigh the number of things I do know. I know that I'm somewhere in the Malay Archipelago, because that's what they told me when they dropped me from the helicopter. Beyond that, what I know mostly comes from the Rust Preventer's Manual. Take Natural Forces, for example: *"Natural Forces of sun, rain, snow, seawater, mist, perspiration, humidity, and corrosive fumes are eternally at work—attacking, deteriorating, and destroying man-made things."* Today, the Natural Forces are heat, humidity, and sweat. And oxygen. Let us not forget oxygen. Iron plus water plus oxygen yields rust. It is only a matter of days before the onslaught. The ferric-oxidic disease.

To keep the Natural Forces at bay, I pretend I'm hard at work. I enter fake statistics into the Log; I open the door for the delivery of materials each morning as if I can still hear the plane streak across the sky; I routinely rearrange the rust on my front lawn. I don't want whatever's out there to know that I have nothing, whatsoever, to do.

At least I'm not alone. I've got a companion. She's kind of a mischievous thing: the way she darts so masterfully in and out of the shack. The way she can kiss one moment and growl the next. But I always forgive her. Because there can be no debating it: She is a monkey. A monkey is she.

I have named her Pamela.

Pamela is small, with powder white hands. She likes to listen as I tell her all about rust prevention. She does this cute little jumping dance whenever I start talking from the Manual. I memorized the

Manual ages ago, and it's nice to pretend that I am the teacher and she is my pupil. I am teaching her to say my name, and her name. She is Pamela, Pamela is she.

"Pa-me-la," I say.

"Ba-ba-ba," she says.

We haven't had any jumping today though. Today it's so hot we can barely move. Right now Pamela is snoozing on my cot, curled up in a little ball, and I don't want to wake her. But with evening comes a cool wind off the river. It's quite refreshing. When Pamela wakes up, she's excited to begin the jumping. She jumps so high she swipes the ceiling of the shack.

"Little Bobo," I say, scolding. We have lots of nicknames for each other. Mostly I call her Little Bobo. She calls me Chee-Chee with a cluck sound at the end.

It's our own special thing.

"Do you know about Natural Forces?" I say.

Pamela hops on top of the Log and gurgles.

I recite out loud: *"The attack from Natural Forces is unrelenting and occurs everywhere. To enable these man-made products to last for any significant amount of time and to function properly, they must be protected."*

Pamela jumps like crazy on the cot, going nuts.

I grin. "There's a whole section on Natural Forces in the Manual," I say. "I think it's very interesting. What do you think, *ma singe*?"

Pamela spits on the floor and shows her teeth. "Oyanyynynm," she says.

I just adore her pretty little monkey language.

I met the Monkey-Pamela the first time I went for a run down by the river. She was nibbling her nails in the big tree that hangs over the swell. She waved at me and I waved back. We've been friends ever since. More than friends, to be perfectly honest. It's kind of a simple relationship: I share my Chompy Nut chocolate bars; she keeps me company. She hangs out with me all day, but returns to her family at night. I get nervous when she leaves me, because at night I can hear the Natural Forces turn:

Cracking noises—what was that?

Lilting, unfamiliar odors—Bodies! Bodies!

Stay back, quick shadows with long tails.

I'm not telling Pamela my concern. My concern is that there are days when the Natural Forces are so strong I'm sure that I'll be swept away by them. I have visions of myself being picked up by the wind like a dirty handkerchief and dropped off to sea. And with the wind is this voice that says, "You do not belong here." When the voice comes and I quake from uncertainty, I turn to her, my Beloved Bo, for reassurance.

I wonder sometimes what my family would think about me and Pamela. Pamela's a monkey and I am a man. I'm from Hobiskobie Falls, New Hampshire. I grew up in a house with a mother and a father and running water. I've turned on lamps and made fires in a fireplace. I've smoked cigarettes. I've written poetry. I can speak a little French from when my family went to Canada:

"La pomme de terre est sur la table."

I used to know a Girl-Pamela, way back in high school in New Hampshire. The Girl-Pamela had long gold hair. It lay flat on her back like a two-by-four. I remember stroking it with my fingers, how she smiled with a frown, and how when we made love, I'd hold her lower back like you hold a baby. The Girl-Pamela had beautiful, ocean-colored eyes. Or were they brown? Earth-colored. Was there a mole above her upper lip?

I think so, yes.

When I came to the jungle, I was given a refrigerator-sized box of melted Chompy Nut bars and a smaller, red bin of gasoline. They said that the gasoline was for personal use, but they also said that it would come in handy if the enemy ever found the shack. For burning the rusted materials. That way they wouldn't be able to see American weaponry in a decrepit state. That way they wouldn't think that America had failed in rust prevention.

Pamela's *very* interested in the Chompy Nut bars. This afternoon, after a recitation from the Manual, we share one: She climbs up the back of my chair, places her small head on my shoulder, and peeps until I unwrap the wrapper and unfold the insides, slippery with chocolate.

She licks, I lick.

Before the PORC (Preventives Officers' Radio Communication) radio broke, it kept saying over and over again that the workers must not lose heart. It said that the war was not over and that the Rust Preventers were needed.

I wonder for the sixty-ninth time today if it is 1950.

I stand up from the table and walk a few paces to the end of the shack. I pick up a winged hexnut from the small pile of specimens that I keep inside with me. It's new-looking and shiny. I hold it up to the window. The sun hits the hexagonal sides and the reflection sends a bright light into my eye, making me blink several times quickly. Then I go outside with the specimen in my hand and lay it on the ground with the rest of the specimens. They all line up, thousands of them, from silver to orange to red to dust.

But behind the rows of these mixed metals is a mountain of rust—the pile of the bigger tests: the rifles, propeller blades, rifle barrels, all crusted over, decomposing.

"Pamela, come look at this," I say. I look down and she's not there. But something is shaking in my tropical bushes by the side of the shack. All I see is a flick of the tail before Pamela scampers off where I can't see her. I know exactly what will bring her back:

"*Hutton & Hutton provides a complete line of 'Hutto-Clean' metal cleaning compounds,*" I say out loud. "*Three general classes of alkaline cleaners are included in the Hutto-Clean series: Light Duty, Medium Duty, and Heavy Duty types, which clean by saponification with very little emulsifying.*"

When Pamela shows herself, she starts hopping like crazy on my front jungle lawn. We spend the rest of the day together. Me at the table entering statistics into the Log, her sniffing gasoline. We share another Chompy Nut. One of my duties is to hold a galvanic couple corrosion test. The test uses a combination of dissimilar metals that are put together for no other useful purpose than testing rust prevention. It's supposed to show whether one kind of metal becomes more passive or aggressive than the adjacent metals. The materials that I use for the test are one Bakelite washer, one standard brass washer, one quarter-inch-long piece of Bakelite tubing, and one RHBMS with brass hexnuts.

I don't know exactly what an RHBMS is, but it looks like a screw and that's how it's labeled on the box.

At sunset, we walk outside. I sit down between the mountain and a small pile of propeller blades. She sits in my lap, and together we smell the rust. When the spirit moves, she hops off my lap and goes digging through the lines of couple corrosion tests. She chooses a few to bring over and drops them on my lap. I get orange all over my pants. She gets it all over her tiny white paws. Then it gets late, and I try to give her a rusted couple corrosion test for her to keep, but she scowls at my choice. She shakes her head and bounces around the newest one, the one that still has all its shine. I slap my forehead for being so stupid. I kneel down on the lawn and cup my hands around the newest one, and the dying pink sun shines on it and it sparkles pink. I give it to her just like in the movies. With her monkey paw stretched out, I place it in her palm and then close her fingers around it.

"Barm," she says, softly.

On cooler days, I go out running. I used to run in my underpants, but since no one can see me anyway, wearing the Fruit of the Looms was...fruitless. They've long since become a rag for bug-mooshing. Now I run naked.

Pamela clucks. It looks like she wants to come with me today. She's small and darts through holes in the jungle. I'm big and break the mossy ground with my feet. I know that she's with me, even if I can't see her. Today we're running to the river, about eight miles there and back. We tear through the brushwood, long grass, and tangled vegetation. Branches snap. Trees blur. Mosquitoes sigh. The bottoms of my feet callused over a long time ago. The heavy breathing starts, but the sweat can't start because it never really stopped. If there were wind, I would feel it between my legs and over my shoulders. If there were another person to speak to, I might have an original thought. Instead, the Manual spins through my brain like a Ferris wheel in a hurricane: *"Proper packaging to preserve metal parts against the ravages of corrosion—ever a problem—became critically acute when men's lives and the success of our armed forces depended on such packaging of vital war materials."*

If I close my eyes I can imagine myself home, as a boy in New Hampshire. My name was Jonah Freed. Jonah Freed used to go through the nail tin that his father kept on the workbench. Grabbing a fistful of nails; dropping them on the floor; staring at the powdery, orange residue left on his hands; wondering why his father kept so many rusty nails around. But I've imagined Jonah Freed dropping those nails so many times I wonder if that boy really *was* me at all.

I'm not sure if these pictures in my mind really *are* memories. It's like saying a word over and over again until it loses all meaning completely. "Nails," I say, because that's the word that comes to mind. "Nails, nails, nails, nails, nails."

Deep down, I know that Jonah Freed has been forgotten. I've been rationing the few pieces of silvery metal I have left because that is all there is to do. Dump the metal. Wait. Rust. In the meantime? I run. My muscles are thin and my stomach's distended. The little cage of ribs that protects my heart feels pliant. And the voice hangs over me like a wet towel.

"You do not belong here."

But I can shake it when I run. When I run, everything pulls together, all of my damaged and disparaged parts, and I get somewhere. When I don't run, the parts squeak, pop, and grind, and they could fall apart at any moment.

It's a precarious situation.

When I get to the river, I'm happy to see that Bobo beat me. She's perched on a branch of the tree where we met, wagging her thumbs. The branch hangs over the river like an outstretched arm. The river itself is thick and muggy today. It glides oafishly in the heat, seeming to move only when it wants to. Pamela waves a paw—at me, I think, or maybe a bug. She blinks her small eyes. Her tail dangles low and curls at the bottom like a fishhook.

"Hullo!" I shout. A cacophony of birds in the distance.

After all the running, I'm sticky and tired. I feel like stirring something in this hot kettle. I dive in and swim underwater, all the way across the river. It isn't far. The water's warm and murky, but it's water. I will bring some home to boil because the drinking filter they gave me when I came here broke a long time ago and now sits on a shelf in the shack like a knickknack.

I'll find a purpose for it someday.

When I appear naked at the other side of the river, I don't think twice about it. I start reciting from the Manual, and Pamela starts bobbing on the tree. She's been coming to see me every day, except when it rains. When it rains she goes to the cave with other monkeys. They are her family: two brother monkeys and the mother monkey. The father monkey is rarely home, but I've seen him. He has a long white circle around his neck. It looks like he's wearing a royal necklace. I call him King.

If I stop reciting, for even a second, Pamela barks impatiently.

"Okay," I shout and continue reciting while the jungle bugs gleefully nip me in the ass. But I do it for Pamela, because she feels like hopping to the Manual. *"There are numerous general methods for accomplishing rust prevention,"* I say, *"such as Painting, Plating, Chemical Treatments, Porcelain Enameling, and certain types of easily removable coatings, including oils, greases, and solvent mixtures."*

Then Pamela does something funny. She runs to the end of the branch and points at me. The branch sways with her and I worry that it's going to snap. I take a few steps toward the water. I'm ready to go back in again and save her. I have a vision of diving low in the crud and lifting her tiny body up with one hand and swimming back to shore. Then I give her mouth-to-mouth resuscitation, or something dramatic like that.

"What is it?" I say.

"Chee-chee," she says, and a cluck. It's my name!

Then she runs back from the end of the branch, toward the trunk, away from me and disappears into the jungle. My eyes spin, searching for a glimpse of her between the trees. I wonder what I've done to send her away. My neck becomes hot. The sun pushes harder.

"You do not belong here."

Out of nowhere, a ball of fear rises in my throat so big it feels like

I'm choking. The whistles and jungle chatter that serve as a backdrop every day suddenly sound closer. I swear I smell fire. Hunger overwhelms me. I drop to my knees and press my hands on the ground because I'm too dizzy to stand up anymore. The earth is an amusement ride. I grab the grass and hold on, saying, *"A product should be cleaned in as simple a state as possible. A product should be cleaned in as simple a state as possible. A product should be..."*

I say it over and over again. I say it until the grasses part and Pamela is standing right in front of me, hopping on her two hind legs with her little feet pointed inward.

I give her a look that says, "Don't you *dare* do that again."

She gives me a look that says, "Hey, Jack, I'm just a monkey."

Then she jumps into my arms and my heart relaxes. For now, the worry I had about abandonment is nipped in the bud. Don't think that I haven't noted, however, the shape of our love. Tactile and fleeting. I haven't told Pamela that we're out of Chompy Nut bars.

I am holding a hard grape with oily hands.

So Pamela hasn't come today. Even though I tell myself that she *will* come, I have to say I'm not too certain. I'm trying not to think about it. I decide to spend today getting organized. I eat three bananas and sweep all of the flying roach carcasses off my floor. I go outside for a short walk and find a few tropical flowers, which I pick because I'm human, and humans like things to look nice. I put the flowers on my windowsill. I look out my window and smile at the large pile of decomposing materials and try to feel better.

Now *that* is a man's job. I am Man! I am Science!

I talk out loud to keep myself company, the way I used to before I met Pamela. *"The reasons for application of any protective coatings are essentially a) to preserve dimension, b) to preserve surface condition, c) to preserve appearance. The third reason is very obvious: Even if corrosion did not affect dimension or surface, no one wants a deteriorated, rusty-looking product."*

But it isn't the same.

I stare at my reflection in the window for the first time in a long time. I see a handsome face looking back at me. The odd, trapezoidal jaw. Two thin eyebrows. Hair the color of bleached sand. But the hair is wild—too long. I decide that a shave and a haircut are definitely in order. I set up a small bowl of boiling water underneath the window and scrounge around for the razor I used to have. It's in a small box underneath the springs in my mattress. I hold it up to the window. There are no blades, only two stripes of orange residue where the metal used to be. Rusted, of course. I go outside to hunt down something sharp. There's that propeller blade that arrived with a crack through the tip. It snaps off easy.

It takes a while, but slowly dollops of hair drop to the ground. It's not a close shave by any means, but I've gone from looking like a man who looks like an ape to looking like a man. A lumberjack. A scruffy insurance salesman. A college professor. And I'm satisfied. For the moment, I'm satisfied with anything. But when I look in the mirror closer, I see myself without hair and feel awkwardly light. Human. Familiar. I look like Jonah Freed, the boy who went bicycling to the junkyard and drank a beer that he stole from the fridge; the boy who pressed his crayons so hard the tips were round and crumbly; the boy who sang his father's songs.

But Jonah Freed had brown hair, and my hair is blond. So blond, I don't know where my head ends and the heavens begin. My shoulders droop as the sun plummets. Hope: the bewitching combination of expectation and desire. Hope, hope, hope, hope, hope. If I say the word enough times it will lose all meaning.

I feel a wave, a tsunami of loneliness.

———

There are a billion shuffling stars in the sky tonight. I lie in my cot and stare out the window, wishing that Pamela were here. I know that it isn't right for a person to be in love with a monkey and pretend to have all kinds of human memories and enter fake entries into a Log that is supposed to be serving the war effort. I look at the broken PORC radio that I used to listen to as I fell asleep. It's coated in rust. Bitterly, I realize that no one bothered to rust-prevent my radio before I came out here. My eyes become wells, and I cry a little. I hold up my hand in the moonlight to make shadow puppets. My dexterous fingers easily maneuver to create the animals.

Dog. Gator. Rabbit.

It can't be 1950.

I haven't seen Pamela for a week, and it's been a week of hell. The bugs get bigger every season, I swear to God, and I can't battle them alone. When Pamela is with me at the wooden table, she'll catch the flying roaches in her paws and eat them. She's remarkably adept at flying-roach catching, and without her, I find myself seated at the wooden table not even able to get any pretend work done for the arthropodan traffic around me. I crack their armor with the hard-backed Manual and moosh them with the Fruit of the Looms. They're also bolder without her presence, lingering on the goddamn ceiling of the shack until they are certain that I'm immersed in my rust prevention and then falling, back-first, onto the pages of the Log, startling me clear out of my chair. Or they'll take the more direct approach: circling at high speeds and dropping out of the sky onto my neck.

My sweat is their ambrosia; my pheromone is their frigging nectar.

I've spent the morning sitting very quietly in my chair, waiting for roaches to fall, crack-mooshing hundreds. I decide that I have to get out of the shack before the death toll reaches a thousand. I'll swing by Pamela's cave to see where in the hell she has *been* lately. It's a route I could follow blindfolded.

I walk a few paces around the front of the monkey lawn and shout, "Hullo?" But there's no answer. I go inside. It's dark in there and—phew!—reeks of monkey sweat and scum. I can see why Pamela likes hanging out at my place so much. Hers is a small cave, with a low ceiling and these dirt patches on the ground that have been scratched up all over the place. I wonder if that's what monkeys use for beds. I touch a wall and grime flakes off onto my hand. I wonder if Pamela's been thinking about me.

Jonah Freed's family might think that monkey-hankering is a pretty low deed. But me? All I do is think about her. The tremulous fur. The bright eyes. The perfect mouth that's shaped like an upside-down V. I, contrarily, am big and white and plastic-looking. I stink of humanness: barbarity, indigestion, and intelligent thought. I stink of rust. Homo sapienus Hideosus.

"Hoo, hoo," I say, feebly.

Man trying to imitate monkey. Failing.

Then there's a lot of whooping and swinging of branches. I hear the family coming home. I wish that I'd brought something. (Banana, coconut.) I sit down in front of the entrance to the cave to wait, to think about how I'll have a heart-to-heart with King. I'll spill my guts and tell him about how Pamela and I met, how we need each other, how I am going to take her out of the cave and give her a job at my shack organizing the rusted iron plates, or something just as professional. If she'll have me. I get so excited thinking about bringing Pamela home for good that I stand up and start pacing again, thinking even crazier thoughts, like marriage. Some cool evening there could be a wedding, down by the river. The moon gets so big in the jungle.

But it isn't the family at all. King's nowhere in sight. My Pamela is there, though, making my lungs flutter. She! Furry, Old World goddess! My white-throated, four-handed Primate!

"Pamela!" I shout.

She stops fast. I see that she's not alone. There's a he-monkey with her, all brown, with an unusual downturned proboscis.

L'étranger.

Pamela has found a lover. Maybe she found him a long time ago. They hold on to branches with their halluxed paws and blink at me, as if *I'm* the one who's the foreigner. And I can't bear to see them. I feel the filthiest that I've felt for the entire time I've been in the jungle. In desperation, I try to think about the Girl-Pamela, with the long gold hair. I try to imagine myself on a bed with her, making love or even just fucking, but the thought of it makes me gag and retch. The ache to hold Monkey-Pamela in my lap and breathe in her fur is so real I'm quivering. I'm quivering, while she, the Philistine, is *blinking*.

I give her a look that says, "How could you do this to me?"

She gives me a look that says, "You ran out of Chompy Nut bars."

My eyes drop and my face burns and I grip my fists so tight that my fingernails puncture my palms. I stand there for a second, simmering, until I realize that my feet move. I can still run. I run all the way back to the shack. But I don't go in. I can't face the buggy swarm. Instead I'm out in the machinery, attacking the rust. I kick a Stage 10 rifle barrel like a ball, but it's so rusted that it doesn't even move; it just disintegrates into a powdery pile on my sprawling jungle lawn. So I swing my leg at a propeller blade, Stage 2, which, it turns out, does *not* go propelling off my lawn in a satisfactorily airborne manner, but slices neatly across my ankle instead. A dark spout of blood spreads onto the lawn. I'm draining. I collapse in a messy pile and let the blood run. It is my blood, I think.

It is mine and I am its.

———

I'm lying on the cot in the shack in the jungle. I haven't moved for days. The ankle is not healing nicely. The large slash exposed the bone and the wound is swampy and swollen and extraordinarily painful. The red is spreading up my shin. At night the ankle sticks to my sheet and the flying roaches consider me their frigging banquet. That's when I can smell it, feverish and all sour. Every time I close my eyes I think about her. I'm trying to pretend that she's here with me, but the ankle hurts too much and my wincing always brings me back to reality.

The reality is that Pamela and I were never in love; the reality is that love is not company; the reality is that the sun goes up each day and the moon goes up each night. Time, now, spins faster than ever before, like a record playing on the wrong speed. *"All metals,"* I think before fainting, *"with the exception of the noble metals such as gold or platinum, corrode. The difference between them is in the degree and rate of the corrosion."*

I'm awake. The red has reached my groin, and these small, strange white numbers have taken over my ankle. I huck the Manual into a corner. I pick up the red bin of gasoline and throw what's left of it over the leg.

My kingdom for a match.

Old sun. Old moon.

There they go: up, up.

The Natural Forces are closer than ever, rustling my bushes and crashing my iron. The voice gets louder, always saying, "You do not belong here." I hear its hot breath on my door and I cannot run. I hoist myself out of bed, sweat running off me in smooth sheets. I crawl on my arms and good leg to the door. The bad leg drags behind

me. I'm a half-winged plane, an injured fly. A pretty little POW. I
bust open the door with my fist and pull myself outside.

"Who is keeping me captive?" I shout. But there is no answer.
There is only the mountain of rust, so brilliantly red it glows. I'm not
a Rust Preventer. I don't prevent anything at all. I am a Rust Enabler.
"I may not belong here," I say, "but I *am* here." And I'm amazed. By
the way it just painlessly happens. It could so easily be 1950.

I wouldn't even know.

VANYA RAINOVA

University of San Francisco

TRAMPOLINE

First they built the wall. Then they shot a man trying to climb over it. Then the wall fell. Or, to be precise, they undid it, stone by stone. They say that east and west of the wall's footprint people cheered. They cheered again, a month later, when a man dying of AIDS conducted Beethoven's Ninth twice, one time on each side of where the wall had been. Between the concerts, on Christmas Day of 1989, they shot Elena and Nicolae in front of a different, less meaningful wall.

The static light of an electronica transmitted the execution to the living room of a two-bedroom apartment on the eighth floor of Building 415 in Solidarity—a large development of oversized matchbox concrete structures scarring the periphery of Sofia. The Danube River ran in the living room. It began, roughly, from the center of the wall and seeped out and down until it met the black and white checkers of the floor tile. Once the photo wallpaper had captured the lush green of vineyards on the banks of the longest international river in Europe. But the morning sun had baked the blues and greens out, leaving behind an arid scene; only the rocks looked comfortable. To Liubo it was more familiar that way: Where the Danube marked the border between Bulgaria and Romania, its waters were thick with history and gray with environmental waste from the Communist industrial complex, running through Eastern Europe, dumping everything into the Black Sea some one hundred kilometers north of the Bulgarian border.

Like the river, the picture of the execution arrived solemn and gray and in that way it was not too different from other pictures the world west of the wall had seen of the world east of the wall. Soon after the wall fell, General Motors shot a commercial in Prague, where filming was cheaper. Only then, in commercial breaks, did those who could afford to buy General Motors cars see that Prague was not a city permanently encased in smog. It was indeed golden.

The firing squad assumed position on the screen. Liubo sank in the couch facing the wallpaper and the TV. He was wrapped in a blanket and there was something both pitiful and intimidating about the woolen fabric that covered his body from his ragged loafers to the thorny stubble of his beard. To Liubo's right, his mother, Vera, sat cross-legged and erect. Everything about her was tucked—her opaque stockings, her white collar peeking out of a dark sweater, her bun, the cigarette between her index and her middle fingers. Only her top leg disobeyed; it swung back and forth from the knee down. To Liubo's left and slightly forward, his father, Stefan, occupied his armchair the way he always had, yet not quite: His legs were spread apart, his arms hung outside the armrests. None of them flinched when the soldiers shot, none of them believed it had happened. The family remained still and arranged, as if in a portrait, as if one day they would say, "And here we are celebrating our first Christmas." And perhaps this was a fitting way to begin celebrating Christmas, no longer weary of such nonsense as the opium of the masses.

So on:

August 1992, Slanchev Briag, Bulgaria.

Stefan penciled in a word and looked above the edge of his newspaper. "For how long has she been on there?" he asked. Liubo glanced at the timer attached to his swimming trunks but said nothing.

Father and son sat on canvas chairs behind the trampoline. Liubo squinted at the bodies arranged on the hot sand. The rim of Liubo's baseball hat framed the scene. In the foreground, a pair of skinny legs that supported the face of Mickey Mouse dropped into the frame, feet touched the elastic surface of the trampoline, which propelled Mickey and the legs high into the air, until only the feet were left in the frame, and, again, down they came. A few meters away, and to the left and right as far as one could see, men and women lay on colorful beach towels. Calves. Those who were in the second week of their vacations greeted the sun with the full length of their stretched legs, torsos, arms. Mickey Mouse. Others sheltered their fair skin under thick canvas beach umbrellas that they could rent for three deutschmarks. Toes.

Liubo had a way of squinting that shifted the beach out of focus. This way, it resembled a patchwork of swimwear and beach towels in bold colors. Calves. Many of the clothing items and accessories were purchased from the stalls that lined the boardwalk and sold Mike, Adibas, and Speed. With blurred vision one could not see that the brand names were a mere letter away from trademark apparel. Mickey Mouse.

Slanchev Briag had evolved into the type of resort that needed signage in English: *Welcome to Sunny Beach*. The once Party-owned apartment towers 1, 2, 3, 4, 5, and 6 had been privatized and re-named. The new names displayed an equal lack of imagination, but did so loudly: Golden Sand, Seagull, Pearl. The resort attracted working-class families from the former East Germany; hairy-legged, tall, blond Polish women; men from the post-Soviet republics who wore gold bracelets and dark sunglasses, and their wives, who sun-tanned topless and who gazed over their shoulders and maintained a bored look while yelling sternly to their kids, "Sasha, *idi suda!*" And then there were the impoverished Bulgarians, who managed through various schemes to hold on to their cherished habit of taking summer vacations by the sea. Liubo had come up with his own plan: He had borrowed two trampolines from the Sofia Circus, had driven them four hundred kilometers east to set them up on the beach. It cost one deutschmark to jump on the trampoline for five minutes. He had employed his parents. Vera was in charge of one of the trampolines, and a kilometer or so north on the shoreline Stefan manned the other. Stefan and Vera drank beer or vodka or gin. They gathered sand under their nails, scrubbed flaky skin off their shoulders, flat-tened mosquitoes under sweaty palms. Liubo met the people he needed to meet and paid money to whom he needed to pay so that the trampolines would not disappear, or break, or hurt someone.

Arms embracing legs and Mickey Mouse partly hidden, then back in the air.

"I think she's been on there for five minutes already," Stefan said.

Liubo readjusted his baseball hat. He braced the sides of the chair, rose, walked around the trampoline, and faced the girl. She jumped up and down with violent joy, striving to land more heavily, so she could fly higher. As soon as she saw Liubo, the girl pushed her sweaty bangs away from her forehead and turned ninety degrees in midair. Liubo walked to the side of the trampoline.

"Have you had enough?" he shouted above "Sasha, *idi suda!*" and the waves. The girl ignored him. "Your time's up."

"What?" she said as she touched the trampoline and propelled herself in the air.

Liubo turned his back on her and looked around. There was no adult waiting for the girl. He returned to the canvas chair.

"There is a building for rent," Liubo said.

"What's another word for *luck*?" Stefan's face was flushed.

"The Community Arts Center in Solidarity owns it, but they've no money to pay the utility bills." Many streets, parks, and neighborhoods in Bulgaria had been renamed to reflect the change of regime. However, Solidarity had retained its name. "The rent's cheap. It has a stage—"

"For how long has she been on there?" Stefan wrote something, then turned the pencil around and erased what he'd written.

Liubo shrugged. "I don't know. Seven, ten minutes. It's hot."

"It's supposed to be hot," Stefan said and stood up. Slim, short, athletic legs supported his almost perfectly round torso. The odd proportion of his body forced him to walk with his feet wide apart and his weight shifted to the heels, pouch first. He wore rubber thongs that slapped his heels as he made his way to the trampoline in tiny steps. Liubo jumped to his feet and caught up to his father. The two men stood beside the trampoline.

The girl looked back at them, stiffened her body, and let it bounce to a stop. She almost lost her balance, but then regained it.

"Nobody's waiting," she said. She eyed the two men and stepped back, away from the shadows they threw on the trampoline. She placed her hands on her hips—seemingly for courage. "There's nobody here to jump." She glanced to the left, to the right, then steadied her eyes back at the men in front of her. "I can leave, but the trampoline will be empty and will not make more money than if I stay. So why do you want me to leave?"

"Mila!"

As if all three of them were called Mila, Stefan, Liubo, and the girl looked in the direction of the voice. A woman ran toward them, almost tripping in the sand, balancing a plastic cup of foamy beer.

As Liubo watched the woman near them, the polylingual screech of the beach subsided. She slowed down and smoothed her dark hair, which sprung back into disarray from under her palm. Her whiteness, her fullness, her softness seemed to Liubo out of place under the high harsh sun. But even that contrast faded in comparison to the sleek scar that spliced the woman's throat. The thin line, divided into five even parts by four marks where the stitches had been, was both delicate and violent in its precision, in the way it rose and fell as the woman swallowed.

"I'm sorry. Sorry," she repeated, looking at Mila then Stefan. "I'm late. How much do I owe you?"

"She wasn't there for that long," Liubo said before Stefan could speak.

"There's nobody waiting," said the girl.

"Thank you," the woman said and stretched her hand out to Liubo. "Maria." Maria rubbed Mila's sweaty back with her other hand. "Do you want to jump for another five minutes?"

Mila nodded. In Bulgaria people nod no and shake their heads yes. The girl sat on the edge of the trampoline and slid onto the sand. She dipped a finger into the beer foam and licked it. Liubo let go of Maria's hand.

Father and son watched mother and daughter negotiate their way through the sand. Even though he was looking at Maria's back, in his mind Liubo saw her scar. He followed them until they disappeared in the crowd and then he rubbed the tips of the fingers of his right hand against each other, gently.

Liubo was a large man, and he felt the awkwardness of his size. He was conscious of his head clearing a doorway, the teaspoon lost in his palm, his shoulder touching that of the stranger sitting next to him in the opera house.

As a child, Liubo had spent many evenings backstage at the opera. Several of Vera's friends had worked there, and Liubo remembered walking in through a narrow door, past a sign that read STAFF ONLY. Disembodied voices beginning a phrase over and over again, men in stockings struggling into wigs, layers and layers of makeup, chiffon, notes, lights, static microphones, powder, the scales of a piano—doremifasollasido—and backward—dosilasolfamiredo...Those were bleeps in Liubo's memory—nonlinear, nonnarrative, intangible, more moods than episodes. But when the lights dimmed and the curtain lifted, the parts became whole, the chaos comprehensible, no one had to speak to make sense, and Liubo's body tingled.

That afternoon, as he often did, Liubo walked to a small tucked-away beach about five kilometers from the resort. There, the seabed was rocky and the water unfriendly. The waves left behind seaweed and empty shells. Tiny flies hovered above the refuse on the shore. The wind spread a subtle odor, both salty and bitter.

The closer Liubo got to the beach's seclusion, the more spacious life felt. He walked along the bluff and down a steep path to a flat rock. He jumped off the rock and landed in the sand. At the beach, Liubo practiced tai chi. The twelve movements blended together into a brief dance, which was light and subtle and in that way very different from his broad freckled back, his wide rib cage, and his dark body hair. Liubo moved barefoot in the sand; he remained stable throughout. After the tai chi routine, he sang. Roles written for a baritone would have suited Liubo better, but he liked tenor arias, especially Puccini's. If he closed his eyes, the waves breaking against the rocks sounded very much like applause and he sang longer.

It was late afternoon and the bluffs cast a shadow on the beach. The water had turned green. Liubo let his body flow in the soft light. His movements were slow and balletlike. He leaned and pushed against the air, and the air seemed to lean and push against him. Then Liubo stopped, grounded his feet hip-width apart, and inhaled.

In the first act of *Tosca,* Angelotti, an escaped political prisoner, takes refuge in a side chapel of the church of Sant'Andrea della Valle in Rome. An elderly sacristan comes to tidy up, followed by Cavaradossi, a painter, who is at work on a portrait of the Madonna. Cavaradossi compares his Madonna's blond-haired, blue-eyed charm to the dark beauty of his lover, the famous singer Floria Tosca. "Recondita armonia."

That was when Liubo saw her. Maria sat with her back against a rock, looking directly at him. She scooped sand in the bowl of her palms, let it sift through her fingers, and scooped again. Some moments feel so fragile that one fears a wrong move, or any move, can shatter them. Liubo regarded Maria with the hesitation he experienced at such moments and dug his feet deeper into the sand. He finished the aria. The silence was audible. Maria smiled and rose to her feet. She walked up the path and away from the bluff.

Liubo waited in the car while Stefan helped Vera dismantle the trampoline and lock it in the wooden shack that the right people had rented to Liubo for the season. The orange Lada exhaled and trembled in the sun, like a mirage in the hot desert air. The Slavs were originally pantheistic, and Lada was the goddess of love. One has to wonder what possessed the Soviet government to choose the name for its car. And it wasn't a car to love, either. One of the first jokes that emerged in the free market was that selling a Lada with its tank full doubled the price.

Liubo rolled all four windows down, leaned against the seat, and let its fabric sponge his sweaty naked back.

Vera got in the backseat and felt the pocket of her shorts for her lipstick. A red tennis bandana held her permed hair into a heavy bunch. Vera was a petite woman—no higher than 155 centimeters barefoot. Before she permed her hair, Vera used to pull it in a bun and walk into the classroom as if she were suspended from the sky with an invisible string, her toes pointing slightly outward—an Audrey Hepburn of the Bolshoi Theatre Ballet. She had taught Russian literature to high school students until the course became an elective. Now, even with the help of her high-heeled sandals, at 162 centimeters, she looked as if the weight of her hair might tip her over. Her actions seemed to occupy more space than her body. She popped open a pocket mirror on her lap, but didn't even glance at it as she shut the car door with her right hand while tracing her lips in deep red with her left hand.

Stefan sat next to Liubo and slammed the door. He readjusted the seat, sliding it back until it pressed against Vera's knees. Liubo started the car.

"How was business?" Liubo asked.

Vera undid the clasp of a pouch belt that she wore around her waist and handed it to Liubo. "Forty marks," she announced. Stefan opened the glove compartment and Liubo tossed the pouch inside.

The family rented a one-story house in the village of Ravda, ten kilometers south of Sunny Beach. The road ran parallel to the water and cut through fields of corn. They drove by the dilapidated construction site of a half-built factory, already deteriorating without ever quite having come into existence.

"Look at this," Stefan said, waving in the direction of the former factory-to-be. "The monuments of a banana republic in the making." The Party had stripped Stefan of his royal blue engineer uniform and dressed him in starched white shirts. He had presided over meetings, and sweaty circles had radiated from his armpits as he had gone over five-year plans for developing and expanding the robotic industry of Bulgaria. The factory they drove by would have manufactured digital recording devices. Stefan would have directed the factory. But then the wall fell and the Soviet Union did not buy CDs and China would not buy CDs, so they didn't need a factory and nobody needed a director for a factory that didn't exist.

"You know the community arts center in Solidarnost," Liubo said, glancing at his mother in the rearview mirror. "They're bankrupt."

Stefan grunted and reached into the glove compartment. He began counting the money in the pouch.

"The building's for rent," Liubo added, this time looking at Vera over his shoulder. Vera pulled a half-smoked cigarette from a weathered leather case. Liubo pressed in the lighter.

"How much?" she asked.

"There's only thirty-eight marks here," Stefan said, and started counting over.

"I had lunch. It's so expensive at the beach." The lighter popped out. Stefan turned to light Vera's cigarette.

"Don't," he said, looking at the fag hanging between Vera's lips. "They smell like burnt plastic when you relight them."

Liubo turned the wheel sharply and stepped on the brake. The car came to a halt on the shoulder of the road. Liubo draped his arm across the back of Stefan's seat and looked over his shoulder, this time past Vera. He backed up slowly. Vera and Stefan followed his eyes. Two women, one of them a girl really, walked on the side of the road.

"Who are they?" Vera asked.

"Oh, that's the woman from the beach," Stefan said.

"Why did we stop?"

"And the other one's her daughter," Stefan added.

"Why are we stopping?" Vera asked, this time looking directly at Liubo.

Liubo pulled the car even with Maria and Mila. He reached over Stefan's lap and rolled down the window.

"Would you like a ride?" The words fell clumsily off Liubo's tongue, as if they belonged to someone else.

"Oh. It's you," Maria said, and Liubo thought that her words, too, sounded to him frustratingly foreign, stolen from one of the Latin-American telenovelas that captured audiences and boosted the ratings on Bulgarian TV stations. "We're not going very far. Ravda's over there," Maria said. Mila stood to the side.

"We're headed for Ravda, too." Liubo reached back and across to open the door. Before he could touch it, Vera pushed the door open and scooted slowly to the left. Maria got in beside her and smiled a hello. "Thank you," she said to no one in particular. Mila sat next to her mother.

Hesitantly, the car accelerated. "There's no air-conditioning," Liubo said. "But at this speed the wind cools you off."

The passengers in the Lada fell quiet. Mila hummed a tune. It all felt so deliberate, as if they were in a movie: the lonely Lada speeding along an empty country road snaking between yellow corn and blue water, the car's shell hovering low above the heated asphalt, Mila's humming. In the stillness of approaching dusk, one could begin to understand why in Bulgarian folktales it is the time when lonely shepherds sing and young brides faint in the fields.

"Who taught you this tune?" Liubo asked, and adjusted the rearview mirror so he could see Maria and Mila. "Do you know what it is?"

"It's *Tosca*," Mila said. Maria straightened out her gold chain and let her fingers linger on the scar on her neck.

"Right here," Maria said. They had entered the village. Liubo parked in front of the house that Maria pointed to. Mila jumped out, and while her mother thanked the family for the ride and bid them good-bye, Mila ran around the car to Liubo's side. "What's your name?" she whispered. Her question was barely audible above the idling engine of the Lada.

"Liubo," he replied in the same hushed tone.

"Liubo," Mila repeated. "My mother used to sing before—" Mila drew her finger across her neck and Liubo wanted to tell her that she was using the gesture inappropriately but Mila's mother was calling her. The girl ran after Maria and waved to the car without turning.

"Nice girl," Vera said.

The house in Ravda had a shack in the backyard that doubled as a summer kitchen. A curtain made out of colorful one-centimeter-wide plastic ribbons hung at the entrance door. The breeze, or a hint of it, shuffled the ribbons, keeping flies and mosquitoes away. Liubo sat at one end of a large table made of raw wood. He peeled potatoes. Next to him, Stefan cut the potatoes into perfect halves, quarters, eighths, new moons. Vera's heels stomped across the tile floor, back and forth between the table and a gas stove top in the corner of the room. The fridge strained to stay cool in the summer heat; its frame trembled and grumbled.

"You're going too deep," Stefan said, inspecting a potato peel that was still attached to half a centimeter of pale yellow flesh.

They were all familiar with this routine, its mindless efficiency, its musty smell of domesticity. They supported each other in their silence, massaging their existence—the bachelor son, the trampoline, the forgetting of things—into what one might call "ordinary."

Liubo looked above the blade at the dance of the ribbons. He thought he saw a shadow cross the door, as if an actor had walked backstage.

"Dad, I think we should mortgage the apartment."

The potatoes dropped under Stefan's hands—half, quarter, eighth, new moon.

"Six thousand deutschmarks. I'll pay them back in a year."

Vera threw a handful of potatoes in the frying pan, then quickly stepped back, away from the sizzling oil.

"That's a lot of money," she said.

"What for?" asked Stefan. "Art? An opera?" His raised eyebrow trembled with overstated sarcasm. "We've no money for art." His speech was gaining in speed and volume. "How old are you? Let's play life, my son, not opera." Liubo knew the pattern well. Stefan would build a tower of bitterness, vexing word upon vexing word, until no statement more scathing than the one preceding it came to mind. Then, in a final theatrical gesture, he would pause, wipe his forehead with his forearm, and sit back.

Liubo was not going to wait for his father to finish tonight. He got up to leave. As he neared the door, he heard a loud thump. He parted the curtain and saw two skinny, nine-year-old legs turn the corner around the side of the house. In their hurry, the feet had tipped over a clay pot. An uprooted cactus lay in a heap of dirt near it.

By the trampoline, each day resembled the one before it, and the one after it, the way each jump traced the trajectory of the fall that preceded it and of the one that followed it.

Liubo had taken to replacing Stefan during lunch break. He sat next to his father's empty chair for an hour and searched the crowd but there were no familiar faces except that of the man dressed in a white T-shirt and white linen pants who plowed the sand with his bare feet every day. The man dug his toes deep, where the sand was cooler. A Polaroid camera was draped across his neck. He stooped over, as if his body was giving in under the weight of the equipment and the impartial sun of August. Alf (or someone who vacationed by walking the beach dressed in the costume of a furry alien) trailed a few meters behind the photographer. All around them, parents reached into their purses and pressed bills into the outstretched hands of children, who swarmed around Alf and waited for their turn to hug the alien and say "cheese" in English into the photographer's camera. Somehow, all children knew they were supposed to say "cheese." At the end of the summer, Polaroid prints of kids with ice-cream mustaches hugging Alf would find their way into family albums across central and Eastern Europe.

"Would you like a beer?"

Sometimes the phone rings or the postman drops an envelope in the mailbox or there is a knock on the door and you just know it is the call you've expected, the letter you've awaited, the visitor you've longed for. In this very same way, without looking up, without recognizing Maria's voice, Liubo knew who was placing a plastic cup full of foam in his hand.

Maria sat in the vacant chair next to Liubo and watched Mila climb on the trampoline.

"Do you mind?" she asked, nodding in Mila's direction.

"I thought you'd left the seaside," Liubo said, without looking at her, only stealing a glance at the scar. It had been almost a week since Liubo had seen Maria on the beach. Each day, he made a point of going there at the exact same time—the curse of knowing the other knows where to find you. Once, he thought he saw her walk above him along the edge of the bluff, in the periphery of his vision. But when he left the beach, an hour later, there was no trace of Maria.

"Cheers." Maria touched Liubo's cup with hers. She sat back and watched Mila jump. Liubo, too, faced forward, but every so often his eyes darted sideways. The silence between them kept the noise of the beach at bay.

"I sang *Tosca* once," Maria said. "Before the surgery."

"What happened?" Liubo's question had the caution of a man reaching out to pet a dog he wasn't sure wouldn't bite.

"Cancer. They took my voice with it." Maria punctuated her sentences with even sips of beer. "I was like fish on the shore. My lips moved but barely made a sound. It was like gasping, not speaking." She finished the beer, scooped some sand, and sifted it inside the cup. Then she placed the cup between her feet.

"They went in again, tried to fix my cords."

"Did they?" Liubo had inched his chair toward hers.

"I have a limited range." She spoke the words as if she had said them many times before. *I have a daughter. I have cancer. I have a limited range.*

"The doctor said that if I strained my cords, I could lose my voice forever. 'Irretrievably,' as he puts it." She laughed, almost.

"I'm sorry," Liubo said.

"One of my professors from the conservatory helped me get a job as a pianist. I accompany the students. It's embarrassing sometimes. Some are passionate, but have no talent. I feel as if I should tell them so."

"Do you think I have talent?"

Mila had come off the trampoline. She picked up her mother's sand-filled cup and poured out the sand.

"Can I go play by the water?" she asked.

"Just stay where I can see you," Maria said.

Liubo was aware of his shoulder touching Maria's. He watched Mila build a castle by scooping wet sand in her palm and letting it drip from between her fingers. When a wave broke and washed her ornate structure away, she started anew.

"Will you work for me?" Liubo asked, more loudly than he thought he would.

Maria laughed. "At the trampoline? It'll save me a lot of money on Mila's entertainment."

"Fuck the trampoline." Maria's shoulder twitched against his. "I'm sorry," Liubo said. "I wasn't talking about the trampoline. I want to have a private opera."

Maria laughed. "Well, you and I could use one, I guess," she said. "Your father's back." Stefan walked slowly toward them with a newspaper under his arm.

"They're renting the Community Arts Center in Solidarnost," Liubo continued. "For six thousand deutschmarks."

"Well, hello again." Stefan greeted Maria with a stretched arm.

"Hi." Maria stood up and stepped aside. "Sorry, I took your seat."

"It has a stage and everything."

"Ah, the opera." Stefan's lips struggled into a thin smile.

Maria bit on her lower lip. "I must go. We haven't had lunch yet."

The next day, when Liubo reached the beach, Maria was already there, sitting in the same place he had first seen her the week before, as if she had never left. Dark clouds weighed above the muddy green water—a dirty mirror held against the sky. Liubo quietly took his place next to Maria. She looked smaller than he remembered her. Mila was nowhere to be seen. Liubo sat by Maria. The air had cooled, but the sand remained warm.

"You want an opera and I have the money," Maria said.

Liubo had never performed, but had made-believe many times; he understood waiting. As a singer waits for the applause to exhaust itself, he now waited for Maria to continue.

"My grandfather owned a lot of land. They'll restitute it now. I'll get it all back. It must be worth an opera house. Fields of corn and pinewood forests for as far as you can see with a small river running through them, flowing into the Danube."

As Maria spoke, her voice subsided into a whisper, inviting Liubo to lean toward her, closer, close enough so he could hear her, so he could smell the forest in her hair, feel its wind onto his cheek, touch its grass, trace the river with his fingers. She was a good storyteller—the type of storyteller who could end a summer by a trampoline.

Liubo and Maria fell asleep on the beach. The small *s* of her body fit snuggly in the capital *S* of his. The gray sky cleared. Its transparency began edging into the earth, the way water seeps into the dry sand, reclaiming the bed of the sea. It crept and crept, erasing the ground beneath Liubo's feet, until he stood suspended in midair, no longer wedged between sky and soil.

MELANIE WESTERBERG

California College of the Arts

WATERMARK

In my ninth month at the aquarium, fish began to disappear. I'd seen a school attack one of its weaker members, nipping at its skin until only bones were left. This was different. No bones lay scattered at the bottoms of the tanks, no scale peelings drifted; these fish simply disappeared, and always from the same room. I suspected Murphy, the octopus, whose two-hundred-gallon tank faced a wall of tropicals: glassed-in columns of starfish, betas, angelfish, clown fish, and their symbiotic anemones.

Disappearance wasn't a new event in my life. My twin sister, Missy, disappeared just over a year ago. Like the fish, Missy didn't leave any trace of a body behind. She left a cabinet of diving ribbons and medals and newspaper clippings from her childhood, a blanket crocheted by our mother, and the closetful of clothes her husband bought her. Missy gave away most of her things when she married.

When she disappeared, she left Mama and me and a weird rich husband who sat in his mansion and didn't say a word.

I decided to investigate the disappearing fish. I started by going back to the aquarium after hours. With the overhead fluorescents shut off and the fish silhouettes cast against the walls, the rooms are brighter at night than in the daytime.

The tropical fish wall splits at its center, forming a doorway to the shark room, with its tank that spans three walls full of Great Barrier Reef sharks. I knew I'd be able to spy on Murphy unobtrusively from inside the shark tank. My day job is to wave razor-slit mackerels around, spread their blood, beckon the sharks that always scatter when I hit the tank. I hand-feed them from inside a little cage, lowered by Miguel, who stands above me dropping freshly slitted mackerel. For the hand feeding I wear special gloves, thick and heavy things scalloped with chain mail. I'd wanted nothing more than to take them off.

I pulled on my wet suit and my oxygen pack and dropped, cageless, into the water. The sharks bolted for their fake shipwreck. I loved shark bodies, perfect flippered cigars, unchanged for millions of years, their worried grimaces and oily stares. Also, I loved the twist of danger when two sharks left their shipwreck holes and started toward me.

I swam to the middle of the tank and a little thresher nosed up, my wet suit so spare I felt its shark shape against my skin. I slid my gloves away. I should have stuck them inside my suit, but instead I watched them float down and settle at the bottom of the tank.

When I lifted my head, there were other sharks around me. I drew my hands along a flank, lingered at the gill, and dipped my finger where the skin caved. I patted a head, stroked down a back, the curve of a dorsal fin.

The water closed around me and I shut my eyes, connected only by the sandpaper of the sharks' backs and the rhythm of the breath I pulled from my hose. When I opened them, I noticed that Murphy was sloshing in his tank. He shoved a tentacle against its plastic lid, bounced it to one side bit by bit, then he inched each arm up and over the tank's edge. When he slid to the floor, I imagined the sound of his body on impact: bones versus cartilage, jelly versus muscle, a slap, rollover, or body-sized shudder.

Murphy dragged himself up the beta wall, ran his tentacle along the top, and dipped in, drawing fish after fish into his mouth. Then he carefully made his way back to his tank. I grinned around my oxygen hose until water sifted into my mouth. Murphy, class *cephalopod* genus *Octopus,* my little star who outshined the others!

The thresher opened its mouth. Perhaps the sharks recognized my faint wet suit scent from feeding time, or maybe it was a convulsion, like a yawn. I put my hand inside its mouth then my other hand between a leopard shark's parted jaws.

I felt their teeth in rows and the flesh of their gums. I wore the sharks like cumbersome mittens, their toothprints edging my palm. Their heartbeats thrummed—how deeply could I reach? My heart went rabbity at the thought and the oxygen I pulled from my hose wasn't enough to keep up with my breathing.

I was the only one ever, I thought, to scrape a fingernail against shark teeth in a living shark mouth. I looked down at my gloves, resting like fallen leaves at the bottom of the tank. Then the thresher gave a little tremor and I pulled my hands from their mouths just before they snapped shut.

Back in his tank, Murphy opened himself up. Baring his underside, his suction cups against the glass, he was shaped like a circle.

"Lenny's running around like crazy trying to find out who was in here last night," Miguel whispered. He injected something into a squirming sea otter and its eyes fell shut. We were standing side by side in the exam room, where one wall was a window that looked out into the aquarium. A pack of children watched nervously.

Still groggy, I pieced together the elements of the morning: Lenny blazing past me when I came in an hour before, the docent's shoulders set stiffly as she herded the children closer to our window, the memory of my gloves. The aquarium, with its baby blue paint job, its peeling murals and soft lamps, didn't house tension well.

Like an epidemic, a vague threat spread from the gloves to Miguel, who, he confessed, had fished them out. That would have been the end of it; he was the first one there most mornings, except that Lenny found him standing on the platform next to the feeding cage, contemplating the gloves in his hand. By the time I arrived, everyone was humming with scandal. Even the children appeared to be buzzing with it.

"Were you, say, petting the sharks last night? Because really, Lea, it would've looked bad if the kids had come in and seen a pair of gloves lying on the bottom of the tank. Really, it would've scared the crap out of them."

Miguel was a Lab Technician IV, so he outranked me, a Marine Animal Care Specialist III. He peeled the wrapper from an otter-fitted splint and unraveled some surgical tape from its roll.

"I just put some medicine inside Elsie so she'll fall asleep. Her leg was hurt today and we need to set it so that it'll heal correctly," he said into the microphone.

The kids looked relieved. Children generally latched onto Miguel because he looked like the kind of scientist they might invent themselves: big glasses that magnified his eyes, his hair thick in its ponytail, a chin that receded into his neck. His lab coat pocket was lined with pens and scalpels and tweezers. He wore dolphin-printed shirts. One of the children smiled and waved.

Miguel was right to suspect me, I suppose. One morning he found me sleeping on the carpet in the middle of the shark room. It was about a month after I started working at the aquarium, when my dreams were so bad I began my nocturnal visits to the shark room.

Most of the dreams were of Missy and me buried to our breasts in earth. We bickered at first, side by side, panicked and unmoving, but once the sand piled to our necks then over our mouths, drying our bodies synchronously, we reached a quiet congruency. These were violent dreams where I wound myself up in sheets and awoke gasping. My walks to the aquarium those nights were rhythmic and contemplative. This was only a few months after she disappeared, and carving her memory into the shapes of my footsteps calmed me. By the time I reached the shark room, the blue of the lamps and the hum of the water lulled me back to sleep.

Missy and I learned to swim at baby swimming lessons at the YWCA. By the time she was eight, she was soaring off the high dive, elegant as a cormorant. I was her fat little shadow, landing prone on my belly, my skin red from the water's impact. When I think of the Reagan years, I think of Missy. She used to sit on a towel in the living room, watching him stumble through the State of the Union address, and dry-shave her body. She wetted her legs with a washcloth and soap and dragged at them with her pink Daisy razor. Then she did her arms. If she had a competition coming up, she'd beg me to shave her back.

When she was recruited to appear in a commercial for the Partnership for a Drug-Free America, it absorbed us for months. Her black tank suit, her white cap. Her gaze fixed and body rigid, she was a ropy sylph of a girl—a perfect dive downturned into the empty pool, then a cut to the cracks on the pool floor. The morning that Miguel found me sprawled like a starfish, I was dreaming of Missy's most memorable dive.

Now Miguel fidgeted with the splint and the tape and the leg X-rays like he wasn't ready to picture my hands abandoning those gloves. I let a hand fall lightly onto the otter's belly. Otter fur is the softest thing I've ever felt. This one was a mother, I could tell from the clawprint scars that lined her flanks and the pink of her nose, a bite mark that never healed.

"So," he said.

"Hm?"

"*Conspirators of Pleasure*'s playing tonight at ten. Do you wanna go with me?"

I froze, imagining us side by side in movie theater darkness, Miguel elbowing me madly during the scene with the woman sticking her toes into the mouths of two pale fish.

I swallowed hard. "I have a better idea."

The otter sighed and opened one eye.

"Why don't you meet me here? Tonight. At ten," I said quickly.

Miguel made a sound like he was pushing all the breath from his body. I watched his eyes narrow. They were brown and huge behind his glasses. He was mapping the spaces between me, a starfish shape on the morning carpet, and me on the other side of the glass, a slip of meat with no slitted mackerel in my hands, without even gloves on my hands. He hedged the connection; I could see it in the twist of his mouth and the way he relaxed his eyes again, a wide and trusting face. Then he said yes, tonight, ten.

"And now it's just a matter of wrapping this splint around the injured leg and voilà! One healthy otter! She'll spend a couple of days here in the lab with us, where we'll keep her safe and warm. Once the bones set, she's on her way back to the sea."

The kids applauded.

Emotional fish are honest the way a body's honest. When Murphy's angry, he flares red and inflates. When he's threatened, he clouds himself in ink. Miguel found me later that afternoon in front of

Murphy's tank, watching the circle of his body with one hand dipped into the water. He flitted from subject to subject, then asked if I knew what was going on with the disappearing fish. I said no, but my body said yes the moment a blush crept over my nose and across my cheeks.

I never went home that evening, just waited in my shared office. There'd been talk of installing a new alarm system or hiring someone to keep watch at night. But how could they guard against someone who never left, whose skin took on the water's low-lit pallor and whose eyes were as steely as a shark's?

There were spaces behind the tanks, passages in the walls that led like arteries to the center of the aquarium, walled in and long disused, where I could make myself a home. I considered this until the last person went home around eight, turning out the lights behind her, and then I left my office and walked the aquarium's bright halls. A twinge of anxiety settled in my stomach; I'd spend the night alone or Miguel would look me in the eye. But if Missy clawed her way back into my thoughts, I was afraid I'd lose my skin like a weakened fish.

I went back in with the sharks, not bothering to put on my gloves. I did this quickly, like a routine, not even waiting for my senses to unfold the way they had before. I half expected them to attack this time, the way a school knows how when a member falters: unravel the skin and let the bones fall. Their mouths yawned open and I slipped my hands in and out, but the thrill was muted this time. I concentrated instead on being suspended, liminal; I opened my mouth to let the water rush in. When I clambered out of the tank, I put away my oxygen pack but kept my wet suit on and arranged myself flat on my back in starfish position. The shift in pressure was palpable and I welcomed it.

The room was cool without the crowds of children warming it, but my body in its envelope felt nothing. It wasn't that I wanted

Miguel with me as much as I wanted my actions to be followed by consequences. I was tired of feeling nothing punctuated by the thrill of contact with something alive: flesh, teeth, or fur, or the fall and rise of pressure, the rise of my breath in response.

I counted sharks as they floated by and, maybe because I remembered preparing for sleep on that carpet all those months ago, my mind turned to my sister. Perhaps she'd just taken off one night on a red-eye flight to somewhere she could collect her thoughts, or colored her hair dark, changed her name, and started walking until she found a little apartment to rent in some distant city. She may have taken a lover, mothered his children. Probably she was somewhere in the ground. Lost and gone were fathoms apart, but she was never the kind of woman who'd secret herself away. She craved attention and approval too intensely to begin her life over again.

The only shark in our collection I was afraid of was the sand tiger. Sand tiger sharks give birth live. The babies develop as a ball of twenty or more bodies in the womb. They eat each other until only one is left, and that one gets born. I understand this perfectly because Missy once found a lump in the side of her belly. It turned out to be bone and tissue fragments from our triplet, whom she absorbed in the womb. She was distraught, but I was devastated. As we grew up together, she tried to finish the job on me. I didn't like Missy much once we left childhood. We lost touch over the years, but still I could tell the difference between lost and gone. Gone was what seized my body up just then without the touch of anything. Like the snap of a shark's jaw, a megamouth all teeth with its massive head on an eely body. Dark inside, it pulled me to its depth, then a curious floating.

A wet and heavy dragging sound woke me. I thought it was Miguel; the clock on the wall read half past ten. But when I rolled my head to the side, I saw Murphy on the floor in front of his tank. He was agitated. Stripes snaked across his body and two knobby horns poked from his head. These were signs of courtship, a way of testing to see if the female would attack or open herself. But there was no female octopus in this aquarium, there was only me, blushing. Then I started to laugh, the sound of it not leaving my side, sealed in by carpet and glass.

Murphy reared up into a circle that shuddered as he gasped for breath and I thought *why not?* An animal could leave its element when nobody was watching, could become so anxious in its cramped box that it might grasp for anything alive. One body could be exchanged for another, could maybe become another, outside of reason, for moments at a time.

The architecture was so jarring that it was no wonder its creatures behaved strangely. The exam room's supply closet opened onto a passageway that few entered. Thick-walled and dim, this led to a saltwater pool at the center of the aquarium. Only its domed ceiling was visible to the guests, and then only from outdoors, at a middle distance.

The aquarium was built around a large, round pool. Fifty years ago, Esther Williams and her girls performed there in their flowered bathing caps. I'd seen them in a movie when I was seven. I was growing fat and Missy was growing pretty and I remember understanding that my sister wasn't the one I'd synchronize my swimming with. Later, the pool was filled with bath-warm salt water, therapeutic for the elderly, until the aquarium walled it in.

The pool's pull was urgent, turning just beneath my skin. I sat up and Murphy flopped back to the floor. His stripes faded and the knobs receded into his head. I watched him scramble back into his tank. My wet suit had dried while I was asleep and it was squeaky and tight, so I took it off. I was past expecting Miguel.

I left my wet suit on a shelf in the lab, where I collected a large, shallow tray and a few fish from the refrigerator. I carried them to Murphy's tank, placed them on the floor, and wrestled him out. He was as light as a large house cat. He flared red and his tentacles thrashed against my body, a living stickiness, like he himself was water, shaped and solidified. I didn't understand how my own body could contain so much salt water; humans hide it well. Balancing the tray on one arm, I stroked the cups on one of Murphy's tentacles with a fish. He relaxed a little, wrapped his arm around the fish, then pushed it into his mouth.

I returned to the exam room, opened the door to the supply closet, then shut it carefully behind me. It was very dark, but once I located the collapsible wall at the back of the closet and nudged it open, I found that the passageway was gently lit. I carried Murphy in his pan through the corridor, a walk that lasted several minutes. He wrapped four arms around mine. When I opened the door to the pool room, the air was absolutely still, with a clinging humidity. I shut the door behind me and dumped Murphy into the water.

When Missy disappeared, I read everything I could get my hands on about twins. Babies, calves, and snakes attached at the hip, the leg, the head. Twins estranged and reunited, telekinetic twins, twins with secret languages. I learned again what I already knew: That when one looks the other in the eye and sees a tiny reflection of herself, self and other blur. The paired reflections might converge into something more than either of them, a kind of shared self.

The high dive probably hadn't been used since Esther Williams's time. The ladder stretched almost straight up, its metal banisters cool against my palms. When I reached the top, I watched Murphy, a circle suspended in a graduated cylinder of water. He'd purpled again and looked pleased at being able to stretch out. If I could spend the rest of my life wrapped up in water, I imagine I wouldn't feel so strange. Solid earth could swallow one whole. Water doesn't allow for disappearance, it pushes everything to its surface.

I hurried to the edge of the board, sank my heels, hopped three times, and angled my body down. My shape was an arc, then a jack-knife. I shut my eyes and my trajectory from then to now, which was a line that met itself, broadened until the salt water of the pool greeted the salt water in my body.

The water was warm against my skin, and I felt again the suspension of the shark tank: solid as a blanket, pulling in all directions. I didn't meet Murphy's body, but I felt him blurt away. My feet scraped the bottom of the pool and I felt like I could keep moving down, but my body strained itself upward. My eyes stung when I opened them, and the water was black with ink.

When I resurfaced, I floated on my back. I kept my eyes open and followed the contours of the ceiling, held gently inside a round room.

ALBERT E. MARTINEZ

New Mexico State University

USELESS BEAUTY
OR
NOTES ON *ESQUIRE*'S "THINGS A MAN SHOULD NEVER DO AFTER THE AGE OF 30"

1. Use the word party *as a verb. 10. Refer to breasts as "chesticles." 5. Read a book with the words* Zen and the Art of *in the title.*

Max has slept in late, so late that looking at the alarm clock can only prove how much of a loser he is, how right his ex-girlfriend Lori was months ago when she predicted that he would become "the Mission District's biggest shitbag" and then left—for good. At the time he was disappointed that she restricted his title to such a specific geographical part of the city.

Outside his window the sun burns through the Saturday morning fog. The vendors at the Farmers Market near city hall must have already broken down their tables, counted and recounted their stacks of bills, and started their treks back to Mill Valley, Oakland, the peninsula, and other strip mall districts.

Lori is among these people. Her table features beaded necklaces, toe rings, and bracelets she makes on the weekends in the Dubose Triangle apartment she shares with her fiancé. During the week she works as a project manager at a Web company. When she first started her jewelry projects a couple of years ago, Max asked her where she would sell the stuff. "The Farmers Market," she replied, simply and disarmingly. The remnants of an omelet breakfast he'd cooked cooled on the plates between them.

"But you're not a farmer," he said.

"Oh, buckwheat," she replied, shaking her head. She placed a newly finished silver bracelet on her wrist, holding it up for him to see, inviting him to admire its beauty. And Max, not yet fully aware of his own lameness, turned back to the Sunday *Chronicle* to review baseball scores and ads for the expensive electronics he often bought but rarely used.

Now, here in his bed on this morning, though, The Headache announces itself and demands attention. A shower would help immensely, but down the hall one of his three roommates is singing under the steamy stream. Though the tune is vaguely familiar, it takes Max several minutes (as the hot water he was hoping to enjoy disappears) to identify it as Morrissey's "Unhappy Birthday." He's lifting my theme song, Max thinks. Max turned thirty less than a week ago.

31. Live with someone you don't sleep with. 26. Google ex-girlfriends.

A late start, true, yet Max is out the door and striding up the sidewalk, thankful for the sun after a chilly shower, water so cold he shunned his masturbation ritual, or "daily tune-up," as he thinks of it. A toasted garlic bagel sealed in a Ziploc warms his pocket and twenty minutes separate him from his destination—his friend Rand's apartment in Cole Valley.

Rand is moving to the Inner Richmond, across the park, and though The Headache prevents Max from identifying the exact day weeks ago when he reluctantly agreed to help, he clearly recalls the awkward pause on the phone as he tried to conjure an answer to Rand's question, "What are you doing on the weekend of July eighteenth?" It should be illegal to ask such an open-ended question—no one plans that far in advance. This was a particularly tricky situation, since Rand has access to a house in Healdsburg and often invites Max up there for long weekends of boozing, drugging, music playing, and general mischief. Max met Lori at one of these lost weekends four years ago. Max said, "No plans yet."

"Good," Rand said. "You can help me hump my shit over to the new place."

Max hops on the N-Judah as it grinds to a halt near Safeway on Church Street. He finds a handrail in the crowded car. Everyone seems to be holding plastic bags filled with fresh vegetables, bulk grains, handcarved wood. The Farmers Market. The train approaches the tunnel near Dubose Park, and just before Max goes subterranean, he spots Lori's apartment—colorful, wise, occupying the top floor of an old Victorian. They must have an incredible view of the skyline and everything east, he thinks. The subway car lights flicker, the vehicle lurches and goes black, cutting off this glimpse of Lori's imagined new life.

7. Help friends move. 35. Sleep past 10:30. 45. Attend Mardi Gras, Carnival, or Burning Man.

Max and Rand spot each other at nearly the same moment. Rand is lugging a ridiculously huge Balinese wood sculpture of a cat, placing it into a Ryder truck double-parked on Carl Street. Max is carrying his lame, soon-to-be-dumped book—*Chicken Soup for the Webdesigner's Soul*, a book he thought he could read *ironically*, as if that were possible—and munching on the now-cold bagel. He leans forward to prevent crumbs from catching on his T-shirt.

"You partied too hard last night, *dawg*," Rand says as Max approaches. Not a question, a statement.

"That would be a correct assessment of the situation," Max says slowly and articulately, with mock formality. As of last night, his birthday celebration has lasted five consecutive nights.

"I've saved the best for last here," Rand says, looking up at his apartment.

"How thoughtful," Max says. He'd feared a large, empty truck awaited him, but it's half loaded already. He can deal with this.

Max and Rand make an inefficient team. The furniture they carry down the flight of stairs—two oak dressers, two nightstands, a huge TV, an entertainment center, a water bed—gets dropped, scraped, chipped. The building walls look like hell. How can you not get mad while huffing someone else's stuff down stairs? Max finds himself criticizing all of Rand's choices in furniture. "Does anyone—anyone besides you, anyone sane—even use a water bed anymore?" Max says.

"Just place the goods in the truck," Rand says. "No commentary needed."

Max first got together with Lori near Rand's camp at Burning Man. She had been dressed as a Red Flyer, a winged creature covered in red silky material that lapped seductively in the breeze. Max wore a black secondhand sport coat with a giant white question mark on the back, a pair of black shorts, no shirt and no shoes. They dry-humped in the back of Lori's Corolla while everyone else watched Burning Man get torched an hour after sunset. Max said "I love you" not once but a dozen times, motivated by the two hits of Ecstasy coursing through his bloodstream and by the act of having such unexpectedly stimulating clothes-on sex. Later he realized, pleasantly, that saying he loved Lori translated into real love and deep affection long after he returned to the city, after the caked mud on his camping gear left permanent stains, despite severe scrubbing. Around Thanksgiving, Max and Lori moved into the roomiest junior one-bedroom apartment he'd ever seen. Max prepped and basted the turkey, Lori sliced it and made buttered yams. Even now the word *yams* could give him an erection.

19. Use the word dawg *in a sentence when referring to a friend or, worse, yourself. 49. Pick a fistfight by thrusting out your neck, flexing, and screaming, "It's go time!"*

Unpacking a truck is always faster than packing it; an architect's lifelong work can be destroyed with a single, well-placed match. Max is relieved at how quickly the unloading goes on the other side of the park. The two flights of stairs erode some of the relief but not enough to spur anger, not true anger anyway, at having agreed to help. Rand is moving into his girlfriend Kristi's rent-controlled two-bedroom apartment overlooking Lake Street and the Presidio's canopy of trees. Kristi's there with a beautiful, athletic friend named Miranda, who helps out. Max has never seen her before. The phrase "easy on the eyes" pops into his head. "What did *we* do to deserve this?" Max says to her after Kristi introduces them. Perhaps there are more graceful ways of greeting a new friend, but Max can't think of one. Lifting boxes, lamps, and crates out of the truck, the two women keep saying how it's "a great upper body/lower body workout." This kind of talk would usually annoy Max, yet somehow today it doesn't. Sex with Miranda would be a full-body workout, he decides.

Max could take Miranda to Sushi Groove on Russian Hill, they might hit III Minna on Wednesday nights, mountain bike in the Headlands, go snowboarding in Tahoe on long weekends—all the things he enjoyed doing with Lori not so long ago. He and Miranda might move in together, master yoga-inspired orgasm techniques, pick up ceramics as a hobby, take trips to London and Barcelona, run with the bulls in Pamplona, learn how to sail. They would receive holiday cards and vacation postcards addressed to "Miranda and Max." Maybe they could go the distance, get married, have some great years together. Or maybe one of them would get very bored and drop out before it gets too serious. It's hard to tell after knowing a woman for only an hour, Max realizes.

When the truck is emptied, Rand parks it illegally on the curb and the four of them head toward Clement Street for a Korean buffet. Rand is buying. Would Kristi try to prevent Max from going for Miranda? Max isn't sure. Kristi and Lori are friends, yet Kristi never took sides after the breakup. For that small kindness he is overly grateful.

Rand announces that Glasstown is playing at Bottom of the Hill tonight and that they should all go. Max has nothing planned and says yes quickly, hoping that Miranda will get caught up in the enthusiasm of the moment. Miranda says, "Sounds good to me," and that's all it takes for Max to consider the night promising. It's only later, after the satisfying dinner, that Kristi says to Max, "The show's a kind of going-away party for Lori. She's moving to Iceland."

11. Experiment with facial hair. 16. Know the names of the current Real World *cast.*

Before they go out, Max showers in Kristi and Rand's bathroom, and for the second time that day, he restrains himself from masturbating. Though showers are the natural habitat for his sessions, it wouldn't be right. He picks up a bright yellow rubber ducky on the basin ledge and squeezes a squeak out of it. There's no way it would be right. Yet now that he knows he'll see Lori, he wishes he could let off some steam before the encounter. His only chance is to have sex with Miranda in the taxi. He's never pulled that maneuver off, not even with women who've loved him, not even with Lori. He releases his tight grip on the ducky and it falls to the tub floor. With his toe, Max shoves the head of the toy into the drain. He turns off the water and gets out of the shower. It's nearly nine o'clock. He had the water going for more than twenty minutes. Damn. Now they're going to think he was jacking off anyway. He dresses quickly in clothes borrowed from Rand, gargles a shot of mouthwash, rakes his fingers through his hair. Outside the window, the view to the west reveals that the fog has parked itself over the Richmond for the night—tidy, comforting, chaste.

"What were you doing in there?" Kristi says when Max steps out of the bathroom. "We thought you'd passed out." She, Miranda, and Rand are dressed up and sitting on a futon, one of the only cleared spaces in the living room, flipping through magazines and catalogues, drinking cosmos and martinis. A TV set on boxes plays MTV at low volume.

"Nothing," he says. It represents too much denial, though. "Everything," he says, correcting himself. "Cleaning up," he says finally. Kristi, Miranda, and Rand glance at Max, not appearing to believe a word he's said, but also not looking very interested.

"Here's to your cleanup," Miranda says calmly, then holds up her glass. The three of them polish off their drinks and stand, smoothing out their clothes. The doorbell rings. Rand has apparently already called a cab. They're ready to go.

20. Own a futon. 39. Employ any other pickup line besides "Hi, my name is _____. What's yours?"

In the taxi ride to the Potrero Hill bar, the driver talks about the 4.1 earthquake that shook Santa Rosa this afternoon, knocking canned goods to the floor in several grocery stores.

Max knows something about earthquakes, yet it's not scientific knowledge and nothing he needs to bring up in the cab. Earthquakes, or more specifically the potential for earthquakes, is partly what came between him and Lori. One night a year ago an earthquake rattled the peninsula, shaking him from bed. Lori slept right through it. He laid awake considering how their building might come down—would he be buried under lumber and plaster, roofing perhaps? What were their chances of survival? A week later, he couldn't bring himself to have sex with Lori. Every time they moved toward intercourse he envisioned a collapsing building. He focused on oral sex for her instead. While this tactic worked for a while— much longer than he'd expected—eventually she demanded other things.

"Get that cock in there," she said.

Max merely stared back at her in the dark.

"Come on, buddy," she said. "Let's go." She said it the way one talks to a dog, trying to convince it to get up and go for a walk.

"I want to focus on you more," he said, genuinely afraid of the building coming down on top of them. All that weight, so ready to fall. He'd always heard that the Transamerica Building downtown had been designed to "bend and flex" during a quake, but Max's ability to withstand that kind of movement hadn't been engineered so well.

"Focus on me *while* you're having sex with me," she said.

In a stroke of honesty, Max said, "An earthquake's going to destroy the city. Doesn't that worry you?"

"What worries me is that my boyfriend is telling me he won't have sex with me. I can handle earthquakes."

"I don't know what to say," Max said. Lori felt delicious so close to him, beautiful lines and wild hair and earthy scent.

"Do we need to put on the necklace?" Lori reached into the bedside table for the jewelry she'd crafted for Max months before. The turquoise stones fastened to a long length of silver worked as a kind of fetish charm for Max during their sexual encounters. When he wore it around his waist it heightened his control of sexual tension beyond his normal range, which unfortunately was rather limited. She wrapped the necklace around him and closed the clasp. By any objective assessment, the necklace was beautiful, its detail wonderful. Yet, that night it did nothing for him, countered none of the paralysis. Lori tried being patient, then became angry, and then just plain sad. Max couldn't be talked down. Or up.

In a calmer moment hours later, she said, "What are we going to do about all this useless beauty?" Her hand glided over both their bodies. "It's not natural for a man not to want to have sex. Are you a man?"

Max wondered. Men had penises. Max had a penis. Therefore, Max was a man. Yet it was obvious that this wasn't enough. Not between them, not at that moment.

Two months later, Lori moved out. He was relieved to learn that he had no problem with sexual partners after her departure, yet at a loss as to how to explain it. In building elevators or public parks—it didn't matter; the world was his bedroom.

42. *Shave any part of your body except your face.*

Halfway through Glasstown's set, the band plays "The Rack and the Wheel," and Max spots Lori dancing at the front of the crowd. Kristi, Rand, and Miranda are dancing also, alongside Jan and Windy, two sisters Max knows from snowboarding in Tahoe. Miranda spots Max standing at the bar and waves him over. She's so upbeat, Max thinks. He waves back at her and puts up a finger, as though saying he'll be there in just a minute. He's staying where he is, though, at least while Lori's dancing. Lori's hair is radically shorter than the last time he saw her. It's dyed blond and in hair clips. She has morphed, once again finding a new way to look attractive. She smiles. Her bracelets and necklaces jangle as she gyrates, jumps, and wiggles—their brilliance a fluid tattoo. Watching her dance, Max forgets how loud this bar is, everyone crammed up against the speakers. It's a place suited to skatebands and punks. He considers asking the bartender for a pair of earplugs, but that would surely peg him as an aging lout.

Before the band breaks into "Firefly," the singer pauses to dedicate the song to Lori, who, he says sarcastically, is fleeing the warm weather of San Francisco for the warmer weather of Iceland. "You're such a doll and we'll miss you," he says, his whiney voice scratchy over the speaker system. "Bring back Björk for a visit sometime." People clap. Max finds himself clapping also. The music starts.

Later, after Glasstown has finished playing and the next band comes on, Lori finds Max on the back patio. He's been hiding out, bumming cigarettes, lighting them, puffing but not inhaling. It amazes him that Lori has sought him out. Occasionally God grants mercy on the weak and the emotionally pathetic. She wants to say good-bye. She talks about how she's quit her job and will leave within a week. She's moving to Reykjavík, where she'll work part-time for a small publishing house and spend the rest of her time making jewelry. "It's the new Prague," she says.

Just as Prague was the new Paris? he thinks. "That's what I hear," Max says.

"You've got a new goatee-soul-patch thing going there," she says, tickling the hair on his chin.

"That's correct." Something needs to happen between them, yet he can't think what. Maybe he should apologize, tickle *her* chin. Anything can happen. "Hey, look, good luck with your trip. I hope it works out. Or something. What about your fiancé? Is he going?"

"Oracle transferred him to Austin, so things have cooled down a lot between us," she says. "I thought Rand and Kristi might have told you."

"Right."

"Miranda's cute," Lori says, turning to look at her. "She could be interesting."

"I've just met her and we're already over each other. I like to get things finished before they start nowadays."

"Don't be so pessimistic. You've got to have hope in people. By the way, happy birthday. I know I missed it last week."

"Yes."

"Brace yourself, I'm going to give you a kiss." She steps closer to him, he leans in, and Lori's lips meet his cheek. The release Max has craved all day arrives: satisfying, unapologetic, perfect. Then she's gone.

The next day Max receives an e-mail from Lori detailing her plans, offering a forwarding address and a new phone number. He must be one of the legacy contacts in her address book, one of the many people blind-carbon-copied on massive e-mail lists announcing big plans, changes of lifestyle, spontaneous decisions, new zip codes. The recipients form an inside group and yet remain anonymous to each other, tied together by a single, delicate thread.

49. Take advice offered by articles in men's magazines.

An hour after leaving the bar with Miranda, Max is in his own bathroom, moved to brush his teeth in anticipation of sleeping with (or is it merely next to?) her. The roommates laugh too loudly down the hall. Miranda warms the sheets in his bed, as though she's been with him for months. The night resists resigned closure. Max merely desires a moment to himself before life pushes forward. He studies a pair of silver cuff links given to him by Lori; they're perched in the dingy medicine cabinet, staring back at him like soft eyes.

He recalls one Friday night during his time with Lori, a particularly good period he calls "El Año del Oro." They had gotten out of work early, rented a car, and raced to Rand's house in Healdsburg, arriving hours before anyone else. They pulled the hidden key from the fake rock in the driveway and let themselves in.

They showered together, soaping each other's backs, running shampoo through each other's scalps. Without talking about it, they knew they had a limited number of hours before the others got there. They tried to live a whole weekend before nightfall, before the cars carrying their friends pulled up, before the backpacks filled the rooms and house music pulsed out of the stereo, before the first bowl was sparked, beer opened, dose taken. They moved with a grace and purity he'd experienced only on hallucinogens. In the dusty light, they made love on a padded lawn chair on the deck overlooking the thriving valley nearby.

Afterward, they showered again, then took a walk down to the community pond. They threw rocks into the water and sat in the soft sand, running their fingers through it, digging deep then forcing their fingers to emerge from it, the grains falling away steady as an hourglass.

Night approached. They returned to the deck, where they popped the corks of four bottles of wine, two Sangioveses and two Petite Sirahs, all grown in the Alexander Valley below them. Lori flipped through a men's magazine and found an article with a list of things men should and shouldn't do after turning thirty. She read aloud from the list. Max laughed, mostly because Lori got such a kick out of it. Although he was twenty-seven years old, he considered thirty to be as far off as time travel, as distant as Morocco, as unreachable as the Arctic Circle.

The sun faded over all those fields of grapes, organic pockets of sweetness that would grow and grow and soon be changed, then changed again. Max marveled at the world, and his place in it. The shifting of tectonic plates could change things, just as sex could—a relatively minor slip and a fully intentional, yearning movement, a destruction of the old and an opening of the new.

SARAH BLACKMAN

University of Alabama

THE JUPITER'S IN

PROLOGUE

wakes to the golf balls. "Again?" two more slamming into the side of the trailer, and "How Dare!" one pocking the roof, and "What Time?" But when Miss Flora Jean rolls over Buddy is still dead and gone and the alarm glows 12:00 blink 12:00 blink 12:00. The power must have gone out.

Miss Flora Jean flicks on her bedside lamp and listens. A semi revs its engine to make it up the steep hill. Two smaller cars whish by like ice-skaters, or jesus bugs, or leaves. She hears neither golf carts, nor teenagers running, nor anybody, familiar and warm, snoring beside her. No more golf balls.

Miss Flora Jean folds back the covers carefully, so they open into a triangle that will let her out without seams or wrinkles, and switches off the bedside lamp. She makes her way by touch to the window on the side of the trailer that faces the golf course and inches back the blinds. She stands frozen, widening her eyes to let in as much light as there is to absorb on a night with no moon, and stares past the fringe of weedy pine and poplar, the black hulk of the golf cart garage, and onto the empty course itself. It is black, even when the frenetic glare of headlights dazzles across it as cars take the bend: There is so much of it to light, so many low hills rolling. Even if she had a flashlight, thinks Miss Flora Jean, she couldn't hope to see

PART 1

a pity," says Miss Flora Jean. Z. Randall closes the refrigerator door and stares at its blank, white face. Then he opens it again, gets out a package of American cheese, a head of lettuce, BBQ sauce.

"Did you hear me?" Miss Flora Jean tucks her bathrobe closer around her, though the kitchen is warm and the motel's halls are long and quiet. "Z. Randall? About the milk?"

LaSalle snorts, thumbs her shorts down over her ass and her white cotton underwear, and wiggles up onto the counter, but Z. Randall says, "I did, Momma. I sure did," and opens the refrigerator once again to put the milk away.

"Whew," says Miss Flora Jean—who is winning, who has not yet won—as she fans herself with the hand not clutching her robe. "It sure is hot in here at night, and what are you two doing up?" She smiles at LaSalle who is stripping the plastic off a slice of cheese. LaSalle rolls her eyes. She takes tiny bites from around the cheese's edge like a mouse. Miss Flora Jean realizes she can see the tuck and rubble of LaSalle's nipple through her tank top and, as LaSalle reaches out one monkey foot and snags the waistband of Z. Randall's pants, that she is losing if not yet lost.

"I mean hotter than a devil," Miss Flora Jean says over her shoulder as she goes into the motel lobby for a chair. She drags the orange plastic one Z. Randall normally sits in when he is behind the counter into the kitchen doorway and sits in it, fills the space with the hard strut of metal legs, the bony threat of her own knees crossed and poking through the fabric of her nightgown. Z. Randall has his back to her. He is at the stove frying eggs, at least a dozen crinkled strips of bacon leaking grease on the paper towel beside him. LaSalle kicks her heels so that they drum against the cabinet beneath her like thunk thud thunk thud thunk thud thud thud, and sneers at Miss Flora Jean from over the scalloped edge of her cheese. Outside, Miss Flora Jean knows, the night is clear and cooling. She pictures her own trailer, bright and clever in the sporadic headlight glare, and the twenty or so feet of weeds and gravel that separates it from the motel. Trucks rumble up and down the hill. Something has happened.

"Them kids were at it with the golf balls, again," she says crossing, uncrossing her legs, shifting in her chair. "Z. Randall? You hear me? They were hitting golf balls into the trailer again and woke me up. It's been most nights this week now—even with school and what all they have. You'd think something better. But you know how they get so close? to hit my trailer at all? you know Z. Randall? You know that?"

"How," Z. Randall asks as he scoops the eggs out of the pan and onto a plate, then tops them with the bacon and the lettuce (torn in strips), then the BBQ sauce. His food heaps and trembles, and Miss Flora Jean is momentarily distracted by its mass and fragile girth. Z. Randall raises an eyebrow at LaSalle, who reaches into the cabinet below her and passes him a mixing bowl.

"Because the light's out, that's how!" Miss Flora Jean collects herself as Z. Randall scrapes the food from plate to bowl and goes searching for a fork. "The lights! out! For years now, Z. Randall. Ain't you ashamed? No ambition is what you got. And with that N all dark and some of the J. It looks like UPITER'S IN, or something. Like a doctor's sign, and I for one won't stand for, WHAT ARE YOU EATING?"

LaSalle, who has hopped down from the counter and poured them all glasses of milk, hands Miss Flora Jean her drink and pats her hand. "You get your heart all afizzle, Miss Flora Jean. You should shut up." She thumbs her shorts down over her ass and stands in the middle of the floor on one leg, like a stork, or a signpost, or a tattered flag. LaSalle downs her milk in one cold swallow. "Zebbie's just getting him a little midnight snack."

Miss Flora Jean thuds her glass down on the table hard enough to slop milk over its edge and onto the checked plastic tablecloth. "A head of lettuce is not a midnight snack," she tells Z. Randall, who is eating with the salad server, balancing great piles of food on its flat prongs and then trying to stretch his mouth wide enough to accommodate it all. "You hear me, Z. Randall? Not a midnight snack?" Z. Randall nods his head. There is lettuce on his chin and a glob of undercooked egg balancing on the firm globe of his belly.

"Zebbie's got a plan," says LaSalle, who has gone over to Z. Randall and wrapped her arms around his waist. Her fingers strain a little to touch, but they do and rest there, contented. "He got *ambition*." LaSalle is sneering again and Miss Flora Jean likes none of this. She strains her ears for the sounds of golf carts busting through her calla lilies, golf balls smashing through windows, anything to distract and scatter.

Z. Randall struggles to swallow his bite. He is smiling, sheepish, and tinted a delicate pink. "LaSalle," he says, patting her hand and flicking the bit of egg off his shirt and onto the floor, "I thought we weren't going to tell her, yet. Till I knew if I could." LaSalle shrugs and looks away, but Z. Randall doesn't notice. He beams at Miss

Flora Jean and takes a deep breath. "Okay, Momma. Here goes. I'm trying to gain weight."

Miss Flora Jean looks again at Z. Randall's gut, at the crescent gaps between the strained buttons. "Hmmm," is all she says.

"No, Momma, you don't understand. It's ambition, see." Z. Randall is nodding now, as if to make her nod along with him in mimicry if not in comprehension. "I can't be the best. Okay. Face that and move on. But if I can't be the best, are you following here, Momma? if I can't be the best, then who says not the biggest?" Z. Randall spreads his arms to show her how big, and Miss Flora Jean nearly chokes on the sip of milk she has finally decided to take.

"Z. Randall!" she sputters. "But what? But for what? But what for?"

LaSalle thumbs her shorts down over her ass. "He's gonna be the fattest astronaut ever to go

PART 2

to the moon?" The man leans over the counter to peer down at Z. Randall's gut. Miss Flora Jean, who is squirting Windex on the fly-specked front window and eavesdropping, turns in time to see Z. Randall smile proudly and stand to show the guest the prodigious swag of his underbelly, the thick swathes of fat that have begun to swaddle his triceps. Z. Randall turns while the guest signs the book so he can admire the breadth of his back, the double crescents of fat that hang above his hips.

The window clears in swatches. Through the first Miss Flora Jean—who is grinding her teeth, rubbing the paper towel into shreds—sees the roof of the guest's car. Next is the hood, then the windshield, the front door and, her hand shaking, the rear tires, and a part of her front flower bed starting to brown with fall. Finally, Miss Flora Jean clears the window and sees the child freeing the wheel of her bike and tugging the whole thing out of the backseat of the car. The child has red hair, cut short and pulled into two inexpert pigtails that burst from her head like fireworks. She has no socks. As she mounts her bike and rides it through the last brittle stands of Miss Flora Jean's lilies she is not smiling, as Miss Flora Jean might expect, but instead grimacing and concentrating as she hits the planter set in the middle of the motel's turnaround and flips over it onto the concrete.

Miss Flora Jean sucks in her breath and turns to say something to the guest, who is deep in conversation with Z. Randall. "—facts aren't everything, but I can give you facts. Yes sir, encyclopedias are nothing if they aren't facts. This is a project, isn't it? I mean of mammoth proportions. You're going to need help, you're going to need—" Miss Flora Jean notices the guest's bald spot, the shiny seat of his corduroy jeans. Everything he wears is brown, and she does not trust him to tend to a child with hair like fireworks.

Miss Flora Jean hurries to the front door and opens it dramatically, but the child has already picked herself up out of the road and is tugging her bike out from under the planter. Both her knees are skinned and bleeding, and she is grinning like a banshee. Miss Flora Jean notices that she has no front teeth, and that her nose is still turned in the soft pudge of childhood, before bones and finishing.

"What's your girl's name?" Miss Flora Jean asks, turning back to the guest and Z. Randall, who both look up at the sudden rush of brisk air.

"That's Raylynn," says Raylynn's father, his spectacles flashing in the glare of the setting sun. "She'll need a separate room. And can we have an open-ended stay?" he asks Z. Randall. "I don't know how long

PART 4

is sitting on LaSalle's lap in room 13B where LaSalle and Z. Randall have been staying this week. Miss Flora Jean has the blue sheets, the white knit blanket, the comforter with roses. She is changing things up.

"LaSalle? I'm gonna strip this bed, now. I'm changing the sheets." But LaSalle neither looks up nor moves. She is painting each of Raylynn's toenails a different color. Coral Pink, then Fire Engine, then Blushing Rose, then Scream. Raylynn squirms to see over LaSalle's shoulder as Miss Flora Jean flips the blankets off the bed and gathers the dirty sheets into a neat bundle. She drops the whole mess onto LaSalle's cot. Z. Randall is so big now she worries about the doors, about replacing mattresses and who will clean the gutters this year, who?

As she snaps the ground sheet over the mattress Miss Flora Jean can hear Raylynn's daddy lecturing Z. Randall through the thin wall.

- "—minor malfunction of the door seal caused the death of all three cosmonauts.
- "Balloons were the first vehicles by which man approached the edge of space.
- "The Soviet *Luna 3* first photographed the far side of the moon.
- "The Lunar Module landed on the moon on November 19, are you listening Z. Randall? in the Ocean of Storms."

He has a high-pitched voice, thin like a wasp. Miss Flora Jean rests her ear, just for a minute, against the wall, but she can't hear Z. Randall's response.

"Raylynn," she asks the girl, who is still craning over LaSalle's shoulder, still staring, "what exactly does your daddy do again?"

Raylynn shrugs her shoulders and digs a fingernail into LaSalle's arm. It leaves a crescent mark that quickly thins to a mean red line, but LaSalle doesn't move or stop in her painting. She has Raylynn's foot firmly in her grip, pressing the ball flat, splaying the toes so she can get to each toenail separately. She shakes a bottle labeled Paradise Pink and dips the brush twice, viciously, to break up clumps.

Raylynn pokes her again, and when she still gets no reaction she looks back over LaSalle's shoulder to where Miss Flora Jean is tucking the edges of the sheets (midnight blue, Z. Randall's favorite) under the mattress and says, "My daddy is a fireman. He rescues people." Then she cozies back into LaSalle's lap and slings an arm around her neck. Miss Flora Jean can see the flame tips of Raylynn's hair, the inverted bowl of her elbow.

"What about a boy?" asks Raylynn. "What'll you call it if it's a boy?"

LaSalle stiffens and Miss Flora Jean, dropping the comforter, waits for the room to stop spinning and implode.

Behind the wall Raylynn's daddy's voice rises to a high buzz like a drill, or a siren, or

PART 5

Paul. Timothy? Wallace, Herbert, Edward, Tom?" Miss Flora Jean has been doing this for two months now, ever since LaSalle informed her that if it is a girl they will name it Elvis. If it is a boy, she doesn't care.

"Shit," says Miss Flora Jean, as she drops a stitch in the navy blue booties she is knitting. Raylynn, under a blanket in the other lawn chair, doesn't look up, but Miss Flora Jean swats her on the knee anyway, for hearing it. They are outside, though it is chilly and all the plants are dead, because there is a couple in room 5 who drink all day and cuss out of meanness, and the man in room 4, though he's only been there the afternoon, has a look to him that Miss Flora Jean doesn't want Raylynn around.

"What about Jeremy, Raylynn? You like that name?" Raylynn shrugs and kicks her feet under the blanket to make it billow and settle like a tent, or a gown, or an ocean. "What about Howard, or Glenn, or Buddy even? Did I ever tell you about your grandpa Buddy, Raylynn?"

The wind blows tendrils of Raylynn's hair around her eyes and nose and she huddles further under the blanket. "He ain't *my* grandpa," she says, pouting.

"You know, missy, you make an ugly face and people see an ugly soul." Miss Flora Jean clicks her needles and watches Raylynn's daddy and Z. Randall get their golf cart stuck in the mud left over from last Thursday's surprise flurry. They've jimmied the lock on the golf cart garage to "borrow" this cart during the off-season and work on their simulation—a sheet of cardboard painted with the American flag hung over the side, glued toilet paper rolls like scientific robot arms jutting out of the front—but Miss Flora Jean suspects that it is starting to be hard for Z. Randall to get around. She has cried over him, she has begged.

"If Buddy were still here," Miss Flora Jean tells Raylynn, "things would be different. For one thing them lights'd be fixed." She uses her knitting needle to point to the dead N, the still dying J, the S, which glows dim in its orbit as soon as it gets dark enough to see the lights are on at all. "And that boy," she points at Z. Randall, who has snagged his belly on the steering wheel and is balancing half out of the cart, leaning on Raylynn's daddy for support, "well, that boy."

Miss Flora Jean thinks about Buddy—his laugh, the way his shirts always came untucked first in the back and he wouldn't ever notice and she would have to come up behind and tuck them back in, driving the wedge of her hand gently down the back of his jeans, neatening him clean. Once, when Buddy was repainting the front of the motel, Miss Flora Jean absentmindedly walked under the ladder he was perched on and got little comets of white paint all over her sweater. She started to cry, not about the sweater, but about the bad luck, the new doom blotting their future. Buddy came down from the ladder and held on to her, patted her back. He didn't ask any questions, but when she finally told him what was wrong he laughed and said, "Shit, honey. Bad luck can't touch you if you're beautiful." She believed him then, but of course it did.

Raylynn, who is watching her, reaches out suddenly from under the blanket and grabs Miss Flora Jean's hand. Miss Flora Jean looks down at her, but she is staring away now, fixated on the pale half-full moon that has braved the day to ghost over the motel's sign. "I like the name Roger," Raylynn says, squeezing Miss Flora Jean's hand.

"Well, I do, too, honey. Roger is a very handsome

PART 6

- "—was the first manned space shuttle to land on the moon. N. Armstrong stepped onto the moon's surface at 2:56 A.M. GMT and said:
- "*Apollo 12* followed the flight plan of *Apollo 11* and landed on the moon on
- In room 12, Raylynn's daddy is bent over a desk covered in papers and books. He writes, erases, writes, takes off his glasses, sighs, looks out the window, writes,

- "*Apollo 13*, launched April 11, 1970, failed to complete its lunar landing mission due to an explosion in the Service Module that damaged

- In room 15, LaSalle opens a cardboard suitcase she has had since Z. Randall met her and begins to unpack. She takes out an embroidered pillowcase, a mirror, two pictures, a brush,

- "*Apollo 14* continued exploration of the moon, landing within eighteen meters of the last

- In the motel kitchen, Z. Randall, weighing all of three hundred pounds, starts his day with two slices of cake and half a ham. He has tacked a photo of the moon to the refrigerator and looks at it while he chews, traces the mares and dead oceans with the ball of his thumb, begins to cry,

- "*Apollo 15* permitted extensive exploration of the moon's surface by crew members. The weight of material returned was prodigious compared to

- In room 2, Miss Flora Jean is cleaning. She empties the trash can, remakes the bed, takes the Bible out of the nightstand and riffles through it to make sure no one has made any marks. She hums to herself. She stretches. She looks out the window and sees

- "*Apollo 16* landed in the Descartes region, and *Apollo 17* was the last

- Outside, on the asphalt turnaround, Raylynn balances her bike at the top of the steep driveway. She squints at the sun and holds up one gloved finger to test the wind. She pulls swim goggles down over her eyes and then launches herself, pedaling furiously, toward the road. As she rolls

Miss Flora Jean is the first one there because she saw it, the truck not even braking, and no time for her to scream or call out, though she did, running and screaming down the hill because the truck did not even brake and the bike is in a ditch, half up in the slim trees, bending them to snapping, so she thinks "we can fix it, we can fix that," because the child is on the ground and her father is running down the hill with his mouth opening and shutting like he is eating something bigger than his jaws, making impossible words because she is still wearing her gloves and her jeans with the hole in the knee and one of her eyes is... the truck not even braking and LaSalle there now, holding the child's head lifting it from the ground where the asphalt is darker and dear god and darker and pressing the child's cheek to her own swollen belly and Miss Flora Jean goes to her knees on the side of the road because there is BLOOD COMING OUT OF HER MOUTH and THE AS-PHALT IS DARKER AND MY GOD IT'S DARKER and the child's father running down the hill opening and closing his mouth like he is chewing on his own words now, he cannot get there, and LaSalle is rocking her, holding her, she hasn't moved, and her bike's wheels are spinning still, one of them—the truck didn't brake and Z. Randall stands at the top of the hill like a monument blotting the sun because it should not shine here, it should not move and make time move as long as the truck did not brake and Miss Flora Jean, by the side of the road, must look at the asphalt where it is darker and realize it will dry red, and it will dry.

PART 1

the middle of July the motel is hotter than the guests can stand. There are none, but for a couple in room 11 with a baby. They run the air conditioner all day and argue late at night when they think no one can hear. Miss Flora Jean is in the storage room, repacking the winter linens with mothballs. Her trailer is an oven. At night she bakes and thinks of herself as a chicken—an old pullet with stringy legs, tough breasts, no meat.

Z. Randall comes to the storage room door and leans on its frame. He has two canes now, to help him walk, and is always out of breath. Miss Flora Jean listens to him pant for as long as she can stand before turning around.

"Did you unclog that toilet, Z. Randall?" she asks before she notices the wetness on his cheeks, the way his belly jiggles and heaves. But she doesn't have time for this. There is no longer any time for this. "Z. Randall," Miss Flora Jean says, more gently now. She lays her hand on the side of his face like she did when he was a little boy and Buddy had whipped him, or scolded him, or passed him by. "Did you do the things you were supposed to do today?"

Z. Randall nods. He is crying still, but trying to stop it, wiping his eyes on the sheets Miss Flora Jean has sewn into a shirt for him, that LaSalle has embroidered with the United States flag and the military bars of an astronaut.

"Well, then, that's all you can do. That's all anybody needs you to do." Miss Flora Jean pats her son one more time and turns back to her boxes.

"Come on over here and help me pack up these things. Things were so crazy last winter with ... well, with all of it, that I never had time to do this right."

Z. Randall wedges his way into the room and, though it is hot, it is stifling, he leans against his mother and she holds him, as much as she can, with one arm, while he folds and stacks and sets things to order again so they will be ready when they are needed, when

EPILOGUE

her birthday and LaSalle, her hands over Miss Flora Jean's eyes, is walking her out the front door of the motel while Z. Randall calls from the turnaround.

"You're going to love this, Momma," he yells, his voice, strangely, coming from above. LaSalle must strain her arms to keep her hands over Miss Flora Jean's eyes, her belly so large now that it stands between the two of them like a small Earth, like a satellite held in steady orbit around her body.

On the asphalt now Miss Flora Jean can feel the heat coming off the blacktop in waves, and in the breeze just the slightest hint of fall again, the first edges of chill.

"Okay, LaSalle," Z. Randall yells, and Miss Flora Jean feels LaSalle stiffen against her. "Let her see!"

LaSalle lifts her hands away and Miss Flora Jean is momentarily confused. There is no one in the turnaround, in her flower beds, behind her in the motel door.

"Up here, Momma," Z. Randall yells again and Miss Flora Jean notices the cherry picker parked in front of the motel sign for the first time and thinks, "How could I miss that, how could I be so old?" then looks up to see her son spilling out over the edges of the basket. He waves down at her, beaming.

"Z. Randall!" says Miss Flora Jean. "What in the hell are you doing?"

Z. Randall reaches into one of the bags that are hung over the basket's side and pulls out a halogen lightbulb. He waves it in the darkening air above his head like an air traffic controller and, with a theatric flourish, unscrews one of the dead bulbs from the base of the N and twists the new one in. It lights up immediately, breaking through the gloaming to illuminate Z. Randall's face.

"I'm changing the lightbulbs, Momma. I'm doing it for you," he shouts down. He tosses the dead bulb into the weeds at the base of the sign, where it shatters.

LaSalle has pulled up one of the lawn chairs and sits in it, propping her feet on the other. Her belly rests in her lap as if autonomous. "He's been planning this one. For weeks now. Had to get the picker rented and test it out and get the bulbs." LaSalle looks up and moves her feet so Miss Flora Jean can sit. "He's doing it for you."

Miss Flora Jean lowers herself onto the lawn chair and looks on, a little stunned, as her son tosses dead globes down to shatter on the hard earth, one after the other. She thinks to call up, to tell him to be careful, but Z. Randall is maneuvering the cherry picker with ease, flinging the bulbs with obvious joy. She is quiet.

After a while LaSalle, who has seemed asleep, turns to Miss Flora Jean and says, "I'm still naming her Elvis. That don't change none."

Miss Flora Jean nods and still is quiet while night falls and the moon—fat as a peach, or a fish, or a child—rises over the golf course, where the teenagers are racing golf carts through the darkness, over the hulk of her son's left shoulder as it tosses and heaves, over the sign for THE JUPITER'S INN, which lights bulb by bulb into wholeness.

Behind them the hotel is dark, but for one room where a young couple stays up with their baby and argues. And behind them the road is dark all the way down the slope and into the valley, where solitary lights glimmer and fade as people open car doors, switch off porch lights, stand to cook dinner, strand themselves in the blue glow of the television, switch on the lights to the bedroom, switch them off again, hum in the dark, vast and lonely, each one turning into each, or waking up to see

JAMIE KEENE

University of Oregon

ALICE'S HOUSE

I wake up because someone's in the house. It's an old house with an old front door and that's what wakes me up: the sound of the door closing. Right away I think of Alice and her fear of intruders, how I'd laughed at the way she'd set up cookie sheets and frying pans in the window ledges if I was away overnight. And she used to get angry when I forgot to lock the door before we went to bed. *Are you trying to get us killed?* Burglars don't kill people, I argued then. Although now I'm certain I'll be killed.

I open up the drawer of the nightstand and feel around for something, maybe a flashlight. I don't have a gun. I don't even have a baseball bat. All the knives are in the kitchen. I try to think of anything that might be big enough to hit someone over the head with, but all I can think of is the yardstick in the closet. I know there's a metal flashlight in this room and it's heavy enough to knock someone out, but it's not in the drawer. I reach down, feel under the bed, but of course it isn't there either.

I remember this from somewhere: The only criminals to worry about are the ones who enter the bedroom. Don't come in here, don't come in here, I think, reaching for the phone to call the police. But the phone is a cordless and I've left it somewhere in the house.

The burglar isn't making any noise, so I relax slightly, thinking maybe I imagined everything. Maybe it was a dream, that creaking door sound. I do have very realistic dreams sometimes. But then I hear something else. It's a light sound, fast, a step on the floor maybe, and moments later a smell. Cigarette smoke. It seeps through the bottom of the door. And then there's a nervous cough, small and quick, more like a clearing of the throat. But it's enough. I switch on the light. I know that cough.

"I didn't mean to disturb you," Alice says when I walk into the living room.

"You didn't disturb me," I say. "Is everything okay?"

Alice nods. "This place is filthy," she says, brushing dust from the coffee table onto her jeans. "You never were much for keeping things in order."

"Then thank god for you," I say, but no one laughs. This is how we are, Alice and me. She puts me down and I make a joke about how I need her around to get by. That got us through our last year together, but it's an old joke now. "Are you sure everything is okay?" I ask again.

"I wanted to have a look around," Alice says.

"Sure," I say, trying to sound nonchalant. Alice had a moving company come for her things a year ago but now she wants a look around. At almost midnight on a Tuesday, she wants a look around. "I guess I left the door unlocked," I say.

"No," she says. "It was locked. I used my key." She holds it up as proof.

"I forgot you had a key," I say. "You scared me a little. I thought there was a stranger in the house." Alice doesn't say anything. She reaches for the ashtray on the table and puts her cigarette in it, then she gets up from her chair and walks around the small living room half inspecting things she's seen a million times.

"You probably woke right up," she says. "You can never relax." She says this flatly: no affection, no judgment. She used to tell people I vibrated in my sleep. When we were first together, she said it didn't bother her, that she thought it was charming, the way I fidgeted. Later, she complained, said I had a lot of nervous energy, and that my tossing and turning kept her awake at night. The last few months she slept on the couch.

Alice flips through the records on the shelf of the stereo cabinet. "You're probably the only person in the world who still listens to records," she says.

"I'm nostalgic," I say.

"Or afraid of change," Alice says. She doesn't turn around. With her back toward me she continues to flip slowly through the records, picking up an album and looking at the track listing before replacing it on the shelf. The tag is sticking out from her sweater and I think for a second about stepping a little closer, tucking it in, sliding it back against her neck, but I don't.

It's been a long time since I've touched Alice.

I sit down on the sofa, wishing I had picked up before bed. There are two beer bottles on the table, a dirty plate, my discarded running clothes in a pile on the floor, inside out, socks on top. I hope she doesn't go in the kitchen, I think. Or have to use the bathroom. I haven't been to Alice's apartment, but I'm sure it's spotless, everything in its place.

That's how her first apartment was, the one she had when I met her fifteen years ago. Back then, she worked full-time at a dentist's office and went to school, which impressed me because my parents paid my tuition, room and board, everything. I was also impressed by the fact that she lived alone, no roommates. The apartment wasn't my style, too bright and girlish, but it was nice—you couldn't deny that. Plus, it felt like an adult's apartment, not like a college apartment. It had plush blue carpet and papered walls and all these miniatures set up in display cases she hung herself: doll-sized kitchen appliances and tiny pieces of furniture, and dozens of baby animals—porcelain kittens and chicks and puppies no bigger than my thumbnail. Her bedroom had a white wicker vanity and a wicker rocking chair and she'd taken these silk ivy things and woven them into the white wicker headboard behind the bed. She'd even glued little silk flowers into the ivy pieces. She also had a wicker bookcase, which held hundreds of cassette tapes arranged in alphabetical order. When we were first together, she wrote me long letters on lined notebook paper filled with quotes from her favorite songs. I let her play her tapes in my car. Sometimes, when she stayed at my house, she packed a few cassettes in her overnight bag and after we made love she said *Can I play you a song?* and I said yes and she'd put it on and look at me in a sleepy, happy way. At some point, she must have gotten rid of the tapes, because I can only remember listening to my records after we got married.

"Do you want some coffee?" I ask. I say this instead of what I really want to ask, which is *Why are you here?* I no longer feel comfortable making demands of Alice.

Alice turns away from the stereo cabinet. "Coffee? It's after midnight," she says. "And you shouldn't drink any either. You know how you get." Again, the flat voice.

"Tea?" I ask. "I might have some herbal tea." I want something to do, a project. In the kitchen I can boil water and wash cups. I won't feel so awkward if I have something to do.

"I don't think so," Alice says. "I just wanted to look around. When's the big move?"

"Not sure," I say. "Next couple of weeks. As soon as I get this house sold. If I can find a buyer, that is. Nobody's seemed too interested."

"The house needs a lot of work," Alice says. "It's hard to invest in something that needs so much fixing."

She's right, it does need work, but it would make a good starter house for someone. A young couple with energy. It's right outside the city, close enough to downtown, but far enough away from the hustle, in a small town with one grocery store and one bank, one gas station and one decent restaurant. As for the problems, well, the heat is broken in half of the rooms. There aren't a lot of windows. The outside needs paint and there are leaky pipes and faucets that we never got fixed right. Still, I remember how excited we were to have it. We didn't complain then; we knew how to compromise.

We got the house cheap because it's on the main road. You can hear the garbage trucks at dawn and the kids driving up and down the street at night, but we liked having something that belonged to us. And we liked the view. You have it only from the corner room, the attic room upstairs, but you get it all: the pier, the water, the little boats that come in at night. That room is terribly cold in the winter, but in the summer, it's perfect. The people who'd owned the house before us had used it for storage, but we didn't have much stuff, so we bought a love seat at the Goodwill and put it up there. The first few summers, Alice and I spent most evenings up there, reading, or making love, talking; but then we got busier and had less time for each other. I'd tried to explain the room to a few couples—how they could uncork a bottle of wine and sit down by the open window, and smell the salt rise from the harbor, hear the waves lick the old wood dock, and watch the lights on the water; but they weren't impressed.

"What are you thinking about?" Alice asks.

"Nothing," I say. "Work stuff. I've got a lot of work stuff lately. Did you say you wanted tea?"

"No," she says. "I guess I should go."

"You can stay," I say. "I didn't mean I wanted you to go. I want you to stay." Alice looks at me, raising her eyebrows. "I didn't mean it like that," I say. "I mean, I'll go back to bed and you can stay."

She runs her hand across the wall, down the side of the heavy silver mirror. Because of where she's standing, I can't see her reflection in it, only mine.

"I was thinking about using a yardstick," I say. "On the intruder. On you." This is supposed to be funny, but no one laughs, and I realize I'm not making sense, nothing I say makes sense. "As a weapon," I explain. "In case you thought you could rob me blind, take my valuables."

"What valuables?" she says. "You have valuables?"

"Never mind."

"I should go," Alice says. I nod and watch her pick up her things: cigarettes, lighter, key. I watch her walk to the door. She pulls it closed softly so it doesn't make a sound.

The next night, Robin and I are lying in bed and I'm reading aloud, which Robin says is quite possibly one of the nicest things anyone has ever done for her. She says I have a strong voice. One evening we went to a reading at the local college where Robin teaches literature. A bunch of graduate students read from their fiction. Some of the stories might have been good, but you wouldn't know it from the way they read. It was terrible—as if they were too smart for their own work: flat voices talking about love and relationships and death as if they were asking for five more minutes of sleep in the morning.

After I finish, I always have to stop for a minute and think about what I've read. Robin gets the meaning faster than I do and points out things I've missed.

"The end of that story kills me," Robin says. "Every time I hear it." She's not crying, but her voice breaks a little. She says she cries sometimes when she's reading aloud to her students. It embarrasses her. They're undergraduates and easily flustered.

"My god," she says. "I'm so emotional this week."

"There's a lot of changes," I say, pulling her close to me. "Don't get anxious. I don't need to be out of here immediately. We can move me into your house as slow as we please."

"No," Robin says. "I'm sick of waiting. I'm tired of trying to figure out who's coming to whose house and wondering if I've got everything I need for the next day. I'm just nervous," she says. "I've never done this before." Robin is the only person I know who's never done this before. She had lovers before me and was engaged once, but she's thirty-five and has lived alone since college. On our third date, she said, "I'm going to let you know up front that I don't want kids. And I don't think I want to live with anyone. I like being alone." That's how it is with Robin and me. She says exactly what she means. I asked her out for a fourth date and then a fifth. She's never said it, but I think she likes that I don't ask anything from her. It's easy with us. With me and Alice nothing was easy.

"It'll be great," I tell her. She nods and nuzzles against me.

I wake up half an hour later to the smell of cigarette smoke. The clock says 12:10. I can tell by Robin's breathing that she isn't awake. My heart beats against my chest. Now what? Do I wake Robin up and tell her Alice is out there? Do I go out and ask Alice to leave? What is she doing here? Robin's car is in the driveway. She knows about Robin. Just as I know about John. I wouldn't go into someone's house if a strange car were in the driveway.

Maybe Alice will just leave, I think. Unless she needs something and what if that's it? What if she needs something? She must need something because why would she come back here again if she didn't need anything? Here is the dilemma: I don't want Alice to knock on the bedroom door and I don't want her to sit out there alone.

So here's what I do. I slide out of bed as quietly as possible, pulling one leg out, then stopping to check that Robin's still asleep. Her breathing is deep. I move the other leg, watching Robin the whole time. I'm out of the bed. And as soon as I'm not looking at her, she's awake. "Where are you going?" she asks.

"I just have to get up for a minute," I say. "Go back to sleep."

"What's burning?" she asks, sitting up.

"Shh," I say, putting my finger to my lips. "It's nothing."

Robin turns on the light beside the bed. "Something's burning, do you smell that? Did you turn the oven off?"

"Shh," I say again. "It's Alice. She's smoking. In the living room. Just go back to sleep. I'll go talk to her and I'll be right back." I'm whispering and when Robin talks again, she's whispering, too.

"Did something happen? Is she okay?" Robin asks. There's concern in her voice.

"Yes. Maybe. I don't know," I say. "I think she's okay."

"How long has she been here?"

"She just got here. Wait for me. Or go to sleep. I'll be right back."

In the living room, Alice is sitting in the velvet chair she insisted on buying when we first got married and refused to take when she left.

"Hi," she whispers. "I woke you?"

"Alice," I say.

"I'm sorry if I woke you," she says. "I took my shoes off." She points to the hallway. I see her high heels on the floor. Alice is tiny, only five feet tall, and insists on wearing six-inch heels with everything, even with jeans. Most people don't notice the heels; I guess because she doesn't look like the sort of woman who would wear impractical shoes. I remember the first time I saw her barefoot, how startled I was to see her so small. I looked at her for a long time. She got embarrassed and pushed her head into my rib cage, hiding her face in my shirt. Years later, she started getting cramps in her legs at night and I told her she was silly, that she didn't need to wear such high shoes, that no one cared how small she was. "I care," she said.

"It wasn't the shoes that woke me," I say. "It was the cigarettes." I'm looking at Alice, who is looking at the wall.

"Right. The cigarettes," she says. Maybe it's because I just woke up, but the smell of her cigarette makes me think of sex. Sometimes in the middle of things, Alice would reach over and light one from the pack beside the bed. This might sound strange, but it never bothered me. Alice looks up at me and smiles, shyly, as if she's embarrassed, as if she knows what I'm thinking. It's an odd feeling to look at someone you've been intimate with so many hundreds of times and to think: I will never know you again. Like when you realize it was the last time, and you hadn't even known it would be the last time, because if you had you would have done something differently, you would have marked it for yourself somehow, found some way to remember everything better than you do.

"I was thinking this afternoon," Alice says. "About you. How you never once gave me a hard time about smoking. Thank you. I know you hated it." She puts her cigarette out in the ashtray. I haven't emptied it from the night before. I wonder how Robin missed those.

I haven't told Robin that Alice was here last night. Not because I needed to hide it. I just didn't know what to say.

"I didn't hate it. I just worried about you."

"I don't smoke so much anymore," Alice says. "Just at night." She reaches for her pack and lights another. She's not in a hurry to leave. I should mention Robin, but I don't. I'm not sure how to mention Robin or how to mention anything. I wonder if Robin will come out of the bedroom. I'd come out. I'd come out and let a person know I was there. Robin is a better person than I am. Robin won't come out.

Robin trusts me and she likes Alice. She and I ran into John and Alice once about three months ago at the college's art museum. I'd never met John before and Alice had never met Robin. Alice and John got together at the adult education center where she volunteers one night a week, teaching English as a Second Language. "He's an artist," she told me over the phone. We were finalizing divorce papers. Coordinating the signatures.

"Is that his only job? Teaching art at adult ed?" I asked.

"He's got a minor disability," she said, defensively. "He can't work full-time."

"What disability?" I asked. Somehow the fact that John had a disability and taught ceramics to retired people made me feel bad for Alice but also a little superior.

"None of your business," Alice said.

Robin loved Alice when she met her, because everyone loves Alice. Alice is charming and sincere and looks you in the eye when she speaks to you, I mean *really* looks, which is what most people won't do. People always remark what a good listener Alice is. I don't know that that's a measurable quality, but nevertheless, that's what people say. I overheard Robin say that the two of them, meaning she and Alice, should get together sometime. John and I were awkwardly conversing about a painting that he liked and I didn't. I was trying to determine what was wrong with him. He looked fine to me. A bit like a guy who doesn't know how to change a tire, but otherwise fine. When we left, I said to Robin, "Do you really think becoming friends with Alice is the best idea? Aren't there any other women in town you can be friends with?"

"I'm sure it'll never happen," Robin said. "Although wouldn't that be something if the two of us became friends?" They haven't seen each other since, but I don't think right now is the best time for them to get reacquainted.

"I was also thinking," Alice says. "About how quiet it was."

"What quiet?" I ask, sitting on the couch.

"Like this," Alice says. "Here we are, two people in a room, and it's quiet."

"It's late," I say.

"I know," she says. "But in general, things were very quiet."

"That's not true," I say. "There was always some noise or another. My records, the way we always talked. We used to talk so much in the evenings. Other sounds, too—the neighbors, how they fought all the time. There was always the sound of them arguing, their dog barking, their baby crying. There was the traffic outside. And people constantly phoning to talk about something, friends asking us to help with this or that. We never had any quiet."

"There was quiet," she says. "It got unbearably quiet." I look at Alice, who looks at the floor. She crushes her cigarette out and puts her head in her hands. Her pale blond hair falls around her fingers.

"It wasn't quiet," I say, without looking up. "I don't know what it was, but it wasn't quiet."

"You must be tired," she says, sitting back in the chair. She makes a mouth at me—not a smile, not a frown, but a mouth that means *enough.* "And I know you've probably got somewhere to be," she says, looking toward the bedroom. "Go on to bed. I'm just going to sit here a while. I'll let myself out."

"Alice," I say, and that's all I say, because everything else requires too many words.

"Go on," she says.

Robin is sitting up in the bed when I climb in. "What's going on?" she asks.

"Shh. She'll be gone soon," I say.

"Why do you keep telling me to be quiet?" she whispers.

"I don't feel like arguing right now," I say.

"Who's arguing? I just want to know what's going on."

"I don't know, Robin," I say. "I'm tired. I'm confused. I'm tired. I don't know what to say. It's late. This is a very awkward moment. My wife is in the living room. My girlfriend is in the bedroom. I have to sell this house. I have to get up early." I turn over and pull the blanket around me. Robin isn't settling in. She says something, I think, but it's too low for me to make out. I move the comforter and turn over again to face her.

"What?" I say.

"Your ex-wife," Robin says.

"What?"

"Your ex-wife. You said *my wife* is in the living room." She runs her fingers across her throat.

"My *ex*-wife is in the living room," I say. I put my hand on her leg, but she flinches it away.

"What's she doing here?" Robin asks. "Does she know I'm here?"

"I don't know what she's doing here," I say. "And yes, she knows you're here." Robin doesn't say anything. Then there is the sound, thank god, of the front door clicking closed. "She's gone," I say.

"What do you mean the *second* time?" Robin asks. It's already past eleven, I had a late dinner meeting, and both of us are exhausted after last night. Neither of us slept. I could tell Robin was awake by her breathing. It was too soft and even. We're at Robin's house, in her bedroom. Soon it will be our bedroom, but right now I've only got a drawer. I take off my tie and unbutton my shirt. I lay them on the bed. "Are you going to answer me?" she says.

"She came the night before," I say. I sit down next to her and take off my shoes.

"What night before?"

"The night before last," I say.

"She came two nights in a row?" Robin asks. I nod. "Did she call first? Did you know she was coming?" I shake my head no. "I didn't even hear her knock," she says.

"She used her key," I say.

"She has a key?"

"It's her house, Robin."

"It's not her house," Robin says, moving a little farther away from me.

"What was I supposed to do, Robin? She was just sitting there, in the dark."

"I don't know, maybe say 'What are you doing here?' Maybe 'It's a little bizarre to just use an old key and come into the house in the middle of the night.' Or, 'Isn't this something we could take care of in the morning?'" Robin is raising her voice now, which she rarely does. When she gets angry it's usually about other people or things— students who lied to her, budget cuts, parking places, politics.

"Robin, it's complicated."

"Yes, it is complicated. It's complicated because it's abnormal. I know divorce is hard, but it's been over a year. I don't think it's too complicated to call first. You can't tell me you think this is normal."

"I don't think it's normal, but I don't know what to do."

"Why is she coming over?"

"I don't know," I say.

"Didn't you ask her?"

"She said she wanted to look around."

"Look around for what?" Robin asks.

"I didn't ask."

"Why didn't you ask? Weren't you curious? Don't you think that sort of behavior is odd?"

"I suppose it's odd," I said.

"You suppose? What's wrong with you? Can you look at me, please? You're going to have to talk to her. I don't want to be over there worried about her coming in during the middle of the night. What if we were making love, or, worse, arguing, and she just *used her key* and came in. I want you to call her. I don't know what it is with you, but I think you're making an awful lot of excuses here. I can't believe you don't find this whole thing uncomfortable."

"It is uncomfortable," I say.

"Uncomfortable with me or with her?" she says.

"Both," I say. "It's equally hard with both of you."

"What have I done?" Robin asks. And now she's not yelling, but crying, which is worse and she is really crying, which I've never seen. "Alice is the one breaking into the house," she says, wiping at her eyes with the sleeve of her pajama top. "If I remember correctly, you left to go comfort *her* last night. When you came back, you barely spoke to me. And now I'm making you uncomfortable? I think you need to get your priorities straight. I've never questioned anything you've done in relation to Alice, and there have been times. The way you looked at her when we ran into them at the museum, the way your voice lowers when you talk about her, about your life. I know you loved her. And I fully accept that, but this isn't normal."

"I don't know what normal is, Robin. Nothing has ever been normal with Alice and me. What do you want me to do?"

"I want you to ask her what's wrong and tell her not to come to the house anymore. At least not at midnight and not without calling." I get up and walk to the window. This room is hot and I need some air.

"Are you listening to me?" Robin says.

"I can't do that," I say, without turning to look at her.

"You can't ask her not to come over in the middle of the night without calling first?" Robin asks. Her voice is incredulous. And I know she's right. But I can't give her this. Not because I don't understand her but because somewhere, somehow, I need to understand Alice. I walk toward the bed where she's sitting. "Just give me a little time."

I am looking at Robin and she is looking at the floor. She's crying still, but it's so soft. Not like Alice. Alice could really cry. Alice always said that I didn't know how to cope with people being upset, that I wasn't really there when she needed to talk to me. I'm not good at this, I think.

Robin and I sit there for a long time. Neither one of us says anything.

"I should go home," I say. She reaches for the box of tissues beside the bed.

"Where is *home*?" she asks, quietly. "Here, or Alice's house?"

I park the car and walk up to the front of the house. When we bought this house, it seemed so small. Now it seems so big. I turn the key and open the old door. I can see the smoke in the air of the living room. The upstairs light is on. "Alice?" I call.

She's not in her chair. I walk through the kitchen and into the hallway. The bathroom door is open and the light is off. I open our bedroom door, turn on the light, and then shut the door again. I walk toward the staircase. "Alice?" I call, louder this time. She doesn't answer. I walk slowly up the stairs and into the tiny corner room of the attic. There's nothing there. No Alice, no smoke, only the light. I turn it off. The window is pushed open, all the way, and the breeze from the harbor hits my face. I can hear waves lapping against the pier, and somewhere, off in the distance, is a boat, its lights glittering in the darkness, moving farther away into the water.

Robin asked me a few times, "Where did it go bad with you and Alice?" This struck me as strange, that she'd ask where—as if bad is a place you go to as opposed to a thing that happens. When she asked, I told her I didn't know. "You must know something," Robin said. "A marriage doesn't fall apart for no reason." So, I thought about it. I thought about it like I'd thought about it a hundred times before. But I couldn't come up with anything specific. I remembered things we'd said to each other upstairs on the love seat, over a bottle of wine. I thought about the time Alice asked me if I would still love her if something happened to her, some sort of accident or paralysis, the way I said, "Yes, I'd still love you."

"Would you take care of me?"

"I guess so," I said. "Although honestly, you know I wouldn't be that good at it. You'd probably be better off with your sister or your mother, someone who knows how to do that sort of thing. And then I'd keep working and come visit you on the weekends." I'd been half kidding when I said it, but it had hurt her feelings.

I thought about the time the neighbors had the big fight. They always fought, but this time was the worst. They were screaming as if they were the only two people alive in the world. The things they said to each other. "I'm calling the police," I said.

"No you're not," Alice said. "It's just a fight. That's what couples do, they fight." She emptied the last of the wine into her glass.

The fight got worse and I started saying we should really call the police or I should go over there, that we had to do something. He might hurt her. And Alice said it was none of our business, that we didn't need to get involved. That people work things out in their own way. "You don't have to worry about them," she said. "Couples that fight like that are no different than couples who make love all the time," she said, which I thought was ridiculous. "It's the ones who don't make any noise at all that are worrisome." Alice was dramatic like that. I walked downstairs and called the police anyway.

For a while I thought things were bad between us because of her health. Alice had been feeling tired for a long time and, when she finally went to the doctor, we found out she had diabetes. Alice hated needles and didn't like injecting herself. When I was home, she was always asking me to give her the injections, but I never liked having to pinch the fleshy part of her stomach together and finally I said, "You manage to do this just fine when I'm not around. What's the problem now?" After that, she stopped asking.

Once, near the end, Alice said, "Why don't you want to talk to me anymore? Don't you think I'm interesting? You never talk to me anymore." We talked, I thought. We just didn't have as much fun as we used to have. We were tired, weren't we? I looked at her when she said this. She was small and pale. I saw one thin blue vein in her cheek. She told me not to look at her that way and I wasn't even sure what way I was looking at her.

Nights, Alice would lie in bed perfectly still. The lights were off, but I knew her eyes were open. It unnerved me, knowing she was awake, unmoving there beside me. I told her so. She slept in the living room after that.

Were those things enough to make a marriage fall apart? I didn't know. So that's what I said to Robin. I told her I didn't know. I told her that one night in bed, Alice said something and I said something then she said something again. Then we didn't say anything for a long time.

"What did she say?" Robin asked.

"She said she didn't think I loved her," I said.

"What did you say?"

"I said that it wasn't my problem, that I was sorry she felt like that." I didn't tell Robin the rest. That Alice had asked me to say it, to tell her that I loved her and that I wouldn't. I don't know why I didn't tell her, but I didn't.

"Look at me. You never look at me anymore," Alice said. I stood in the kitchen and looked at her face for a long time. It was still pale and there again, the blue vein. I couldn't stop looking at that blue vein. I didn't think it had always been there. It snaked down the side of her face and into her neck, disappearing somewhere inside her throat. "Say something," Alice said. "Please."

The next night, the phone rings at ten.

"Are you there?" Robin says into the machine. "If you're there, pick up. We need to talk." But I don't pick up because I'm waiting for Alice.

Again, the phone, not too much later. The house is so quiet tonight. Alice said it was always quiet. And for the first time, I understand what she meant by quiet. Look at this, I think, *this* is quiet.

I sit in Alice's chair. I flip through the records, but I don't want to listen to any of them. I get up a few times and check the door, making sure it's unlocked. I look at my reflection in the long mirror and wonder how it's possible for so much to change without me even noticing it. I swear it was just yesterday that Alice and I were unlocking the front door, that we were painting the living room walls red, buying chairs and couches and lamps and little things to set up on tables so the house would look like it had been ours forever. It wasn't so long ago, really.

At a little after midnight, I know she's not coming. I walk up the stairs into the corner room. The window is still open. The breeze is there, colder than the night before. There's no movement on the water. Everything is still. No one is at sea. If I squint my eyes, I can almost see them, the flickering lights of the boat. Almost, but not quite.

It's a little after midnight when the phone rings again. It seems as if it's ringing forever, but finally it stops, abruptly and absolutely. And it's quiet again, and I'm alone.

MATT FREIDSON

Wisconsin Institute for Creative Writing

LIBERTY

The morning Phúc first saw Ngoc Anh was like any other morning in the Reeducation Center for Delinquent Youth. The boys were crowded behind rickety desks in the stuffy classroom while old Duc lectured them on history. The concrete walls sweated and the chipped turquoise paint glistened in the penetrating sun that the glassless windows chopped into hot squares. The newest and youngest boys, shoved out of the shadier seats, sat squinting in the glare, their pale blue uniform shirts soaked in sweat.

Our army was no match for the Mongol horde, Duc crowed, but the people had a plan. Each and every citizen painted each and every leaf in honey with the legend: "It is the will of Heaven—the invaders must retreat!"

Phúc drew a Mongol swordsman chopping old Duc's head off. Cuong leaned over his shoulder, his round face shining with sweat.

Phúc, when are you going to let me tattoo you?

After you let me fuck your sister.

My sister's dead.

Your mother, then.

Cuong giggled and shook his head. His stomach rumbled loudly.

The caterpillars ate the honey, Duc droned on, carving the message into the leaves. When the sun rose, it shone through the characters, like a message from the gods themselves! The Mongols were scared to their bowels, and turned back.

Chinh sat at Phúc's left, cleaning his fingernails with the point of his pencil. It's time you joined up, Phúc, he muttered. You can't stay friends with us if you won't take our mark.

He tapped the pencil on the long joint of his middle finger, where Cuong had tattooed a T. All of Chinh's group bore the mark, which stood for *tinh, tien,* and *tu do*—love, money, freedom. Their contingent lorded over the fifty boys in the prison with fists and fear. Phúc had been in the center for six months, but he had declined membership—thus earning their respect and resentment.

You think you're better than us? Chinh hissed. You think people won't know you're a convict when you get out because you've no tattoos? You're wrong. They'll know.

Phúc pretended to concentrate on Duc's lecture. It was hard to know when Chinh was angry and when he was simply polishing his ferocious theatrics.

Duc's hands shook and spit flew from his lips as he worked himself into a frenzy: The unity of the Vietnamese people is what has kept our nation strong and inviolate! But one worm can ruin the whole pot of soup!

You listen to old Duc Cong, Chinh muttered. You're that worm, Hanh Phúc.

They called the teacher Duc Cong—Pile of Shit. Against the chill of approaching old age, he had wrapped himself in Communism's coat. Phúc was known by the derisive Hanh Phúc: Happiness. Only Chinh was called by a reputable nickname, Chinh Chanh: Fistfight.

You're lost to our nation because you don't know your history! Duc shouted. That's why you've fallen to social evils and petty crimes! You're disgraceful! You disgrace our nation's freedom! You are the children of 1975—the children of liberation!

He snatched up his pointer and charged, smacking the boys asleep at their desks.

Trung! Duc laid the wooden pointer like a sword at a frightened boy's neck. You're from Hanoi. What street do you live on?

Ly Thuong Kiet Street, sir! Trung's chubby cheeks quivered.

And who was Ly Thuong Kiet?

I don't know, sir!

Duc whacked the pointer across Trung's neck. He whirled around and raised it above Cuong's stubbled head, as if about to cleave a melon.

What street do you live on, Cuong?

Le Duan Street, sir!

Who is Le Duan?

I don't know, sir!

Silver beads of sweat flew off Cuong's head. The pointer left a bright red welt.

Phúc! What street are you from?

Chicken Alley, sir!

The boys burst into laughter. Duc's pointer struck Phúc's ear, then his wrists and fingers as he curled his arms around his head. They laughed until Duc shouted for silence.

I have been a political cadre for twenty-five years, he said solemnly. I have shone the light of our nation on platoon after platoon of young men like you. They fought with their hearts! They spilled their blood for your freedom! Every man in my company was

killed driving out the Chinese in 1979! But you ungrateful—he hit
Phúc once more—thieving—he sliced at Chinh—drug addicts! He
cracked the pointer on Cuong's skull again.

Spent, Duc panted openmouthed. He seemed about to weep in
despair, staring at them as if they were the ghosts of those fallen he-
roes. At last, he marched back to the blackboard, tossed the pointer
aside, and took up a nub of chalk.

Take this down! Duc commanded in a cracked voice. In a waver-
ing scrawl, he wrote out a biography of Le Duan. The boys sagged in
relief. Phúc and Chinh exchanged knowing grins. Cuong rubbed his
skull ruefully, sweat stinging the welts.

Tam, who had turned back to the window as soon as Duc's rage
passed, gave a start and grabbed his neighbor's elbow. Within moments they were all craning their necks and murmuring. Chinh jerked
his head at Phúc to follow, and they padded to the windows. One
glare from Chinh and two younger boys relinquished their seats.

The fat warden jangled his ring of keys as he strode across the
yard. Behind him two policemen escorted a new prisoner. The prisoner's head hung down, and a sheaf of long black hair fell over the
collar of the green and white striped uniform, past the elegant waist.
Excited whispers sprang from all corners of the classroom.

It's a girl!

That's no girl. It's a faggot.

It's Tuan, who escaped last October. He must have grown his hair
out as a disguise.

Tuan was twenty centimeters taller than that, you idiot.

Who are you calling an idiot, dogface?

I'm sure it's a girl.

None of them had seen a woman since their imprisonment; for
some it had been a year or more. Even the oldest boys pined for their

mothers. Phúc could just discern the slim, graceful body beneath the stained, sweat-soaked uniform.

Trung said, I know all about it. She's the warden's daughter, come to visit him.

Why's she wearing a prison outfit then? Phúc hissed irritably.

Fuck you, Hanh Phúc.

Chinh clucked his tongue and shook his head. Trung gulped and turned back to the window. Duc's chalk continued to screech; he remained unaware of the hushed excitement at his back.

She's sick, Cuong whispered hoarsely. He squeezed in next to Phúc. Look at her shiver. She needs a hit of dope, bad.

Phúc glanced at him. Cuong sat chewing his lip, eyes brimming with pity.

You'd know better than me, Phúc said. Maybe she just has dengue or something.

Maybe. Cuong grinned bashfully and shrugged.

Just before rounding the corner to the solitary cell, the girl raised her head and looked over her shoulder. Her eyes were swollen and her full lips trembled. She had high cheekbones and a finely tapered chin, but her cheeks were pitted with angry red pocks. Despite the pocks and her illness she was remarkably beautiful. All this Phúc caught in a fleeting glimpse.

Did you see that? Trung whispered excitedly. She looked at me! She didn't look at you, asshole. She looked at me.

Both you morons are cross-eyed. She was clearly looking at me.

Duc turned back to the class and they spun around to face him. Now, he said. Did you get all that down?

In the cutting glare of noon they hunched in the dirt yard over bowls of thin vegetable soup, talking excitedly about the girl's arrival. The newest boys squatted to the side, ignored, slurping the diluted soup from the top of the pots. Phúc and Cuong and Chinh and the other toughs sat with their backs to the wall.

Who do you think she is? Phúc asked, thinking of those haunting eyes.

Some whore, Chinh shrugged, chewing the tough greens from the bottom of the pot. Probably has AIDS, and a pussy like a broken shoe.

Is that why her face is marked up like that, from AIDS? Cuong asked. No one knew.

Trung strode over from his contingent of lonely romantics, banded by a crescent moon tattooed on the fat haunch where thumbs met delicate, filthy hands. Big Doan stood to intercept him, but Chinh waved him aside.

Chinh, Trung said firmly, everyone agrees that I should visit the girl first. I'm the best-looking and most educated of all of us. My father is a diplomat. He might be able to help her.

Chinh drained his bowl and handed it to Doan. He passed his wrist across his lips.

Trung Tiên, Chinh growled, always farting off your mouth. Everyone knows your father is a traitor who tried to get to Hong Kong. They ought to execute cowards like him.

Besides, Phúc chimed in, you'd probably scare her to death with your ugly face.

Trung stuttered in protest.

I'm going first, Chinh growled. Anyone have a problem with that?

Trung looked to his crew for support but they pretended to be absorbed in eating their soup. Phúc took a breath to speak, but then did not.

Among Chinh's band there were boys stronger than Chinh, yet all deferred to him. Big Doan had assisted his extortion and loan shark enterprise in the Bach Khoa district, but it was Chinh who had stabbed a tailor with his own scissors because he was delinquent on a loan. Though only fifteen, Chinh had originally been sent to the adult prison. There he had put a man's eye out with a sharpened chopstick. The convict's friends swore bloody revenge, so Chinh arranged for his mother to pay a hefty bribe to transfer him to the Reeducation Center, where he was a tiger among mice.

How about you, pretty Hanh Phúc? Think you ought to go see her first?

Phúc met Chinh's cold, hard stare—the dull soulless gleam of a knife blade.

No, friend Chinh Chanh. You go ahead.

Chinh ran his hands through his greasy hair and wiped them on his thighs. He buttoned his shirt over his lean stomach, which was adorned with one of Cuong's most ambitious creations: a heavenly palace with three bulbous minarets.

Don't want to scare her. Nice girls don't go for a guy with tattoos, right? Chinh grinned and winked. Cuong giggled and scratched his head. Phúc looked away. The lean young chieftain loped across the yard toward the solitary cells.

They waited expectantly, murmuring. After fifteen minutes Chinh had not returned and the boys resumed their gossiping and speculation.

Phúc went over to the yard's edge, where two guards, Dieu and Khoi, leaned against the barrack wall, smoking. Dieu's hair stood up at all angles, like a scarecrow's, and the ill-fitting uniform did nothing to mend Khoi's loose-limbed peasant slouch. The pair would have looked more at home in the rice paddies that surrounded the Center.

Uncles, how about a bit of tobacco? Phúc extended a strip of paper torn from his drawing. The two guards looked around the yard nervously, but Phúc knew the warden was napping in his office, as he always did after lunch.

Well, all right, Khoi said. But remember, you promised to ask your brother-in-law about a job for me.

Right. Phúc rolled up the pinch of tobacco and Khoi gave him a light. So, who's that girl you guys brought in this morning?

A drug addict. Dieu hunched the shoulders of his tight jacket. She got transferred from Central Main. They're sending her to the Reform Center the day after next. She should be stronger by then.

Phúc nodded and puffed his thin cigarette. The Reform Center was the hard-labor camp for juvenile criminals, but it had male and female inmates. Most of the boys in Reeducation had sold drugs, failed to bribe the police to allow them to shine shoes, or committed minor thefts or other mild offenses. The Center was dedicated to returning them to civil society. Phúc had been the runner for a black market money-changing ring. The shrewd middle-aged women involved had bought their way out of arrest—only he was serving time.

They had her in solitary with the men, Khoi said, picking a shred of tobacco off the tip of his tongue. I know a guard over there.

You know everyone, Khoi, Phúc beamed. You're well-connected.

Khoi flashed his snaggled brown teeth. Know what he told me? He gave the cons the chance to get in the cell with her for 10,000 a go. The thing is, none of them had that much. But the dumb chicken wouldn't bargain. Stood firm on his price.

That's the problem with Communism, Dieu said solemnly. No one understands the laws of supply and demand.

True enough, Khoi agreed, nodding thoughtfully. But he had a monopoly for his shift, and those guys were desperate. A pretty fifteen-year-old girl!

Yes, but no one could afford his price, so what good was it? That's state-owned enterprise for you. Dieu beamed, pleased by his own brilliant observation.

I suppose, Khoi sighed. The guard on the night shift wouldn't lower the rate either, but he let them jack off through the bars for a thousand dông. Disgusting! Her clothes are stiff with it. When they came to get her, the warden slipped and fell in the puddle of come!

Khoi and Dieu cackled, and Phúc pretended to join in. His throat felt as thin as paper. He thanked them for the cigarette and went around the corner to the bathroom. He screwed his eyes against the stench, so at first Chinh appeared as a pale smear.

Chinh was squatting in the corner, fingering a fresh lump on his forehead. Tears had washed clean tracks down his filthy cheeks. Phúc squatted next to him.

Bastard Tong wouldn't let me near her, he snuffled. Thumped me with his baton.

Phúc put his arm around Chinh. When the young gangster had regained his composure, they returned to the yard, where the boys were playing soccer with a plastic sandal. Chinh projected an aura of steely rage that deflected their questions. For the rest of the hour he sat in a corner of the yard with his hand on Cuong's knee as the younger boy patiently pricked his back with an improvised needle-and-ballpoint-pen instrument. Cuong had been working on the flying dove for the past week. Phúc sat with them, watching the bird take shape with each dot of ink, watching Chinh clench his jaw against the pain, a dreamy smile playing on Cuong's full lips.

Halfway through afternoon math class, Phúc looked out the window to see Tong give Khoi his keys and baton, then go into the warden's office. Khoi disappeared around the corner to the solitary cell. At the blackboard, half-blind Teacher Phan was scratching out fractions. Phúc winked at Cuong and slipped over the window ledge, then bent and crab-walked along the wall. He stopped by the water pot and dipped in two cups, then made his way over.

Khoi was sprawled in the dirt next to the solitary cell, his head tilted back, fanning himself with his army cap. He scrambled to his feet as Phúc approached.

Hot day, Phúc said, offering one of the cups. Thought you might like a drink.

Thanks, little brother! Khoi gulped it down, his sharp Adam's apple bobbing across lines of dirt on his neck.

Mind if I take a peek at her?

Khoi scratched his chin. Sure, why not? I'm going to take a piss. You better not be here when I get back, though.

Fair enough, Uncle Khoi.

The front of the cell was barred but otherwise open to the world. The girl lay pressed into the corner with her back to him. Shadows of the bars cut across the green and white stripes of the Central Main uniform; the shape of her was crumpled beneath. The cell reeked of vomit, bitter with an edge of cloying sweetness.

Hello? Phúc called tentatively. Are you all right?

She turned over and raised herself on her palms. Her hair tumbled across one shoulder, and the overlarge shirt exposed a wedge of sweaty skin gleaming in the sharp afternoon light. Her eyes wavered, then found his. He gripped the bar, weak from the force of her gaze.

I brought you some water, Phúc said softly, holding out the red plastic cup. She rose unsteadily, and he could see she was trembling. Cuong had told him of junk withdrawal, the grating of bone on bone, the terrible crawling of flesh trying to flee itself. She staggered and grabbed the bars for support. He held the cup to her cracked lips as she drank. Her skin was pale gray and the pocks marking her face were almost black, like the dark pips scattered in the flesh of dragon-fruit. But beneath the awful sickness and the plague of pox was a del-icate beauty, marred only on its shallowest surface.

What's your name? Phúc whispered.

Ngoc Anh, she murmured. She wiped her nose with a grimy hand, leaving a shiny track like a snail's.

I'm Phúc.

She looked up at him, and he saw now an impregnable solidity, the steel skin of a woman who survives any hardship.

I have to go now, but I'll try to come back again.

She nodded. He looked back, but she had already vanished into the darkness of the cell.

That night in their sleeping barracks, Phúc was surrounded by a ring of boys who made him repeat again and again every detail. Eventually Phúc lost track of what he had embellished. Chinh lay on his mat, propped up on his elbows. Phúc glanced uneasily at him from time to time and saw that Chinh was eavesdropping, but he had ignored Phúc all evening.

Ngoc Anh: the name flitted up and down the long hall. Tong came on his round, and found them awake and chattering excitedly. He charged along the line of mats, boxing ears and cracking his hard fists on heads. In the fearful silence of his wake, most fell asleep. Phúc slipped onto his mat, exhausted, wary of Chinh next to him.

There must be some way to get in there and fuck her, Chinh muttered, scratching his chest.

I wish I'd seen her, Cuong moaned longingly. I could do a portrait on your arm, Phúc.

Cuong, you know what? Chinh said. Sometimes I think you're a goddamn queer.

Phúc was unsettled by all their talk; they had stolen a private moment and shredded it among them so only useless scraps remained, just as when a boy got hold of a newspaper—they tore it into strips for cigarettes. He turned over on his stomach and rested his chin on his folded hands.

Hey, Cuong, he whispered. If you can get a picture of the Statue of Liberty to copy from, I'd let you give me a tattoo of her.

What's that?

She's in America. I saw her in a movie once. She's huge, amazing. Remember those Chinese students two years ago, in Tiananmen Square? They built one.

Draw it for me; I can work from that.

No, I want her to be real. It has to be the real Liberty—or I don't want her.

He had never wanted a tattoo before, but the image of that proud figure with her arm upraised appeared before him in the dark. He felt the need to mark the day permanently, record it on his very flesh.

The breath of a hundred boys sleeping and rustling on thin mats was broken by the whine of mosquitoes, the drone of cicadas. The boys stifled sobs and coughed and murmured in dreams.

A high, lonely song cut the restless still of the night, rang across the dark prison. She sang in English: It was an American song, a modern song. A song of youth and longing. They did not know the meaning of the lyrics, but it was a tune they all knew. It spilled from cassette players, from karaoke machines, and from cafés where young lovers lingered over coffee—as ubiquitous as Uncle Ho's proverbs but speaking so much more powerfully to their fierce desires and plaintive secrets.

The boys sat up in their beds as one, rapt and silent. She sang "Hotel California" without quaver or flaw, with necessity and strength. At the chorus, Phúc raised his voice with hers and thus her lonely cell and the barracks that housed the boys were joined.

There was a clatter of steel on steel, boots on packed earth, and the brute Tong screamed: Shut up! Stop that fucking singing right now! I'll beat the life out of you!

———

The next day Duc was much pleased; the boys seemed focused on their lessons, copying down every word he said. They were writing love letters to Ngoc Anh: dreamy declarations of love, poems cribbed from sugary songs, protestations of burning hearts. They scrawled impassioned pleas with dull nubs of pencil on creased, dog-eared scraps of paper. Cuong fashioned a bouquet from dead grass and brittle leaves. Only Chinh did not compose a message; he said he hated romance. Phúc had long suspected that he was illiterate.

At their lunch break, Phúc, Cuong, Trung, and five other boys gathered all the letters. The boys pooled a sufficient bribe for the guard—scraps of loose tobacco and withered bills in undignified denominations. Chinh leaned on the wall beside thick-necked Doan, ignoring them, picking at the scabs of his new tattoo and spitting into the red dirt.

The delegation crowded and jostled at the cell door: They showered her with their letters; they sang loudly and lustily. Cuong reached between the bars to present his pitiable bouquet.

Ngoc Anh crouched in the corner of the cell, eyes wide with terror, her hands clawed before her as if to ward off blows. The sprinkling of marks on her face blazed red and she gulped the dusty air. Drunk on infatuation, the boys paid no mind, calling out to her, holding out their hands, shouting and crooning joyfully. At last, calmed, she stood and threw back her long tangled hair. She laughed with the deep relief of joy returning after a long misery. With delicate grace she plucked the bouquet from Cuong's hand and bowed as if they were an audience lauding her fine performance. She met Phúc's gaze and smiled, her eyes full of promise and warmth.

That night, the barracks rustled with rhythmic slaps as Ngoc Anh bloomed in the boys' fevered fantasies. Even the youngest—bodies disqualified from comforting release—took satisfaction in the animal tang that rose from their elders' beds. All sighed with longing and contentment and slept the deep rest of children who know they are loved. Phúc lay awake, fashioning elaborate plans for escape, elopement, a life rich and full and far from concrete cells. The particulars were vague but Ngoc Anh's face was clear enough to see each scar's edge, to trace constellations in them.

When the guards came to awaken them the next morning, the boys heard the wheeze of the warden's jeep. They rushed into the yard but she was already gone. During morning exercise, tears flew from faces with each jumping jack. As they sang the national anthem, only Chinh's voice failed to break, and he barked spitefully:

> *Ceaselessly for the People's cause we struggle*
> *Hastening to the battlefield*
> *Forward! All advancing as one*
> *Our Vietnam is strong for eternity...*

For days their hearts smoldered; the loneliness Ngoc Anh had banished now returned with doubled might. Old Duc wrung his hands in despair; Tong tried to thrash the self-pity out of them; Dieu and Khoi smuggled in a bag of hard candies. Only half-blind Phan failed to notice, lost in his fog of divisors and prime numbers. When they whimpered too loudly in the night, Chinh flew at them in a storm of blows. For days he taunted and tormented Phúc over his lost love, but Phúc refused either to show his tears or to put up his fists.

A week later, an outbreak of scabies swept through the Center. The boys were rounded up and stripped; their heads were shaved and they were doused with a burning white liniment. The barracks were emptied of bedding and clothes, the boys locked inside and told to lie still for twenty-four hours. They lay on the cold concrete, shivering and joking and looking very much like corpses, their white shaved heads like skulls atop their skinny bodies. Phúc and Trung sang and some boys hopped up to dance, genitals bobbing as they swung their arms through the air. The black spirals of the parasites' tracks were evident beneath the pale chalk ointment, as if Cuong's tattoo needle had inscribed long, lazy strings over their limbs.

The passage of the scabies carried with it memories of Ngoc Anh. Chinh claimed she had infected them; this was a matter of fierce dispute. Boys were discharged and new ones incarcerated; the story of her stay was shattered and reassembled into something between rumor and legend.

Some months later Phúc was released, still unmarked by any tattoo, but with Ngoc Anh and her song etched into his spirit. On the day of his departure, he hugged his friends good-bye as Chinh stood glaring, his arms crossed over his chest. At last Phúc went up to him.

I'll see you, Chinh Chanh.

You better hope not, Chinh replied, turning his back on Phúc and stalking off toward the barracks with angry chops of his feet.

It was spring of the following year and the flame trees were in bloom—blossoms the university students gave each other for luck on their exams, blossoms Phúc crushed under the wheels of his motorbike.

A friend of Cuong's rented him a Honda Super Cub at an exorbitant rate; Phúc made his living taxiing students and teachers from school to home. Sitting at tea stands near the high schools, he searched the knots of young girls in uniforms or white *ao dais*. But he never saw the angry red sprinkling of pocks among the faces. The students spoke to him haughtily, deflecting his attempts at conversation.

When he braked short and the taut bodies of his young female customers pressed against his back, he shivered, imagining them to be Ngoc Anh. She would swat his head playfully and tell him to be more careful. She would wrap her arms around his waist and lean her head against his back. Her perfume would envelop them, and her laugh would drown out the roar of engines and the blare of horns.

Phúc believed that Ngoc Anh had been chastened by her imprisonment, and that she had enrolled in school after her release. She lived in a concrete dorm with innocent, giggling girls from the countryside: the silent, wise older sister who sang them to sleep. He was sure of this. His mother had always impressed upon him the importance of an education, and Ngoc Anh's mother must have done the same. Perhaps her father, like his, had drunk all the money away, so there was none to graft the teachers with when it came time to graduate. When he tried to picture her family, his imagination rolled away like a ball of twine.

The school year ended without any sighting of her.

On summer nights, men paid Phúc to drive them across the bridge to Gia Lam. He tooled past nightclubs, karaoke bars, and hourly rate hotels—all operating brothels behind their seedy facades. Ngoc Anh's fierce stare never leaped out from the glazed faces of the hardworking women, and for this, at least, he was glad. He could not bear to think of her lying beneath some paunchy man for a few thousand đông. But the image returned to him so often that he found himself staring at the women with a lustful hunger.

One hot night in Gia Lam, a burly man in a flowered shirt flagged him drunkenly, as if swatting away a swarm of bees. It was his brother-in-law, Binh, blinking in a haze of whiskey. They stared at each other for a moment, stricken, then Binh laughed and climbed on the back of Phúc's Cub, hugging him tightly.

Take me home, Phúc. No charge for me, right?

Of course not, he replied. He did not know what else to say.

You won't mention this to your sister? Binh mumbled into his shoulder; Phúc could feel the hot breath through his T-shirt.

Phúc thought of Ha Yên, her weary, fearful eyes. After their father had died, their mother went south in search of work and was never heard from again. Passed from cousin to aunt, Ha Yên had married as soon as she was old enough. He could not tell her.

No, Phúc said at last, and his shame made him sweat. But why...?

Binh laughed heartily. You'll be married someday. You'll understand that a man gets tired of the same old rice. I love your sister, but since she gave birth to Qui Anh...

He trailed off. Long Bien Bridge was dark and the Cub's headlight played along a silent procession of peasants in the adjacent lane. They pushed bicycles loaded down with baskets of produce to sell at the morning markets.

Binh, why didn't you pay off the police when I got arrested?

They knew I owned a laundry. They wanted a hundred thousand.

The metal plates of the bridge hummed and clattered when the wheels hit their edges. Phúc wanted to dump Binh off the side, into the Red River. An accident. That was what Chinh would do. Phúc hit fourth gear. Binh had forbidden him from coming to the house, claiming Phúc was a bad example for his young son. Ha Yên had visited him in the Reeducation Center once, but Binh prevented her from returning.

After he dumped Binh into the river, he and Ha Yên would go to Ho Chi Minh City and find their mother. He and Ha Yên and Ngoc Anh would find her, and they would all sleep in one bed under the soothing wind of a ceiling fan.

Binh coughed and spat. I'll make it up to you, Phúc. You can come work in the laundry and sleep in the back.

Riding had cooled the sweat from both of them. It was a winner's bribe, a paltry offering. But if Phúc worked hard and continued driving the bike at night, he could save enough for something big, something good. Something he could be proud of. When he found

Ngoc Anh he could support her, and Ha Yên could move in with them.

All right.

Good boy, Binh said.

The Cub's engine hammered away the shell of his sweet fantasy and beneath it Phúc felt a sickening truth: that Ngoc Anh was a whore, rubbing herself on grinning men and pawing through their trousers for money.

Phúc pulled to a stop in front of his house and Binh stumbled off and puked in the gutter. Ha Yên came to the door with Qui Anh in her arms. She looked frightened; she always looked frightened. He thought of her and Binh rutting like two dogs. Unable to face her, Phúc waved and drove away.

Days, in Binh's laundry, Phúc prodded steaming vats of cloth with a bamboo pole, cranked the presser, folded and sorted. Nights, he skimmed across Hanoi on his bike, taking fares. Since his release he required little sleep. When he did sleep for an hour or two, he curled up on piles of clean cloth while his coworkers sang songs of war, romance, and patriotism. The constant slosh of water gave the laundry the air of a ship at sea. Bare lightbulbs smeared halos in the fog of bleach and steam. The chill of winter cooled the steam on Phúc's skin, so that he shivered constantly.

Late one December night, Phúc answered a loud knock at the laundry door. There stood chubby-cheeked Trung and dim, thick-necked Doan. Lurking behind them, shivering in a thin jacket, was Chinh.

We got out of the Center last week, Trung whimpered. Doan's parents won't let him stay with them; they're afraid of what the neighbors will say. My folks are happy to have me, of course, it's just that...

Phúc stared past them until Chinh met his eye. Chinh shrugged and looked away.

Vinh took over my corner, he muttered. I'll get it back soon enough.

Phúc spoke to Binh, and they were hired on. Chinh and Doan often came in bruised and bloody. The days flew by more quickly; Big Doan stole a cassette player and Trung filched tapes for them to sing along to: Elton John, Air Supply, the Eagles. When "Hotel California" came on, they taunted Phúc mercilessly and made him feel like a child longing for a shiny, expensive toy. It was warm in the laundry in the winter, steam rising from the wet concrete floor. He was building muscle from hefting the heavy stirring pole; his small roll of savings began to germinate.

He had stopped searching for Ngoc Anh, but he still cherished her in quiet solitude. Nights, he tooled about on his Cub, taking fares just for the easy human contact. He imagined the crooked lines he drew across the city, a sprawling web that was sure to eventually cross whatever path she traveled.

One cool spring night, Phúc picked up two Belgian backpackers. He drove them to a house in the Old Quarter and led them down a dark corridor into Cuong's studio. The walls and ceiling of the tiny room were plastered with photos torn from magazines, drawings and sketches, snapshots of Cuong's work on young muscles. Cuong looked up from his cluttered worktable, a grin spreading across his wide melon face.

Hanh Phúc! he cried. What have you brought me?

Two backpackers. They want to buy some dope.

They're cute. Like two tall girls. Cuong bobbed his head and they flashed stricken grins. They haggled by fingers, frowns, and smiles, and grunted English numbers. The Belgians leaned over the measure he laid out for them, snorting like pigs, holding each other's hair back in turn. Cuong watched them as adoringly as a father watches his children at play. Phúc felt a fascinated disgust. Laughing low in their throats and moving with slow undersea grace, the Belgians drew wads of cash from their pouches, shook hands formally, and staggered out.

Phúc clasped Cuong's wrist before he could stow the money. I'll take my cut of that, all right?

I have something else in mind, Cuong said, smirking.

Phúc twisted Cuong's skinny arm behind his back and took him in a playful headlock.

No more of your blow jobs! You almost chewed it off last time!

Better! Cuong's giggle was muffled by Phúc's armpit.

Your mother? Too old for me.

Better! Better!

Phúc released him and Cuong took down a postcard from the haphazard collage. He gave Phúc the card reverently, with both hands. It depicted an enormous green crowned statue. Gray buildings taller than any Phúc had ever imagined sawed the sky behind her.

Ah! It's her! Phúc cried. He read the caption in an awed voice: *New York!*

I got it from Tam, Cuong crowed proudly. His cousin sent it.

She's green!

Of course. You said she was green.

No, I didn't.

Yes, you did.

What's she holding? Phúc curled an arm to his stomach in imitation.

Two cartons of Marlboros?

Don't be an idiot. Phúc slapped Cuong across the back of the head.

So, what do you think? Will you let me do her on you? It's been a long time coming.

Phúc studied the stern face, carved in peppermint iron. There was a majestic loftiness he recognized as Ngoc Anh's. He imagined Liberty emblazoned on his chest like armor. Tattoos were for gangsters, convicts, and in his dreams he and Ngoc Anh lived respectably with no reminders of their captivity. Still, he wanted Liberty badly. She was blue jeans, rock and roll—green as dollars, her arm soaring up into the air like the guitar in "Hotel California." Ngoc Anh could be found, the postcard showed him: She was as real and true and solid as the Statue of Liberty.

I'll tell you what, he said. Hold on to her for me, but promise me you won't give her to anyone else, okay?

She's all yours, Hanh Phúc. Cuong pinned Liberty to the wall, high above the sketches of doves and daggers and palaces he etched on bare skin.

Binh laid off the day manager and installed Phúc. The day shift began stealing clothes and blamed it on the former inmates, who rankled under Phúc's authority. Chinh and Doan came late one afternoon and Phúc took them to task.

What's with you, Phúc? Big Doan whined. You're like one of the damn guards in the Center. King of your little pile of dirty towels.

Just come on time, Phúc snapped. They resumed work in angry silence.

He had a headache from the detergent fumes. He'd never imagined work could be so boring and so unrewarding. In the Center they had pretended to disdain working for a living, but beneath this apparent contempt Phúc had always imagined a good job, a fruitful life. As he counted his stash he found himself again including Ngoc Anh in wistful, vague plans.

On rare nights he was now invited to Binh and Ha Yên's for dinner—more quarrels, the sharp judging eye of Binh's aged mother,
and guilty looks at Ha Yên, silent and cowed.

He could find no place for himself among folk, but in his private
reveries Ngoc Anh neither deserted nor forsook him. When he could
not stand it he got on his Cub and lost himself in the hazardous ballet of Hanoi's traffic, dodging and weaving among frantic machines
until at last he could sleep.

Binh had connections in two of the larger hotels in the city, and the
laundry workers often made a guessing game of the stains.

Russian! Trung would say, holding a towel aloft like a banner. He
claimed he'd spent his childhood in Moscow, where his father had
been an ambassador.

Ugh! Doan grimaced as he lifted shrouded hands to pass a stained
sheet under his nose. American! Like rancid butter.

Oof, Phúc hooted. Cheap cologne and too much of it. Chinese, or
maybe a businessman from Ho Chi Minh City.

Mmm—French woman. Phúc, I'll bet your sister's butterfly
smells like this.

Shut up about my sister, Chinh.

Chinh flung the pillowcase onto a heap and rolled his lean, mus-
cular shoulders.

I'll say what I want. And what I want is your sister.

Piss off, Chinh. Pick up that pile and start sorting.

With quick animal grace Chinh shouldered Phúc into the wall.
He cracked Phúc's head against the concrete with a palm to the
chin, put his forearm across Phúc's throat and grabbed his balls, and
twisted.

You squirt of duck shit, Chinh hissed. Did you fuck that pepper-
faced whore in the Center or not?

Chinh squeezed again, harder, and Phúc's knees buckled, his whole weight hanging from Chinh's arm on his neck. The room leached of color, turning pale and hazy. He could not draw breath but only gulp the syllables:

Yes ... I did ...

He didn't know why he said it. In his panic he only wanted to give the answer that might save him further pain. The knife scar on Chinh's eyebrow twitched like an earthworm and his breath smelled of roast pork.

You lying no-dick. Chinh let him fall and drew back one foot and kicked him hard in the nose and mouth, and Phúc felt a tooth crack.

Chinh stepped over him to get his jacket. Phúc stood shakily, grabbed one of the bamboo poles, and swung. He missed, the pole whistling as it cleaved the air. He swung the pole madly. Chinh put his hand out on the next pass to catch it, but Phúc caught him across the ear, raised the pole, and cracked it across Chinh's skull. He landed hard on the tile floor.

Phúc stood over him, panting, blood dripping from his split nose. Trung and Doan stumbled for the door, eyes wide. He had seen that glazed fear on their faces when the wrath of Chinh or the guards was aimed at them. He had seen it on Ngoc Anh's face when she had thought they were coming to degrade her. He lifted the unwieldy pole and struck Chinh again and again. Chinh curled into a moaning ball, but Phúc beat him harder. Finally, the quivering pole flew from his hands and clattered on the floor.

Phúc rode to Binh's and sat on his motorbike in front of the house. He had nowhere else to go. The night air stung his split nose, blood cold on his shirt. At last he rang the bell. Binh came to the door, looked at him through the metal gate, and turned away. Phúc heard the couple bickering, voices rising with an anger that made him wince. Ha Yên pushed open the gate and he clenched her hard, her tears soaking through his shirt. A fierce impulse rose in him, a roar like the bike's engine, a rush of wind.

Let's leave, he said. Just go.

She leaned back and stared at him, blinking wetly. Where? Where could we go?

Anywhere.

There's nowhere to go, Phúc.

Why don't you leave him? he asked.

I love him, she sobbed. He's the father of my son. She was just as weak as he was. Worse, she had no dreams left. Phúc stroked her hair and wept. Wept for Ha Yên, wept for himself. Wept for Ngoc Anh.

Summer rains overflowed from the sewers, making creeks of alleyways. He was no longer welcome among the tea stands frequented by detention center graduates; he was not welcome among the money changers and shoeshine boys around the post office. Some nights he went to Cuong's, but there his friend and fellow addicts slumped in ghostly silence, scratching themselves lazily as they parceled time into burnt spoons.

In the hours before dawn Phúc's legs sweated on the Cub's vinyl seat. He came up behind a girl in a short black skirt, a red tank top, and platform shoes. She weaved slowly along the pavement, head nodding as heroin stroked her eyelids shut. Then she tossed her hair over one shoulder, like a horse shaking its mane. An electric shock ran from Phúc's chest down his arms, and he gripped the brake.

She turned and gave him a lewd, crooked smile, figuring him another customer.

Don't I know you? she said.

Her hair hung limply in the heat and she scratched at oozing scabs in an elbow's crook. Her face was as flat and round as a plate, pale, and coated in a sheen of smeared makeup and sweat. She looked nothing like Ngoc Anh.

I don't think so, Phúc said.

Weren't you in the Reform Center?

No. He hesitated. I was in the Reeducation Center.

Ah. I knew you had that look. Her clouded eyes wavered as she struggled to arrange her homely features into a sly look.

Did you know a girl named Ngoc Anh there? he asked.

The dead-faced whore scratched her bare shoulder, leaving long red welts.

There was a fat dyke named Ngoc Anh, a murderer, is that who you mean?

No. A girl with scars on her face, like from smallpox.

Didn't know her.

Phúc mumbled an apology and curled the bike back into the street.

At least give me a fucking ride! the whore screeched. What's the matter, afraid I'm too much for you? Asshole taxi boy!

He rode back to the laundry in the sickly dawn, shaking, her curses ringing in his ears. His coworkers had gone to deliver a load of clean sheets to the Army Hotel; he was alone and glad for it. Phúc stripped to his shorts and lay on a pile of laundry in the storeroom, a cigarette hissing between his sweaty fingers. Through the tiny window the city grumbled, itching under a thick, humid blanket. Phúc tried to imagine Ngoc Anh's high breasts and the down between her legs, but all that came to him was a jumble of green and white stripes, a cascade of hair like spilled oil and the face of the whore, as swollen and pallid as a drowned corpse's.

You're ridiculous! he shouted to the cramped, empty room. You should have screwed that whore, any whore! What's the difference? She didn't care who you were. She wouldn't even remember you. You didn't even have the balls to get into the cell!

He cursed himself, cursed the whore. Then he cursed Ngoc Anh at the top of his lungs, calling her a fox-tailed whore, dog shit; he compared her privates to a urinal and her face to a maggoty pig's head. Hoarse and exhausted, he dropped into fitful sleep.

The day shift arrived but did not wake him. During their lunchtime card game, he sat bolt upright and stared at them as if they were spirits wagering for his soul.

Dreaming about pussy? one asked, slapping down a card.

Ooh, Hanh Phúc! another cooed, kissing the air. I'll make your canary sing!

Screw your ancestors, he growled. And deal me a hand.

With each card that smacked down, Phúc felt a little lift in his heart. He won hand after hand. Binh came in, pushing his Honda Dream through the door.

Come on, you bastards, he said. There's work to do.

Give us a minute, Binh, one of the day-shift workers said. Your brother-in-law's killing us.

That right? Binh looked at Phúc appraisingly. Deal me in. I know how to take care of little convict cardsharps.

But Phúc's luck was steadfast, and that afternoon he won the shift's wages for a week. Elated, Phúc took them all out for noodles in the pearly cool of dusk. His coworkers grumbled over their losses, but softened after he bought a few rounds of beer.

Binh ordered another bowl of noodles. I'm taking some Chinese guys out tonight; they own the West Lake Hotel. Why don't you come along?

Sure, Phúc said.

Sitting on the rough wooden bench, slurping the rich broth, Phúc saw the city shine anew. A rich artery of traffic flowed by: husbands, fathers, mothers, sisters. A girl jogged by with two baskets of mangoes suspended from a pole over her shoulder. She smiled at him and the perfume of the fruit lingered after she'd passed. There was a whole life to be lived in this world, he thought.

Phúc wore his best shirt and made a point of being early. Binh had him drive the borrowed Daewoo sedan. Binh sat in front, leaning over the plush seat to talk to the Chinese. The four older men ignored Phúc. They nosed across the bridge. Bicyclists steadied themselves by resting hands on the car's flanks.

Phúc parked in front of the Cactus Restaurant and Nightclub and hopped out to open the door for the Chinese. Binh gave him a dark look, and Phúc realized he should have opened his door first.

They were seated in a plush booth. The brown vinyl couch curved around the table; all around the dim club the booths' backs hid all but the tops of heads. Mr. Han wanted to discuss the laundry contract, but Binh gave him a pained, indulgent look.

First we eat and drink, he said. Then tomorrow we'll do business, as friends.

A slim waitress plunked cold beers and plates of squid jerky before them. Mr. Jiang dunked a strip of jerky into the sauce. As he chewed the red chili paste smeared around his lips. Binh ordered a feast that the older men devoured with relish; Phúc waited until his elders had sampled the dishes before tasting anything. He sat quietly, drinking cold beer but unable to lave his dry throat—unsure if he should join the conversation, and unsure what to say. Binh and the Chinese polished off several large bottles of Hennessy and knocked bowls to the floor, slopped more drink into their glasses.

Phúc and the two slightly more sober Chinese helped Mr. Jiang to the bathroom, where he vomited copiously while the others laughed from the urinal trough, pissing in loud, lordly arches. Phúc propped Mr. Jiang against the sink and wiped his face, sponged off his tie. Mr. Han and Mr. Chan made derogatory comments in Chinese as they combed their hair at the mirror. As Phúc was drying Mr. Jiang's face, the thin businessman grabbed his shoulders and puckered as if to kiss him. The three Chinese roared with laughter and Phúc smiled grimly.

When they returned to the table, Binh called over the proprietress, and a few moments later three young women squeezed into the booth. Binh and the Chinese groped the women under the table.

Not a word to your sister, eh, Phúc? Binh said.

A young woman with a long neck paused by their table and cocked her head at Phúc, the only one unpaired. He smiled thinly at the goose-necked girl and shook his head. She shrugged and moved on to the next table.

The lights went up on the small stage and three glum-looking musicians began to play—a long-haired guitarist, a slicked-up young bassist, and a plump, balding keyboard player. At first they plunked tunelessly, but soon they converged on a melody that bubbled through the dark club, laying notes across drunken conversations. A singer in a red cocktail dress sparkling with sequins stepped up to the microphone and sang "Remembering Hanoi at Night."

The young woman on Mr. Jiang's lap wriggled off and raised her hand to slap him. Jiang grinned dementedly, his eyes glazed. The girl's lip trembled, but the proprietress came over and spoke in her ear. The girl put her arms around Jiang, pinning him. He tried to lick her ear but she leaned back, shaking her head indulgently. The band struck up "Let It Be."

Phúc stared blearily at the singer, her hips tipping like water in a glass. He had not eaten much, and the beer made a cold roiling ball in his stomach. The band took a break, and then the singer returned in a red and gold *ao dai*. For a drunken moment Phúc thought her a different woman entirely. As they played "Four Great Sorrows," Phúc peered carefully at her. Her mouth was carved in deep red lipstick and she was enveloped in the music, disdainful of her audience. He had been searching for Ngoc Anh for two years now and his memory of her had warped and faded. But it seemed that the strong jaw and those deep eyes were hers. Did he catch hints of sprinkled spots on her cheeks, beneath the white mask of thick makeup? The singer raised her face to the spotlight and sang.

Her outstretched arms welcomed them all to the Hotel California, and Phúc saw it was the same girl who, long ago, had held the bars of the solitary cell as he'd trickled water past her lips. The same girl who had scrambled back and forth in that cage in terror at their loud protestations of love, the same girl who had been sentenced to hard labor in the Reform Center. From the audience came a dim smattering of applause, which Ngoc Anh accepted with an icy stare and an arrogant wince.

In the bathroom, Phúc smoothed the tails of his yellow shirt, hiked his belt, and primped his hair in the mirror. He put a cigarette in his mouth and affected a casual, worldly air.

Ngoc Anh was sitting in a booth with her trio at the back of the Cactus. When Phúc came to their table only the long-haired guitarist looked up, and he shook his head sadly.

Hello, Ngoc Anh, Phúc said. Remember me?

Ngoc Anh got up and strode toward the stairs that led up to the private rooms. Phúc stepped nimbly in front of her.

Hey, don't run away.

Her face was a cold mask of resentment. He could see the angry hillocks of her scars beneath the cracked alabaster sheath of cosmetics.

Don't you remember me? From the Reeducation Center?

She hissed and flapped a hand at him. Her eyes darted to see if anyone had heard.

We wrote you letters. I brought you water. We sang together.

For a moment her gaze wavered; she bit her scarlet lip softly, and he saw her: desperate, selfish, human. Then she fixed him with her steely glare and sucked her pitted cheeks.

I don't date little boys. And I don't date convicts. So fuck off and get out of my way before I have you thrown out.

She swept past him in a flash of carmine and gold. He stood there in a waft of sickly sweet perfume and the sharp tang of her sweat. His eyes stung, and a husk of that whitened face hung before him. It floated above the curled vinyl booths cupping drunken laughter and feigned titters and sighs of passion and empty promises.

Cuong was high when Phúc arrived, but he insisted heroin's slow current steadied his hands. Phúc did not mention finding Ngoc Anh. He stripped off his shirt and said, I'm ready for her now. Cuong took a rag and laved Phúc's chest with alcohol.

You have such nice skin, Cuong murmured bashfully. It's so pale and soft. She'll look wonderful. Her torch will end here—he touched a fingertip to where Phúc's collarbone met his shoulder— and I'll do just below her breasts, to here. He stroked Phúc's nipple, hard from the chill of the alcohol.

I want her in red and green. So no one will think it's a prison tattoo.

The young tattooist nodded thoughtfully and wiped his runny nose. He took the postcard of Liberty down from the altar of his decorative endeavors. When he had assembled his gun, inks, and blood-spotted rags, he sat staring, as if he had forgotten their purpose.

I'm going to take a little shot. Do you want one? It'll take the pain away.

Phúc shook his head and reached for the bottle of rice whiskey under Cuong's worktable. He took long pulls of the harsh, fiery liquor while Cuong hummed over his boiling portion, then stroked the needle into a bruised vein. He unwrapped the belt from his arm and let it fall, sighing with ecstasy. A dreamy smile twitched across his lips.

Why do you like that stuff so much?

Cuong giggled, his face tilted to the heavens in abandon. Sometimes I think it's just the needle I like.

Cuong filled the tattoo gun with red ink; it looked very much like the blood-filled syringe he had just sprayed on the stained floor. He leaned over Phúc's chest and stared at the expanse of skin, searching with an artist's intuition for the proper starting point. He looked up into Phúc's eyes, pupils as tiny and black as the end of his needle.

Are you ready?

Do it.

The gun whined with a desperate animal sound. The needle poked his skin insistently. The pain of each stab was negligible, but the unrelenting sequence was torture. He clenched his fist and swigged the burning whiskey with his free hand.

Don't move, Cuong chastised him in a low soothing voice. Stay still, keep still now.

Each prick of Cuong's needle was like one of Ngoc Anh's pocks, a star in a galaxy of tiny agonies, from which Cuong fashioned a constellation of Liberty's contours. When Cuong moved to a new bit of flesh the momentary relief was immediately replaced by fresh pain.

Cuong completed the outline and part of the face as dawn broke. They could hear the mutter of traffic, the songs of birds, the coughs and grumbles of Hanoi awakening. The Party loudspeakers belched first static from the electric poles, then songs of the revolution, and finally the morning's propaganda. Cuong wiped the blood from Phúc's chest and took another injection. Phúc tilted the whiskey to pour the last warm, burning swallow past his lips.

To hell with her, he said. There are plenty of other women out there.

For a bleary moment an array of women's faces spooled before him, as jumbled and scattered as the montage on Cuong's wall—a rich and varied multitude of warm, inviting smiles.

But Cuong had not heard him; his eyes were closed and a loose grin hung crookedly on his wet lips. His face dipped down and he wavered precariously in his chair, swaying with the eddies of the paradise coursing in his veins. Phúc was alone in his new dawn of bewildering possibility. On his chest, the thousand pocks of the needle itched. The new Liberty sweated and oozed and wept blood, engraved painfully on his chest in rich, glossy ink.

GREGORY PLEMMONS

Sewanee Writers' Conference

TWINLESS

In the end, I thought it best to lock my brother, Nate, down in the root cellar. It was cool and dry down there, even in August, and it would certainly hold him for the hour or so it would take for our father to get remarried. My brother liked to get stoned there on summer evenings after work, brooding in the hazy darkness with the flower bulbs and fertilizer, and I knew I would find him there on our father's wedding day as well. All summer long, Nate had threatened to cause a scene during that part of the ceremony where the minister asks if there's anybody present who knows why the couple in question should not be joined in holy matrimony.

"If he marries that woman, there'll be fireworks," my brother had declared soon after hearing the news of our father's engagement. And then, one afternoon, while cleaning out the root cellar, I discovered he had meant the real kind. Roman candles. Bottle rockets. Black Cat Brand. Not just your standard six-shot Chirping Orioles, but nineteen-shot Toot and Twirls. Plus Screaming Dragons, Jumping Tigers, Moon Travelers. I found them all in a feed sack, next to the narcissus bulbs, cornered away, still wrapped in red cellophane, intact and unexploded, waiting for their special moment down at the Wando Baptist Church. I immediately pictured them exploding in the apse, fireballs hurling down the aisle straight toward our father's fiancée, Lila, she and her bridesmaids (myself included) annihilated in a rapid conflagration of baby's breath, crinoline, and Aqua Net. Of course, my brother would never hurt a flea and I hoped he would have the sense to aim them away from the bridal party, but you get the point. So you see, I had no choice but to lock him up. My brother lacked self-control at times, more so, it seemed, since Mama had died. I was here to protect him from the world, the world from him. Arson is a federal offense, and besides, I reasoned, Baptists almost always press charges.

My plan was near perfect. No one would miss Nate at the wedding, since he had already made it clear to my father he would not be attending. All I had to do was catch him down in the cellar that day, where I knew he'd be at some point, fomenting and probably high as a kite. Sure enough, I spotted him heading across our backyard as I was slipping into my poofy bridesmaid's dress, a tea-length monstrosity in crepe that rustled and flapped with every movement I made. I dove downstairs and scampered across our backyard barefoot, reached the root cellar in seconds flat, and slipped my sturdy Kryptonite bicycle lock through the hasp on the door, clamping it shut. The lock was heavy and felt solid in my hands. Like a big black behemoth safety pin. I tested the latch. It felt snug. I kneeled down and peered through the cracks in the door slats, down into the darkness. Splinters stung my cheeks as I squinted. Unable to make out anything at first, I waited for my pupils to adjust. Then I saw a glimmer of ember and ash.

"I really hate to do this to you," I stammered, slightly out of breath. "But it's for your own damn good." I waited several minutes. No response. Not even a protest. Just my breathing and the rustle of taffeta. The late afternoon sun slipped across our backyard and light began to spill through the chinks in the door. Soon I could spot the faint outline of Nate's body down below, in the shadows. He was shirtless, in cutoffs, lying on the ground, looking up. The light clipped his face into stripes as he squinted at me.

"Fireworks are illegal inside the city limits," I said. "Especially at your own father's wedding." I took a deep breath. The smell of weed and fertilizer wafted up from below, faintly acrid and herbal. "Nate, you know I don't care for her any more than you do. But we're grown-ups now. Daddy has the right to do whatever he wants."

"Traitor," he mumbled. I watched his shadow take a drag in the shadows, then exhale. "She is the enemy and must be destroyed."

"Not by fire," I replied. "I promise I'll let you out as soon as it's over with."

He didn't respond. He just looked up at me. Then he moved his face out of the light. I thought I saw some flicker of lucidity there that seemed to say *thank you for stopping me,* like when Old Yeller gets that look at the end of the movie. But now I think I just imagined it. I stood up, straightened the straps of my dress, and headed back across the yard. And that was the last time I saw him, down there in the cool earthy bosom of Mother Earth and Mama's root cellar. When I got home from the wedding later that evening, his Toyota was gone and the cellar door was wide open, not a whiff of weed remaining. Even my Kryptonite bike lock, which had a $500 guarantee, had vanished. Without a trace.

Nate and I are both nineteen. He and I are twins, biologically speaking, but that is *it.* He got the good middle name—Nathaniel

Audubon Gibbs (after that bird guy) and I got the bad one—Leona Linnaeus. Leona after our hypochondriac aunt and Linnaeus after some eighteenth-century Swedish scientist who designed what amounted to the Dewey decimal system for flora and fauna, the Father of Taxonomy, thanks to our dweeby biologist father, Louis Gibbs. Exciting, huh? I go by Linny. I am Twin A, which is what they designate the first one in line for the exit door to this world, Nate's breeched little butt twisted up in the rafters, refusing to come down, so I got to be the oldest by seven minutes and fifteen seconds. But who's counting? Nate is Twin B. I weighed less than he did, and they thought I would be the sickly one. I figured my parents gave me the throwaway middle name (Linnaeus) just in case I didn't make it. I've heard it's the opposite in Africa, where mamas name their favorite babies Trash and Dogshit (in respective Swahili or Bantu, of course) so the gods will be fooled and not snatch them away. But who wants to go through life named Dogshit? Linnaeus is bad enough.

Nate and I both had to go to the Special Care Nursery down at Roper Hospital—which is a polite way of saying that your babies are sick as stink and might not make it to cut their first teeth. But we survived anyway. Turns out Nate ended up being the sickly and scrawny one, needing oxygen, his fingers small and gummy as boiled peanuts and his chest bowing clear down to his backbone with each breath, according to Mama. While I got to go home in one week at four pounds, Nate spent his first month of life curled up under an oxygen tent in the nursery. Mama always said she had never seen a child take to camping out like he did. Like that oxygen tent did something to him.

Nate and I are fraternal twins, which means, if you don't already know, Not Identical. Fraternal twins don't even have to come from the same egg, but they can. It turns out I got shortchanged here, too, chromosomally speaking. I got the X and Nate got the Y. Which is just fine, except not only did I get stuck with the bad name and a life-time of gender bias, but also, part of my X chromosome's missing, which they didn't figure out until tenth grade, when I had still not gotten my period and remained eighteen inches shorter than my brother. So my parents took me down to the medical university where they ran all these tests, which are kind of hard to explain. Suffice it to say I have almost all of the same plumbing and accompanying heartbreak and cramping as any other female—that is, if I get my estrogen injections every three months. I'm even a D-cup, but apparently my uterus will remain as infertile as the moon in winter.

Still, twins are special. I don't know whether we just started to believe that because everyone told you that from the get-go. But it's true. Ask any twin. There is something magic about us. Nate always said there was no way you could share the same womb with someone else for nine months and not be connected after the fact by more than just bloodlines and childhood. As if the amniotic fluid we breathed together had evaporated into the universe afterward, sublimated itself into little particles that could transmit thought as clearly as radiowaves. Don't get me wrong. It's not like Nate and I could bend spoons or anything, although we tried that once after seeing *Escape From Witch Mountain,* a Disney flick about orphaned siblings who could levitate Winnebagos just by simultaneously *thinking* it. Nate and I have nothing as special as that. But sometimes, I get a thought, or a feeling, that doesn't seem entirely *mine.* Usually unannounced and subtle, but still an extrasensory moment that I can't explain. Sometimes we dreamed the same dreams. Sometimes Nate knew what I was going to say before I did, even. Mama had always claimed twins are special and mystical. After all, who else had their own Zodiac sign? But our father, while acknowledging our gift, claimed that ESP would turn out to be biologically innate someday, it was just we hadn't figured out all the ways that humans and animals communicated, not yet.

When I returned home from taking my father and Lila to the airport to begin their honeymoon, that open cellar door gaped like a wound. I grabbed a flashlight, and went underground, looking for clues. But there was nothing. All I found was a single Moon Traveler. I glanced at its Chinese writing, rolled it ceremoniously between my palms like a prayer stick, the way I'd seen psychics do, on TV crime shows, with personal belongings of the kidnapped or missing. But nothing came to me. That was the bummer with our little gift, you could never just summon it. It came when you least expected it. Like those people who could get radio stations coming in on their dental fillings from time to time (and I don't mean the kind of messages that told you to go down to the elementary school and start shooting randomly, or head over to the Mojave to wait for the comet to pick you up). Even when a broadcast comes, it lasts just a millisecond. More like a feeling than anything else. But there was nothing that night.

I climbed back up into our yard, single Moon Traveler in hand. I wasn't so much surprised Nate had vanished. He had done that plenty of times, without warning, from our lives. But somehow, each time, I had known he'd return. It felt different this time. I should have hidden his car keys, I thought. I never could think a step ahead of him. We walked in tandem. And Nate had always been the consummate escape artist. Growing up, he idolized magicians. In seventh grade, when we were asked to write and perform our own dramas based on our favorite biographies, Nate chose Houdini, while I got drafted to play Anne Sullivan by Wanda Hacker, my best friend at the time, who had already slid into puberty two summers prior and towered two feet above me in an unkempt red wig, Orphan Annie on steroids. While I had to trace letters onto Wanda's sweaty palms in front of the class while wearing granny glasses and with my hair in a bun, Nate performed magic tricks. He poured milk that vanished into cone-shaped napkins, pulled quarters from ears, slipped out of handcuffs as the classroom oohed and aahed. It shouldn't have come as a surprise, really, that he had escaped from our simple root cellar. But somehow I knew there was nothing to pull him back, this time. Not Mama. Not me. I hid the Moon Traveler in the dresser in Nate's room and shut the drawer.

That night our house was empty, eerily quiet, and I couldn't sleep. I watched infomercials till the wee hours of the morning, ended up with the entire Lori Davis line of hair care products as well as a Thighmaster, but nothing relieved me. I even dialed up the Kryptonite bike lock people, after rambling through my closet at two in the morning until I found the warranty slip and their toll-free number. I spoke to an operator named Doreen who politely informed me that the guarantee only applied to stolen bikes, not people.

"Have you contacted the police?" she asked.

"*He's* not stolen," I said.

"Well, I thought maybe you could file a missing persons report."

"Look, I don't even know if he's missing," I began to sob. "I think he just bailed out on me." I proceeded to tell her about the events of our last two years, Mama's cancer and dying, my father's engagement. It's funny, how you can spill out your guts to complete strangers about such things. Nate and I had rarely spoken of Mama's death. When I finally got to the part about the fireworks, Doreen had to cut me off.

"Miss Gibbs, I'm sorry, but I think I really need to let you go," she apologized. "But I can send you a coupon for ten dollars off your next bike lock."

I hung up the phone. Here I was, the entire house to myself for the first time I could remember, with sixty-seven channels, a liquor cabinet undepleted by mostly teetotaling guests, and a freezer full of wedding cake. All those acts of debauchery I had been anticipating from Nate and his friends, a postwedding blowout that could have achieved new heights in terms of blood alcohol levels, decibels, and craziness, had now dissipated with him into thin air. I was orphaned. I was twinless.

I got a clue, at least, to his whereabouts, a week after the wedding, when I went to our mailbox. Inside, there were not one but two obsequiously cheery HAVING A WONDERFUL TIME postcards. The first was from my father and Lila, greetings from their Holy Land honeymoon, a photo of the Wailing Wall. "We haven't eaten a vegetable in days," health-conscious Lila had written on back. My father, the biologist, had added a few arcane comments on the ecology of the Sinai Peninsula. I learned that the Wailing Wall is not even an actual wall that wails—something I had attributed to some mystic Middle Eastern weather phenomenon—but a place where people go to weep and gnash their teeth. How is that for a honeymoon?

More importantly, the second postcard was from my brother. I immediately recognized his telltale scribble, a deceptively straight-ruled script that became miraculously illegible when you actually viewed it up close. The postcard was from Tupelo, Mississippi, three states over from our home in Charleston. It was a snapshot of Elvis's birthplace. Nate had scribbled on the back: "Dear Linny, The McDonald's here has Elvis etched onto the sneeze guards at the salad bar. Is nothing sacred? Love, Nate. P.S. If Lila asks, say yes it's all her fault even if it isn't. You owe me that. P.P.S. I have your bike lock."

None of it made any sense. I tried to think if Nate knew anyone in Tupelo, but no one came to mind. Nate had never been an Elvis fan, although Mama had owned most of his records. Granted, Elvis made some people crazy, like he did our high school home ec teacher Miss Parnell, who had been past president of the South Carolina Elvis Fan Club and had devoted an entire room in her house to Elvis memorabilia and had even contemplated charging admission at one point. But Nate was immune to religiosity of most all kinds. I turned the postcard over, looking for a clue. On the front, there was a tidy snapshot of Elvis Aaron's clapboard boyhood home, pre-Graceland, under an artificially tinted blue sky, unclouded by Priscilla, drugs, obesity. But nothing else. Just Nate's scribble and somehow the intimation of an innocence gone astray.

I had no idea what my brother was doing seven hundred miles away, but as I sat on our porch, I relished that postcard, turned it over and over in my hands. I ran my fingers over its scalloped edges as if they were Braille, as if they could somehow offer up a tactile explanation for why Nate was there and I was here. There was no explanation. I stared out at our front yard, at the spot where Nate's Toyota had sat for most of the summer, now a rectangular swatch of yellow grass gaping through the green, parched and lifeless. I plopped my feet up on the porch rail and began to paint my toenails an unexciting shade of French Beige. The August air felt bloated and unflappable, like breathing cotton, and suddenly I wanted to take off, too, somewhere—Holy Land or Graceland, it didn't matter, as I watched our sprinklers spritz and arc across the lawn. I sat there for what seemed like a millennium, waiting for my toenails to dry.

Another week later, no word from Nate. It was time to pick up my father and Lila from the airport. I greeted them outside their gate. As we moved toward the baggage claim, I made small talk. We watched the suitcases plummet down the chute. Thankfully my father didn't seem surprised that Nate wasn't with me. We stood politely as the luggage streamed by, my father watching the procession of bags with all the intensity he usually reserved for one of his redbellied woodpeckers or rufous-sided towhees. *There they are,* Lila mouthed and motioned with her hands, pointing to the end. She bounced to the front and hoisted off the three pieces of luggage in no time. She was wearing a sleeveless white blouse and when she gripped the handles I could see her biceps, her shoulders tanned and compact, perfect cylinders of health. Lila taught aerobics to the seniors down at church three mornings a week. Our bodies are God's temples, and you need to take extra special care of them, she incited the 55 Alive Group between reps. My father had started attending her sessions after our mother died. Lila had said it would help him to get out of the house and into the healing properties of low-impact. Funny thing is, he honestly did look healthier than ever, his waist an inch smaller, his gait a bit springier. He stepped over to help her, but she had already popped out the luggage handles and was ready to roll.

"Got it," she smiled. "Let's get out of this place and get us some real food. I've been dying for a glass of iced tea since we left." She slipped a bag onto her shoulder and fluffed up her hair. "It's like ice was against the law over there. Nothing but hot tea. I never could see how those poor women could stand to wear those black veils. Even in the middle of August."

"It's part of their religion," I informed her coolly.

"Well, religion or not, I think I'd be a bit more sensible when choosing what to wear."

"We'll stop at Shoney's on the way home," my father said as we headed outside. Somehow I ended up walking in front, and I couldn't remember where I had parked the car. It felt weird, walking ahead of my father and Lila, like I was chaperoning. We stood there a moment while I tried to get my bearings. All the cars looked the same, bleached out in the afternoon sun, their migraine glare rattling my composure.

"I think we're over there," I pointed.

Lila put down her bag by the car and opened her purse. "My skin is all dried out from this trip," she said, rubbing lotion into her hands. "I never thought I'd appreciate this humidity again." She inhaled a deep breath through her nose. "Where's Nate?"

"He's fine," I mumbled. I unlocked the trunk and watched my father sandwich the luggage squarely. He always had a system for packing, even on the way back from places.

"If he didn't show up at the wedding, I hardly expected him to greet us at the airport," he said as he rearranged the bags.

We got into the car. My father slid in front and Lila took the backseat, thank goodness. She was rummaging through her duty-free shopping bag before we even got out of the parking lot, making irritating crinkling noises. Halfway down I-26 the air conditioner finally kicked in and I could breathe a little as we entered the outskirts of Charleston. Everything was hazy in the afternoon light, the city washed out like a premature Polaroid. I took a deep breath and prepared myself.

"I lied," I said. "About Nate." I hit the lock button for dramatic effect, all four doors making a resounding click of entrapment. Like I halfway expected my father and Lila to leap from the car at sixty-five miles an hour when I told them the news.

"I really don't know where he is. I think he's run away." I wanted my words to plop out hard and stony, but my voice crackled, dehumidified, drowned out by the AC. No one said anything for a moment. I cracked open a window. The air smelled marsh-funky, like old tea that's been setting out for a while. I cleared my throat and continued.

"As best I can figure, he ran away during the wedding." I decided not to mention the root cellar, or locking him up. No need to go into unnecessary details. My father lowered his head and arched his brow, the way he always does when he is feeling slightly incredulous, and he scooted down his eyeglasses a twinge. The way I see it, it is always best to give news like this in moving autos, especially when you are the driver, because you have a good excuse to avoid all direct eye contact and focus on the road. Plus you can scan the people in the backseat in the rearview for quick reaction as well. I glanced at Lila in the mirror, tried to make my eyebrows darts of vengeance, tried to muscle them into arrows on my forehead, with a sort of half-sorrow, half–Vivien Leigh scowl. But she wasn't even looking up—too busy with her compact mirror. I looked over at my father. He stared out the window, leaning his head back against the seat, his bald spot grazing the headrest as he scratched his temple.

"I see." Silence. "So where," he paused a moment, "exactly has he run off to this time?"

"Tupelo, Mississippi," I said. "Maybe it's a temporary thing. I don't know."

"What part?" he asked. "Mississippi, or the running away?"

"Louis, don't be so hard," Lila piped up from the back. "I'm sure Nate's still working through some things."

"We're all working through things," my father said. "I just don't see why he feels the need to run off every time he thinks the world's falling to pieces." He ran his fingers inside his shirt collar, scratching his suntanned neck. "He'll thrash about for a while, I suppose, like he always does. Our little june bug on a string." I watched as my father fiddled with the radio, trying to find a station. "And then he'll get tired and come back."

"I don't think so, Daddy," I said. "Not this time." Something told me I was right. Something told me that the string had snapped, that some centrifugal force had now flung my brother far away, into a hidden and separate orbit, inaccessible even to me. Our car wheels galloped over the bridge joints in rhythm as we headed across the river. Ca-thunk. Ca-thunk. Ca-thunk.

"Have you called the police?" Lila asked.

"It's not like he's missing," I said. "I mean, we have a general idea of where he's at."

Lila let out a sigh. "I can't help but think this has to do with us finally tying the knot," she said, shaking her head. "I know he can't stand me."

"This has nothing to do with you, Lila," my father interjected. "This is just Nathaniel Audubon Gibbs. Pure and unadulterated."

I didn't say a word. I continued to drive, looking occasionally down at the river. Pearman Bridge is the highest point in Charleston, which isn't saying a lot. You can't see to Summerville, much less Tupelo, on a humid August day. But you do get a fine view of the city and the river. Just in cautious glimpses, though, if you're the one driving. The lanes are so narrow and unpassable it's dangerous to look away from the road for long. It makes me anxious, like it did Mama. She had rarely ventured over the bridge after she got sick, except for doctor visits, hyperventilating by the first rise if we weren't careful to put down the seat and keep her horizontal. Funny, ever since she died, I've forced myself to look down just a little whenever I cross. I can't help it. Like the way you can't help but look underneath a scab, or watch those surgeries on TV. So I looked down. Cathunk, ca-thunk sang the bridge joints, snowy egrets at the bottom of the pylons, small and glinty as pinheads as they swirled in shards of sunlight. I was queasy. I looked back at the road. Lila was gawking out the window like a tourist even though she had been across this river a thousand times, and my father stared out at the clouds that were gathering over the bay.

"My classes start on Wednesday," I said. "I'm taking eighteen hours this semester."

"You know we'll be glad to help you move in," Lila offered. We. Like now it was automatically a package deal. "It's going to be odd. With both of you gone."

"Yeah, well, it's not like I'm going anywhere," I sighed. "Just across the river." I was attending the College of Charleston, but suddenly I wished I were going to school across the Atlantic. Two more days and I'll be moved in, I tried to tell myself, as we crossed over the bridge and entered Mount Pleasant, and my father said it felt good to be back home. It didn't hit me till our driveway that Lila was still right there with us and she was home now, too. Whatever that meant.

By the time I pulled into our driveway, it had started to rain, one of those slow, deliberate sprinkles that rarely came in August. My father and Lila headed upstairs to unpack their things. Her things. I went into Nate's room and lay down on his bed for a moment, watching the dabble of shadow and raindrop on his window. I nearly drifted off to sleep. But in that eddy between unconscious and conscious, I somehow started getting a signal. Like I said, I never know when the tuner is going to trip across a transmission from Nate. It's not like we can will it. I closed my eyes and tried to concentrate. Suddenly the image of a big western sky flashed before me, then suddenly went dark. That was all. If I'm lucky, maybe a word will rise at the bottom of the screen in my mind, like a movie credit. I wasn't sure. This much I knew, though: Nate was no longer in Tupelo. He was across the Mississippi River. I could feel it in my bones. As I listened to the rain and jiggle of distant thunder on the windowpane, finally the rest of the signal wobbled on through, scratchy as an old record, the word suddenly flung forth from the darkness like a luminescent Frisbee as it shimmered across my brain. Texas, I said to myself. He is in Texas.

A map of the United States hung on Nate's bedroom wall. He had marked all the states he had ever visited with a bright yellow highlighter, and Texas was still uncharted territory, as was most of the West. I sat up from his bed and traced its border with my finger. Texas was the only state that seemed to be pointing in three directions at once. It was shaped like a moth-eaten pinwheel, a disintegrating cross. When I ran my nail over the squiggle of the Rio Grande, I felt a slight jolt. I know that sounds crazy, but at that moment I felt a current. I also felt a compulsion to go down to the water, to the river that flowed behind our house. The sound of my father and Lila unpacking upstairs was suddenly unbearable. I slipped on Nate's raincoat and smiled when I felt a Bic lighter in one of the pockets. I grabbed the Moon Traveler from his top dresser drawer, then snuck quietly outside, into the drizzle.

Wet blades of grass clung to my sandals and soles as I passed by the root cellar and headed down to the dock. I stood at the edge of the creek for a moment before I finally slipped my sandals into the water. The familiar warm ooze of the pluffmud blanketed my toes. I carefully untethered and flipped over Nate's yellow kayak. I was somewhat surprised he had left it behind. Perhaps he had known that he wouldn't be needing it, where he was going. Or maybe it had just slipped his mind. It didn't matter. I was glad for it. I awkwardly squeezed my big butt and legs into its waterproof lips, the neoprene hugging my hips as tight as a girdle as I paddled on out to the middle of the creek. The marsh percolated with life as I slid back my hood and listened as the rain hit my cheeks. Nate's Moon Traveler remained as snug and dry as a baby, tucked inside my bosom, under his jacket, as I paddled downstream with the tide. I hoped he was warm somewhere tonight.

By the time the rain had let up, I was nearly at the Cooper River. I spotted the spidery silhouette of the Pearman Bridge ahead in the distance. Headlights and taillights began to shimmer as the dusk settled around me, and I withdrew my paddle and drifted a moment, out into the river, away from the bank.

Fireworks are illegal inside the city limits, I reminded myself, as I unzipped Nate's coat and pulled out the Moon Traveler. My alibi was ready, if needed: Bottle rockets were a lot cheaper than emergency flares, and they came in more colors as well—exciting, luminous tones. I was lost, Officer. Lost and confused.

I took aim at the sky. The rocket lurched instantly out of my hands like a rodeo bull, even rocking the kayak, and I watched as it climbed into the descending darkness above me, waiting for its promise of light. A starburst, a chrysanthemum, even a paltry brief sputter and spark would suffice. Any small gift of illumination would be welcome, would not be asking too much of a single Moon Traveler. Gemini was nowhere to be found.

MICHELLE REGALADO DEATRICK

University of Michigan

BACKFIRE

Think about it: two kids in a car, alone, in late summer. That Friday, my mother went into the bank to withdraw twenty dollars, just like she did every Friday. She said it went quicker if Maria and I stayed in the car. In 2005, a lot of folks seeing two kids unattended in a station wagon would whip out their cell phones and call the police. Or Child Protective Services. But it wasn't all that out of the ordinary in 1968. What's more, nothing happened. We didn't die of heatstroke. We weren't kidnapped. I didn't have my mom's car keys, so I didn't start up the engine and drive into the front of a house where a middle-aged man slept alone after eating his bowl of canned tomato cream soup, thereby granting him his semiconscious wish for oblivion. Nothing happened, not then and not ever, in the car.

The fire was later that day. And it was a house fire, not a car fire, though I've seen plenty of both in my line of work. It wasn't even our house that burned until it was a blackened shell.

Of course, this was before all that bullshit came along about it takes a village. Before each little thing down to the minimum number of smoke detectors and their precise placement in a residential dwelling was legislated. The truth is, I'm not someone who should complain about how every stumble over a sidewalk crack, every sore wrist from playing Tetris on company time, every nosebleed from the decking a secretary gives her boss after he grabs her ass is reported to an insurance company. Liability, litigation, and malingering—these keep me in a job. And you better keep those smoke alarms functioning and stocked with fresh batteries, or else when your house burns to a crisp in the middle of the night and you have nothing left except your second favorite pair of pajamas, I might be the one helping your insurance company avoid paying out on your claim. I'm an independent, specializing in freelance evaluation of accident and disability claims. Companies call me in when they don't want to pay out to an insured. Detective Andrew Wade—that's what one claims manager calls me for a joke. I'm based in Hartford, Connecticut, because that's where insurance was at when I finished college and got started in this business. It's also three thousand miles and four climate zones away from where I was born and raised. It's almost far enough.

It was so hot in the station wagon that Friday that I couldn't think and couldn't stop looking at that dumb sign in front of the bank: 100°F...HAVE A NICE DAY!...11:27AM...LOW-INTEREST LOANS AT SACRAMENTO SAVINGS!...100.5°F...HAVE A NICE DAY!...But it was too hot to be a nice day, no matter what the sign said. Mom had parked beneath a tree that spattered the car with shade, and Maria and I had cranked the windows down, but the only place the air moved was just above the dash, where it shimmered a little. I liked the look of that dash. It was the same dark gray green as my army men. In the sun the dash got superhot, though not so soft as the army men. I'd lost a whole platoon to the sun just the week before.

They got left outside after my friend Joey and I played war. By late afternoon, they were just a lumpy pile of plastic, the figures melted together so you couldn't pull them apart or even, in some cases, make out which saluting arm or booted foot belonged to which figure.

Usually, Mom was in the bank for ten minutes. We were at twenty and counting. I'd forgotten my copy of *Encyclopedia Brown, Boy Detective*, and there was no way I wanted to talk to Maria, who was gripping her crotch with both hands, trying not to pee herself. I needed to get home and see Joey. It was the last day he was good for his naked lady picture offer.

When Mom came out, she didn't go to the grocery store as usual. Instead she walked straight and quick to the car and got in. The dark half circles under her eyes that Joey said made her look like a prizefighter had darkened, almost as if she'd been hit, which in a way she had been. She slammed the door, something I couldn't remember her ever doing before. Maria and I looked at each other. Mom had promised us a rare treat, nickel ice creams at Thrifty's, but we didn't dare ask.

I didn't worry about how Mom was acting. Maria was too little to be told just yet, Dad had said, but Mom was going to have a baby. That was why she was tired and cranky. It was fun having this secret from Maria. I wanted the winks and nudges and little, knowing nods between me and Dad to go on forever. And so I did not want the baby to be born, did not want October to come.

As soon as we got home, Maria ran to the bathroom. I waited my turn outside the door, but Maria always used amazing amounts of toilet paper and took forever. Finally, I said, "Hurry up, would you?"

"Let's play pretend when I'm done," Maria said. She opened the door.

I really had to go, and I pushed past her into the bathroom. "What do you have in mind this time?" I asked, shutting the door.

I'd opened my lips just enough to let the words out, in a way Maria called "snarly" but that I claimed kept the hot air out of my mouth. The truth was that I took a mean enjoyment in annoying her. What's more, I knew what she'd say before she said it. I understood even then—though I couldn't have put it into words—that people are seldom very complicated, that they generally run true to type.

"That's the Nile River," she shouted at me through the door. I knew she meant the dented beige dishpan on the linoleum. On August mornings, Mom filled that dishpan with tepid tap water and set it in front of the big floor fan. She pretended this cooled the house nicely, and she liked Maria and me to pretend that, too. "We can sit on the banks and eat a picnic lunch. After we eat, I'll be Pharaoh's daughter."

I flushed for both of us and washed my hands. "So who am I? Baby Moses?" I was joking, of course there was no way I was going to be a baby, but she gave it serious consideration.

"No. Barbie will be Moses. I'll wrap her up so you can't tell she's a girl. You're Moses's big sister. And his mommy, too."

I wanted to be Pharaoh, who was powerful and rich and grown up. He was also, now that I think about it, an insurance man's nightmare—disaster-prone and in denial. But I liked that he refused to take orders from Moses. And Maria was definitely trying to annoy me. She knew I would never, ever, take a girl's part. I raised my fist. Would I have hit her? I don't know. Probably the only thing that saved us from a fight, and me from a thorough belting when Dad got home, was Mom coming out of the kitchen.

I thought I was in big trouble, but Mom just looked at us for what seemed like a long time. "Can you tell me," she said, but not like she expected an answer, "what in the world your father has done with our savings? Imagine!" She smiled, but not in a happy way. "Imagine six thousand dollars gone just like that!" She snapped her fingers.

I didn't know what she was talking about. She started crying and stroking her belly all over with both hands. It bugged me, the way each stroke pulled her dress tight so she looked even bigger, even more taken over by baby. And then Maria started sniveling. "Oh, please, Maria," Mom said, "not now. Don't cry right now." Then, instead of picking Maria up and rocking her to happiness with a reading of *The Frog Prince,* Mom shut herself up in the master bedroom. I heard the lock click.

Maria's sobs quieted. She leaned on my leg and wiped her nose on my shorts. "I'm hungry," she whimpered.

I wanted to shake her off but knew she'd start crying again if I did, so I took her into the kitchen. Mom was big on wholesome, regular meals. For lunch she usually made us thick, moist sandwiches with lettuce and cucumber slices on homemade wheat bread that actually tasted good. But that day she hadn't started our lunches though it was well past noon. Maria wiped her nose again, this time on the back of her hand, and dragged a chair up to the Nile. She put her feet in. "I want my lunch, please," she said carefully, as if she were talking to a teacher. Then she began rocking back and forth, looking sad. I wished I hadn't almost hit her. She'd have been cute if she'd been someone else's sister.

The fridge was pretty bare. There wasn't any ham—Maria's first pick. No cheese, no tuna fish—her second and third choices—so I made her a PB&J, the way she liked, cut corner to corner with the crusts off, the peanut butter thin, and the grape jelly thick. I even put a few potato chips on the plate. At least, I think I did. It makes me feel so good to remember those potato chips that I'm suspicious. Maybe it was just nothing, just air that I left on the scratched-up melamine plate next to the sandwich. It's possible I didn't cut off the crust. Or that Maria didn't like grape jelly at all, which was what my father said the next morning, when I told about the sandwich, trying to prove I'd loved Maria, too. But there's no way to figure it out. No way to triangulate the truth. And sometimes that's how it is: The other witnesses die or disappear and the only story you have is less fact than you'd like.

"Don't you dare go play in the back," I warned her. Then I rolled a slice of bread around a piece of bologna and headed out front to see if Joey was around. I had to get that picture of his.

I was nearly in third grade and I was tired of Maria, who had only finished kindergarten and was childish even for her age. It was bad enough that I lived on what the older kids called The Street of the Retards—half the neighborhood kids went off in one of those little buses to the so-called special school five days a week. Only one of them, Joey's big brother, Cal, was what today we're supposed to call learning disabled. He'd had water on the brain as a baby, Joey said. But we had so many "special" kids on that street that a statistician might have been interested. The teenager next door was a big fat pale deaf girl with a faint mustache and dark eyebrows almost grown together across her forehead. Her mother had come down with German measles when pregnant with her. Every day after school, and all day long in the summer, the girl sat unmoving, her face pressed against the one front window in her house. Her lips were big and round against the glass and Maria, who occasionally said something both smart and funny, once compared her to the albino goldfish in the principal's fish tank. Joey and I sometimes joked about his big brother taking Miss FishFace to a movie.

There were plenty of damaged adults around, too. Dawn's uncle had lost a leg ("And," Joey once asked me, snickering, "what else?") in Korea. He wore a camo jacket in winter and taped a flag to his wheelchair on the Fourth of July. Brenda's second cousin had cut off his own pinkie and part of his ring finger with a chain saw, supposedly while logging redwoods near Eureka but really to avoid the draft.

Joey's dad wasn't around often—he kind of floated in and out of their house when he felt like it—but he'd shot off the front half of his foot while deer hunting. In summer, he limped around in sandals, and we got to see the lumpy pink, sore-looking scar tissue where the front half of his foot should've been.

I felt a little left out when other kids bragged about mutilated relatives, and sometimes I'd offer up a description of my dad's appendix scar or the foot-long reddish ridge up and down my mom's stomach from her C-sections. But like all my attempts to raise my standing with the other kids, this failed. They thought the appendix was dumb. The C-section thing was gross, they said, but they weren't impressed. They couldn't see it.

Maria wasn't special ed, but it was almost as bad for me as if she had been. *Crybaby!* the other kids on the school bus shouted at her whenever the mood took them. Then they'd keep at it until she sobbed. She was the kind of kid who set up hospitals for baby worms stranded in the gutter after a rainstorm and then cried when, left all day in their leaf beds, the worms coiled up and dried. And so the name, being accurate, had stuck. Worse, Joey had told me the kids at school were saying she'd peed her pants one day. I definitely didn't need Maria's reputation dragging me down. I was the only boy picked for recess baseball games after red-faced, asthmatic Billy Parkin, who—Joey had showed the entire second grade—wiped so many boogers on the bottom of his desk that it was coated with a thick greenish crust. No, I didn't want to play with Maria. Not that afternoon, not ever.

So I left her inside with her dishpan Nile and headed over to Joey's. I never bothered with knocking. No one could hear the doorbell anyway. They had a one-bathroom, three-bedroom ranch just like us, but they had three TVs, and usually all three were on. At noon Joey's mom watched *One Life to Live,* at 1:00 *General Hospital,* and at 2:00 *Dark Shadows*. Like my mother said, Mrs. Murkel was trash. My mom never watched the soaps until the lunch dishes were washed, wiped, and put away, and not even then if she needed to sew our clothes or bake or call someone about church stuff.

My mom didn't like me going to Joey's house, but he was my only friend in the neighborhood, and in school for that matter, so she didn't forbid me. Sometimes I wonder how it would have turned out if she had. "Something doesn't smell right about that family," she'd said a couple of times. And I agreed with her, though I was in high school before I understood she didn't mean a physical smell. Maybe she'd gotten a whiff of what Joey put me through, how every summer I had to prove myself worthy of him, and of how every summer he upped the ante. But Joey's house did smell like cat pee. And by the end of August, even he admitted it was about a million degrees in there. His mom didn't have a fan like ours, let alone a swamp cooler like all the other neighbors did. The heat made the stink in his house worse. As I stepped inside, I had to hold down the bologna and bread that wanted to come back up. Loud enough to be heard, I shouted that I wanted to talk to Joey, and then I stepped back out the front door and gulped the clean air.

I realize, now, what a powder keg that house was. Twenty years later, finding an insurer willing to write a homeowner's policy on it would have been a challenge. To begin with, the architecture was bad. No exit from the bedroom wing except through small, high windows. Only the front door offered clear egress. The other two exits were blocked by furniture. And fuel was everywhere. Newspapers and comic books stacked in corners, wall-to-wall shag carpeting, heaps of dirty laundry. What I didn't know about, what couldn't be seen, was even worse: all kinds of flammables stored in the attic and crawl space—firecrackers left from the Fourth, bullets for Joey's dad's hunting rifle, paint cans—stuff that exploded later on.

Joey's mom yelled at him to take out the garbage, but he stepped out just the same and kicked the door closed. He grinned at me: I'd be grounded for the day if I did something like that, and he knew it. He parted his lips over those two squirrelly teeth of his and patted his shirt pocket, the one where he kept the postcard of the naked lady that he'd stolen from his big stupid brother. Another thing Joey knew was how bad I wanted that postcard. I'd watched Maria during her baths, and I'd walked in on my mom during her showers a couple of times, so I had a basic idea of how a girl's body was put together, but I couldn't get that naked lady off my mind. And there was no time to spare. There were already deep creases like scars across the lady's waist where her belly button had been. This was caused by Joey pulling her out, looking at her behind his hand so I couldn't see, then folding her back up. It seemed like he did this about a thousand times a day. His comments were enlightening, even when I didn't get to see the postcard. "Great bazookas," he'd say, or "I'd love to give her a poke, all right." Expressions you'd never hear around my house. Today, though, he patted his pocket in a way that seemed different, more possessive, as if he knew I would never have enough guts to do what it would take to get that lady. "So," Joey said, "you gonna do it, or are you still chicken? Today's your last chance. Brenda's leaving for her cousin's tomorrow."

Brenda Panighetti lived at the bottom of our dead-end street. Her house was the biggest on the block, and Joey and I thought her parents must be rich. Behind her house lay a flat green lawn that ended all of a sudden where a levee began. The levee was just piled-up dirt. Chicken wire kept the sides from crumbling into Brenda's backyard. It rose up about forty feet, holding back the river that otherwise would have spread over the bottom half of our street even in summer and covered most all of it in a wet winter.

Brenda was only in fifth grade but she wore a bra, and not one of those trainer types, either. Joey told me about that. After he'd said so, I looked carefully one day at the bus stop and saw the little metal hooks that held her together in back. This was no camisole like even Maria had for winter; it was the real thing and sometimes when Brenda wore a white T-shirt I could see the lace trim circling around in front. She also liked to climb trees but didn't wear shorts under her dress like Maria did. Joey had promised that if I'd go under the tree when Brenda was climbing and look up her dress, he'd let me have that postcard. He said I needed to stop being a Goody Two-Shoes, and I thought he was right. Of course, he knew I wouldn't just be grounded if my dad ever found out. Joey's mom never did anything but yell, usually for things that were actually his brother's or his little sister's fault. "I'm no tattletale," he'd say afterward, to me. This was a point about him that I admired.

"Okay," I said. I wanted to, anyway. Brenda smiled a lot; she didn't even get mad when Joey called her Spaghetti Heavy Panighetti with Meatballs. She was one of two girls who sometimes played football with the fifth- and sixth-grade boys at school. I didn't think she'd be too mad at me. And maybe my dad wouldn't find out. Maybe Brenda herself wouldn't figure it out. Mostly, though, I wanted the naked lady.

The bright brass thermometer hanging next to Brenda's front door read 106 degrees. Joey shook his head and whistled. The thermometer wasn't even in the sun. It was well shaded, and I wanted to whistle, too. It was what the moment demanded. But I have never been able to produce a good, clean note.

"It's a scorcher," I told Joey instead. "At breakfast, my dad said it was going to be hot enough to fry an egg on the sidewalk if Mom would let us."

"Did she?" he asked, sounding interested.

I shook my head. I hadn't bothered asking. Every Friday morning, when my mom made her shopping list, she calculated the number of eggs she needed that week and then she used them all. Joey's fridge was usually stuffed full of things featured on TV—Fudgsicles and Cokes and Pop-Tarts—piled on top of older stuff that sometimes smelled bad. "Food stamps," my mom had said when I asked why Joey's family could afford stuff we couldn't. Joey's mom would have let him have the egg, if she'd had any, but it might have been rotten.

Joey said he'd get Brenda up that tree by daring her to climb higher than he could. Brenda was not the type of girl to turn down a dare like that from a boy two years younger than she was. She might not even notice what I was doing. It would be fun to see her panties, and maybe more. I wondered what color she wore, if they would be sprinkled with little pink and blue flowers like Maria's were. I wanted the picture. I had a place to hide it, an envelope I'd rescued from the trash and taped to the bottom of my pajamas drawer. It would be worth it, I decided, even if Dad gave me a belting, even if Mom found out and went around praying under her breath and asking the air what she'd done to deserve this.

But all this, like most insurance, was to no end. Brenda's mom opened the door. Cool, damp air flowed toward us from the open doorway, but Brenda wasn't home. She'd left for her cousin's a day early. She'd be there the rest of the summer, taking swimming lessons.

Swimming. Joey looked at me. I knew how he'd get his teeth into some random idea like that and wouldn't let go of it until he got what he wanted. That was how he'd been about the naked lady picture, which I hadn't even wanted when he first showed it to me. He'd wanted me to want it, though, and before long, I did. I thought about it all the time, about the one time he'd let me hold her and I'd gotten a really good look, about her mountainous breasts topped with nipples the color of bubble gum, and her shining yellow hair coiled on top of her head and one strand coming loose like she didn't care, and the brown curls between her legs, and her mouth partly open, and her eyes shut but not like sleeping. If swimming was what he really wanted to do, it was going to be tough to stop him. Joey's mom let him go down to the river, but I was forbidden. Mom said there were currents and rattlesnakes and drunks down there, and if she ever caught me going near that godforsaken place, or even climbing up the levee to take a look at it, she'd give it to me. So, several days that summer, Joey had gone off to the river by himself. Sometimes he let his little sister Robin come along, and they'd returned with their lips and tongues purple with blackberry, hair and shirts and shorts soaked with river. One time, Robin had picked a little bucket of berries for Maria. All this was okay by me. Though I pretended to be mad, I was scared. I didn't like snakes, and I'd never seen a drunk. And I was a lousy swimmer.

"Stay in the shade, boys," Brenda's mom said.

"Thank you, Mrs. Panighetti," I said just before the door shut and the cool air disappeared like it had never been there.

It would have been reasonable for Joey to give me a little more time, at least until Brenda returned at the start of school. But he wasn't reasonable. He was getting tired of being jerked around. I'd better get serious or he was going to give it to Tony Jacobs, a boy he'd been playing with recently. Tony went to the river a couple times a week, and he'd already looked up the dresses of three girls at school. Joey named them, and I was impressed. So if I wanted the lady, I had to prove myself, and right away.

"What about the river?" I asked. I was willing to try even that, if it meant getting that postcard.

His eyes lit up a little. He did want to go swimming, but then he shook his head. "No. Not enough chance you'll get caught." He needed to think about it, and I needed to check on Maria and my mom, so we went to my house.

The bedroom door was still locked. I could hear Mom turning over on the bed, so that was okay, but I couldn't find Maria. Sometimes she liked to hide, and I wasted a lot of time poking around in closets and under the beds. Joey watched me a while, then said, "Isn't that her on the hill?"

I hadn't thought that she might disobey and go out there. The backyard was swampy that summer. Flies and frogs were everywhere, and it stank. Dad thought he'd finally figured out why, and when he told Mom, she flat out forbade us to go back there. Above the floodplain on which we lived was a big ranch where a doctor and his family lived. The doctor had put an illegal septic tank right at the top of the hill behind our house, and it was overflowing into our yard. Dad had called the county health department a bunch of times before he'd gotten an inspector to come out. The inspector put on plastic gloves, then scooped samples of mud and water from various places in our yard into clear jars and screwed lids on them tight. Then he told Dad not to let us play back there until the test results came in, "Just in case."

Joey thought it would be funny to sneak up on Maria and scare her, so we climbed the hill, bent nearly in half like Indians on the warpath. Then, at Joey's nod, we jumped up, yelling that we were going to scalp her with our tomahawks. Maria screamed, then started crying. I felt bad, but not Joey. He was staring at the ground. Maria had dropped a little red bottle with something inside.

"Where'd you get that?" he said.

Maria looked very scared, and I thought it was because of what we'd done. I put my arms around her, very gently as I remember, but she pushed me away and kneeled down, grabbing at the bottle. "It's mine!" she said.

"That's my sister's!" Joey said. "It's Robin's, and you know it, you lying thief."

We didn't have many toys, and though I'd never seen that bottle before, I believed Joey without question. I grabbed the bottle from Maria. I wondered what she'd wanted bad enough to steal. I held the bottle up to the sun. Inside was a doll about as long as my middle finger. The doll was naked, jointed where arms and legs met the body, and very pink. Even the hair, longer than the body, was pink, or maybe it just looked that way in the light shining through the red bottle. I turned on Maria and swatted her bottom hard with my free hand. "How could you do this, you little stinker? After all the nice things Robin has done for you."

Thinking back now, I can't recall anything nice Robin did for Maria except that one bucket of blackberries she gave her. I don't know why I said that, why I acted the way I did. The psychologist types I sometimes consult on my insurance cases would probably say I was worried about my mother and was taking it out on Maria. Then again, they might think my repressed anger at having to play along with Maria's baby games all summer was finally being expressed. Whatever the reason, what Joey and I did next was run away from Maria, laughing.

She stumbled down the hill after us, sobbing and shouting, "Give back my baby doll! What are you doing with her?"

"None of your beeswax!" I shouted back. "And you better get yourself inside before Mom comes looking for you or you're in big trouble, little Lady Jane."

"Don't hurt her!" she screamed. "You don't understand!"

Joey and I kept running and laughing, but we stopped when we saw my dad's car in the driveway. This never happened. Dad left the house around 9:00 every morning except Sunday to go open the shoe store, and he came home at 6:40, after closing it down.

I handed Joey the bottle. "Give this back to Robin, will you? I'd better go see what's going on. Maybe it's my mom."

Joey looked kind of serious and then he said, "Come over soon as you can."

"Promise you won't give it to Tony Jacobs?"

"Bring your army men."

I'd left my bag of army men on the front porch. Mom had pieced that bag together out of Dad's old jeans and it was pretty neat, with the original jeans pockets on the outside. I kept the lead WWI figures that my grandpa had given me swaddled in aspirin bottle fluff, in those outside pockets. A piece of yellow paper was tacked up on the door but I paid no attention. Even if I'd thought about it, I'd have assumed it was a note from some neighbor lady or a church deacon. I could hear Mom's voice through the open window. She was talking very fast. I sneaked in and stood in the entry, pressed against a wall so Mom and Dad wouldn't see me. They were in the kitchen, where they had their fights.

"You did what?" she said.

Dad's voice was so quiet I had to cup my hands around both ears to hear. "I told you, honey. After I got the phone call from the Health Department, I withdrew the money and gave it to the lawyer. For a retainer. So he can make Dr. Fatass up there fix his goddamn septic tank and stop using our yard for a toilet."

"And you let me find out about this from the bank manager?"

"I know I should have asked you. I got carried away, that's all. I went to the lawyer and he said he could help and I just got carried away."

I've seen that kind of lawyer at work on people, and I can imagine the lawyer's bad suit and fake sympathy for my father. But my mother wasn't the type to get carried away or understand when others did. When Dad got angry at us, it was a quick, bright flash in the pan. If you stayed away ten minutes, it was over and you were safe. But Mom was something else. I'd never seen her really angry and didn't think she ever had been. It's taken me years to figure her out. Her anger was a slow, cold burn, the kind that smolders unseen and unheard, until one day it explodes.

"Get it back."

"I can't." Dad sounded tired. "Look at the contract yourself."

Silence. Mom looking at the contract, I guessed. "And what am I supposed to buy the groceries with?" she said. "Have you noticed your son needs a haircut, or am I now supposed to do that myself, too? Maria's dresses are so short they're indecent. You like calling our neighbor Dr. Fatass—it makes you feel like a big man, I suppose, but I bet his wife knows where her next week's groceries are coming from. Oh, how could you be such a fool?"

That sounds like rage, but Mom hadn't even raised her voice. Still, just for a second, she'd sounded as if she might swear. That would be something amazing, so even though this argument was about money just like they all were, I kept listening.

"Try to understand. After I got that call, I couldn't breathe right or see straight. The county tried to sugarcoat it, telling me they didn't have manpower to deal with a one-yard problem, that they'd sent someone out with that notice for our door, telling us not to use our own backyard. So I called this lawyer and he did a little poking around for free. And it turns out our doctor neighbor is the mayor's best golfing buddy. Honey, if we don't have a lawyer deal with this, we'll never be able to use our backyard again."

What my father didn't know was that the lawyer would keep that retainer plus the additional payments Dad had agreed to in that contract—and would do nothing. The yard would stink for years.

It was very quiet for a few minutes, and I peeked around the corner. Mom's back was to me. Dad was in a chair and she was standing over him, stroking his hair.

"Look, we'll work something out," he said. "There's got to be enough in the cupboards to feed us for a couple weeks. It's just until payday. Only ten days away. And I always get good commissions around back to school."

He should never have mentioned the commissions. My mother hated remembering that he was a shoe salesman. She liked to call him the store manager, which he was, but generally he just sold shoes like the rest of the men who worked there. "Commissions!" Mom said. She took her hand off his head. "I've been scraping and scrimping for three years and this is what you do with our savings."

Dad started to stand, so I ducked back in the entry. The fridge door slammed open against the wall. "Nearly empty," she said. "So why don't you figure it out this time? You try stretching a pound of hamburger into three meals. All so we could move out of this pit and get the children away from these hoodlums. Do you even care that your son is probably out with Joey Murkel right now, drowning in the river or setting off firecrackers or pouring gas down ant holes? Did you look at the letter Maria's teacher sent us in May? What do you expect when you send a sensitive, imaginative child like that to a Title One school with a bunch of children whose parents can't be bothered to pack their lunches? And now you've spent our down payment on some damn lawyer who'll use it to take his wife to Hawaii."

She'd done it. She'd sworn. Proof, perhaps, that even before the fire, not all was as usual, that it wasn't only because of what I did, or what she thought I did, that she left us.

"Don't you go upsetting yourself. Not right now, honey." Dad sounded feminine, I thought, like a nurse on *General Hospital*. It made me feel uncomfortable, sort of itchy, to hear him talk that way.

I thought he should have taken a stronger line, like one of the doctors.

I edged quietly out the front door, grabbed my army men bag, and ran across the street, wondering if Joey still wanted to play war. Breathing through my mouth against the stink, I went in. Joey was in the living room, watching a rerun of *I Dream of Jeannie* with Robin. Jeannie's astronaut husband was holding a monkey that was supposed to go to the moon or something. I wanted to watch more, but Joey got up. "Give them here," he said, gesturing toward my bag, and I did. "Come on, let's go upstairs."

I had no idea what he was talking about. His house was a one-story just like all the others on our street. I was still more confused when he led me to the door of Robin's room. It was a mess, of course. Maria's room was small, but Mom made the bed every morning, and even Maria knew to put her dirty clothes on the closet floor and then shut the door.

Joey's mother had actually let him put a ladder in Robin's closet, up into the attic. He said he had a secret club. Bag in hand, he climbed easily up the ladder.

I wasn't sure I wanted to follow but he said, with the impatience he used for scaredy-cats, "Come on!"

The heat hit me like a club when I stuck my head into the attic. He'd made a floor near the access hole by laying down sheets of plywood he'd salvaged from the riverbank and gotten Cal to carry up there. We sat across from each other. It was dark except for where the ladder came up, and between us, where the roof fan above dropped wedges of light and shadow that kept on chasing each other round and round. That and the heat made me dizzy. Joey pulled the naked lady out of his pocket, unfolded it, and smoothed it. He put the postcard to the side, but not before I'd seen that the crease across the lady's stomach was so deep it was beginning to shred and show the bare white paper beneath. He also had the bottle we'd taken from Maria, a tiny cooler full of Cokes he'd swiped from the fridge, a magazine, and a box of long-stemmed matches left from setting off fireworks on the Fourth.

"Aren't you going to give Robin her doll back?"

"Probably. Eventually," he said. "But I always wanted to see if I could get that doll out of there. And I think I've discovered a way." He picked up the magazine. It said *Playboy* on the cover. He shook it until the centerfold opened out and turned it toward me. The light was bad, and he shut it up again in less than a minute, but I'd seen enough to know why he didn't mind giving up the naked lady postcard. For the second time that day, I wished I could whistle.

"Where'd you get that?"

"My dad left it in the bathroom."

"Won't he miss it?"

"He already did. But he thought Cal took it. And Cal's too stupid for Dad to bother yelling at him."

I was a little surprised. I'd been around when Joey took the blame for things that he later told me Robin or Cal had done, but I'd never thought about them catching the blame for stuff he'd done.

"So what do I do?" I meant about getting the lady of course.

Joey handed me the box of matches. "Light one," he said, "we're going to burn up some army men." I wasn't supposed to play with matches. This was far worse than peeking at a girl's panties or even going to the river. I took a drink of Coke and it was cold in my throat and almost too cold in my stomach, but even so I was hotter than I'd ever been in my life. I was thinking it was my fault for letting Joey see how angry I was when he'd left my army men out to melt in the sun the week before. I'd been pretty upset and I'd called him a dickhead. He'd called me worse than that lots of times, but I should have known how he'd take it. No one, he often said, got mad at Joey.

He stuck his hand in the bag and brought out a foot soldier holding a flamethrower. Then he pulled an ordinary stainless steel dinner fork from the dark and stuck it hard into the soldier's belly. A thought flickered: Maybe I'd never really understood him. And of course I hadn't, of course none of this was really about proving me worthy of his friendship, of making me into less of a Goody Two-Shoes. But he laughed and said, "No more Miss Priss, right, Andy?"

"Right." I struck the match at the side of the box. It took a second try and a third before it lit. I was afraid of burning my fingers. I held it under the figure. The flame leaned to the side a little, bent by the air that flowed up from the hole in the closet and out the roof vent. The plastic didn't burn as I'd expected. It darkened and dripped, then the base of the army man slowly fell off in blackened threads. This was fun. I wanted to do more and was glad when Joey pulled three matches out and lit them all at the same time from my dying one. They puffed and hissed together like a shook-up can of soda popped open, and in their large, joined flame the figure glowed a little and then fell in big snotty clots. I didn't even mind when Joey pulled out two more figures and then another two. Everything seemed exciting and unstoppable. The fire at the end of the matches I held was exciting, and so was the sound of match striking box and the sulphury smell that came just after the matches flared. The mound of blackened plastic between us grew, all odd coils and black and silver streaks where the heated pigments had separated a little. My eyes were tearing from smoke and I had to breathe through my mouth because of the awful smell of burnt plastic, but I wanted to go on. It was then that I heard a noise, something like a cough, behind me. It was a little spooky and suddenly I felt as if someone were watching us. I looked around.

"Just the house creaking," Joey said. "Happens a lot when it's really hot or cold."

But that one sound, that single thing that was there when it shouldn't have been, destroyed the dream. Like for my mom when the phone rang during a really good episode of a soap, when a man was about to uncover the murder committed by the woman he loved. Or learn of her child, long lost and now grown up, by a previous marriage of which he'd known nothing. Even when she didn't get the phone, Mom said, it wrecked the show for her. And this show was wrecked for me. Suddenly I started worrying that Joey would find my grandpa's lead figures in the outside pockets, or the one blue figure, a rare machine gunner I'd gotten as a prize in a box of cereal. That his mother would smell the plastic and come looking for us. That my mom or dad would come looking for me. I needed a way to get out.

"I wonder how fast this stuff cools?" I said, and caught at a bunch of strands just as they fell. I didn't have to fake my reaction.

"Shut up, you stupid fuck!" Joey said. "You want Cal and Robin bugging us?" But for once I didn't care what Joey had to say. I dropped the match and grabbed the picture of the naked lady with my unburned hand. Joey snatched at the picture as I got on the ladder, but I tugged it away from him and shoved it in my pants pocket. Then I ran home, where I jerked the cold faucet on and stuck my hand under the water.

Dad was still home but there was a calmness that hadn't been there before. A haze of cigarette smoke hung above the table, and the smell of coffee began to clear the stink of burnt plastic from my nose.

"What's going on? " Mom said, coming to me. And then, "Oh, Andy. What happened to your hand? If it was that Murkel boy..."

I didn't know what to answer. I couldn't tell the truth. My hand throbbed and hurt like hell, so I went ahead and did what I wanted to anyway. Mom got the ice tray. "It's okay to cry. You can tell me about it later," she said. "This has to hurt terribly." Then she turned to Dad. "Look at his hand. Maybe we better take him to the doctor."

The plastic had burned deep curving lines that were beginning to blister across my right palm. I suppose to cheer me up, Dad said, "No one'll ever tell your fortune from that hand anymore." Mom gave him a look that meant *How is it you always manage to say the wrong thing to the poor child and just when I was getting him to feel a bit better?* It was a look that was half exasperation and half love, and very familiar. For years, I've replayed in my mind that look, the feel of her hand on my shoulder. It was the last moment before everything changed. And then the first explosion came, a little pop that I thought was backfire from the Panighettis' old van or Joey setting off caps, but more pops came, louder and faster, and then a series of loud, echoing whistles that we later learned were the Whistling Moon rockets Joey's dad had put in the attic after the Fourth. When Mom and I looked out the kitchen window toward the noise, we saw smoke pouring out that roof vent on top of the Murkels' house.

"Dear god," Mom said. She ran out the front door. I was glad Joey couldn't see her. He would have made fun of her, and she did look a little funny, with that big belly out front and that swaying, dangerous gait of late pregnancy that reminds me of an overloaded pickup with low tire pressure. Dad went after her and caught her by the arm. They struggled.

My burnt hand was feeling a little better, so with the left I pulled the picture of the lady out of my pocket. "Fuck," I said for the first time, ever. When I'd grabbed the postcard from Joey, it had torn where the paper was most creased and weakened. I only had half of the damn thing.

My mother was pointing at the fire. She wanted someone to go in, after the Murkel kids, but my father thought it was too dangerous. Sometimes I still wonder what would have happened if he'd tried.

The explosions were louder, coming one atop another. Neighbors had begun to gather. Black smoke poured out the windows.

Dad told me later that Mom whispered prayers over and over as the house burned. None of us had any idea that Maria was in there. Joey stumbled out, and then Robin. It took the fire trucks six minutes to get to the Murkels' house, a completely unacceptable response time. The house was already a near total loss when they arrived. Joey told them Cal had been asleep in their room, and they broke a window to get to him. An ambulance took him away. Joey's dad hadn't been around and no one knew where to find him. The firefighters searched the bedrooms but couldn't find Joey's mom, and after that it was too dangerous to go in. Someone called Mrs. Murkel's sister; she took Joey and Robin to her house.

It was late afternoon before the firefighters began mop-up, checking neighboring yards for smoldering vegetation, gathering names of witnesses, walking through the blackened house looking for Joey's mom and evidence of the fire's origin. They found her, what was left of her. And Maria.

That was when Mom started screaming. I'd never heard her scream before, but that night she didn't stop until long after I'd gone to bed, the sheet pulled over my head, my burnt palm throbbing, and my fingers stopping up my ears.

I told the fire investigators about that coughing sound, how Maria was almost certainly in the attic, listening and watching us. And about the bottle and how Joey had hidden it in the attic instead of giving it back to Robin. About burning my hand and leaving the attic before Joey, not after. The fire chief nodded his head and called me "son," and I thought he believed me.

A month later, his report arrived. I watched Mom slit open the envelope with her fingernail and read it, and I could tell from her face that he hadn't believed me. Mom hid the report after she'd shown it to Dad, but I found it where she kept all the other things I wasn't supposed to know about—her black slips and see-through red panties and the new-looking copy of *Life Can Be Sexual*. I've got the report now, open in front of me. And what's clear is that the fire chief not only thought I was a liar, but he never bothered putting together a timeline to be certain that the story he believed was conceivable or consistent. He should have considered the physical evidence—the shape of the burns on my hand. He should have considered the temporal evidence—when I left the Murkels' for the last time, and when Joey did. He should have considered the interviews—not only what I said but what Joey said, and what Joey left out. Most of all, he should have considered the characters of the suspect and the witnesses—whether it was likely or even plausible that Joey's friend Andy, a boy who'd never been in serious trouble, could have found a ladder in that mess of a house, hauled it to Robin's room, opened the attic access and crawled in with his little sister, lit fireworks he couldn't know were there, then run away before the first explosion, leaving his little sister to take the blame and burn to death. Because that's what he thought. It's what everyone thought.

But no one considered the evidence. They never looked beyond the most superficial explanation:

Our investigation concludes that the fire that destroyed the Murkel residence at 3462 Grantwood Way, Sacramento, California, was begun by Andrew Wade of 3461 Grantwood Way, age 9, a child without prior history of fire play, interest, or arson, at approximately 3:07 pm on August 23rd, 1968. Despite Andrew's efforts to beat out the flames with his hands, which left him with second-degree burns to the palms, the fire spread rapidly through the home, feeding on large amounts of combustible and flammable material and igniting the supplies of ammunition that Mr. Murkel kept for hunting and recreational shooting. The

death of Cal Murkel, 17, at Mercy Hospital eight hours after the fire re-
sulted from complications of smoke inhalation. The death of Maria
Wade, 6, who apparently entered the house with her brother, Andrew
Wade, resulted from third-degree and fourth-degree burns sustained over
96 percent of her body, according to the coroner's report. The body of Mrs.
Jessie Murkel, 37, was found in the hallway. She had fallen face-first into
the fire, not away from it, and it is the coroner's opinion that she was en-
deavoring to reach the bedroom in which her retarded son, Cal Murkel
(see above), was sleeping. Mrs. Murkel's death resulted from blunt
trauma when a portion of the roof fell on her skull; death was nearly
instantaneous.

Based on fire department records, the time of response to the blaze was
6.5 minutes after the first notification call, placed by Mrs. Donald
Panighetti. The company was called to respond to another fire shortly be-
fore this one and this response time was not ideal.

What I wondered about for a long time was why, even if Mom believed every word of that report, she didn't see there was plenty of
blame to go around. What was Joey's dad doing with that huge stash
of bullets? And what about the state of the Murkels' house? What
about Maria, who shouldn't have left our house without telling someone? And Mom herself, who should have been keeping track of Maria
and maybe even me? Or Dad, who started everything by withdrawing
that money from the bank? Even if Mom thought I'd started the fire,
which she and everyone else did. Even if she didn't realize I couldn't
have gotten those burns the way the report said I did. Even if she
couldn't see that I was a boy being sucked down and swallowed up,
who was hoping, hoping, someone would see the truth and save him.

But she didn't. Like I've said, people run true to type. My mother
was plenty smart, but she wasn't the sort to wade deep into this mess
or any other. Not the septic tank situation, not the fire. The evening

after the fire chief's report came, she walked out the front door. Dad and I followed her. We were afraid to leave her by herself. Her body was growing larger every day it seemed, but she herself was going away to where she no longer saw or heard us.

She pulled the Health Department notice off the front door. Then she ripped a corner from it, put it in her mouth, and chewed. She swallowed and tore off another piece. I tried this once myself, wondering what it was like for her. Eating paper dry is a terrible thing, but she kept on. It didn't occur to me to do anything but watch her as she ate the paper bit by bit. It was as fascinating, in its own way, as playing with fire. She looked at me, not Dad, the whole time. Like she wanted to show me something. But when she was done, she turned toward Dad. "That's how to take care of it, honey."

I like to think that she was trying her best to do one last thing for me, that she was telling Dad to get rid of that fire report, not to spend his nights at the kitchen table, reading it over and over all the years of my growing up, but I'll never know. Maybe she meant the contract with the lawyers, not the report. Or maybe she was just crazy with grief and hormones.

But after that, it wasn't really a surprise when Mom disappeared the following Friday, the first day Dad went back to work at the shoe store. Dad told me not to worry. She'd taken some clothes as well as the station wagon, so nothing awful had happened to her. She'd left because she was upset and needed to get away. Because she couldn't think of a reason to stay. It was understandable. I knew then that in his eyes, I was no longer a reason for anyone to stay. She was still pregnant when she left, and he did call the hospitals. Maybe she was in one of them, having the baby. But she'd gone farther away than that. Probably, he thought, somewhere close to where she'd grown up, in Indiana. He telephoned her cousin there, but the cousin never admitted to hearing from Mom. I thought Mom had maybe gone somewhere warm and sunny, like Los Angeles or New Mexico, because she'd left behind her raincoat, but Dad didn't want to hear my speculations.

Dad never moved, so I grew up in that house, in that neighborhood, and I was always the boy who'd burned down his best friend's house and killed his own little sister. You can imagine how many pizza sleepovers I was invited to, how many dates I had in high school.

Joey and Robin were adopted by their aunt, who lived north of San Francisco on the coast somewhere. Joey came back to the neighborhood only once, on a Saturday afternoon about three months after the fire. I was in the living room, staring out at the ruins of his house, when I saw him. The sky was gray, puddles stood in the street, and I was miserable everywhere, but especially at school. No one would play tetherball or dodgeball with me at recess, and when I came in, little notes littered my desk. I'd stopped unfolding them, but I knew what they said—MURDERER, ARSONIST. Brenda Panighetti wouldn't join with the other kids in singing, "A brother and sister sat in a tree, B-U-R-N-I-N-G. First comes love, then comes death, then comes time in the penitentiary." But even she wouldn't speak to me or try to silence the others.

So I was glad to see Joey, although he'd lied to the fire chief, had told him that I'd been up in that attic alone with Maria while Joey and Robin watched TV. Joey knew, or I thought he knew, the truth, and I figured he'd be grateful. Admire me for taking his rap. But it wasn't like that. I grabbed a jacket and ran out to him. He wouldn't say hello, and when, unable to think what else to say, I asked for the bottom half of that postcard, he wouldn't give it to me. He faked a look of puzzlement at first, then laughed significantly and patted the pocket where he'd kept it when it was whole.

"Sorry, dickhead," he said. "I don't give things away to the guy who murdered my mom and my brother."

He believed it, what he was saying. I could see that in his face. He'd always been good at seeing the world as one in which he could do no harm, and he'd done it again. He'd forgotten, or nearly forgotten, that—except for Maria—he was the last one out of that attic, not me. So I didn't argue with him. No good ever came of arguing with Joey anyway.

The Murkel house was finally bulldozed after the insurance fights were over, but Joey and Robin's aunt didn't sell the lot so it was never rebuilt. Sometimes teenagers went there at night to make out, and the lot became an eyesore littered with whiskey bottles and dog poop. Shortly after my twelfth birthday, which my dad and I celebrated with two store-bought cupcakes, our mailman, a big balding man who'd delivered our mail since before I was born, told me I should have to look at that bare footprint in the grass where the building had been every day for the rest of my life.

The police came around for years afterward, whenever they found the unidentified body of a woman even vaguely my mother's age. I was scared the first few times this happened, but you get used to it. Still, Dad and I were both amazed at how many of these women there were. At how many unidentifiable bodies appear by roadsides and in riverbeds. Bodies that are a gender, a hair color, an approximate age.

Dad had to go down to the morgue a few times, just to be sure. Up until the day he died of lung cancer, last year at the age of sixty-eight, he thought we'd find her. He pinned his hopes on her coming back when I married or had children, but of course I've done neither. I live alone and I prefer it. I eat a lot of canned soup and microwaved lasagna. I've no interest in the murky position that marriage or any similar commitment places you in.

Hard to believe, but it took Dad seven years to hire a PI to look for Mom. I was applying to colleges, and maybe he thought she'd return after I left home. But he claimed he hadn't had the money until then. First he'd paid off his debt to the lawyer who lost the septic tank case. And the funeral home for the Murkels' funerals. He gave several thousand to the aunt who was raising Joey and Robin. I told him I'd pay for college myself, with work and loans, and I did. So he finally hired a PI. But I knew we wouldn't find her. She'd never been one to fudge something. When she made meat loaf, it was good meat loaf with an egg and minced onion and fresh ground pepper. When she sewed my Halloween costume, it was the best in the neighborhood. When she left, she was gone.

It was only this week, as I was going through Dad's papers, that I finally realized the truth about why Maria took up that matchbox and lit a match after we left. She'd seen Joey melting the plastic figures, maybe even heard him talk about getting the doll out of the bottle. She wanted to melt that bottle, set the doll free. It happens that way sometimes, when I'm working on claims that puzzle in some way. Once you put that key piece into place, all the apparent muddle—the inexplicable facts, the hazy motivations—is resolved. You see it all. The difficulties disappear.

I believe the living and the dead deserve the truth if we can uncover it. But no one did that for me or Maria. And yet it was all there, if only they'd tried.

What I notice again and again in my line of work—sometimes it feels as if someone, somewhere, is rubbing my nose in it—is how catastrophes blindside most people. Prophets like Moses may build reputations out of catastrophe, but when the unthinkable happens to you, it's like being struck by lightning. You don't know when, or where, the knife will be planted in your back. It's after the heart attack, the explosion, the fire, that the predictable comes: how people try to control the damage, what they hold on to, what they let go of.

I still have that cardboard torso. I don't look at it much anymore, but I keep it in a drawer, under my winter socks. And somewhere out there, Joey has the bottom half, taped to his bathroom mirror. I'd bet on it.

KAUI HART HEMMINGS

Stanford University

BEGIN WITH AN OUTLINE

SETTING

My dad still has the secret ranch on the Big Island. It looks like a banana plantation but it isn't. The plants don't extend very far within the ranch's perimeter. The bananas are a lie.

I am asked to reveal what I remember. I remember red dirt roads, steel gates, and signs painted with the words NO TRESPASSING. I remember the large holes in the ground, ambushes covered with blankets of grass. One of the holes was filled with sand so I could have a sandbox to play in. I remember the bananas—apple bananas, small and sweet. Lies can taste good. I haven't been to the ranch for fifteen years.

Besides the bananas my dad raises chickens and grows red ginger and marijuana. I'm not sure how large his drug operation is or how much money he makes. I know that he smokes a lot of pot, but not so much for recreational use. It's more about him testing his wares. He rolls joints. He doesn't own a bong, hookah, smoking pipe, chillum, vaporizer, scale, dugout system, grinder, or steamroller.

I currently live in Colorado and am about to graduate from a liberal arts college where people try their best to look dirty and poor. These kids love their pot accessories and they like to make sure their apparatuses are unique. They buy pipes with unusual shapes and give them names such as The Purple Devil or The Reverend.

There are many types of potheads here—the hippie smokers out on the quad tossing Frisbees, the blunt and Old English variety sitting on porch steps, mouthing Eazy-E lyrics and dipping their heads in time to their tight inner beat breaks. There are the wake and bakers, those few who roll out of bed and feed immediately, loading their devices with such ease and normalcy it's as if they're preparing bowls of oatmeal. The most common type of smoker: the kind that lives by the clock, practitioner of the righteous four-twenty dorm room bong hit.

What kind of smoker am I? I'm none of the above. For me pot is something else entirely—it's my home, my original setting. It's my father. It could be my inherited trade. Like steel or plastics, or the blacksmith; it's all in the family. It gets passed on.

My dad used to send me samples from his plantation every now and then, reminding me he was still in business—this message via shimmering buds, hairy and fat and, beneath the brown packaging and coffee beans, seriously reeking.

CHOOSING A SUBJECT

I shouldn't talk about my father. In one of his novels Charles Dickens created a horrendous character modeled on his father. When people read the novel, they sympathized with this character. I don't want to make that mistake.

I guess I'll say that he's Hawaiian, Tahitian, Samoan, etc.—a mutt—but I won't give him a name. I guess I'll say that he no longer sends me packages because four months ago he was arrested and he currently lives in jail. The prosecutor, Allen Bernard, wants me to reveal what I remember. I tell him I remember red dirt roads.

When I was six, my mother had to leave him, admitting she needed essentials like a BMW and white leather pants. She was twenty-one and over the slumming-it stage. It was time to return to her roots, and she took me with her. We moved to Oahu and forgot.

Her name is Madeline. Maddie. She is what you would call a go-getter. She plans parties. That's her job. She focuses on details. She wraps tent poles with tea leaves. She puts glitter in pools. Nothing is spared. To make up for an infanthood spent in squalor, she treated me to good things—tennis camp, private school, a miniature horse named Rambo, and a white Cabriolet. In our new life there were ladders everywhere and my mother climbed them with ease. I can't imagine her living on the ranch: my bleached blond mother in generic jeans gazing upon the fat of the plantation from her spot on top of the food chain. She says she was rebelling against her parents, but grew tried of it because they weren't watching and, in her words, "rebelling was so *unfashionable*. I always looked like an activist, or a *feminist*."

When I ask her about our old rustic life, she tells me how cute I was, running around naked. My chore was to feed the chickens and she said I would stand on a footstool to scatter the corn so the chickens knew who was boss.

Now she is married to a strapping banker. He's heavy in the ass, a slurper of soup, and a parader of small running shorts. Hugh. He used to be an infamous lifeguard who entertained lady tourists by saving them when they weren't drowning. He was known for wearing slacks and collared shirts to the beach, and for a brief time in the late sixties the look caught on. Gucci loafers and Sex Wax. Polo shirts paired with board shorts. Hugh influenced dress codes.

SIGNIFICANT DETAILS

On Oahu, people raised restaurants instead of cattle.

My dad called me on some birthdays—my tenth, my thirteenth, and my fifteenth. The conversations were always an exercise in call and response, similar to the blues, yet without the passion and distress and only the humor and cover-up. There hasn't been a phone call in a long time. Before he went to jail there were just smelly packages with the occasional note. His last note read: *They got planes circling my property. Planes with heat detectors. I don't use heat lamps, you lolos! Keep on circling! Aloha, Dad.*

The note also said that the police were destroying his crops and that weed was decreasing in popularity due to the ice epidemic, in his words, *5.0 went bus' up my goods. Locals like tweak now. Factory jobs. Pot, fo' get it.*

The prosecutor, Allen Bernard, wants me to testify against my father. I don't know all of the details, not even what he's charged with, but I know Allen Bernard isn't concerned with the crops or if my father has sent me marijuana. He wants to know what I remember about the ranch. What was it like growing up there? What did the property look like? Were there traps covered with blankets of grass? Did I ever fall into one of these traps?

Apparently a little girl wandered off from her house and fell into a very big man-made hole. My dad got her out. My dad says he wasn't aware of any holes skirting his property. He would have covered them if he had known of their existence. Allen Bernard is sure he did know of their existence.

Allen Bernard doesn't understand that I don't know my father. He doesn't understand because I'm too ashamed to tell him. He says there's no stronger bond than the one between a father and a daughter and that he understands if my memory isn't "up to par." "But you know what's right and what's wrong," he says. "And you'll do what's right because you love him."

"Yes," I say. "I love him." I want to please Allen Bernard. There's something about his voice that makes me want to wear an apron and cook meat loaf. I tell Allen Bernard that I'm highly conflicted and tormented. *I don't know if I remember holes in the ground. I remember the roads, the chickens. I was just a little girl.* I love our dramatic conversations. I imagine him on the other end of the phone—chestnut hair, a wad of gum on his tongue, fingers snapping at his assistant to hand him a notepad and pen. Sex-y.

"Does your father frighten you?" he once asked.

"Oh, yes, Allen Bernard," I said. "Very, very much."

REGIONAL DIALECT

Since age six, I have seen my dad twice. He's like a whale that way. My most recent sighting came the year I graduated from high school. My grandmother on his side invited me to their family reunion that summer—she said it was about time I met my relatives.

At the reunion, my dad and I talked between rounds of drunken ukulele fun. He had an earring, a tattoo, and a beer. He was tan and muscled. He looked like someone I would make out with. That was weird. I asked if I could visit him and he said, "Yeah. We'll see."

I asked for his phone number. He said he'd give it to me later. I wondered why he didn't want me, why he didn't invite me to the ranch. I could clearly picture myself there. I imagined living with him—being an outlaw, being wanted. Sometimes, in my fantasies, I brought my life on Oahu. In my imagination, it all worked out. My mother would be there, redecorating the ranch house, creating the illusion of more space with mirrors and bold stripes. Hugh would be there, too, adding that special yucky something, a key ingredient, like baking soda. The banker, the decorator, the drug lord, and the child. An odd, yet functional assembly line.

We ate sea urchins and opihi shells—creatures he had plucked from reefs earlier that day.

"Why don't you want me to visit?" I asked.

"Here," he said. "I got something for you."

He searched through his backpack and brought out a jean jacket that had a distinct eighties style, but not in a cool retro sort of way. It was obviously from the children's department, perhaps the young teen racks. I put it on. The cuffs were at my elbows. The waistband was about five inches below my boobs. I turned up the collar.

"A cropped jean jacket," I said. "I love it, Dad." I wanted to say the word *dad.* I had never called someone that before. His effort made me so hopeful. It made me feel normal. I didn't care that the jacket was acid-washed; supplied by Sears, demanded by New Kids on the Block. I thought that this must be what families did—buy each other bad gifts and say thank you. Thank you, Dad. I gave him a hug and pretended I was a girl with a good father. I asked for his phone number again and he squeezed me hard and began to sing. He had a falsetto voice, beautiful and steady. He sang the Queen's Prayer, a haunting, mournful song the last Queen wrote in jail while the monarchy was being overthrown. I knew the English translation; in grade school we were forced to memorize it in chapel. *Forgive the sins of man,* the song said. *Your mercy is as high as heaven.*

"Why are you singing this?" I asked. Was he sending me a message?

"It's what the band's playing," he said, and I heard the faint strumming. At *Amene* we stopped hugging. Our eyes were wet. We looked away from each other. "Sad song," I said. "Going to get a beer," he said.

I never got his number. I wasn't angry with him, though I wanted to be. It's hard to commit to logic. Logically, I should have been upset. All I have wanted, then, and for some time now, is for him to want to see me. I have wanted to return to my original home, but at the reunion I wasn't angry. I was drunk. I sat at the table and looked at the food—the black lumps of boneless bodies coming out of their hard shells. I felt my own body, arms paralyzed by the unyielding jacket, my back pushing against the seams. I thought that maybe this was how life was supposed to be—nothing's supposed to be contained. Structures will stay the same, but the insides will grow and grow. Nothing will ever fit and that's the way they'll fit—by not fitting.

That night, a little cousin introduced me to everyone as her auntie and kept trying to hold my hand. I walked around among the strangers, my family, thinking of liquids—the sperm that made me, his blood that's in me, the sweat on this cousin's small hand, all hidden. I had to talk pidgin or not talk at all with this side of the family in order for them to like me and not think I was some white bitch. Here's a bit of conversation:

Them: "Keolani girl, how you been? Long time no see, ah? You going go schoo on da mainlan? Ho, you smart, ah? Like Erin Brockvich."

Me (K): "Yeah."

Minor Characters

Quotations from Nathan:

"Families are like bony shoulders we're supposed to be comfortable sitting on."

"I am in love with you."

"Do you want to have sex?"

I think Nathan loves my background, but not me, necessarily. He loves the fact that I'm in pain, though I'm not sure he believes it's real. He says my desire to see my dad and return home is a "classic plot" and that he "understands my need to journey into the heart of darkness."

He wants so badly to be compelling, tries to distinguish himself by talking endlessly about Bakhtin and Foucault, Keats and sestinas. Doesn't he know that all schoolboys are impassioned by the same things—Oil, Tibet, Thelonious Monk, Fritz Lang? High school boys were this way also—constantly repeating themselves. Yet they were dumb and angry—masculine. But I can't love them; I have to love the Nathans because I'm growing up. Lately, at the coffee shop, I force myself to eat biscotti instead of the fudgy cookies. I have to take these small steps.

Nathan would hate this outline. He'd say that it's clever, but gimmicks are keeping me from true emotional content. "How does this self-deconstructing form explain your emotional life?" he'd ask, and perhaps I need this voice in my head.

QUOTATIONS FROM LYDIA DYER:

"You're crying 'cause your dad grows herb? Shit."

"You're crying 'cause your dad won't give you his phone number? My dad used to *hit me,* okay?"

"You had a Mongoose bike and a Cabriolet. You want to know what I had? A doll made out of chicken bones."

Lydia Dyer sits in front of me and Nathan in Intergenerational Equity: Budgets, Debt, and Generation X. She gives me perspective. She definitely has me trumped with the whole abuse and chicken bones thing. She is the opposite of Nathan. I believe poignancy gives her hives. Hers is another voice I like to have in my head. *Be distant,* it says. *Don't articulate the thing that's most upsetting. Allocate your scarce resources wisely; use irony, an unorthodox structure. Make it funny. This will make more sense.*

QUOTATIONS FROM PLAYWRITING TEACHER:

"You have great experiences to recall from."

"Take advantage of your pain."

"Do you want to have sex?"

I interpreted his advice: *Exploit pain. Become phony and superficial, indifferent like stage directions or the parentheses that contain them.*

After a while I tore up these directions. There is nothing worse than comparing tragedies, competing. He said I had misunderstood—he meant that I could create art from tragedy. I could paint, dance, act, or write it into form. Begin with an outline, he said. A blueprint, or a frame.

And then he added: "But don't write about college. No one wants to read about Life in College, and you're not going to write about *us,* are you? Don't write about us."

I told him that I wouldn't say a word, and I won't, at least in this outline. But he has given me other advice that I plan on taking one day: *Give yourself permission to say anything you want; once it hits the page, it's fiction.*

The last of the minor characters are my roommates, Tim and Jolene. They're amazing. They solve problems using Hacky Sacks, ropes, and carabiners. They climb mountains as if they're apartment steps. I try to see things through their eyes—life as something to belay across. Row through. Their postgraduation plans include heli-skiing in

Alaska, then moving to some large city (they're not sure which one) to help homeless people.

They say "I love you" each time they part. I scoff at them. I envy them. They take turns doing each other's laundry and take turns buying her birth control pills. They play board games, they do fun runs, and they loved my dad's packages so I usually gave it all to them. I passed it on.

SCENES

ONE (NARRATIVE DRIVE):

When K first gets to Colorado, she drives. She drives on icy roads. She drives on highways and over coiled passes. She reads the signs— I-25, LOVELAND PASS, LOW VISIBILITY, SNOW ROUTE. NORTH, SOUTH, EAST, WEST. These words are exotic. These are real directions. In Hawaii, it's either *mauka* or *makai*—mountains or ocean. She cannot stop driving. She can't believe that you can drive for an hour and be in a different place.

ONE MORE:

K is flying home for Christmas.

The stewardess announces that she will be passing out pencils and scratch paper for those who want to play Halfway to Hawaii. Whoever guesses the time they'll be halfway there, or whoever comes closest, will win a bottle of champagne. The stewardess tells them the exact time they left LAX. She tells them how fast they are going and how much headwind they are receiving. She tells them the distance the flight covers, and when they are expected to arrive.

K writes down the facts. She wants to win, and she tries to remember the equations from high school. She's an econ major for Christ's sake—she should know this. Is it distance equals rate times time? Then, to find the time, distance must be divided by rate? She doesn't know. She has no idea how headwind is supposed to fit in. Plus, she forgets about time zones.

5:27 P.M. is the answer. D12 is the winner. She can see parts of him, the winner, from where she is seated. She can see his fingers drumming a beat on the armrest. She can see the top of his head, his brown hair gelled to one side, except for one strand that points to the roof of the plane and trembles under the ventilation. When the stewardess comes by with his reward, K sees his hand grip the neck of the bottle.

"That should've been mine," K says, and the man turns to look back at her. He has good bone structure, whatever that means. He has the kind of face that winners and bankers have. K smiles to let him know she's joking. Ha. Ha. She's a funny girl. She's full of wisecracks.

"Should've, would've, could've," the man says, then turns to face forward.

K looks at her watch and waits. At 5:27, she looks out her window, and for a minute she sees what halfway looks like—ocean and air. No landmarks, nothing at rest. From the height of the plane, the ocean is calm, inviting even. But she knows that up close it would be choppy and nearly impossible to swim in. Up close it would be exhausting.

WHAT DOES SHE WANT?

Soon I will have a piece of paper saying that I majored in Economics and minored in Creative Writing. I don't know what I'll do with this information. I'd like to follow in my parents' footsteps. Pot Grower and Trophy Wife are decent professions—they're practically recession-proof and they get awesome fringe benefits.

Earlier this year, before the arrest, I called my mom and told her I wanted to see my dad. I asked for directions home. I'd never asked her for his phone number before, because I always wanted him to be the one who gave it to me; but this time I asked. She told me she thought visiting him wasn't a good idea.

"You have a different life now," she said. "Don't you like what I've given you? What have I done wrong?"

My senior thesis explores Congress's unwillingness to apply basic economic principles to drug policy, and how ignoring economic forces will prove unsustainable over the long term. This isn't earth-shattering but I enjoy its relevance to my father's career.

I told my mother I was going to see him to claim my inheritance, my trade, and that this wasn't about who was the better parent; it wasn't about love. This was economics. This was about utilizing my BA.

CRITICAL MOMENT

But it was about love. And forgiveness. I wanted to go to my father, sit him down, and tell him that I didn't know half of me—I didn't remember the ranch; the lessons in getting by, the importance of wearing camouflage. I didn't remember how to speak as he did and I didn't want to feel like a tourist or like President McKinley when I was around his half of the family. I wanted to belong. I wanted to know that part of me. When he wouldn't let me see him, it seemed that an entire history, an entire culture, wouldn't let me in.

So here's what I wanted: I wanted access. I wanted postgraduation employment. I wanted to stand before him on my little painted foot-stool, evoking my old chore—feeding the birds. I'd tell him that I wanted to start from scratch and I'd say, "Should I feed the damn chickens or should I tear them apart?"

I didn't do that, of course, but I did get his number and I did call, and I'm sure that now that he needs me to be on his side he regrets our conversation, because whenever I think about the call I think of Allen Bernard and my strong desire to please him. I think of how badly I want someone in this world to understand where I'm coming from.

CRITICAL ANSWER

He said he no longer raises chickens.

He asked how I got his number.

"I'm resourceful," I said. "I'm a good worker." I prepared to launch into my Big Proposal. This was a big day for me; it was the day I would ask him if I could come home and it was the day I would finally get an answer.

"I sampled the last batch," I said.

"Good stuff, right?" he said.

"You should really consider growing pot that allows a functional high. You know—weed you can smoke during the day." I reminded him of the people in the factories, working longer hours. I suggested he branch out to the states, target students and professionals. "Kids here look at this stuff as if it's legendary, island lore," I said. "Why not cultivate the romance? Kona Gold, Puna Butter. These are magical words to hippies in Saabs. The money they drop on an ounce is often more than twice the price of gold."

"I only grow," he said. "Do you need money?"

I was on the deck of my apartment and Pikes Peak, a glimmering bulk of rock, was giving me courage. I had done my research. I continued: "No. I don't need money. I would like to help you on the ranch. We can get to know each other this way. I studied economics. We can teach each other things. Tit for tat or whatever. For example,

I'm thinking, instead of growing plants the size of Christmas trees, we could try crossbreeding small, fast-growing plants in pots that can be quickly moved so the narcs can't pull them up."

My father didn't respond.

"We could even plant decoys," I said.

I envisioned the house, remembering it was made out of tin. I imagined it rusting beautifully—the blues and red oranges against the surrounding green banana and marijuana leaves. I imagined him greeting me, stepping from a small clearing between patches of tall ferns, carrying a stalk of red ginger. His hair would smell like mud, and walking beside him to the house, every now and then I would get a punch of scent, familiar yet unfamiliar; the flat, plant scent of marijuana not yet plucked, but harvesting in the wetness.

UNEXPECTED AND INEVITABLE

I found out I had a stepmother. She was on the phone, listening. After my last comment she said, "Stop suggesting things. You sound like one missionary. Next thing you know she going buy us out then name the ranch after herself." Click.

"Wife," my dad said. "Sorry."

"Oh," I said. "Congratulations."

"She helps me out," he said.

"Listen," I said. "I don't care about learning the business. I was just trying to find a connection. Forget everything I said. I want to visit and we can talk then. We'll talk about anything you want to talk about."

What came next is predictable. Everyone wants the person or the parent that is absent. It's the best way to be desirable, something I should have known from economics. Things are valuable when they're hard to find. Marijuana and my father are essentially weeds; if legal or easily attained they'd be less valuable than corn. My distortion of basic supply and demand dynamics rendered otherwise worthless crops extremely profitable. Like the drug war, I, too, provide price supports for organized crime.

"I'm glad your mom took you," he said to me. "You're smart. You got one nice house, I bet. You can be someone one day. You don't want this."

"I don't know what *this* means," I said. "Forget about my stupid pot suggestions. I just want to visit. That's all." I swallowed a pain in my throat. "What's that noise?" I asked.

"Water boiling. I'm boiling peanuts."

Boiled peanuts—I remembered eating them at the family reunion—the soft shells, the salty straw smell. The sound of the boiling made me feel breathless and pale, the gulping sound suggesting someone exhaling underwater, drowning.

"Why can I hear the water? It's so loud."

"Phone picks up background noise. Mess with recordings just in case, you know, someone went tap the line."

"Oh," I said.

"Keolani girl," he said. "You too good for this place."

"No, I'm not," I said. "It's where I'm from. Just one visit. Just one time."

"Nah," he said. "You know. The wife. Getting you here. Bumbye one hassle. Too dangerous."

My father, I realized, was breaking up with me. "You make no sense," I said. "I can barely understand your language. And my name is K. Just K."

The secret ranch. The secret rainforest. I suddenly remembered the discarded cones of marijuana, using them instead of dolls in my sandbox. I'd make the cones hold each other's stems and kiss. I'd squeeze the shampoo out of the red ginger plants and wash their rough green skin. I'd have the cones talk to each other. One would say, "I'm not happy here," and the other would say, "But it's paradise."

"Don't send me anything anymore," I said to my dad. "And don't call." I realized my mistake. I didn't have to tell him not to contact me and he hasn't contacted me since.

Now I have the power to hurt him.

I also have the power to forgive him. I think of the Queen's Prayer. *Your mercy is as high as heaven. Behold not with malevolence the sins of man but forgive and cleanse.*

DENOUEMENT

I retrieve my dad's last package from my closet. I invite Tim and Jolene, Nathan and Lydia to join me in smoking the last of him. It's my big finale. It's cleansing time.

I sit next to Nathan on the living room couch. Lydia takes the recliner. Tim and Jolene sit in chairs made out of inflatable sleeping mats. They wear identical outfits—fleeces and shorts, socks and Tevas.

Like me, Nathan doesn't smoke very much, but unlike me he has poor pot etiquette. He says, "Like, groovy, man. Like, pass the ganja," and he coughs for so long it scares all of us.

We talk about our aftergraduation plans. Nathan is going to Nepal to get closer to his soul and to help those whom he sees as less fortunate. I imagine him bartering for their lesser fortunes on the narrow streets.

Lydia is going to Georgetown law school. She takes the joint from Nathan and shivers as she inhales. "Reminds me of my ghetto youth," she says.

Nathan rolls his eyes. "People just love to talk about when they were bad," he says. "Or the bad things that happened to them."

I take the joint—suck, swallow, blow, pass.

"Wow," Tim says. "That was elegant. You're like the John Coltrane of smoking."

"Lydia's the Whitney Houston," Nathan says. He imitates her quivering inhalation.

"All I want to do is eat salty foods," Jolene says after she takes her turn.

"I know," I say. "My dad is growing the wrong kind. I tried to tell him."

"Your dad's awesome," Tim says. "Did he go to career day at your school?"

Everyone laughs. Nathan sounds like a sheep bleating. A stoned sheep bleating.

No one knows he's in jail. No one knows I could help keep him there.

"Oh my god," Nathan says. "Show them the yearbook."

"No," I say.

"Come on," Nathan says.

Nathan always urges me to resist humor, and now he's urging me to get the yearbook. He's insisting on funny.

I get the yearbook and return.

It's my mom's yearbook from her senior year at Kalaheo High. I turn to her glossy, dreamy photograph. Her eyes sparkle; her blond hair is ironed straight. She wears a dress stamped with bold floral prints and a puka shell necklace. Every senior picture floats above a statement, a quote meant to illustrate the person you are or the person you want people to think you are. A saying to encapsulate you in 1972. The girl next to my mother—her statement says:

I'd like to teach the world to sing in perfect harmony. I'd like to hold it in my arms and keep it company.—New Seekers.

The quote under my mother's senior picture reads: *I've got a book of matches.*

"It doesn't make sense without him," Nathan says, and he flips through the pages and points to my dad. My dad wears a stiff palaka shirt and a puka shell necklace. He looks so strong and young, ready to pounce right out of the pages and into real life. The quote under his picture: *Come on baby light my fire.*

It shocks me every time. They don't seem to be my parents. They could be my friends, a couple like Tim and Jolene or me and Nathan, young and childless. I glance up and everyone is laughing, silently, and I feel ashamed.

"You know they were stoned when they wrote that," Tim says. "They were totally high."

EPIPHANY

I think about my mother's beautiful house, my bedroom and its sliding glass door with wood trim. Every morning, I would wake to the sound of chattering birds and the looming greenness of the mountain range upon which battles between Hawaiian tribes were fought. On my four-poster bed, I'd inhale the scent of lychee bleeding through the wire screen behind the wooden jalousies. I would walk to the kitchen where a woman named Lehua would be making me breakfast, and I'd have trouble looking at her. This is where I belong. This is the place I love. I've always been embarrassed of my father and he has been embarrassed of me. His half of me is extinct.

It's not so much an epiphany as an admission of guilt. I do not have any other major insights or overwhelming feelings; the sky does not assume a white radiance; my soul does no slow swooning, and generous tears do not fill my eyes as I contemplate my failed attempts at merging my two halves into one. This merge seemed more critical than the decision I have to make now. Hurt him or help him? Was my father aware of the pits skirting his property? Well, yes, he dug them, of course. Do I remember falling?

I imagine the other little girl at the bottom of the hole. He could have buried her. That's what the holes are for. I wonder if she saw earthworms squirming through the walls, if she rested on the bed of grass and looked at the sky and the passing clouds, a drifting plane. I wonder if she held her pee or if she let it go. I wonder if my father hesitated at all or if he saved her right away and brought her home without thinking of the consequences. He saved me; or rather, he got me out of the hole he made. He didn't find me until it was dark and I was very afraid.

My mother told Allen Bernard she remembers me having nightmares about falling into a hole. She didn't tell him anything else. She has left it up to me.

What happens to my father? Will I testify against him? What do I write in? What do I omit? Will I keep telling this story, in one form or another, over and over again?

I just want someone to understand me.

I look outside at Pikes Peak, the falling sun, the sunset swept over the mountain. Reds and oranges, bruised yellows, dark silver clouds. The sky looks like rusting metal, like bananas—small sweet lies. This is as close as I'll get to his home, my home, a place I truly don't remember that well, Mr. Bernard, but I hope this outline helps.

SEAN ENNIS

University of Mississippi

GOING AFTER LOVELY

On Christmas Eve, Dad came home from the mall and hammered up a bedsheet in the doorway to the living room. No one was allowed in, and there was crashing and cursing behind it. I had been scanning TV commercials for any last-minute gems I might have missed during my six weeks of Christmas requests, Mom was locking the windows, and my older sister, Lovely, was talking on the phone with her boyfriend, Roger, a kid who would mainly twist my ears whenever he saw me, saying, "Now hear this!"

Finally, Dad came out from behind the sheet and grabbed me by the arm. "I need your help."

A dozen long sheets of frosted plastic, four fluorescent bulbs and rigs, and two big bags of potting soil were laid out on the carpet in the living room. "We have to put this together for Mom," Dad told me.

I recognized the equipment. It was an indoor greenhouse, something my mother had smiled over in the Sharper Image catalog. But I knew—even at twelve—that she didn't really want it.

The greenhouse was flimsy and everything snapped into place, but assembling it was still a two-man job. I held a piece and Dad tried to plug another into it, cursing like I'd never heard him. None of the plastic was cut perfectly, but he hammered the pieces together anyway. Then he hung the fluorescent bulbs and I poured the soil into the bottom when he was finished. He plugged the lights in and they buzzed and glowed white purple above the dirt. I guess the idea was you could have a garden inside.

"She's gonna love this," Dad said.

I realize now that Mom was well on her way to becoming completely agoraphobic. She made only one frantic daily trip outside, never at night. The rest of the time, she stayed deep inside the house, reaching into the dryer, organizing cans in a closet. She had stopped working in October. At the time I thought it was a move of choice—that people either wanted to work or they didn't. But Mom was probably incapable of holding a job at that point.

Two other conspicuous packages sat in the living room; one for me and one for Lovely, I assumed. Dad always did his shopping on Christmas Eve, and he bought everyone exactly what he thought they might want, no questions asked. It was a strange, vomiting kind of charity. He was helpless and well-intentioned, working two jobs now, confused about why his family seemed to hate him.

But I didn't hate him.

Dad turned off all the lights in the living room except for the fluorescent bulbs hanging inside the greenhouse. He meant for it to be pretty, but it wasn't. It was more like someone had put a pay phone in our living room. He looked disappointed for a second, as if he suddenly saw that the gift was ridiculous, and then he just switched off all the lights and we went to bed.

Lovely came into my room and demanded to know what I'd helped Dad build. I wouldn't tell.

"It's something stupid for me, isn't it? A dollhouse or something. Know what I really want? A backpack. A big sturdy backpack."

I didn't know why anyone would want that. She had been hinting all fall that she wanted a car, but even she knew that wasn't going to happen.

"Weird things are going on, little brother. I found Mom under her bed when I came from home school yesterday. She said she fell asleep. What do you think of that?"

I shrugged. I had seen Mom throw her car keys in the trash two days earlier. I took them out when she left the room and set them on the counter. I didn't mention that, though. I just said, "Don't sleep too late tomorrow. I want presents."

The next morning—Christmas—the sheet was still up in the living room and we waited outside until Dad came down. Rather than pulling the sheet aside, he plucked at each nail until the curtain finally fell, and there, framed by the doorway and lit up by the sun through the windows, was the indoor greenhouse.

Mom approached slowly, peering into it as if it might contain some sort of animal. It did look like a drained aquarium, eight feet high and long, four feet across. I remembered then that I'd dreamed of a tank like this once—a nightmare—the fish hovering out of the water and swimming in the air and me trying to catch them before they got too close to the ceiling fan.

"What the heck's that?" Lovely said. "What's it do? Who's it for?"

"It's for Mom. It's a greenhouse," Dad told her. "For inside."

Mom opened the door and looked in and then looked back at Dad. He smiled nervously, teeth gritted, and made a sort of "voilà!" gesture with his hands. She shut the door, and Dad handed her a small package. There were seeds inside, and Mom shuffled through the envelopes nonstop like they were playing cards.

I guess at that point Mom was on medication. She seemed fainter and fainter, almost blurry to look at, charged with a purpose none of us could understand and focused on something just above our heads and out of the frame.

Lovely opened her package from Dad: a telescope. She didn't hide her displeasure. Dad gave me an archery set. Considering we lived in a row home in northeast Philadelphia, there was no sensible place to shoot an arrow. Also, there were no stars above the lights of the city, telescope or not. A brown smog hung above the neighborhood that purpled occasionally under a full moon. Our stars were only as high as the streetlamps, the floodlights at car dealerships, the blinkers at the tops of factory smokestacks.

And when Lovely and I looked around, we realized there were no other presents to open. Christmas was over.

Lovely ran out and slammed the door to her room, leaving the telescope box behind, unopened. Dad walked Mom over to the couch and whispered to her about what seeds to plant. I went to my room, got changed, and took the bow and arrows outside to see what I could do.

All the other kids in the neighborhood were riding their new bikes and playing with their new remote control cars in the street. I had never shot an arrow in my life—had never even thought of the possibility—and I was excited. Targets hung everywhere: street signs, parked cars, the occasional city tree. A thin groove at the end of each arrow seemed to fit the string, so I settled one in and pulled it back, but the tension became too much and I let go with both hands. The contraption fell to the ground with a clang, and all the neighborhood kids looked up. I had something, for sure.

After a few more tries, I managed to launch an arrow across the street without much speed. It hit the Kramers' garage door with a thud. Everyone cheered. My friend Clip dropped his new hockey stick and followed me around, begging for a turn.

When I went back inside, Mom was on her knees with a little spade, planting seeds in the living room. Lovely's door was still closed, but Dad had taken the telescope out of the box and was setting it up. He pointed to my bow.

"How's it work? Kill any Indians?"

Mom looked up. "The Indians used arrows. Cowboys used guns."

"Right, right," Dad said. "Well, maybe there's fighting between Indians. They did that, too."

Mom said nothing and climbed farther into the greenhouse.

I said, "I hit the Kramers' garage from over here."

"Good. They need to be brought down a few notches." Dad turned the end of the telescope toward me. "Here, look at this. Wanna see Pluto?"

I looked in and saw that Dad had cut out a space scene from the telescope box, taped it to the far window, and lined the scope up perfectly. A flying saucer was frozen in front of a green planet with rings, and moons and stars were everywhere in the background.

"Just kidding," he said and tore the picture off the window. Lovely hadn't even seen what he had planned for her, and I could tell he was sad about it. He slapped the end of the telescope and it spun and wobbled on its hinge. "Well, merry Christmas, family."

Mom hadn't bought us any presents. This was clear, though Dad made no mention of it—maybe because he was surprised, too. In the past, we just shrugged at his bizarre holiday attempts: the rock tumbler Dad got me the year before was unopened in the garage, and Lovely had never plugged in the massaging chair he gave her. But we were always happy because Mom got us all the right things. And if we were happy, Dad was happy. Not this year.

Lovely, insulted and incredulous, told me privately that Dad could use the telescope to look up his own ass. She said she was going to run away from "this fucking crazy-house." And though Lovely was only five years older than me, she seemed infinitely wiser and, better yet, meaner—mean enough to survive, to cut all of us out of her life, just like that. I still felt too tied and dependent to follow her, though I was beginning to understand that I was only one or two people away from being completely on my own.

But unlike Lovely and her telescope, I liked my archery set and was getting better at using it. The back of the package was a target, so I tied it to the telephone pole outside our house. That week after Christmas, I spent most of my time outside with the set, and scored two bull's-eyes. I didn't shoot the arrows at other kids, like Clip had encouraged me to. Instead, I stayed focused on the target and shot hidden from behind different obstacles on the street—parked cars and trash cans, the occasional city tree. I liked the target because it cataloged each good shot with a ragged but unmistakable hole. I was the Indian Dad said I was, always aiming, on the attack, never at home.

Lovely went to a party on New Year's Eve and never came back. Dad was devastated, mainly because of a cruel note she had written that he never showed me. She had taped it to the far window across from the telescope, and the next night, after a day of worrying, Dad saw what it said, real big.

Mom rarely came out of her indoor greenhouse. She invented tasks that needed to be performed inside it, since nothing actually needed to be done. It would still be weeks before anything appeared aboveground, if at all, so she Windexed the walls and tightened the lightbulbs. I was beginning to worry that she slept in the greenhouse, but I never stayed up late enough to check. Plus, Dad was staying in the living room late, too, using the telescope at night to scour the neighborhood for Lovely.

My block was just different shades of gray, the row homes whitish gray, the asphalt dark gray, cars brownish gray with soot. But my arrows had color, red tips backed with orange and yellow and green feathers. Shooting them was like planting flowers.

Some of the other fathers in the neighborhood came to talk to my dad about me. The street was littered with arrows at this point, some stuck too high in a telephone pole or tree for me to get down. The fathers were worried about the safety of their kids and pets and property.

They were also upset because all their kids wanted archery sets, too.

Dad ignored their complaints. Every Friday there was a new box of arrows on my bed, and a new present for Lovely as well, left unopened of course. When the fathers came to the door, Dad rarely took his eye from the telescope, but instead just aimed the telescope in the direction of the visitor, never spoke. Then for a second he would turn the eyepiece toward Mom—always buried in the greenhouse—then point it back out the window in search of some clue. After this happened a few times, the other fathers stopped coming.

"They got nothing better to do than worry about our problems?" Dad would say. "Must be nice."

School started back up and Lovely still wasn't home. Outside, winter came on harder, but, miraculously, tiny green buds began pushing their way through the soil in the greenhouse. Mom was delighted and talked only about this event. Conversations at dinner—now prepared by Dad—were strictly about the new plant food she was going to try and the centimeters of progress each plant made. She took her meals seated in the doorway to her greenhouse.

Pushed out of the living room by the greenhouse and telescope activity, I spent most evenings in my bedroom. Some of the fathers on the block had warned me that they would take the bow and arrows if they saw me with them, even if my own dad wouldn't.

The first time I shot an arrow into my bedroom door, it made so much noise I thought for sure Mom and Dad would hear, but no one came. After that, I drew a bull's-eye on every wall.

"Where's Lovely?"

Mom talked to me a little. Her voice was muffled through the plastic walls of the greenhouse. "You know, don't you?"

"She went to that party." I was walking through the room, dropping off my schoolbooks. I tried to avoid the living room as much as I could.

"A week ago. She told you she was going to leave, didn't she?"

I shrugged. "She said this is a fucking crazy-house."

Mom pressed against the plastic. "Do *you* think so?"

Dad was in the kitchen fixing dinner, humming his cooking song. I knew he wouldn't like this conversation.

"I think it's not that bad." I started gathering my bow and arrows, making to leave and end the conversation.

"You like your present though, don't you? I told Dad you would. I know you're an angry boy."

I had never thought of that. But I supposed I was.

"When Lovely comes back, we can all live in here. Dad could put a lock on the door, and you could protect us with the arrows and Lovely would watch everybody with the telescope and tell us what's happening out there. I'll grow the food."

I wanted to ask her if she had actually picked out the presents for us that Christmas, but Dad came though the door, carrying cauliflower soup and crackers, and Mom receded into her plants, disappearing almost completely.

"Your mom is busy, Sitting Bull," he said. "Let her eat her supper."

I hustled out of the room knowing Mom's plan for the future was crazy, but scared it might come true.

That night—a school night—Dad knocked on my door. I was actually aiming at the door when he came, so it's a good thing he did. By then my white walls were practically black with holes. I fantasized about the day I would lean on one of the battered walls and it would fall over. I let Dad in.

"Know what I think about all this?"

"My arrows?"

"No. Lovely. I think she's with that Roger." The suction from the telescope's eyepiece had left a sweaty pucker around his right eye. "I found his house with the scope. I say we go get her. Right now." He pointed to the bow. "Bring that."

I bundled up quickly, thrilled to be a part of Dad's plan. I collected as many arrows as I could carry and found Dad in the living room, in the doorway of the greenhouse, whispering to Mom. He kissed her cheek, and then we headed out into the cold.

We walked three or four blocks without speaking. I noticed he was looking around the neighborhood at all the arrows I had planted.

"Getting pretty good with that thing, I see."

I shrugged.

"You miss your sister?"

"Not all the time."

"I'm gonna fix this family. If I have to do it one at a damn time, then so be it. You hear me?" He was smiling when he said this.

"Do you want me to shoot Roger?" I asked. It wasn't an impossible thing for me to imagine doing. Once, to impress Lovely, Roger had choked me until I passed out.

"I want you to come as close to shooting him as you can without doing it. Understand? I won't be made a fool out of by someone that rides a damn skateboard."

It suddenly occurred to me that Dad hadn't gotten any presents at all that Christmas because Mom usually bought our gifts for him, too.

"I'm sorry I didn't get you a Christmas gift, Dad. Mom usually—"

"I know. It's okay. Consider this it."

We got to Roger's house at about ten that night. It looked exactly like our own except the trim around the garage was white instead of black. Dad banged on the door and Roger's dad opened it. He was dressed in a white undershirt with yellow armpits, and dress pants— an out-of-shape man, but still bigger than Dad. I recognized him as one of the men who wanted to take my bow and arrows from me.

"We came for Lovely," Dad said. I held the bow slack at my side, but with an arrow notched, ready to go.

"What's Lovely?"

"My daughter. I think she's here." Roger's dad just shrugged. It didn't seem like he was lying. "Can I at least speak with Roger?"

"Roger's asleep. He has school tomorrow. What's this about?" He looked down at me. "That your kid with the bow and arrow?"

I glared at Roger's dad from behind my own. I was waiting for some signal from Dad to shoot this guy in the belly. We hadn't decided on one, but I assumed I would know it when it came.

"This is important. My daughter has been missing for over a week."

"Hey, call the cops. And keep that bow and arrow away from around here or I'll snap it in two pieces." As he slammed the door, I heard Roger's dad mutter, "Fucking nuts, all of them."

I realized then that my family was gaining a reputation in the neighborhood. I looked at Dad and saw the same thought flash across his face.

"Come on." He led me by the shoulder across the street, and then we stopped and turned around. He pointed to a lighted window on the second floor of Roger's house. "See up there? That's where that nice man sleeps. Think you can hit it with one of those?"

I considered the trajectory and factored in my puny sense of wind effects. I nodded.

"Well, smash that damn cowboy's window, Geronimo!"

I pulled back and launched. The arrow hung in the air until the tip tapped the window with a *plink!* and fell into the shrubs. Dad cheered and picked me up and spun me around. "That's the way to do it!" he sang. "Score one for us finally!"

As we walked toward home, I heard the window open behind us and Roger's dad yelling, "Okay! I'll call the cops *for* you, asshole! Have fun in jail!"

It didn't matter. Dad kept recounting the shot like it had been a field goal kicked in the last seconds of the game. He made an arrow out of his hand and, whistling, sailed it into his other hand like it was the window. "Boom!" he yelled when the two touched.

But Dad stopped cheering when he saw the police car in front of our house.

"What the hell? How'd they get here so quick?"

I thought I should hide the bow, but was afraid to part with it. I considered another Wild West fight—their bullets and my arrows. I readied an arrow and looked up at Dad.

"Easy, Tonto. Let's see what this is about before you make them start pushing up daisies."

I hung back while Dad talked with the cops. I wondered if I would be going to jail. A younger police officer came over to talk with me.

"That's some toy you got there, buddy. Are you a good shot?"

I shrugged, not wanting to implicate myself.

"I bet that was a Christmas present. What else did you get for Christmas, little man?"

"Nothing," I told him.

"Well, don't worry. Everything's gonna be all right. Why don't we hang around out here for a while and you show me how that works?"

Dad had disappeared into our house. I walked up and down the block, pulling arrows out of everything I could reach while the cop tried to make conversation. I imagined they had found Lovely, blindfolded and plugged full of arrows, tied to some tree somewhere. They got her.

Finally, Dad came out and called, "Hey, Last of the Mohicans! Come over here." He gave me a big hug, and thanked the cops. I overheard our neighbor telling one of them, "I didn't know what else to do. All that screaming..." The frame to our front door was splintered and the lock lay on the ground. Dad took me aside.

"Listen, your mom got a little upset that we were gone for so long tonight. She thought we left like your sister. I guess she misunderstood me." He had a phony-looking smile on his face that was ready to crack any minute. "But she's in the tub now, so I need you to be quiet and go on to bed."

I nodded and went inside, the drama of the evening slowly deflating. Dirt from the greenhouse was spread throughout the living room, one of the lightbulbs was smashed. I headed for my room, hoping Dad would be in to check on Mom soon.

He walked past my door on the way to the bathroom and peeked in.

"Good job tonight, Sitting Bull. See you in the morning."

I lay in bed listening to the tub splashing a little next door, and the calm, indecipherable words Dad spoke to Mom. I decided I would sleep on the floor that night, naked as an Indian, and imagine that I lay in the dirt and there was no ceiling above me either, but instead, that picture Dad had cut out on Christmas—all those stars and moons and planets.

Over the next few days, Mom had visitors. All the mothers from the neighborhood came and admired her indoor greenhouse—hastily reassembled by Dad—and made small talk. Mom was pleased. Dad strutted among all these women, his phony smile seeming a little more genuine now, serving snacks and drinks. He demonstrated the telescope for the other mothers, even played the same gag with the window he'd tried with Lovely. Mom's pallor was moving back into a pinkish sort of gray, and Dad winked at me over her shoulder whenever she said something that sounded normal. She still held most of her conversations half inside the greenhouse, but her plants were really coming up now, and seemed like they might actually need her attention.

One night, half awake, I swore I heard them both go back to their bedroom to sleep, giggling a little, and at a decent hour.

These moments of peace couldn't last, though. Lovely was still missing, close to two weeks by then. Dad had filed police reports, but it was just paperwork. He still felt in his own strange way that this was his case to solve. With Mom doing better, in a sense, and busy in the greenhouse, Dad started taking his telescope to different spots in the neighborhood to look for my sister. I followed along and would shoot arrows for distance wherever he pointed the scope, hoping to benignly tap Lovely on her butt, reminding her to come home.

The police arrived one night when we were perched on top of Arnold Street, the tallest hill in the development. The cops recognized us and were kind, aware of all our dilemmas. The younger cop winked at me over his boss's shoulder. Dad, though, got angry.

"If you deputies would do your job, I wouldn't have to be out here looking for my daughter in the freezing cold!"

The lieutenant hinted that Dad could be arrested for a couple of things and should at least call off the search for the evening. Dad relented, muttering under his breath—a frightening, new habit of his. They insisted on driving us back home in the squad car, a move that my dad declared "ridiculous pageantry." But it was obvious that the police's patience with our family was wearing thin.

I started playing a new game with the bow and arrows. I would shoot straight up in the air and stand perfectly still, waiting for the arrow to fall, a game of chance. I didn't get hit, but came very close a few times. If the arrow fell down the right way, its weighted tip would bury itself deep in the ground.

After a long school night of searching for Lovely, Dad began looking down the wrong end of the telescope in the living room and got newly amazed.

"Take a look at this! Try this end!"

Looking down the opposite end made everything smaller—the entirety of our living room appeared to sit at the end of a long, dark corridor. Dad was in there, an inch high now, manically waving, like he had been shrunk.

As I turned the scope, Dad maneuvered to stay within the boundaries of the lens, as if to keep his stature small. He smiled weakly like I was taking his picture.

"Look at your mother, too."

I panned to the greenhouse and there she was: a woman inside a house inside a room inside a telescope. A strange sight. I imagined shooting a tiny arrow down that long corridor to *plink* against that tiny greenhouse.

"See what I mean?" Dad said.

I nodded. "Look at me," I said. I posed and drew an arrow back in the bow. I tried to look fierce as Dad looked through the telescope.

"That's perfect." He held me in it for a moment and then swung the telescope toward Mom. "Now you!"

She smiled between her plants, cupped a daisy in her hands, and batted her eyelashes. We all laughed. The snow picked up outside and scraped the windows, but it was warm inside and I felt safe in that house for the first time in a while.

If only it had been that easy, if something could have shrunk our trouble into something small and containable, something funny, we would have been okay. If Dad had been just a simple man, happy in his own living room with his family, if Mom had been just a pretty woman with her flowers, and me just a boy with his toys, we could have had more of these moments. But that was the wrong way to see things. Our laughs were fed by exhaustion and despair, and when the phone rang in the kitchen, it was like an alarm clock—crisp and abrasive—waking us up out of our dreams.

The call wasn't good, like most that come so late at night. Lovely from a train station in Baltimore, needing money. Or a faraway aunt to say Lovely had shown up in the middle of the night with a strange friend, only to disappear in the morning. Or the police. I forget which call came first, there got to be so many. She's out there still, living, we think.

I lost interest in the bow and arrows by that March, never hitting anything worth much. I tried other forms of violence over the years: broken windows, junior high fistfights, girlfriends with bruised arms. The arrows were just a good start.

The greenhouse stayed up another year and became filled with more and more monstrous plants—sunflowers, strange corn, even what I think was marijuana. But when Mom fashioned a lock for its door, Dad finally intervened.

That night he knocked on my door and I came out to the living room, groggy with sleep. Mom stood in the greenhouse, threatening with her spade, the door padlocked from the inside.

"Your sister called again," he said and then gestured toward the lock. I saw the problem. "Don't think I haven't thought of leaving myself. We could, you know, you and I." He rooted through his toolbox, which was lying open on the floor. "I've been trying. You know that. But then I think, maybe I should just let them all go ahead and get what they want. Some things can't be fixed, I'm sure you've realized. Can't shoot it. Can't even be nice to it." He pulled a hammer from the box. "I mean, when I tear this thing down, your mom may come at me with that spade."

"She won't," I said, but I wasn't sure. Mom's hair was matted with mud, her hands cut and bleeding. "And Lovely will come back, too, Dad."

"She might. But I got news for you. We're all nuts. You shouldn't be the last to know that. When I take this thing apart, you should get out of here. That's why I got you up."

He had never been so honest, and at that moment Dad became a hero of sanity, a rarity in my world. None of us had ever made the right move except for Lovely, and Dad and I both worshipped and hated her for it. She knew a bad situation when she saw one. Dad and I had just banged and fired at it all, stubborn, trying to make it work.

Lovely would not come back. And now the greenhouse, that last monument to good intentions gone awful, had to come down.

Dad approached with the hammer, and Mom slammed the blade of her spade into the plastic on level with his face. Dad looked back at me, sunk the claw between the greenhouse's wall and roof, and said, "Run."

SIAN M. JONES

Mills College

PILOT

Their mother was at home when the stroke hit. She was traveling from the kitchen to the living room. It was early morning on a Tuesday. She had a cup of coffee in her hand. She was going to watch the local news. Her leg must have been raised as she stepped, and when she put it back down, it must have been as if it weren't there. Half of her didn't work. She broke her arm falling, bruised all along one side of her body, her face. The mug shattered, and the coffee on the floor ran toward her and soaked her clothes. She landed near the couch, where the phone was sitting on one of the cushions. She dragged herself to it, dialed 911, and said, "Pilot."

Calla was first at the hospital, coming in out of the gloom of an overcast day to the emergency room, bright and cold. The nurses took her to the bed, where her mother, immobilized, blinked with one eye. The right side of her face was bruised—black, deep bruises with edges like cranberry jelly. Through the tubes, over the railing of the bed, Calla reached and put her hand on the bare spot she could reach, her mother's forehead. Her mother didn't say anything, just closed the blinking eye. The other eye stayed loose, half open, but Calla guessed she'd fallen asleep.

Calla heard Boyd talking to the nurse, asking appropriate questions, before he parted the privacy curtain. "Hey," he said.

Calla turned to look at her mother, at the monitors. "She's fine. I think. I think she's fine. Boyd, is she fine?"

"You tell me." He came to the same side of the bed and laid his hand over Calla's. "This is too much." He removed his hand. "This is too much like Dad."

Calla shook her head, like her hair was wet with rain. "No. She's awake. She is. This isn't like Dad."

When she was sixteen and Boyd twelve, their father had been taking out the garbage, dragging the wheeled can down the uneven driveway to the curb. It was December and there was snow on the ground. He slipped on some ice, keeping himself upright only by holding on to the can, wrenching his shoulder. "Are you all right?" their mother called from the porch, where she stood in the open door.

Their father moved his shoulder in soft circles as he came back in. Calla turned from the television to see what had happened. He ran his hand along his upper arm, massaging. "I'm fine," he said. "I think I may have pulled something." Which is why no one noticed anything when the pain spread to his chest and back and ate into him, ate up his heart. He died later that night, laid out on the living room carpet, Calla and Boyd dipping in and out, in and out, breathing for him, trying to push the blood through his body with the force of their palms against his chest. Their mother, crying, opened the door for the paramedics, who had arrived too late.

Now, in the hospital, Calla moved her hand from their mother's forehead, and their mother opened her eyes. "Audubon."

Calla and Boyd looked at each other, then at their mother.

"Polyphyry," she said, out of half her mouth.

"Did you get that?" asked Boyd.

"She did what with her keys?" asked Calla.

Their mother's internist, Dr. Rubin, had an office in the hospital, and it was there he took Calla and Boyd to talk. The office smelled like the books on the shelves that lined each wall. Calla and Boyd sat on leather chairs the color of claret. Dr. Rubin, wearing a yellow tie the color of an early crocus, leaned across his desk at them, his hands extended toward each other in a pyramid.

"Your mother," said Dr. Rubin, "had a large middle cerebral artery stroke this morning. Since she was brought in to us, she has continued having a series of smaller strokes. We're working with her blood levels now, but I have to acquaint you with the worst-case scenario."

"Which is?" said Boyd, attentively.

"One massive blowout?" said Calla.

Dr. Rubin smiled paternally. He'd seen Calla once or twice as a teenager for regular physicals. He'd had black hair, then, and asked her about boyfriends during her first breast exam. "That—or she just continues as she is, losing more function gradually. She's suffering paralysis throughout the right hemisphere, and you've noticed her speech has been severely affected. It's more than just the distortion related to the hemip lagia—she's suffering from what we call global aphasia. Her vocabulary has been cut loose from grammar and meaning. With these secondary strokes we're seeing, I'm not sure how much recovery we can really expect at this point."

It was quiet in the room, as cool ventilation blew down at them from a ceiling grid.

"Can she understand us?" asked Boyd.

Dr. Rubin looked at the papers on his desk for a moment. "It's one of those things where we don't know. She may seem to be re-sponsive to you when you speak, when in fact what you're seeing is an autologous biological response. A reflex."

Calla looked at Dr. Rubin, noticing the size of the pores in his nose, the faint hint of gray stubble at the turn of his jaw. She looked at Boyd, who didn't look back at her.

In the afternoon, their mother was transferred to a room in the in-tensive care unit. The walls of the room were mostly window glass, so the nurses at the center of the wing could see all the patients just by looking up. The room gave a false, unconvincing privacy.

"Blue quick loose," their mother said, pointing to the end of the bed with her good hand. Calla decided she was pointing at her foot, which had been bruised in the fall.

"That sounds pretty accurate to me," said Calla.

"Stop encouraging her," said Boyd.

Calla looked at her brother, not moving her face. "This is my poker face," she said. "Why? Because I'm a poker." She poked at the air in his direction.

Though he was several feet away in another waiting chair, he crossed his arms unconsciously to defend himself. "I like how mature you are about all this."

"I know you are, but what am I?"

Their mother's right arm lay in a complicated splint across her stomach. Her feet turned up, pigeon-toed, under the blue sheet. Her head seemed never to be at the right angle, so Calla moved the bed up and down using the control box.

"Calla," said Boyd. "It's not like the problem's a crick in her neck."

"Pasteur," said their mother.

"What she said," said Calla and let the gears grind on the mecha-nism some more.

Their mother had been treated for very high blood pressure for twenty years. Now the hospital staff was working to thin her blood like they were making sauce: add water, let simmer, add more.

"Oh, great," Calla said. "She'll have thin blood to go with her thin skin. It'll make it easier to see the clots. They can just hold her up to the light."

"You're very funny," said Boyd.

"Cistern. Custard." Their mother raised her left hand, pointing to the corner of the room.

"I see." Calla sat in the chair at the foot of their mother's bed, trying to figure out if the good left eye was blinking out Morse code.

"So," said Boyd.

"So," said Calla.

"Pariah salts," said their mother.

Calla got up and opened the curtain farther, so the outside light fell across the bed, struck sparks in the gray green iris of their mother's half-mast right eye.

"So," said Boyd. "You want the house?"

A few days later, Calla cut her mother's hair. Her mother liked to keep her hair short like a Buddhist nun's, and she'd been putting off having it cut when the stroke hit. Calla remembered her mother, complaining that it was getting too long the last time they'd talked on the phone, the evening before the stroke. Even though the nurses bathed her, her hair stuck up like cake frosting. Half her face didn't work, a half-moon of bruise. At least, Calla thought, her hair could be symmetrical. Calla brushed the clippings, like broken tinsel or very fine glass, off her mother's shoulders and neck. The skin of her neck was soft, pale near the new silver hairline like grass leached of color at the edge of melting snow.

"Bare east corner," said her mother, tilting her head, trying to look up at her.

"I know," said Calla. "I get that."

On Saturday, when Calla arrived at the hospital, Boyd and his family were already there—Boyd and Dara and the five kids. Calla was avalanched with hugs by the four youngest children, but the eldest, her niece, Pleasant, stood by her grandmother's bed, holding her hand. Calla joined Pleasant, giving her a hug. When Calla kissed her mother on the cheek, her mother looked up at her, her half look. "Comets apparatus underling," she said.

"You bet, Mom," said Calla.

"She's talking to Grandpa," said Pleasant. "He's in the room here. He's waiting for her. She's talking to him in angel talk. She's dying, you know."

Calla shifted slightly on her feet. "Who told you that?"

"I did," said Boyd.

Calla looked at him. "Do you know what dying means, Pleasant?" She kept her eyes on Boyd.

"Yes. She's going to be with Jesus Christ. Jesus taught her to talk like this. So when she gets to the"—she paused over the words she'd learned in Primary—"Celestial Kingdom, she can talk to everybody there."

"Goats," said their mother. "Rise."

"Yeah," said Calla. "They do."

Three weeks after the stroke, their mother was moved from the hospital to a rehabilitation center out in the south valley. The center was a nursing home with a fancy title, and it was a thirty-minute drive from work, but Calla went there each night when she got off. The remains of her mother's dinner would still be on the table that swung over her bed. Calla would turn off *Wheel of Fortune* on the television in the corner, which the staff had left on. She'd help her mother drink water from a paper cup with a bendy straw, lifting her mother's good hand to the cup until she grasped it herself. Her mother would half smile at her, and her head would dangle a little to one side, in a way that Calla took as a nod.

"Pierces corrugated."

"Yup," said Calla, tucking in the blanket around her mother's feet. "Point taken."

Calla went to her mother's house to bring in the mail. She opened the front door with her own key and walked inside the old house, turning on lamps. The house smelled like dusk. She stopped herself from calling out to her mother, who, it seemed, should have been there. When her father had died, it had taken years before she stopped expecting him to walk around certain corners. As a teenager, she'd tiptoed around the house, whipping her head around like a dog hearing a noise, trying to catch sight of her father before he slid away once more.

Since her mother had gone into the hospital Calla hadn't been to the house more than a few times. Dust collected over her mother's books, the curlicues and curves of the frames holding the family photographs on the mantel, the flat surfaces of the piano and television, the unswept hardwood floors. When she opened the back doors to look out at the dark yard, the hinges seemed to resist a little, the lock stubborn. When she closed them again, the doors fell together in relief.

She stood over the answering machine, red digits blinking up at her. She'd stopped listening to the messages after the first few weeks. The people who were important knew her mother wasn't there. Those who didn't, Calla figured, didn't deserve to know.

She knew the refrigerator was empty, but she opened it anyway, inhaling among the plastic fumes the residue of old cheese, the smell of hard apples her mother had been keeping in the crisper, and butter. She'd stood in front of the refrigerator so many times as a teenager, swaying back and forth, researching the food. Habit had not been broken.

The dishes were all done and put away. She ran the tap into the sink for a moment, to make sure it still worked. The water fell against the stainless steel, a resonant drum.

In the upstairs and downstairs bathrooms she flushed the toilets, heard the speed of the water as it rushed down and out of the house pipes toward the sewer.

She'd done all her mother's laundry, which she'd found in piles around the bedroom. Everything was hung up or in drawers. Her mother had very simple clothing needs now—the loose sweatpants, the hospital-style V-neck top, the fuzzy slipper socks.

She'd made her mother's bed, paid her mother's bills, raked the flat, wide sycamore leaves in the front yard into orange bags to be picked up by the city.

She was out of things to do at the house. It wasn't so strange that she only came here like a security guard patrolling the museum that was her mother's life.

The phone's ringing woke Calla. "Hello?" It was dark in her apartment. She'd gotten to the phone through the darkness, suddenly an adept sleepwalker.

"Hello, dear. What am I doing here?" The voice on the other end was clear, brisk, precious.

Calla shivered in her pajamas. "Mom?"

"Where am I?"

Calla wrapped her ribs with her free hand, trying to warm herself. "I don't know, Mom. Where are you?"

"Well, it's a room. It's draped. Someone has draped fabric from the ceiling. That's strange, isn't it? Remember, dear, how we used to do that for you, your father and I? We'd make a stage between the living room and the dining room by hanging that sheet, and you and your brother performed 'Tarzan.' And you wore my beads—faience, weren't they?"

"I was the African queen."

"That's right. You wore a towel for a dress. You used to like doing that, didn't you? The towel as the dress. You were so dramatic. Well, you still are."

The objects in her apartment began to rise out of the darkness, gray geometry asserting itself. She blinked. "Mom, where are you?"

"I told you, I don't know. A room. It's draped. It's not by any means dark—oh, there's a door open, and light from the hallway. A woman just walked by the door."

"Oh, good. A nurse. It sounds like you're in your room."

"This isn't my room."

"Not your room at home. You're in a hospital, I mean, a rehab unit."

"Am I ill?"

"You have been. Has the nurse come back? She must have heard you."

"Shut up!" Calla heard in the background. An old woman's voice. The woman with the clicking dentures, her mother's latest roommate. "Shut up!"

"Someone just threw a pillow at me," said her mother.

"It is kind of late to be calling," said Calla.

"Shut up!" said the roommate. "You don't make no sense! Shut up!"

Calla shivered again. "Mom, go back to sleep. We can talk in the morning. I'll come by. Do you think you can sleep?"

"Well, yes. You know me when my head hits the pillow."

"Okay. Good night."

"Good night."

The next morning, when Calla arrived at the rehabilitation center, a senior citizen group was playing harmonicas in the entryway. They were playing "Oh, Susannah," as she made her way up the ramp of the hallway to her mother's room. She knocked before swinging the door open. Her mother's roommate was out. In her own bed, Calla's mother leaned back against pillows, looking at the sway of the blinds in the ventilation draft. The swinging blinds cast cutout rectangles of shadow across the room and back. "Hi, Mom," said Calla, kissing the cheek that was toward her, the good cheek. "What does Dr. Rubin have to say about your fancy self talking?"

Her mother turned to her, half smiling. "Parallel overboard."

Calla stood very still.

"Bus, bus," said her mother.

"Oh," said Calla, dragging a chair from the wall to the bedside. The chair was so low she couldn't really see up on the bed where her mother was. "I see."

About half an hour later, one of the nurses brought the clicking dentures back into the room. Dentures was groaning and had to be helped into the bed. "We've just come back from physical therapy," said the nurse.

"Not torture, then," said Calla. "Thanks for clearing that up."

Dentures made a few noises. The nurse turned. "Where did you see it last?"

"Are you looking for this?" Calla reached under her mother's bed for the pillow that had been in her line of sight since she'd sat down. "Is this yours?"

"Thank you," said the nurse. "Old folks' pillow fight, I guess."

"She don't make no sense," said Dentures, clicking loudly. "Talks all the time, but she don't make no sense."

"Below asphalt carousel," said her mother.

Later, Calla dropped by her brother's house. The kids were already in bed. Dara was doing the dishes by hand. The sound of the water flattened and broadened each time a plate or cup was introduced into the flow.

Boyd and Calla sat at the kitchen table. "Mom talked to me last night," said Calla.

"Hmm," said Boyd, biting into the bologna sandwich that was his late dinner.

"I don't mean gibberish. She called me on the phone last night."

He put down his sandwich. "Mom's talking again? You didn't call me?"

Calla reached for the packaged bread and pulled out a slice. "She's not talking anymore. I mean, she is talking—just gibberish again."

"So it was just temporary? Is that common? What'd Dr. Rubin say?"

"I don't know. I didn't talk to him."

"What?"

"I didn't think he'd believe me. She's not talking now."

"You should have told him. It's got to mean something."

"Okay. I'll tell him. Tomorrow." She pinched pieces of bread off and put them in her mouth.

Boyd took a meditative bite of his sandwich. "Well," he said through a mouthful, "what did she say?"

"Nothing really."

"Nothing?"

"Not really."

He took another bite, nodding. After swallowing, he said, "What did you say?"

She popped the last of her bread into her mouth. "Not enough."

Calla caught Dr. Rubin in the hall outside her mother's room, while he was on his rounds. They stood at angles on the ramped floor.

"I can't say that I detect any improvement," said Dr. Rubin.

"She talked to me."

Dr. Rubin clicked his pen closed and put it in his pocket. "Calla, isn't it possible you were asleep?"

Calla decided she hated his tie. It was the color of asparagus. "So, in your medical opinion it was a dream."

"I'd like to anticipate that level of recovery, but I can't." He shifted patient charts from one arm to the other.

"Isn't there anything in the literature—some kind of transient recovery? I mean, maybe there's still blockage there, but it's floating." Calla held on to the image of a cloudburst, gutters overflowing, sewer grates blocked with leaves, clearing, blocking again.

Calla called Boyd at work. "Don't you think that there are things called miracles?"

"This from the atheist?" said Boyd.

"Sorry, I meant, random inexplicable confluences in a kind of chaos theory sense."

"So, it was a dream."

"I was awake."

Boyd breathed a little into the phone. "It's okay that it was a dream, Calla. I get it, you know? I wish I'd dreamed it, too."

She twisted the phone cord around her finger, released it. "Well, I was awake, but thanks anyway."

———

Calla watched her mother sleep Sunday afternoon away. She'd brought books on speech therapy, the physiology of speech, the anatomy of the brain, studies of brain damage cases. In the end, she returned to her mother's copy of Eliot's "The Waste Land," which had been by her mother's bed at home, half read, on top of a copy of Joyce's *Ulysses*. She was reading and rereading. Her mother breathed, her sheet-covered chest lifting and closing like a valve.

Before she left, Calla kissed her mother and whispered, "What I really want is an explanation before you go, if you can manage it."

As she was in the doorway, she heard, "Of what?"

She turned back. Her mother was looking at her, both eyes tracking. "What shall I explain?"

Calla leaned out the door into the hall, looked both ways. There was no one in the halls except, at the far end, a man with slippered feet walking his wheelchair forward. She looked back. Her mother was struggling to sit up in the bed, using her good arm. Calla rushed to her and propped the pillows up behind her.

"Well," she said, "you can start with my father."

Her mother nodded, the late winter sunlight sparkling her hair. "Well," said her mother. "Your father and I met—is this what you want to know? Through mutual friends—only they hated him, and I loved him. They had talked so badly about him—he was arrogant and conceited, he had no respect for what others thought. But I was tired of them, I suppose, tired of people who said the same thing and thought the same thing. I was a bit of an iconoclast, myself."

"You were not," said Calla. "You lived your entire life in one place."

Her mother tried to straighten both shoulders, but the right one stayed slumped. "I was."

"I know all this," said Calla. "You went hiking on Antelope Island. Up in the rocks, you cut your hand on a broken bottle. Dad wrapped your hand in his handkerchief—clean, presumably—and then he wouldn't stop holding your hand for the rest of the way down—to maintain pressure, he told you."

"Yes," said her mother, laying her good hand in her lap. "He was a bad liar."

Calla lowered the nearest railing on the bed and sat on the edge of the mattress. "Is this okay? Does my sitting here make you tip?"

Her mother fluttered her good hand dismissively. "He wanted to do things, he wanted to publish books and change the way people thought about history. So he could change how they thought about the present, I guess." The skin around the bad eye drooped a little, but the lids held the iris straight forward at Calla.

She knew these things, this list of her father's aspirations, the weight of them in boxes in the room that had been his old office. "But what about me? What about Boyd? What about us?"

"Oh," said her mother, half smiling to herself. "You know how he felt about you."

"I don't. I know all the things that people said—I know what all his colleagues said at the memorial. But they'd have to say that, wouldn't they? They'd have to say to a sixteen-year-old and twelve-year-old, they'd have to say—he loved you. He loved you more than anything else in the world. Because he wasn't around to contradict them."

The right corner of her mother's mouth pointed to the floor, twitched a little. "You're wrong, Calla. You have it mixed up."

"I'd hear you two talking in the night, in the bedroom, but I couldn't hear what you were saying. Sometimes I'd hear my name, and I'd try to make up what it was about, based on the way he said my name. I didn't know."

"He was a reticent man, that's all. He wasn't very demonstrative. But you knew—you have to know how he felt about you. You were the best thing in his life."

"Then how," Calla asked, "could he have left us?"

Her mother was quiet. She sat in the hospital bed, her good knee pulled up under the sheet, her back resting against the pillow. The hospital gown was a soft semicircle at her neck, a soft checker-print over her chest. She touched her head, rubbed the stubble a little. "He didn't leave us, Calla. He died. You can't resist dying."

Calla leaned close. "Well, try, damn it."

"Ah," said her mother. "Bellicose ashland bay."

"Don't you think you're just hearing what you want to hear?" said Boyd. They stood in the hallway outside their mother's room.

"She did tell me that you're adopted."

"I'm serious."

"Me, too. You were actually a Cambodian boat baby."

"Calla. Are you taking your medication?"

"My sense of humor cannot be treated by antidepressants."

"Calla."

"Yes, and besides auditory hallucination was never a component of my mental illness. Obsessional fantasies about killing you, however..."

Boyd leaned back against the wall, arms crossed. "Look, I'm pretty close to the brink myself, okay? I don't need you flipping out, too. I mean, this is—" He looked down at the utility carpet, the loops tight so the rubber-tipped feet of walkers slid easily, didn't catch. "I've been so involved with life, you know—with the kids. Adding to life, not taking away. I didn't want to feel death again. I don't want to feel this." Tears shunted away from his eyes down his throat. She could hear them.

She stayed on the opposite side of the hall. "Doesn't your religion give you some way to deal with this?"

"Yup." He wiped the tears from under his nose. "I wish you believed."

"Yeah," she said. "Right back at you."

On a notepad in her purse, Calla would write a series of questions to ask her mother in case of isolated coherence: *When did I take my first step? What were the extra spices Grandma put in her pumpkin pies? What was the best day of your life? What does it feel like when you can't talk? Does it feel like you're trying to fit into clothing that's too small? What do you think about when I'm not here? Do you think about dying? Tell me about death.*

She would ask the questions even though her mother wasn't making sense, and sometimes when Boyd was in the room, just to annoy him. She'd pull out her pad and read, "How wrong is Boyd to think that he's your favorite?"

"Spruce, parsley, center." Their mother's head would tilt back and forth, a little unsteady.

Calla stood at the end of the bed. "And when do you think Boyd will start losing his hair like Grandma's family? He already has the gut."

Boyd would sit in the chair by the side of the bed, looking not at their mother, but at Calla. "How'd you manage to get Calla promoted out of special ed, Mom? What grade in high school was she when she could finally dress herself?"

"Mom, Boyd thinks you left him your millions, but I know that's not true. You've buried the gold bullion in a secret location in the backyard, near the graves of all our parakeets, haven't you?"

Boyd snorted. "Not so secret anymore. I know where the graves are."

"Ha! Was Boyd always this easy to throw off the scent?"

In the early spring, like an ice floe thawing, clots began traveling through their mother's bloodstream, and lodged again in her head. She was transferred back to the hospital.

Boyd was there first this time, and he met Calla at the front entrance.

"I thought they had this under control," she said.

"Me, too. Dr. Rubin says—"

"Fuck Dr. Rubin," said Calla. "Where's Mom?"

Boyd led her through the populated daytime halls of the hospital, doctors standing along the walls talking to each other about their golf games and their white-water rapid trips, candy stripers with rolling trays full of flowers and balloons, other family members wandering with blank faces toward the cafeteria.

Their mother was in a different room than the last time, but with the same glass walls. She was at the center of a series of tubes again, with a new tube at her nose because one lung had shut down like an unplugged vacuum. Her right eye was open, and tears ran from it slowly, like they weren't water but Karo syrup.

"Mom," said Calla, entering the room, Boyd right behind her.

"Calla," said their mother, half her mouth whispering.

"Are you in pain?" Calla crossed the room to hear her better.

"Yes," she said. "No," she said. "I can't feel except—"

Calla touched her mother's cheek, pushing away the tears. "What do you want me to do?"

"Cover my knee," said her mother. "It's cold."

Calla reached down and pulled the blanket over the knee, straightening the leg so that it lay flat. "Better?"

"Yes," said her mother. "Yes." The lid on the good eye lowered, and on that side, her face relaxed.

"Uh, Calla," said Boyd. "Can I—can I talk to you out in the—"

Calla nodded, touched her mother's hand where it lay against the blanket, followed him out.

Outside the door, she noticed he was shaking. "Oh, Boyd." She reached up and put her arms around him. He tucked his head against her neck, and she could feel his breath in and out, rough and smooth.

"It's all right," said Boyd. "I believe you."

Calla watched the nurses in their loose circus-print scrubs turn in and out of the transparent rooms. "You believe what?"

He stood back from her. "You don't—" was all he said for a moment.

Calla felt cold, the way she had that first night, during the phone call, standing half awake in her room.

Boyd said, "She isn't talking. But, Jesus, Calla—you are."

Dully, she said, "Well, yeah."

"In gibberish."

Calla stood for a moment, blinked against the fluorescent lighting. "What did I say? What did she say?"

"She said—" He frowned, his eyebrows closing downward. "'Pilot,' and you said, 'Hour plus microfiche,' or something like that. I can't remember exactly. What were you saying?"

Calla listened to the monitors in her mother's room, audible beeps through the doorway, marking out her mother's life. "Oh," she said. "Enough."

A third stroke swallowed their mother whole that night. The morticians came to the hospital in fresh suits, and drove her body north to the cemetery where their grandparents and their father were buried, in among blue spruce decorated with buds like Christmas lights. When they were choosing the inscription for the stone, Boyd made Calla write it: *Blue teeth gas wire.*

"I can see myself explaining this to the kids," he said. "When they're older. But it's clear enough to me."

CONTRIBUTORS

ANDREW FOSTER ALTSCHUL is a former Wallace Stegner Fellow at Stanford University and teaches creative writing at the University of San Francisco. His work has appeared or is forthcoming in *Swink, Pleiades, The Florida Review,* and others. "A New Kind of Gravity" is included in his collection of short stories, *The One Life.* He is currently at work on a novel about punk rock, poetry, and suicide.

JESSICA ANTHONY grew up in a small agricultural community in upstate New York, sandwiched between a Native American reservation and a cutlery factory. This has shaped her worldview. Her stories have appeared in *McSweeney's, Mid-American Review, CutBank, New American Writing,* and elsewhere. She has won several awards for her fiction, including George Mason University's Thesis Fellowship and the Summer Literary Seminars fiction contest and nominations for the Pushcart Prize, and she is the first recipient of *McSweeney's* Amanda Davis Highwire Fiction Award. She currently teaches literature at the University of Southern Maine and lives in Portland with her husband, music producer Jon Wyman. She is thrilled to have been selected for inclusion in this anthology, and is at work on a novel, firmly titled *The Convalescent.*

SARAH BLACKMAN was born and raised in the Washington, D.C., area and is currently a student in the MFA program at the University of Alabama in Tuscaloosa. She is simultaneously compiling a collection of short stories and working on a novel.

MICHELLE REGALADO DEATRICK recently received an MFA from the University of Michigan, where she was the recipient of a Colby Fellowship and of Hopwood Awards in fiction and poetry. She has also studied creative writing through Stanford's Continuing Studies Program. Her poetry has appeared in *Poet Lore.* Michelle is working on a novel and on a collection of short stories set in East Africa, where she lived for several years.

AMBER DERMONT is the Faculty Fiction Writer-in-Residence at Rice University in Houston. Her fiction and creative nonfiction have appeared in *Alaska Quarterly*

Review, The Georgia Review, The Gettysburg Review, Open City, Seneca Review, Tin House, and *Zoetrope: All-Story.* She has completed a collection of short stories, *A Splendid Wife,* and is at work on her first novel.

SEAN ENNIS is a Philadelphia native and now an MFA student at the University of Mississippi. His work has appeared in *Pindeldyboz* and *storySouth* and is forthcoming in *Stories from the Blue Moon Café.* He is currently working on a novel in stories.

MATT FREIDSON lived in Hanoi, Vietnam, in 1997–1998 and managed a Vietnamese refugee center in London in 2001–2003. The first half of "Liberty" draws on the research of his wife, Dr. Rachel Burr. Other sections of his novel-in-stories, *This Side of the River,* have appeared in *New England Review, Confrontation, Virginia Quarterly Review, StoryQuarterly, Ontario Review, Michigan Quarterly Review,* and elsewhere. He is currently working on *Invisible Trades,* a book on refugees in London.

KAUI HART HEMMINGS is the author of *House of Thieves,* a collection of stories. She was a Richard Scowcroft and Stegner Fellow in the Wallace Stegner Program at Stanford, and her fiction appears in *StoryQuarterly, Zoetrope: All-Story,* and *The Best American Nonrequired Reading 2004.*

Born in Salt Lake City, SIAN M. JONES graduated with a BA from the University of Utah. She recently completed an MFA at Mills College, where she was managing editor of the experimental journal *580 Split,* received Ardella Mills Prizes for fiction and essay, and was first runner-up for the Amanda Davis Thesis Award. She's currently at work on a collection of short stories.

JAMIE KEENE received her MFA from the University of Oregon. She lives in northern California and is working on a novel.

ALBERT E. MARTINEZ grew up in Coronado, California, and Santa Fe, New Mexico. After traveling through Southeast Asia and working in San Francisco during the late 1990s, he earned his MFA at New Mexico State University. He currently lives in Berkeley and is completing work on a novel.

GREGORY PLEMMONS received his BA from Wofford College and his MD from the Medical University of South Carolina and is currently an MFA student with Bennington Writing Seminars. He is assistant professor of pediatrics at Vanderbilt University in Nashville, Tennessee. He is currently at work on a novel. Excerpted here is the opening chapter.

Born and raised in Bulgaria, VANYA RAINOVA did not begin writing until moving to her current home, northern California. She is working toward her MFA and also working on a novel that evolved from the completion of "Trampoline."

JENNIFER SHAFF received her MFA from Emerson College in Boston, Massachusetts. She teaches English at East Hartford High School in East Hartford, Connecticut. She is currently working on a novel.

MELANIE WESTERBERG's story "Watermark" first appeared in the *Mid-American Review,* and has been nominated for a Pushcart Prize. She received her BA from the University of Iowa and her MFA from California College of the Arts, where she won the All College Honors Award. She lives in San Francisco, and is at work on a collection of short stories.

PARTICIPANTS

The Advanced Fiction Workshop with
Carol Edgarian & Tom Jenks
P.O. Box 29272
San Francisco, CA 94129-9991
415/346-4477

American University
MFA Program in Creative Writing
Department of Literature
Washington, DC 20016-8047
202/885-2973

Arizona State University
College of Liberal Arts and Sciences
Department of Literature—Creative
Writing Program
Tempe, AZ 85287
480/965-3528

The Banff Centre for the Arts
Writing Studio
Box 1020, Station 34
107 Tunnel Mountain Drive
Banff, AB TIL 1H5
403/762-6100

Binghamton University
Creative Writing Program
Department of English, General
Literature, and Rhetoric
P.O. Box 6000
Binghamton, NY 13902-6000
607/777-2713

Boise State University
MFA Program in Writing
1910 University Drive
Boise, ID 83725
208/426-1246

Boston University
Creative Writing Program
236 Bay State Road
Boston, MA 02215
617/353-2510

Bowling Green State University
Department of English
Creative Writing Program
Bowling Green, OH 43403-0215
419/372-8370

The Bread Loaf Writers' Conference
Middlebury College—P&W
Middlebury, VT 05753
802/443-5286

California College of the Arts
IIII Eighth Street
San Francisco, CA 94107
415/703-9500

California State University, Long Beach
Department of English
1250 Bellflower Boulevard
Long Beach, CA 90840
562/985-4225

California State University, Sacramento
Department of English
6000 J Street
Sacramento, CA 95819
916/278-6586

The City College of New York
Graduate Program in English
138th Street and Convent Avenue
New York, NY 10031
212/650-6694

Colorado State University
MFA Creative Writing Program
English Department, 359 Eddy Hall
Fort Collins, CO 80523-1773
970/491-6428

Columbia College
Department of Fiction Writing
600 South Michigan Avenue
Chicago, IL 60605-1997
312/344-7611

Columbia University
Division of Writing, School of the Arts
2960 Broadway, 415 Dodge
New York, NY 10027
212/854-4391

Cornell University
English Department
Ithaca, NY 14853
607/255-6800

DePaul University
Department of English
802 West Belden Avenue
Chicago, IL 60614-3214
773/325-7485

Eastern Washington University
Creative Writing Program
705 W. First Avenue, MS#1
Spokane, WA 99201-3900
509/623-4221

Emerson College
Writing, Literature and Publishing
120 Boylston Street
Boston, MA 02116
617/824-8750

Fairleigh Dickinson
MFA in Creative Writing Program
285 Madison Avenue, M-MS3-01
Madison, NJ 07940
973/443-8632

Fine Arts Work Center in
Provincetown
24 Pearl Street
Provincetown, MA 02657
508/487-8678

Florida International University
Department of English
Biscayne Bay Campus
3000 NE 151st Street
Miami, FL 33181
305/919-5857

Florida State University
Creative Writing Program
Department of English
Tallahassee, FL 32306-1580
850/644-4230

George Mason University
Creative Writing Program
MS 3E4—English Department
Fairfax, VA 22030
703/993-1185

Hamline University
Graduate Liberal Studies—MS 1730
1536 Hewitt Avenue
St. Paul, MN 55104
651/523-2800

Hollins University
Department of English
P.O. Box 9677
Roanoke, VA 24020
540/362-6317

The Humber School for Writers
Humber College
3199 Lakeshore Boulevard West
Toronto, ON M8V 1K8
416/675-6622

Hunter College
MFA Program in Writing
Department of English
695 Park Avenue
New York, NY 10021
212/772-5164

Indiana University
Department of English
Ballantine Hall 442
1020 East Kirkwood Avenue
Bloomington, IN 47405-6601
812/855-8224

The Indiana University Writers'
Conference
Ballantine Hall 464
1020 East Kirkwood Avenue
Bloomington, IN 47405-7103
812/855-1877

Johns Hopkins University
The Writing Seminars
3400 North Charles Street
Baltimore, MD 21218
410/516-7563

Johns Hopkins Writing Program—
Washington
1717 Massachusetts Avenue, NW
Suite 104
Washington, DC 20036
202/452-1280

Kansas State University
Department of English
108 English/Counseling Services
Building
Manhattan, KS 66506-6501
785/532-6716

The Loft Literary Center
Mentor Series Program
Open Book, Suite 200
1011 Washington Avenue South
Minneapolis, MN 55415
612/215-2575

Louisiana State University
MFA Program
Department of English
Allen Hall
Baton Rouge, LA 70803-5001
225/578-2236

Loyola Marymount University
1 LMU Drive
University Hall
Los Angeles, CA 90045
310/338-3018

McNeese State University
Department of Languages
P.O. Box 92655
Lake Charles, LA 70609-2655
337/475-5326

Miami University
Creative Writing Program
Oxford, OH 45056
513/529-5221

The Michener Center for Writers
University of Texas
J. Frank Dobie House
702 East Dean Keeton Street
Austin, TX 78705
512/471-1601

Mills College
Creative Writing Program
Mills Hall 311
5000 MacArthur Boulevard
Oakland, CA 94613
510/430-3309

Minnesota State University, Mankato
English Department
230 Armstrong Hall
Mankato, MN 56001
507/389-2117

Mississippi State University
Department of English
Drawer E
Mississippi State, MS 39762
662/325-3644

Napa Valley Writers' Conference
Napa Valley College
1088 College Avenue
St. Helena, CA 94574
707/967-2900

Naropa University
Program in Writing and Poetics
2130 Arapahoe Avenue
Boulder, CO 80302
303/546-3540

New Mexico State University
Department of English
Box 30001—Department 3E
Las Cruces, NM 88003-8001
505/646-3931

New York University
Graduate Program in Creative Writing
19 University Place, Room 219
New York, NY 10003
212/998-8816

Ohio State University
English Department
421 Denney Hall
164 West 17th Avenue
Columbus, OH 43210-1370
614/292-6065

PEN Prison Writing Committee
PEN American Center
568 Broadway
Suite 401
New York, NY 10012
212/334-1660, Ext. 117

Pennsylvania State University
Department of English
112 Burrowes Building
University Park, PA 16802-6200
814/863-3069

Purdue University
Department of English
Heavilon Hall
West Lafayette, IN 47907-2038
765/494-3740

Sage Hill Writing Experience
Box 1731
Saskatoon, SK S7K 3S1
306/652-7395

Saint Mary's College of California
MFA Program in Creative Writing
P.O. Box 4686
Moraga, CA 94575-4686
925/631-4762

San Diego State University
MFA Program
Department of English and
Comparative Literature
San Diego, CA 92182-8140
619/594-5431

San Francisco State University
Creative Writing Department, College
of Humanities
1600 Holloway Avenue
San Francisco, CA 94132-4162
415/338-1891

Sarah Lawrence College
Graduate Writing Program
1 Mead Way
Slonim House
Bronxville, NY 10708-5999
914/395-2371

Sewanee Writers' Conference
310 St. Luke's Hall
735 University Avenue
Sewanee, TN 37383-1000
931/598-1141

Sonoma State University
Department of English
1801 East Cotati Avenue
Rohnert Park, CA 94928-3609
707/664-2140

Southampton College of Long Island
University
MFA Program in English and Writing
English Department
Southampton, NY 11968
631/283-4000

Stanford University
Creative Writing Program
Department of English
Stanford, CA 94305-2087
650/725-1208

Syracuse University
Program in Creative Writing
401 Hall of Languages
Syracuse, NY 13244-1170
315/443-2174

Taos Summer Writers' Conference
Department of English
MSC 03 2170
University of New Mexico
Albuquerque, NM 87131-0001
505/277-6347

Temple University
Creative Writing Program
Anderson Hall, 10th Floor
Philadelphia, PA 19122
215/204-1796

Texas A&M University
Creative Writing Program
English Department
College Station, TX 77843-4227
409/845-9936

Texas State University
MFA Program in Creative Writing
Department of English
601 University Drive
San Marcos, TX 78666-4616
512/245-2163

Texas Tech University
Creative Writing Program
Department of English
Box 43091
Lubbock, TX 79409
806/742-2501

Tin House Writers Conference
P.O. Box 10500
Portland, OR 97210
503/219-0622

University at Albany, SUNY
The Graduate Program in English
Studies
Department of English
Humanities Building
Albany, NY 12222
518/442-4055

University of Alabama
Program in Creative Writing
Department of English
103 Morgan Hall
P.O. Box 870244
Tuscaloosa, AL 35487-0244
205/348-0766

University of Arizona
Creative Writing Program
Department of English
Modern Languages Building #67
Tucson, AZ 85721-0067
520/621-3880

University of Arkansas
Program in Creative Writing
Department of English
333 Kimpel Hall
Fayetteville, AR 72701
479/575-4301

University of California, Davis
Graduate Creative Writing Program
Department of English
One Shields Avenue
Davis, CA 95616
530/752-1658

University of Cincinnati
Creative Writing Program
Department of English & Comparative
Literature
ML 69
Cincinnati, OH 45221-0069
513/556-5924

University of Colorado at Boulder
Creative Writing Program
Department of English
Campus Box 226
Boulder, CO 80309-0226
303/492-7381

University of Florida
Creative Writing Program
Department of English
P.O. Box 117310
Gainesville, FL 32611-7310
352/392-6650

University of Houston
Creative Writing Program
Department of English
Houston, TX 77204-3015
713/743-2952

University of Idaho
Creative Writing Program
Department of English
P.O. Box 441102
Moscow, ID 83844-1102
208/885-6156

University of Illinois at Chicago
Program for Writers
Department of English MC/162
601 South Morgan Street
Chicago, IL 60607-7120
312/413-2229

University of Iowa
Program in Creative Writing
102 Dey House
507 N. Clinton Street
Iowa City, IA 52242
319/335-0416

University of Louisiana at Lafayette
Creative Writing Concentration
Department of English
P.O. Box 44691
Lafayette, LA 70504-4691
337/482-6906

University of Maine
Master's in English Program
5752 Neville Hall
Orono, ME 04469-5752
207/581-3822

University of Maryland
Creative Writing Program
Department of English
3119F Susquehanna Hall
College Park, MD 20742
301/405-3820

University of Massachusetts, Amherst
MFA Program in English
Bartlett Hall
130 Hicks Way
Amherst, MA 01003-9269
413/545-2332

University of Memphis
MFA Creative Writing Program
Department of English
College of Arts & Sciences
Memphis, TN 38152-3510
901/678-2651

University of Michigan
MFA Program in Creative Writing
Department of English
3187 Angell Hall
Ann Arbor, MI 48109-1003
734/615-3710

University of Minnesota
MFA Program in Creative Writing
Department of English
207 Church Street, SE
Minneapolis, MN 55455
612/625-6366

University of Mississippi
MFA Program in Creative Writing
English Department
Bondurant Hall C128
Oxford, MS 38677-1848
662/915-7439

University of Missouri–Columbia
Creative Writing Program
Department of English
107 Tate Hall
Columbia, MO 65211-1500
573/884-7773

University of Missouri–St. Louis
MFA in Creative Writing Program
Department of English
8001 Natural Bridge Road
St. Louis, MO 63121
314/516-6845

University of Montana
Creative Writing Program
Department of English
Missoula, MT 59812-1013
406/243-5231

University of Nebraska, Lincoln
Creative Writing Program
Department of English
202 Andrews Hall
Lincoln, NE 68588-0333
402/472-3191

University of Nevada, Las Vegas
MFA in Creative Writing
Department of English
4505 Maryland Parkway
Las Vegas, NV 89154-5011
702/895-3533

University of New Hampshire
Creative Writing Program
Department of English
Hamilton Smith Hall
95 Main Street
Durham, NH 03824-3574
603/862-3963

University of New Mexico
Graduate Program in Creative Writing
Department of English Language and
Literature
Humanities Bldg., 2nd Floor
Albuquerque, NM 87131-1106
505/277-6347

University of New Orleans
Creative Writing Workshop
College of Liberal Arts
Lakefront
New Orleans, LA 70148
504/280-7454

University of North Carolina at
Greensboro
MFA Writing Program
Department of English
P.O. Box 26170
Greensboro, NC 27402-6170
336/334-5459

University of North Carolina at
Wilmington
MFA in Writing Program
Department of Creative Writing
601 S. College Road
Wilmington, NC 28403
910/962-7063

University of North Texas
Creative Writing Division
Department of English
P.O. Box 311307
Denton, TX 76203-1307
940/565-2050

University of Notre Dame
Creative Writing Program
340 O'Shaughnessy Hall
Notre Dame, IN 46556-5639
574/631-7526

University of Oregon
Program in Creative Writing
P.O. Box 5243
Eugene, OR 97403-5243
541/346-0509

University of San Francisco
MFA in Writing Program
Program Office, Lone Mountain 340
2130 Fulton Street
San Francisco, CA 94117-1080
415/422-2382

University of South Carolina
MFA Program in Creative Writing
Department of English
Columbia, SC 29208
803/777-4204

University of Southern Mississippi
Center for Writers
Box 5144
118 College Drive
Hattiesburg, MS 39406-5144
601/266-4321

University of Tennessee
Creative Writing Program
Department of English
301 McClung Tower
Knoxville, TN 37996
865/974-5401

University of Texas at El Paso
MFA Program with a Bilingual Option
English Department
Hudspeth Hall, Room 113
El Paso, TX 79968-0526
915/747-5731

University of Utah
Creative Writing Program
255 S. Central Campus Drive
Room 3500
Salt Lake City, UT 84112-0494
801/581-7131

University of Virginia
Creative Writing Program
Department of English
P.O. Box 400121
Charlottesville, VA 22904-4121
434/924-6675

University of Washington
Creative Writing Program
Box 354330
Seattle, WA 98195-4330
206/543-9865

University of Wisconsin–Madison
Program in Creative Writing
English Department
Helen C. White Hall
600 N. Park Street
Madison, WI 53706
608/263-3800

University of Wisconsin–Milwaukee
Creative Writing Program
Department of English
Box 413
Milwaukee, WI 53201
414/229-4243

Unterberg Poetry Center
Writing Program
92nd Street Y
1395 Lexington Avenue
New York, NY 10128
212/415-5760

Vermont College of Union Institute &
University
MFA in Writing
36 College Street
Montpelier, VT 05602
800/336-6794

Virginia Commonwealth University
MFA in Creative Writing Program
Department of English
P.O. Box 842005
Richmond, VA 23284-2005
804/828-1329

Washington University
The Writing Program
Campus Box 1122
One Brookings Drive
St. Louis, MO 63130-4899
314/935-5190

Wayne State University
Creative Writing Program
English Department
Detroit, MI 48202
313/577-2450

The Wesleyan Writers Conference
Wesleyan University
Middletown, CT 06459
860/685-3604

West Virginia University
Creative Writing Program
Department of English
P.O. Box 6269
Morgantown, WV 26506-6269
304/293-3107

Western Michigan University
Graduate Program in Creative Writing
Department of English
Kalamazoo, MI 49008-5092
269/387-2572

Wisconsin Institute for
Creative Writing
University of Wisconsin–Madison
Department of English
Helen C. White Hall
600 N. Park Street
Madison, WI 53706
608/263-3374